Praise for the Masters of the Shadowlands

Lean on Me

"Ms. Sinclair's stories are rare gems that continue to haunt the reader even as the last page is read."

– *Love Romances and More*

Make Me, Sir

"*Make Me, Sir* was a gripping story that kept me entertained all the way through to the end."

– *Whipped Cream Erotic Reviews*

To Command and Collar

"Get ready for the most emotionally wrenching MASTERS OF THE SHADOWLANDS book to date."

– *Romance Junkies*

This is Who I Am

"[I] came away super satisfied..."

– *Fiction Vixen Reviews*

"[S]urpasses what I expected..."

– *Under the Covers Book Blog*

Rated Purest Delight! "Cherise Sinclair...wrings emotions from her reader like a dishrag."

– *Guilty Pleasures Book Reviews*

LooseId®

ISBN 13: 978-1-62300-497-2
THIS IS WHO I AM
Copyright © July 2013 by Cherise Sinclair
Originally released in e-book format in May 2013

Cover Art by Christine M. Griffin
Cover Layout and Design by April Martinez

Printed in the U.S.A. by
Lightning Source, Inc.
1246 Heil Quaker Blvd
La Vergne TN 37086
www.lightningsource.com

THIS IS WHO I AM

Cherise Sinclair

Dedication

Dedicated to those brave souls who have abandoned the conventional trail to find their own way. Your courage will ease the way for those who follow.

Acknowledgment

I want to thank my crazy street team, who keeps me laughing with tales of pouncing on unwary readers to pimp my books. Y'all are the best!

Thanks to my fantastic beta readers: sweet Rosie Moewe for her encouragement; Monette Michaels, who forces me to stay with the plot; Bianca Sommerland, whose wicked pen keeps me from fatal errors *wiping off blood*; and Fiona Archer, who kicks critting and brainstorming ass.

It was a long winter and a long wait for this book. To all of you who sent encouraging and scolding e-mails, who filled Twitter and Facebook with cheers and hugs as well as photos for inspiration, laughs, and kitteh fun—you have my gratitude and love.

Hugs to Robyn Peterman for the generous gift of Frank. Frank, without you, this book would have been years in arriving. Bless you both.

Cheers to my editor for dropping everything to get Master Sam's story off to a quick release date.

And, as always and for always, to my wonderful husband for his enduring patience and love.

Author's Note

To my readers,

The books I write are fiction, not reality and, as in most romantic fiction, the romance is compressed into a very, very short time period.

You, my darlings, live in the real world and I want you to take a little more time in your romance. Good Doms don't grow on trees and there's some strange people out there. So while you're looking for that special Dom, please, be careful.

When you find him, realize he can't read your mind. Yes, frightening as it might be, you're going to have to open up and talk to him. And you listen to him, in return. Share your hopes and fears, what you want from him, what scares you spitless. Okay, he may try to push your boundaries a little—he's a Dom, after all—but you will have your safeword. You will have a safeword, am I clear? Use protection. Have a back-up person. Communicate.

Remember: safe, sane and consensual.

Know that I'm hoping you find that special, loving person who will understand your needs and hold you close. Let me know how you're doing. I worry, you know.

And while you're looking or if you're already found your dearheart, come and hang-out with the Masters in Club Shadowlands

Love,

Cherise

Chapter One

Linda grabbed the chair arm of the witness stand, fighting to pull in a breath. Under her silk blouse, sweat dampened her back, and black spots danced at the edge of her vision. As her knees threatened to buckle, she tightened her grip on the curved wood. *Will. Not. Show. Weakness.* Another breath. She pretended to look around, stalling and hoping she'd be able to walk.

Whispers skittered around the courtroom, but the jurors were silent, watching her with concern. The white-haired grocer's expression was outraged—for her. The tiny housewife wiped tears from her face.

The prosecuting attorney stepped forward to help, but the jury's warmth had put strength back into Linda's body. She straightened, stepped down, and her legs held. *Thank you, God.* Surely she could walk to the door.

She glanced at the defense attorney and his client— the balding, older man in his European-cut suit and diamond-encrusted watch—who was on trial for the murder of a nineteen-year-old college student.

Holly had been kidnapped. Enslaved like Linda.

Linda swallowed hard. She'd held the sweet-faced girl as she'd cried for her mother. She'd told her it would be all right. She'd lied. When the FBI raided an auction, freeing the slaves, it had been far too late for Holly.

The bastard sitting there so smugly had whipped her to death.

As Linda walked past, his patronizing gaze slid down her body, making her shudder and remember her own screams. Unable to escape, unable to fight. Beaten. Raped. She already felt dirty all the way to her core; his stare added another layer of filth. Ignoring the bile burning her throat, she forced herself to give him a dismissive look. Testifying had required all her strength, but she'd done what she'd come here to do. Chin up, head held high, she strode toward the exit.

The sandy-haired FBI agent, Vance Buchanan, waited there. "Well done," he said in a low voice. "Only a few steps farther." He reached out to assist her.

She flinched away.

As his hand dropped and he opened the door, she cursed herself for showing weakness. But she'd been a slave. She didn't want to be touched.

After the overcrowded courtroom, the fresh air in the hallway was bracing, and then suddenly too cold. Her legs went boneless, and she dropped with a jarring thump onto the wooden bench. When she pushed her hands between her knees to hide the trembling, it only made the shaking of her knees more obvious. The dancing black spots had returned. *Lovely.*

"You did great, Linda." Vance's voice was washed away by her pounding pulse, and she—

"Goddamn fool, she's shocky." A voice from her dreams grated across her nerves, snapping her into the present. The bench squeaked a complaint as someone sat beside her. Arms closed around her, trapping her.

No! She shoved at his wide shoulders, panic rising like a flood tide.

"Don't move, girl. You need to be held. Slap me later." The rough growl of Sam's voice was the rumble of an 18-wheeler carrying a truckload of safety.

Not trapped. Sheltered. He was warm—so, so warm. She sagged against him. *I hate you.*

"That a girl. Take a break for a second. You earned it."

His chest was a brick wall, his arms iron bands, not comfortable in the least. Her body didn't care, more secure than in the long, long months since she'd been freed from the slavers. With Sam's arms around her, nothing would hurt her.

Except him.

"What are you doing here, Davies?" Vance asked.

"Kim told me the asshole who'd killed their friend was being tried. I figured this one would testify." The silence that followed sounded accusing.

Vance sighed. "Linda didn't want to see you."

"Yep. I can see that." The dryness in the gravelly voice came through loud and clear.

When had she put her arms around his waist? She was gripping him as if he were a lifeline over an abyss. Her arms loosened.

His tightened. "One more minute, missy. Be a shame not to get your strength back before you bust my chops."

Another minute sounded...just right. As she rested her cheek against his chest, the lazy *lub-dub* of his heart tried to coax hers into slowing. His soft cotton shirt smelled of the outdoors, of hay and leather and sun. So very different from the stench of fear and sex. Of pain. Her stomach clenched.

He gave a hissing sound of annoyance.

She looked up.

In a face tanned to old leather, his eyes were a startling pale blue. His silvering hair needed a trim. "Whatever you're thinking, stop." He curved a hand over her nape and tucked her head back under his chin.

Okay. For a few more seconds, she'd... What in the world was she doing? *I hate this man.* As her mind cleared, she tried to push away. "Don't touch me."

He grunted as if she'd hit him, and released her instantly.

Expecting to see amusement in his gaze, she saw only concern. It didn't matter. She rose to her feet, rattled when he did the same. But he was the kind of man who'd observe that old-fashioned courtesy. A gentleman sadist. His aura of confidence—and menace—was disconcerting. She took a step away from him.

Distance didn't help. He trapped her easily with the power of his gaze, his posture, his voice. "I want you to call me."

"No," she whispered, unable to give her refusal the strength it deserved. "I don't want to see you." The one hour of knowing him had been enough for her. He'd seen right to her core, and she'd learned how deep humiliation could go.

His hard mouth tightened, but he merely tapped her chin with a finger. "Submissives don't get what they want. They get what they need." He might as well have said the rest of what he was thinking: *And you need me.*

But she didn't. She wouldn't.

* * * *

Sam left his battered truck in the parking lot and strode across the street to the small city park. Beyond the palms lining the entrance, massive live oak trees cast dark pools of shade. The air was cool with a slight crispness. Almost into February, Tampa still had a few months before the daily rains would send the humidity to sauna-like levels.

He spotted Nolan King on a picnic bench across the green swath of grass. Sam glanced at his watch. Late. Linda's testimony had lasted longer than he'd planned.

As Sam sidestepped a toddler chasing a beach ball, her mother on a park bench gave him a sharp look. He approved of her vigilance. The world held too many monsters. But Sam wasn't someone she needed to worry about. He might be a sadist, but he only played consensual games.

Except for one time.

The scene he'd done at the slave auction with Linda hadn't been what he would call consensual. To lead the FBI to the auction, he'd convinced the slavers he was a buyer and gotten himself an invitation. But the cops had needed time to block the roads, which left Raoul, his sub, and Sam in a nightmare. Wealthy buyers had roamed a ballroom, sampling the "merchandise"—the slaves chained to the walls.

Linda had been up for sale. Since Raoul's sub knew her, she'd asked Sam to care for Linda. But there was no care to be had in a place like that. Disguised as a buyer, Sam's only hope was to pretend to *check* her out prior to buying her. To whip her himself. He couldn't risk telling her that he was a good guy and help was on the way.

Seeing Kim's nod of approval, Linda had known Sam wasn't a complete bastard. But was the scene consensual? Hardly. Not when her only choice had been him or another slaver.

Sam ran his hand through his hair. He was too damned old to play James Bond. He was a farmer, not a spy. He'd done his best by her, and she'd been the sweetest, most responsive submissive-masochist he'd ever met. The chemistry between them had been a bonfire. She'd trusted him, given him what he asked for, and in return, he'd transformed what might have been a nightmare of pain into something wonderful for her.

And then he'd made a mistake; to this day, he wasn't sure exactly what. He had ideas, but hell, he could be totally off base.

Sam sighed. For the past few months, Linda'd lived out of state with a sister, and this morning, he'd had her in his arms again. She'd trusted him to hold her. The sound of her low voice, her citrus-lavender scent, her yielding body had been even better than his memories. Until she'd pushed him away.

As Sam approached the picnic table, Nolan looked up. From a small cooler, the hard-faced Dom removed a Mountain Dew and handed it over. "Figured you'd need something to wipe the taste out of your mouth. How'd the trial go?"

"The goddamned defense attorney took his questions into the gutter trying to shake her. Bad enough she gets raped by the slavers. To get raped again by a sleazy interrogation?" Sam popped the top as he sat. The icy drink washed the bitterness from his throat. "I wanted to shove a boot in his foul mouth."

And then rip apart the balding slaver who'd killed the youngster. Holly had only been nineteen—the same age as his little girl. *"I'm an adult now, Daddy,"* his pretty Nicole often reminded him. He growled under his breath. No matter what the law said, his daughter's life had barely begun. And because of the slavers, one young woman wouldn't grow any older. The police had found Holly's body in a ravine where the killer had dumped her like garbage.

But after Linda's testimony, Sam had seen the bastard's conviction in the jurors' faces. And he wouldn't live long—not once the other prisoners saw pictures of the sweet-faced college student. "Linda held up like a trouper."

"May have less muscles, but women got more guts than most men."

"True." They'd endure where a man would give up and die.

As a light breeze swept the park with the scent of brine, Sam listened to the children on the swing set.

"Push me."

"Look how high I can go."

He relaxed. He'd needed the reminder of happiness. "Why the park?"

Nolan jerked his chin to the left. "Great scenery."

Sam followed his gaze. Beth, Nolan's submissive, knelt nearby, planting bright yellow flowers in a newly tilled garden. The glint of her red hair reminded him how Linda's thick mane had brushed his fingers when he held her shoulders. Her hair had grown.

Nolan's contented, possessive smile sent envy through Sam. He'd never had that kind of happiness with a woman. Probably never would since just the thought of his ex-wife drove ice shards into his gut. But he had a good life now. Wanting more would be stupid. "Beth ignoring you?"

"No. I brought her lunch and made her take a break. She just went back to work." Nolan glanced at Sam. "You going to go after that submissive? Linda, right?"

"She's not interested." But dammit, the way she'd clung to him said otherwise.

"Want to tell me why not?"

Nolan's sub had been abused. He might have advice. Didn't matter. "No."

"And they say I'm closemouthed."

Sam shrugged. Nolan didn't like to talk. Period. Sam just didn't talk about personal shit. Too risky. Back in 'Nam, trails often held trip wires and mines. He'd seen friends blown to bits. Then when he married, he'd learned booby traps could be made of confidences. Could kill the spirit instead.

And wasn't he a bitter fool on a sunny day? He nodded at the rolled-up sheaf of paper sitting on the table. "The plans?"

"Yep. If they suit you, I can have the concrete guys start in another week." Nolan spread the paper out on the rough wood. "I think you'll like the suggestions the architect made."

Sam rose to take a better look. Good timing for this. Construction of a new stable would keep him busy for a while. Give Linda a chance to settle back into her life.

Then he'd see what was what.

* * * *

As the breeze off the Gulf toyed with her hair, Linda wiggled her toes in the sand and listened to the hissing of the waves on the shore. Compared to the energetic Pacific

Ocean, the Gulf of Mexico was wonderfully peaceful. Yet she felt distant, as if she were watching life through a frosted window in a frigid alpine castle. "Nice place."

Kim was settled in a weathered Adirondack chair with her German shepherd sprawled at her feet. "It is. I love Raoul's house, but his beach here is what saved my sanity." Her black hair spilled down her back as she tipped her face up to the sun. "Sooo, was Sam at the courthouse?"

Odd how even her anger felt bottled up. "I should wallop you for telling him." But how could she be mad? She and Kim had been slaves together, and then Kim had risked her life to free Linda. "Yes, he was at the courthouse."

And he'd been more overwhelming than she remembered. Heavens, if she had to see him again, couldn't he have been...less? Less strong, less commanding. In the last few months, couldn't he have picked up a potbelly and sagging chest?

Or at least been a jerk? Instead, he'd simply held her. He'd shown up just to be there for her, and how was she supposed to deal with that?

"I'm surprised he made it. Over the winter, he got grumpy." Kim dug her toes into the sand and flicked some at Linda. "Okay, more grumpy than normal. Raoul says he hardly leaves his place except for business."

"Place?"

"Bunch of acres. A ranch or farm or something."

A rancher. She might have guessed. When several gulls started bickering in loud screeches over a washed-up fish, the dog raised his head, ears pricked, his whole body tensing. He gave Kim an entreating look.

"Oh, fine. Go chase the birds." As the dog launched into action, Kim smiled at Linda. "We don't let Ari chase the other shorebirds, but gulls are fair game."

As the dog ran up the beach, gulls flapped into the air with annoyed squawks, and Linda relaxed. *Thank you, Ari, for changing the subject.* Even with someone as understanding as Kim, she didn't want to discuss Sam. She sighed. If he'd simply whipped her at the slave auction, she'd have no problems sharing with Kim, but the damage he'd caused hadn't been from his whipping her. It hadn't been physical.

That night, when Sam had stepped up to her, she'd trusted Kim's approving nod. He'd told Linda she could have him or another buyer. If she chose him, he would hurt her, and he'd known she was a masochist. He'd driven everything out of her mind except him, the sensations he gave her, and the sound of his growling voice.

The Overseer had called her a slut and whore. Sam had made her feel like one in an emotional rape far worse than the physical ones.

Earlier today—although months had passed—her body had still reacted to his voice, craving the safety he offered. The rest of her had wanted to hide in a cave.

With a happy bark, Ari ran back and shook, sending water and sand over them both. Kim gave a token grumble. "Stupid dog."

Panting, Ari dropped down over her feet. His wagging tail thumped on Linda's ankle like a metronome.

After ruffling the dog's fur, Kim gave Linda an irrepressible grin. "So about Master Sam. Do you suppose he got so good at a whip because he's a rancher, or did the sadist come first?"

Linda choked. She remembered all too well how competent the man had been. "You know, a few months ago, you'd never have made a joke about a whip."

"I'm better. Not all fixed, but better. Raoul made a huge difference." She tugged at her shepherd's ear. "Ari helped too."

"Nice to have a four-footed counselor." Kim had been kidnapped off the street, and afterward she'd panic if outside alone. Raoul had bought her a doggy escort.

Kim gave her a worried frown. "I figured you'd come back all tan and happy after being at your sister's in California, but you look exhausted. Not sleeping?"

"Not much, no." Linda managed to smile. "Maybe I should buy a dog. At least I'd have something to keep the bed warm." But no pet would solve her problems.

"Well, maybe that guy you were dating last fall will want to heat up your sheets."

The thought made her skin crawl. "Not going to happen."

"Yeah, I'm not surprised. I felt like that too. Did you get counseling in California?"

"Um-hmm. It helped." At least at first. But now the ice encased her more each day, no matter what she did. Over the past few weeks, she'd tried journaling, talking. Screaming.

Needing something to do with her hands, she pulled some grasses up, weaving them together in patterns she'd learned as a teen. Basketry had given her an escape from rigid, fanatical parents, given her a world she could control and a way to make beauty. Later, in college, she'd discovered running and how the throbbing of exhausted muscles could break through her stress and help her reconnect with her own feelings.

She'd needed that help then. Occasionally since.

Because I'm a masochist. What an ugly label, though, with its implication of perversion. Last fall, when she'd realized she needed something more in her life, she'd wanted to experiment. Why not? She was a widow. Her children grown. No real partner.

But she should never have taken that first step, never have visited a downtown kink club to learn if her fantasies and needs had any basis in reality. *They did; they did.* She stared down at her hands, remembering the wonder of that discovery. Even as part of her was horrified that she'd actually asked to be flogged, she'd embraced the pain. Had flown with it, and for a brief period she'd felt...whole. Alive.

Her throat tightened. Then she'd walked out of the club. *Night air, so clean and salty, so quiet after the sounds of the club. In the parking lot, a low cry. Racing over. A woman, unconscious, being tossed into a van.* Linda had run, screaming, and everything had gone black.

She'd been kidnapped herself. Right into slavery, rape, and abuse.

Now she wanted to feel whole again. To feel alive. She knew one way to accomplish that, but no matter how wonderful that brief experience of pain had been in the BDSM club, how could she let anyone hurt her again? She'd panic...wouldn't she?

Yet how could she go home like this? So different from who she really was, with as much emotion in her as a wooden post. Her children would be horrified. And Lee, the man she'd dated off and on? What would he think?

Every day was growing worse. Recently, she had trouble even laughing. She couldn't continue like this.

With a shuddering breath, she rubbed her hands over her face. She knew what she had to do.

That night at the slave auction, she'd been more closed off than now, yet Sam had blown her walls wide open, as if his cruel whip had cut fissures to relieve the pressure.

Maybe if I...if I could get help one more time, then I'd be all right. Back home, with life returned to normal, I'd never need it again.

She couldn't allow herself to need it again. When she returned to Foggy Shores, she would need to go back to being normal. To pick up her life and habits and keep everything quiet. Sane.

But she wasn't home yet.

If she could just find someone to...hurt her. Just one time. If she could endure it. Her stomach turned over as she thought of returning to the Tampa club, the one where she'd been kidnapped.

She realized her hands had clenched into tight balls. Finger by finger, she opened them. Earlier, Kim had mentioned that she and Raoul belonged to a BDSM club. A private one.

No one would know her there. And she wouldn't be alone. If Kim was there—and Raoul—maybe she'd feel secure enough to...do something.

Slowly she turned to face Kim. To meet her compassionate eyes. To force out the request. "Would you and Raoul take me to the Shadowlands?"

Chapter Two

Flanked by Raoul and Kim, Linda walked into the exclusive BDSM club known as the Shadowlands. Light from wrought-iron sconces flickered ominously over the dungeon equipment lining the walls. The overwhelming scents of leather, sweat, and sex slapped into her and stole her breath. The sounds of pain were like a kick to her stomach. Even the music held a savage bite.

At least no one would see her reactions—or who she was. The black mask she wore concealed her face, leaving only her lips and eyes revealed. Now, if she could only get her feet to move. The little voice inside her screaming *get me out of here* grew louder.

When Raoul put his hand on her shoulder, she jumped. "*Chiquita.*" His dark brown eyes were worried. "You would be safe in the Shadowlands, no matter what. But you're also with me."

"Thank you." Considering the man had more muscles than the beach had sand, he was a reassuring presence.

"Linda, let's go home," Kim said. "We don't have to stay." Her blue corset matched her eyes, and her black collar held a silver engraving: *Master Raoul's gatita.* Of all the women in captivity, Kim had seemed the least likely to want to be a slave. But the love between her and

Raoul was so strong it almost shimmered. Somehow, Kim had moved on and found happiness.

Linda hadn't. Even worse, she was unraveling as emotions ripped through her. She cringed at the sound of a paddle against flesh. A woman's screams made her hands turn cold and numb. As the trembling in her belly worked outward, her knees started to shake. She couldn't escape the memories of horrors. This was the stupidest thing she'd ever done.

"Raoul." A gray-eyed man blocked their way, and his gaze swept over her face, her shoulders, her hands. "What are you doing? She's terrified."

Well, sheesh. She could have sworn she'd hidden her fear fairly well.

"She wanted to come," Kim protested, then closed her mouth when Raoul tugged her collar.

The stranger was lean and graceful, wearing all black as a Dom would—only he had no need to wear black to establish his authority. Power surrounded him like the scent of aftershave. "You must be Linda. Little one, you should go home."

Raoul squeezed her shoulder. "Linda, this is Master Z. He agreed to give you a temporary membership, and he's the reason you are safe here."

"It's nice to meet you, Master Z." So this was the infamous Master Z who owned the Shadowlands. She swallowed. Kim hadn't come close to describing how intimidating the man was. "Kim's right. I wanted to come."

He lifted an eyebrow in an unspoken command to continue. In just one night at that other club, she'd discovered how a Dom in full command mode could turn her spine into jelly.

"I wanted…" Why had it been easier to explain to Raoul, even if she hadn't explained everything? "Wanted to remind myself that people do this for fun. Consensually."

"You want to replace the images in your head with better ones," he said gently.

"That's it." *And maybe find someone to hurt me.* God, that sounded so sick.

He held his hand out, and her fingers were in his grip before she realized she'd moved. He studied her for a minute, then nodded. "All right, Linda. I think you have the strength, but don't push yourself into a panic attack." He arched a brow at Kim. "Your companions are quite familiar with the symptoms."

Kim actually giggled. The beautiful sound showed that healing could happen, even after horrors.

"I'll be careful," Linda said.

"Very good." He released her hand and moved off with the lethal grace of a big cat.

Linda blew out a breath and glanced at Kim. "Well. You tried to warn me." If nothing else, Master Z had broken into her nightmare and got her moving again.

Kim grinned. "And you didn't believe me."

Linda laughed and looked around. The place was certainly different from the one she'd gone to before. True, her single visit to a BDSM club hardly made her an authority, but she'd spent hours there before doing anything. This place was more expensive. The equipment was padded with leather, the burnished hardwood floors reflected the flickering of the wrought-iron sconces. The general populace was older and quieter, although—she enjoyed the spectacle of a woman in a full catsuit followed by a naked submissive—the costumes were just as outrageous.

"Do you want to wander around or settle somewhere?" Kim glanced over Linda's shoulder, and her eyes widened. "Uh, let's just go to the bar."

Linda turned. The nearest scene was a man on a St. Andrew's cross with a Mistress putting clamps on his nipples. The spiderweb next to it held a restrained submissive struggling to evade the flick of a crop. Then a spanking scene. Then several people watching a Dom with a flogger.

When the Dom turned slightly, Linda's lungs felt as if they were being pinched in wickedly tight clamps. *Sam.* Sam was here. She'd forgotten the dangerous vibe he gave off in dominant mode. Almost half a foot taller than her five-seven, he wore black jeans, black boots, a black belt, and a black flannel shirt with the sleeves rolled up. His silvery hair didn't make him look old—just really, really experienced.

He was using a full-sized, heavy flogger with brown leather strands. No fancy colors for him. The woman on the cross was in tears, her back reddened. As Sam flogged the blonde with a smooth rhythm, Linda wanted to hate him for inflicting such pain.

Yet, as the woman went up on tiptoes, she pushed her bottom back to get more. Her face gleamed with sweat and tears, but her half-agonized, half-blissful expression was that of a masochist getting what she wanted.

I want it too. Linda felt like a shaken soda with the cap screwed on too tightly to let out the increasing pressure. Pain might give her a way to open up and spew everything out. *I need that.*

Not with Sam though. *No no no.* And yet... She shivered and wrapped her arms around herself over her silky shirt. Watching him with a woman made her feel odd. Wanting and angry and unsettled. After a minute, she forced herself to turn away. Thank heavens she'd worn a mask.

Raoul was watching her, his dark eyes narrowed. "Shall I find you a Dom to play with?"

How had Kim found someone so sweetly protective? But she wouldn't—couldn't—have another person make those choices for her again. "Thank you, but I'd rather choose my own if I decide to...do anything."

And she'd be very careful. She'd pick a sadist, but not one who was also a Dominant. During her night at the club, the Dom she'd spoken to had told her she was submissive as well as a masochist. *As if one perversion wasn't enough, I've got two.*

But it had been Sam who had showed her how a powerful Dom could push her limits—could go past her limits. At the auction, she could have handled being whipped, but he'd done...more. *Damn him.*

"As you wish. Then let us have something to drink while you decide." After pulling Kim to his side, Raoul guided them to the bar.

Linda glanced longingly at the bottles of tequila, scotch, and rum.

Raoul shook his head. "You may have water or a soda." He turned to Kim and settled her on a bar stool, kissing her hair lightly.

But I want a drink. Linda sighed but had to admit he was right. Alcohol, in this place, might do as much harm as good. She needed to stay on top of things. In control.

The bartender's assistant came over to get their orders. As Kim talked with her, Linda looked over her shoulder at Sam. Again.

He'd finished the scene. The blonde with spiky hair who might have looked tough at one time was trying to bury herself in his chest. When he rubbed her undoubtedly tender back and she cried harder, he grinned. Definitely a sadist. But a caring one. And strong. She remembered the steel-like feeling of his arms. He might be in his fifties, but he was all bone and muscle.

A shiver ran up Linda's spine. *Don't look.*

Turning away, she let herself sink into the sounds of the place. The slap of paddles and floggers and canes. Moaning and groaning. A shriek. Low conversation. A half-heard man's laugh—the sound familiar and horrible—sent memories oozing through her. Caged on a boat. Men talking about—

She shook herself loose, feeling cold sweat trickle down her back. *I'm free. At the Shadowlands.* And as she listened, she realized the noise was different from the slave auctions. The sobbing was that of a release; the shriek had excitement accompanying the pain. There were none of the hopeless cries, the pleading, and the screams of pain that wouldn't end. She shuddered.

"Linda. Look at me." Raoul's gaze was watchful. Measuring.

"I'm okay." And she wasn't lying. His voice, his steady eyes had settled her. She gave him a shaky smile. "Thank you." Her deep breath calmed her further as she carefully cataloged more differences. She'd thought the downtown BDSM club smelled of leather, sex, pain, and fear. Now she knew fear stank of piss and blood and sour sweat. Nothing like here.

The Shadowlands held laughter, and not only from the male Doms. There were women laughing. To one side, some submissives giggled as one negotiated with a Dom. Linda took a quick survey of the room before turning to Kim. "The percentage of Doms to submissives seems pretty even."

The bartender's submissive grinned at her. "Good eye. I'm Andrea, by the way." She glanced around the room and answered Linda's unspoken questions. "Master Z keeps the membership balanced, no matter how long the waiting list gets. It's nice. I've visited clubs where I felt like a sheep surrounded by a pack of wolves."

"That's it," Linda agreed. "There's no sense of being stalked." In fact, the unattached subs were having a good time with each other. More weight lifted from her shoulders. She'd be safe here, if... Could she really do this? Let a sadist hurt her? Her fears and needs seemed to twine together, creating a macramé of self-loathing. Why couldn't she be normal?

Her gaze fell on a man by a St. Andrew's cross. Tall. Thin. He was packing up his toy bag after using a cane on a younger woman who'd quickly wimped out. But he hadn't tried to dominate the woman. As he picked up his bag, he met Linda's gaze and nodded politely.

She continued to stare at him, and he tilted his head, reassessing her.

Raoul's hand covered hers. "Are you sure, chiquita? Edward is a sadist but not a Dominant. Sam might be—"

"Not Sam." When his eyebrows rose, she winced at her bluntness. "I'm sorry."

"Do not apologize for being honest." His gaze stayed on her face. "Continue."

"Just...I don't want a Dom. Or Sam."

His jaw tightened. "Did Sam do something that—"

"*No*. No, it's nothing. I just like making my own choices." To escape more questions, she kissed his cheek in a hasty apology, then went to meet the sadist halfway.

AS SAM CLEANED the equipment and kept an eye on Dara, he half listened to the sounds from the adjacent scene. Holt was using a cane on a submissive, pushing her boundaries and heightening her arousal. From the noise the brunette was making, the Dom was doing an excellent job.

After putting the cleaning supplies in the stand, Sam went down on one knee beside Dara. With a blanket around her shoulders, the Goth trainee had eaten her chocolate bites and was sipping the sports drink he'd given her.

"How you doing?" Sam asked, running his knuckles over her cheek.

"I'm good." Her eyes were clear, skin warm, speech coherent. He'd learned Dara didn't want much aftercare, didn't want to be held. She liked moving around and enjoying the buzz. She grinned at him. "That was really fun, Master Sam. Thank you."

"All right then." He stood and helped her to her feet. After giving him a quick hug, she trotted off toward the restrooms—undoubtedly to admire the stripes he'd put on her thighs and ass.

Feeling a tad deprived, he headed to the bar. What was the world coming to when a Dom enjoyed aftercare more than the submissive?

"Hey, Davies."

Sam looked around.

Special Agent Vance Buchanan and his partner, Galen Kouros, were sitting at the bar.

Sam leaned an elbow on the bar and greeted the linebacker-sized agent, "Buchanan," then nodded at the lean, dark one. "Kouros." They were both in jeans and white button-up shirts. "Here on Fed business?"

"Not this time," Kouros said. "Our transfer to Tampa came through, so we're talking to Z about membership here."

"You'll be welcome." Sam had seen them play a time or two. Although it wasn't common for two Doms to link up permanently, they'd made topping together into an art. And Kouros had some serious skill with mind-fucking games. "Is the Harvest Association belly-up?" Although the Feds had netted the bastards who'd kidnapped Linda and Kim, the slave-trafficking association's reach extended across the entire United States.

"Not quite. The northeast is still going strong." Buchanan scowled. "We think that area has some highly placed contacts."

"Bad news."

"A bad crime." Over the past months, the lines in Kouros's face had deepened.

The Harvest Association dealt in human trafficking with a twist. They kidnapped intelligent middle- and upper-class submissives, ones already in the lifestyle, and sold them to wealthy buyers who wanted trained slaves or—even worse—toys to be broken. Linda and Kim had been slaves. Other Shadowlands submissives had been targeted. Like Z's Jessica and a mouthy trainee named Sally.

Sally was cute as a button. He spotted her, hands on hips, apparently giving a newer Dom a lesson in something. Sam chuckled. Although he preferred to scene with masochists, he'd topped the little brunette a few times. She took a bit of work, but then she would surrender beautifully.

All of the Shadowlands Masters worked with the trainees, filling their needs, instructing and evaluating. The goal was to get them matched with suitable Doms, but Sally was too damn smart and independent for her own good. She needed a powerful Dom, and so far Z hadn't found one who would meet her needs.

Buchanan's gaze followed Sam's, and the FBI agent nudged his partner, pointing out the trainee. The girl loved role-play games and today had dressed as a biker chick...probably hoping for someone to take on the cop role. "Want to give her a treat?" Buchanan asked.

Kouros smiled slowly before shaking his head. "Members have more privileges than guests," he reminded Buchanan. "We'll wait."

"Yo." Wearing his brown "I'm a Dom and don't need black to prove it" leathers, Cullen looked up from drawing a beer for someone. "You agents plotting something?"

"Not tonight," Buchanan said.

After giving the Feds' glasses a bartender's assessment, Cullen grinned at Sam. "'Bout time you graced us with your presence, buddy. What can I get you?"

Sam considered. Did he want something? Was he finished for the night? His arm was tired; his need to make a woman cry was satisfied. He didn't want to do a more intense scene—hadn't wanted to in months. *Damn the redhead.* "How about a beer?"

"How about not?" Cullen leaned a big arm on the bar top. "Raoul's here with Kim and a friend of hers. An older redhead. Would she be the Linda I've heard rumors about?"

His Linda? Sam straightened. "Where?"

"She's doing a scene with Edward." Cullen jerked his chin toward the right.

Sam spotted her easily. Dark red hair. White skin. Despite her mask, she was easily recognizable—at least to a Dom who'd run his hands all over her beautifully curved body. What the hell was she doing? A hard-core sadist, Edward had a good technique with a single-tail, but... "He's no Dom, and she's submissive."

"Yeah? She told Raoul she didn't want a Dom—or you."

The words sliced through his flesh like a fillet knife. "Then why the hell did you point her out?"

"All her fire at just hearing your name? You got unresolved business there, buddy."

Not any revelation, at least on Sam's side. But she wasn't going to let him close enough to do anything about it.

Cullen was laughing.

"What's so goddamned funny?"

"Check out the scene." Cullen nodded to the cross. "That's one frustrated subbie."

Sam looked again. Linda's back was to the room as Edward used a cane on her jeans-covered ass. Gorgeous body. Maybe not to the fools who wanted their women young and tight and bland. No, Linda's body was past prime. Soft. The highlighted streaks in her hair were probably there to cover up the gray. He remembered she had fine wrinkles beside her mouth, on her neck. And he wanted her with every cell in his body.

With a grunt of annoyance, he shut his dick down and studied her. Cullen's comment held truth. She was flinching from the blows. Not welcoming them. In the way a woman might be unable to have an orgasm, the sweet masochist wasn't hitting the place that would let her ride the pain. Why? Sam watched awhile longer, and his jaw tightened. "She doesn't trust him enough to go with it. And he's not dominant enough to break through to her."

"That's my take."

Sam saw Z approaching the scene. The owner of the Shadowlands rarely interrupted a session...unless he felt the play was harmful to the submissive. And that scene certainly wasn't doing Linda any favors.

Sam pushed away from the bar and strode over to intercept him.

Z gave him a level look. "Samuel."

He didn't need to hear Z state what he already knew. "No, she doesn't want to see me. But I'm the one she needs right now."

"You have a history between you. I've heard it's not a happy one."

Submissives loved to gossip, and Z's Jessica would be at the heart of it. "I screwed up, but there was a connection between us. It's still there."

Z's frown deepened, and he crossed his arms over his chest as he considered. "You may offer. If she accepts, you will emphasize she has a safe word. And I intend to monitor."

"Considering what she's been through, I'm good with a backup." Sam turned. Butting into another Dom's scene wasn't done, but...she needed him. His protective instincts pushed him closer.

Edward wasn't into the scene at all, or he wouldn't have noticed Sam stand one foot too close to the roped-off area. He walked over. "Friend of yours?"

He'd give his left nut to be able to say yes. "Not quite. But I might be able to get through to her. She's submissive."

"No fucking way. She said she wasn't."

"She lied."

"You've got to be shitting me." Edward scowled. "I should have spotted it. But she was so insistent."

"The truth isn't always comfortable. May I?"

"Go for it. I'm fucking tired of being lied to." Edward tossed his cane in his bag, picked it up, and stalked away.

Well, that was easy. Sam moved slowly as if approaching a wild mare. They had a connection from before, and she needed what he had to give. Was it enough to get past her anger? To let her trust him? His shoulder muscles knotted as he approached from the side where she could see him. If she'd open her eyes.

He took a minute to enjoy the sight of her. She still wore her jeans and an ugly black mask but had removed her shirt and bra, leaving her lightly freckled back bare. In the courthouse, she'd been dead white, but now he saw she had a fading tan. Kim had mentioned she'd been in California to recuperate and escape the asshole newspeople. *Welcome home, girl.* His mouth tightened when he saw the faint white lines—scars—on her back, left from her trauma.

He gripped her chin gently but firmly enough that she'd recognize the touch of a Master. "Linda. Look at me."

Her eyes popped open, and her body went rigid. "No. Not you."

Dammit, he'd had submissives fearful of him, especially nonmasochists, but at the auction, he'd given Linda only as much pain as she'd needed. Anger might be warranted, not fear. "Goddammit, I've never hurt anyone who didn't ask me to."

She closed her eyes as if she couldn't stand the sight of him, but restrained on the cross, she had no choice except to hear his apology.

"I'm not sure what I did." Where were all the arguments he'd come up with over the past months? "But I did something wrong. I'm sorry, girl."

Her body shuddered as if trying to throw off his words. Her eyes opened. "It's okay. It doesn't matter."

The anger and shame in her gaze was far more honest than her words. Her forgiveness wasn't even close. "Yes, it does. I hope you'll forgive me. But for right now"—with her chin cupped in his palm, he stroked his thumb over her jawline below the mask—"you need to hurt. And you need someone to push you hard enough that you can relax into it."

She bit back an obvious denial, and her eyebrows drew together.

He held himself immobile, not touching the bright strands dancing on her shoulders, not tracing the ridge of her spine with his fingers. He permitted only one touch; she needed the dominance of his hand controlling her face. Nothing more. Not yet. "Tell me I'm wrong, girl."

Tiny puffs of air hit his palm as her breathing went shallow and fast. And then...she shook her head.

He wasn't wrong. The surge of satisfaction held him frozen for another moment. "All right then. Here's how it will be. Your safe word is red. Say it."

She swallowed and then whispered, "Red."

"Good." This time he ran his thumb over her puffy lips, seeing her pupils dilate until her eyes were as dark as the cross on which she was bound. "I'm going to touch you, but your jeans will stay up. Your pussy will be out of bounds." *This time.* "I'll leave your mask on." Although it annoyed the hell out of him. "I won't try to get you off. Agreed?"

"What about my...breasts?"

"Those are mine to play with." He leaned in closer until all she'd be able to see was his face. "To hurt."

A flush swept upward from her chest to her face. She was aroused.

The knowledge gave him a finer satisfaction than coming after a long fucking. The connection they'd had before was intact. Working with her this time would be like sliding a new hickory handle into the eye of an ax head. Knowing it was a perfect fit. Then hammering in the wedge to prevent their bond from coming apart again. That's what she'd lacked with Edward. She needed dominance as much as she needed pain.

He'd give her both before he was done.

"Your mouth is mine as well," he growled before taking her lips. Soft, plump lips, and he wouldn't enjoy them in anything but a kiss. Even if tonight was all she'd give him, he wouldn't betray her trust.

After a moment, her lips moved under his. He took but stepped away before she was satisfied. Next time he kissed her, she'd offer him more and sooner. He needed to keep her off balance and slowly gather in each tiny piece of her until he had it all. And then, reins in hand, he'd use the spurs.

MIND SPINNING AS a disconcerting arousal swelled within her, Linda tried to look at Sam, but he'd moved behind her. As he gathered her hair, which brushed her shoulders, his grip was firm, pulling hard enough that she felt each hair follicle waken and protest. God, what had she agreed to?

She'd agreed to *more*. When Edward had caned her, the hurt had done nothing for her. She couldn't understand why. Yet somehow Sam knew what was wrong. His gaze reached right to where her soul hid from the outside world.

Just his voice and the way he'd gripped her face had dissolved the floor beneath her, leaving her sinking in quicksand. "Sam."

"Yes. That's my name." His deep voice sounded at one with the bass of the techno music. He pushed her hair forward so the strands tickled her collarbone with each breath. When Edward had done the same, she'd felt nothing. Now her skin was in a shivery, anticipating state, feeling the coolness of the air, the brush of his arm.

As he ran his calloused fingers down her spine, the abrasive sensation started to melt the ice inside her. When his touch moved over her jeans to where the cane had left sore areas, heat pooled low in her belly. How did he do this to her? She shook her head and craned her neck, trying to see over her shoulder.

He'd obviously been waiting for her to do just that, and the shock of his intent gaze was like a blow to her chest. "Those big eyes won't help you, missy. You're where I want you. We both know you'll be crying before I'm through."

His harsh words compressed her ribs until she had to struggle for her next breath.

"I'm going to take a look at you first though." As his hands slid over her wide hips, delight lit his gaze like sunlight through a stained glass window. "You got a beautiful body, missy."

The compliment shoved her off balance, as if she'd missed a step.

His grip on her hips tightened, holding her immobile, and the strength in his fingers was terrifying. Arousing. He could hold her...down. She'd been afraid to think about that when coming in here, and now she wanted it? Not logical. She shook her head, wanting—

The whapping sound was simultaneous with the shocking sting on her bottom. He'd swatted her hard. "You don't think unless I tell you to think," he growled before slapping her other ass cheek.

The burn spread out from her bottom. Her brain blanked as if he'd shut off a switch.

Before she could reorder her thoughts, she heard him say, "Good girl." Leaning against her from behind, he rubbed his chest over the strips of hot flesh on her back, sending fitful sparks of pain through her like a malfunctioning lighter. The ground dropped another foot.

He reached around to cup her breasts in his big hands, and the caress shook areas deep inside her, places that had dried up and died. "Sam." It sounded like a protest, but she heard the plea beneath.

His teeth closed on her shoulder, biting the muscle, holding her as he moved his hands in a milking pattern, increasing the blood flow to her nipples. When his fingers closed on the engorged peaks, the exquisite sensation buckled her knees. He gave a rough laugh. "I've dreamed about your breasts." His voice was low, his breath warm on her ear. He pinched harder, continuing the pressure until every molecule inside her liquefied. She moaned, losing herself as the burn wrapped around her nerves.

He growled in enjoyment, then moved away, leaving her breasts throbbing. After taking a flogger from his bag—a heavier one than what he'd used on the other woman—he tickled it over her back. The scent of leather swept through her, the smell reminding her of the other BDSM club. Where the pain had been good. Her eyes closed as she took a bigger breath.

When he gave her a couple of experimental flicks over her shoulders and ass, the light thudding was wonderful.

"Edward warmed you up well. Let's get some red going on those shoulders."

Her husband'd had that matter-of-fact tone. *"Looks like it's going to rain."* But Frederick would never have talked about hurting her. *"That's not something nice people do, Linda."* She wasn't a nice person. She was perverted and—

The nasty swat on her bottom made her gasp and fragmented her thoughts. "Don't listen well, do you, little girl?" Sam said. He drew his hand back, and three more hard slaps followed.

Tears burned Linda's eyes, and as the stinging warped into intense pleasure, the feeling that swept through her was glorious. Her nerves drank in the hurting like flowers in a drought, and her body started to shake. This wasn't right. She couldn't take this. She'd break. But Sam...Sam would keep her safe as she fell apart.

A hard hand caught her chin and examined her face. "There we go. You're ready to cry now."

He ran his hand down her back, and she had a moment of panic when nothing touched her, and then the flogger whapped against her bottom. Where the strands hit the places he'd spanked, her skin seemed to inhale the impact, breathing in the sensation like air.

Left-right, left-right. The flogger moved in an easy rhythm up her butt, skipping over the area below her ribs to avoid the kidneys, then her upper back—harder, increasing slowly from thumping to something heavier. Each strike hurt enough that she'd tense before feeling the bite. Each sear of pain expanded deeper inward and settled low in her belly. Then her muscles would tighten again in anticipation. A few fast blows removed her ability to tense between them.

The sound of the flogger on flesh turned harsher when it hit her jeans. The dance-floor music had changed, the bass turned up to reverberate against her bones. The strands moved down to her ass, upping the deep burn as if the sadist took glee in seeing her hips move. *Whap*; pain; pleasure. *Whap*; pain; pleasure. She started to settle into the rhythm. Her head felt light, her body heavy.

"You have the prettiest round ass. Let's see it dance, girl."

The strikes came harder as he drove her out of her comfort zone, harder until her hips were trying to evade yet tilting up for more of the sharp-edged sweetness. Tears rolled down her cheeks as a massive glacier of agony dug deep, pushing everything before it as it carved out its passageway. A wail of distress escaped her.

He *laughed*. "Nice. Give me more."

The strands moved lower, sending fire across the backs and sides of her thighs. Wonderful hurting. She heard low crying, and it was hers. Then she was choking on sobs as everything inside her bubbled up and out. He didn't stop, keeping up a steady rhythm she could depend on as the rest of her dissolved.

Sometime later, she realized the flogger was only caressing her lightly with a whisper of sweet pain, enough to keep her connected. She lifted her head, amazed at how difficult it was. Tears still streamed from her eyes as she sank into the sensation, the heat. She could feel her body, every inch of her skin aware and sensitive in a way she hadn't felt in a long, long time. Slowly she gathered her senses, sliding back into reality.

So, so wonderfully relaxed.

The flogger dropped onto the floor with a *thump*, and Sam leaned against her again. His body warmth and the abrasion of his shirt set her back to a happy burn even as he pulled her tighter. His erection pressed against her backside, but he didn't rub it on her or even seem to notice as he teased her nipples into hard points. One hand opened, flattened on her waist, just above her jeans. "You're a wonderful armful," he growled in her ear.

Her body shook, urgent with arousal. Her clit throbbed, needing his hand to move lower. Her body remembered exactly how his experienced fingers had felt when he brought her to orgasm.

In front of a room of slavers.

No. When she stiffened, his hand stilled. She wanted more. *No, I don't. No. Not ever again.* What was she even doing here? *This was sick. Unnatural.* "Let me go, Sam," she whispered, wanting, wanting.

He fisted her hair and tilted her face to study her. The firmness of his grip said he knew she was fleeing from herself. The liquid warmth inside her said he could stop her. Please her. His ice-blue gaze swept over her. "All right."

She realized the horrible feeling inside had disappeared. The pressure and the shadows were gone from her spirit, washed away with her tears and pain.

What kind of a perv was she that she needed to hurt to be able to empty her emotions?

His hand tightened on her jaw. "Don't think. Not now. Tomorrow is soon enough." He reached up and unsnapped her cuffs, then helped her away from the cross. Her back burned where his arm around her waist rubbed the tender skin. Her legs shook as if she had been sick for a year, and she sagged against him.

He walked her to the edge of the scene area. "Kneel here."

Her whole body went stiff as nausea surged. The Overseer had made her kneel for everything. Always. Or crawl. Would he— "I'm not your slave," she hissed.

He gave her a look, and his tone was firm but mild. "I don't need or want a slave."

Slave. Just the sound made her sicker until his words registered. *"Don't need or want a slave."* Her spine found strength, and her shoulders straightened. "Then why make me kneel?" Her mouth was so dry that her voice came out in a whisper.

"You can't stand by yourself, baby. You need to be close to the floor." His rough voice held an odd tenderness. "And I want you where I can keep an eye on you as I clean up."

Oh. "I'm sorry." She let him help her down, her right knee, as always, stiffer than the other. To her surprise, when he returned with a bottled water and blanket, he squatted down to wrap the fuzzy fabric around her. Warm. Wonderfully concealing. "Thank you."

"Right." His hand stayed on her shoulder, holding her firmly.

She frowned and looked up.

"You're kneeling for one more reason, girl, and you might as well learn to deal. You're submissive. That's part of what you need...and kneeling is an acknowledgment of that. Submission isn't slavery."

Her chin tightened. *Yes, it is.*

He breathed out, then opened the water and wrapped her fingers around the bottle. "We'll talk later."

As he cleaned the equipment, she watched. Not young at all, older than her. But he moved with a rancher's strength and a strong man's confidence.

She didn't have that kind of confidence. Not anymore. Hard to believe she'd run her household and a business. Now she was in a BDSM club. Asking to be beaten. She really was the pervert that a lover had called her. Or the dirty slut that the slavers had named her.

Her hands started to shake. She'd done what she'd set out to do. Broken through all the walls. Could feel again. But now she needed to leave. This wasn't what she wanted in her life. With an effort, she looked around for Kim and Raoul.

They stood just beyond the rope beside Master Z. They'd all been watching.

A flush warmed Linda's face. Kim might be submissive, but she wasn't a...masochist. A pain slut. Humiliation swept through her as she set down the water and struggled to her feet. "Raoul, please. Can we go home now?"

A moment of confusion showed on Raoul's face, and then he nodded. "If you want." He gripped her arm, steadying her, as Kim went to get her shirt and bra.

Sam saw them and returned. "Raoul." The anger in Sam's voice was suppressed but present.

The way Raoul tensed showed that even a weight lifter didn't want to take on an angry Sam.

Guilt made her shoulders hunch. She was causing a problem between friends. "It's not his fault, Sam. I asked them to take me home."

When he reached for her, she flinched back. His arm lowered. "You're not ready to leave. You can barely walk...and we need to talk."

"I'm...sorry." She pulled on her bra, feeling the sweet tenderness of her back. Wanting more. "What you did helped," she admitted. He'd earned her thanks. In a way, an ugly way, she'd used him. Except...he liked what he'd done, hadn't he? Had he received as much pleasure from seeing her pain as she had from receiving it? "But I-I don't do this...stuff. I was just here to learn to put it behind me."

"Put it behind you?"

"Yes. This isn't who I am." She forced her chin up, her spine straight, even though she'd felt so, so much better on her knees. "Thank you for"— *for hurting me. For making me cry, making me feel—*"for your time."

He lifted his chin in acknowledgment. But was that hurt she saw in his face for a moment? Surely not from this harsh man who'd called her "baby" and wrapped a blanket around her. Her eyes burned. Why had she ever wanted to feel? Her heart hurt, throbbing as if it had taken the beating instead of her back.

He shot Raoul an unreadable look. "Take care of her."

Raoul's fighting stance relaxed. "As if she were my own."

I'm no one's. The knowledge didn't sound independent—just lonely. Linda pulled on her shirt and led the way to the exit to show Sam she didn't need help. As his gaze burned into her back, she forced herself not to look over her shoulder, not to run and kneel at his feet. Why couldn't she just have been a...normal person and him a normal person? Then, maybe...

NEAR THE far wall of the Shadowlands, the spotter watched Adrienne wipe down the sawhorse. Tears still ran down her face. Quite nice. Even nicer were the welts on her ass and thighs. Red marks over her hips showed where his fingers had dug in as he fucked her. Used and abused, just the way he liked them.

She hadn't been a bad fuck, considering her youth. And getting off put him in an excellent mood, despite settling for a woman so thin her breasts were almost nonexistent. But the plumper women had already been picked. Perhaps he should speak to Z about getting a wider variety of submissives.

Or perhaps not.

He preferred to avoid the owner of the club, since the psychologist displayed a disconcerting competence at reading people. In fact, it was good that Aaron had joined soon after the Shadowlands opened. Over the years, the club's application and interview process had grown more rigorous than he'd be willing to risk.

After all, a man who selected submissives to be sold into slavery must exert a modicum of caution.

Adrienne put away the cleaning supplies in the stand and then knelt at his feet.

"Good enough," he said.

Biting her trembling lower lip, she gazed up at him. Probably hoping he'd hold her and pet her. Did he look like a pathetically weak-willed Dom?

"I told you before we started, I don't do aftercare. Take yourself off." Since he'd been clear about his inclinations, she could hardly bitch about the lack. Z couldn't fault him if the sub knew the deal.

Without speaking, she scooped up her clothing and scurried away, probably to cry over her injured feelings. Or the welts. Given his choice, she'd be bleeding rather than welted, but she'd been about to use her safe word, so he'd throttled back. Because the Shadowlands had *rules*.

He smiled, remembering the last whore he'd bought. Paying for his fun annoyed him, but at least he wasn't forced to stop. Not with fucking the slut, not with hurting her.

As he cleaned his toys, he glanced around the room and spotted the ex-slave leaving with Raoul. Yeah, maybe his next prostitute should be a redhead. Soft. Older.

Interesting that she was here. And wearing a mask, no less. He laughed. Did she believe hiding her face would conceal her identity? Hardly. Her hair and breasts were quite memorable. He ran his fingers over the cane he held. Smooth. Flexible. Would mark that pale skin nicely.

Now where had he seen her? He rubbed his finger over his upper lip. On the slave boat. Seems as if she'd been kidnapped a couple of weeks before, and the association had permitted select buyers to preview the merchandise. The redhead had been in one of the kennels, her head turned and eyes closed to shut out the leering buyers.

Strong woman. He'd liked that.

No one had bought her at the first auction—most buyers preferred the young ones—so he'd bided his time, waiting for her to be devalued and then used as a reward for spotters and guards. But the Overseer had insisted on putting her up for sale again, and Feds had raided the auction.

Stinking Feds. His source of cheap, disposable slaves had disappeared that night. With a grunt of annoyance, he tossed the thin cane into his bag.

As he strolled to the bar, he considered asking Cullen for the ex-slave's name. No, showing interest in her would be unwise, at least until the Harvest Association ceased to be newsworthy.

He'd have to settle for whores. For now.

Chapter Three

Tears prickled in Linda's eyes as she drove down the cul-de-sac and pulled into her driveway. Home at last. And mercifully alone. She'd have no witnesses if she burst into tears.

At first she'd thought she'd have to spend a mint for a taxi to get to Foggy Shores, but Raoul had arranged for someone to bring her car to his house. Obstinate, overprotective Dom. *Bless him.*

Linda slid out of the car and regarded the pretty one-story house where she and Frederick had raised their children. Deep inside, she'd harbored fear that it might have been destroyed—like her life had been. Inhaling slowly, she wrapped the peace of the tiny coastal town and her quiet neighborhood around her like a blanket. So familiar. Next door, dolls and cars scattered the sidewalk like a toy explosion. Across the street, the Smiths' impeccably trimmed yard made the Brendans' appear even more straggly. Music trickled from Adele's home where she gave piano lessons.

Not everything stayed the same though. A FOR SALE sign was planted in Myrtle's front yard. Brenna had mentioned the old woman's death.

Twenty years ago, the starchy woman had been the first to welcome Linda and Frederick to the street. *I didn't get to say good-bye.*

Linda blinked back tears. She'd been in captivity two months and spent another three in California. Almost half a year. She'd changed—oh, she had—but she'd counted on Foggy Shores to stay the same.

But no matter. She was home now, ready to pick up her life. To be the respectable mother of Brenna and Charles, the owner of Foggy Treasures, a good neighbor, a member of the Methodist choir. A normal woman who dated nice normal men.

Not a *pervert.*

Pulling her suitcase, she entered her house. Here, everything was the same. Brenna and Charles had checked on the place every week.

"I'm home." She pulled in a shuddering breath as her voice echoed in the silence. She should be grateful her sweet terrier had died a while before her kidnapping, but now there was no excited yapping to welcome her home. No one at all. Maybe she should have let the kids come today, but unsure of the trial's length, she'd told them to hold off. They both had college classes, after all.

They'd visit next weekend. No reason to feel so...let down. Ignoring the hollowness in her chest, she went to the bedroom to unpack. Time to get back to routines. She'd wallowed in her emotions long enough.

Sunlight filtered through the sand-colored draperies in her bedroom, danced over the cream-and-white, lacy bedspread. Peaceful, lighthearted colors.

So different from the Shadowlands last night. She bit her lip, trying not to remember Sam's voice. His hands. The pain he'd given her in such a mixture of caring and roughness she'd had no choice but to submit. She closed her eyes, hating herself for wanting more. For wanting a sadist. For not being *normal.*

The phone's ring made her jump. She glanced at the display. *Unknown number.* "Hello."

A shrill man's voice said, "This is Italy's Pizza, calling to confirm your order."

Linda laughed at the familiar game. "That's a good one, Charles. Yes, I'm home."

"Aw, Mom. How come I can fool everyone else?"

"Your friends aren't singers, sweetie."

"Guess not. I'm glad you're back, Mom. I missed you."

She smiled. Since being freed, she'd talked to him every few days, and he and Brenna had joined her in California for Thanksgiving and Christmas. "I missed you too." *More than I can say.*

"Are you going back to work now?"

"I'm going to spend today setting things in order and restocking the refrigerator, and then go in on Monday."

"Oh good. I was hoping your vacation would be over."

Her fingers tightened around the phone. Vacation? Depression so black that she'd stared at the ceiling, unable to find a reason to get out of bed. Erratic crying fits, throwing up, panic attacks. She was hardly having fun. Charles knew she'd gone to her sister's to recover from the kidnapping. Well, he was only twenty, and she'd tried very hard to hide her shattered mental state from the children. He wouldn't know she'd needed all that time to pull the pieces of herself back together. "Not much choice, I'm afraid. My funds are pretty exhausted."

"Does that mean you don't have any money to spare?" A long sigh came over the phone. "Fuck."

She closed her eyes. Exhaustion was setting in, and she sagged against the dresser. "Watch the language, my boy."

"Sorry. But...I'm broke."

"I transferred money into your account on the first. That was supposed to last you all month."

Silence. "Well, it didn't. Things cost more now. I need some money, Mom."

She frowned. "For what?"

"To eat, dammit."

"Your job at the cafeteria pays for your meals."

"I quit, all right? It was taking too much time and—" He broke off.

And his friends didn't have to work. She frowned. Frederick's life insurance paid for the children's tuition and books, and she took care of their rent and gave them a small allowance. He wasn't being abused, despite his whining. "I'm sorry, Charles. You'd better get the job back. I don't have the money to spare."

"I... Fine." The silence grew. Then he muttered, "Right."

She blinked back tears, unable to speak, and after a second heard the brat turn back into the sweetheart she'd raised.

"I'm sorry, Mom. And I really am glad you're back. See you next weekend."

"Bye," she whispered to the dial tone. She listened to the hum for a while, too tired to set the receiver down.

Too afraid of starting to cry. Normally she'd have taken his behavior in stride. It was just...now...that everything seemed to abrade her feelings.

Saying no was the right thing to do. Even if she'd been rich, she'd make him work for part of his college expenses. People didn't value anything unless they themselves put some effort into getting it. Which meant if she handed him all the money, he'd actually be more liable to flunk out.

Logic didn't help. She'd disappointed her baby. *Welcome home, Linda.*

* * * *

At the end of that week, Linda stood behind the counter in her beachfront store, ringing up the sale of a canvas, hand-stitched beach tote. Her feet were screaming at being forced back into her favorite high-heeled sandals, her legs ached from standing so much, and her shoulders were knotted from evenings spent on the accounting backlog. Yet it was wonderful to be home. Her life was returning to normal.

"You have a lovely store." The customer signed the charge slip.

"Thank you." Linda beamed as she handed over the receipt. "Have a wonderful day on the beach."

After growing up in a tiny Florida town, she'd thought she'd simply be a teacher. Or maybe a preacher's wife like her mother had been. Who knew that she'd love running her own business, love the interactions with customers? And after the slavers had tried to convince her she was nothing more than a slut, she needed the reassurance that she was good at what she did.

The store door was latched open, letting customers on the boardwalk flow in and out. Inside, a young couple, hand in hand, were checking out the etched coffee cups. A trio of older women studied the wall of Florida shore paintings. On the right, her clerk was restocking the glass case holding the handcrafted jewelry.

Linda inhaled, enjoying how the sand candles' scents mingled with the salty air off the Gulf. Her tiny store specialized in handcrafted items for tourists. It held no shot glasses or T-shirts made overseas by the thousands. Instead, everything was created by Florida artisans. She even commissioned some of the more popular items. To her delight, the baskets she made also sold well.

She'd never make a fortune but had enough to pay bills and help the children with their expenses—although not working for five months had come close to being a disaster. Thank goodness that after Frederick's death, she'd set up her affairs so the children and business would be handled in case of her death or disability.

But even though the accounting firm had handled the bills and payroll, everything else was behind. In fact, she'd only managed to join Lee for lunch once. Seeing the guy she'd dated off and on before her kidnapping had been...awkward. But Lee was a nice man. He hadn't pushed her and had turned their conversation to local affairs, letting her fill in as she wanted. Although he'd asked her out, she'd put him off for another week. She really did have too much to do.

In fact... She frowned at the window display, which needed to be redone as well.

By the open door, two townspeople slowed to look inside. As their voices dropped to whispers, Linda stiffened.

Her four part-time clerks had been overjoyed to have her back. She'd needed that reassurance since her kidnapping and return had created ripples through the town. The beachfront shop owners and clerks formed a small community of their own, and her acceptance there and elsewhere had changed. She heard ugly whispers everywhere, even with customers in her own store, and the sound was wearing her down.

She'd started to feel like the prostitute in *Pretty Woman*—the one who had discovered that a respectable appearance didn't mean she could ever belong.

"All done." At the jewelry case, Maribelle straightened, patting her short gray hair into place. "I might have to buy my granddaughter those pretty shell earrings. What do you want done now?"

The store suddenly felt confining, and Linda wanted out. "If you'll watch the store, I need to make a coffee run. Want one?"

"No. I've had too much caffeine already." Maribelle took up position behind the counter as Linda stepped into the back to grab a few dollars from her purse.

The small coffee shop was a few stores down, and Linda had always enjoyed the short walk. Even in late January, the sounds of the beach were heartening. Children's shrieks of joy as the gulls dipped down to look for food, a small dog's high yapping, the *thump* and yells of the young men playing volleyball. Under it all, the shushing sound of the waves. She stopped to simply savor the cloudless blue sky over the blue-gray ocean and the white sand bedecked with brightly dressed tourists.

Could anyone who hadn't been imprisoned truly appreciate the glory of just being outside?

When she entered the coffee shop, the scent of newly brewed coffee zinged across her senses.

Waiting at the pickup counter for her order, the toy-store manager nodded at her. "Good to have you back, hon."

Linda smiled. She didn't like the reminder of her ordeal, but the warmth of friendship was never unwelcome. "Thank you, Sandy."

Behind the counter, the coffee-shop owner handed Sandy her drink before looking over. "Linda, what can I make you? The peppermint drinks are on sale today."

"Um." Be virtuous or go for indulgence? She considered. Her body hurt and not in the happy way Sam had given her. *Don't think of that.* "Peppermint white chocolate mocha." Caffeine, fat, sugar, and chocolate—all the essential food groups except salt. "Thanks, Betty."

"Coming right up."

As Linda wavered over buying a scone, she heard whispers from a threesome at a table. Lawrence, who managed the upmarket art gallery, an older woman, and a woman from Linda's church.

Keen hearing was sometimes a curse, she thought. And hating herself for the weakness, she listened anyway.

"That's right. They kept her as a slave." The older woman.

The churchwoman said, "A sex slave."

Linda felt as if her legs would give out.

"Really?" Lawrence leaned forward. "You think she—"

Tears prickled in her eyes as Linda fought the urge to flee. To simply walk away from the coffee shop, her store, everything. To hide in her house and never come out. But what would that achieve except losing her business? The gossip would certainly continue. *Tough it out, girl.* Eventually, some new, ground-shaking scandal would replace hers.

She unclenched her hands and moved to the other end of the counter, close to their table, to wait for her drink.

The table went silent as the two women concentrated on their doughnuts. Lawrence gave her a slow perusal that made her skin crawl. "Hi, Linda. Taking a break?"

"Just a coffee run." She forced her lips into a smile, then accepted her cup from Betty. Turning her back to the room to hide her trembling hands, she added extra sugar and eventually managed to get the plastic lid snapped on.

When she turned, the two women gawked at her as if she'd worn pasties and a thong rather than her cream-colored, button-up shirt and tan slacks. When she stared back, their attention turned to their food.

She headed for the door.

"Nice to see you again," Lawrence said.

She glanced over and nodded. "And you."

"We should get together sometime." His gaze dropped to her breasts, and he licked his lips.

Her anger flared. *I'm not a slut. Not.* Taking a sip of coffee, she let her gaze slide down his body. After deliberately checking out his crotch area, she gave a dismissive sniff—*way too small*—and left the room.

Well, way to make yourself an enemy. She didn't care. At one time, she might have ignored Lawrence's sleazy stare. But the constant verbal abuse she'd suffered as a slave had erased her tolerance.

"*Slut, that's all you are. Nothing else.*" The Overseer's voice, like putrid oil, still oozed through her memories. "*Just a convenient hole to use.*" She shuddered.

Then she recalled a different voice. "*Linda, I don't see you as a slave.*" The memory of Sam's rough words was like an afternoon downpour, washing the gutters clean of debris. His intent blue eyes had been hot, but he'd shown respect as well. He'd given her a safe word, mapped out what he'd do, how far he'd go.

The need to have his arms around her, his sandpapery voice in her ears, shook her so hard she stopped on the boardwalk. *Breathe. Get it together.* She drank her coffee, letting the burn settle her. How annoying for that sadist's voice to be so darned calming. What Sam sought from her might not be enslavement, but it wasn't what she wanted. Her life was normal now. She needed to keep it that way.

The comfort of her store wrapped around her as she entered. Since Maribelle was handling the customers, Linda picked up a wide basket and headed for the display window. *Florida winter. What would look appropriately seasonal?*

"Linda? Hey, Linda!" The man who walked in wore dark slacks and a long-sleeved shirt with garish red and purple stripes. His brown hair needed a trim.

"Hi, Dwayne." Before she met Lee, they'd dated a few times until their one time in bed had shown her that they didn't suit. He made love as badly as he reported the news.

"You haven't returned my phone calls." He halted a step too close.

She retreated a pace. "I've been busy. How are you?"

"I watched your testimony about being a sex slave."

Her mind blanked. *Sex slave.* She had never, ever called herself that.

"I want an interview. You tell me what it was like, what they did to you, and I'll make you famous."

Startled at his insinuating tone and unwholesome interest, she couldn't speak. Did he really think she'd give him a *Penthouse*-worthy report of the horrors she'd suffered? "I don't do interviews."

"How about the other slave—the blonde college kid? Were you close with Holly?"

The name was a hammer blow to her heart. Her inability to protect the girl had been far more devastating than her powerlessness to protect herself. Holly had been so terrified, had pleaded with the Overseer to let her go home. She'd been sold and died under the lash instead.

Linda blinked hard. "I'm busy. Please leave." As customers turned to look, she set her face into an expressionless mask.

Dwayne swept his gaze down her body. His voice dropped. "I gave it to you good, so why'd you dump me? Cuz you'd wanna be tied up when you're fucked? Did you have a better time with them than with me?"

Her stomach twisted. "Get out of my store!"

"Did you—"

Swallowing against the nausea, she yanked her cell phone out, punched two numbers, and turned it so he could see the display. *Nine. One.*

He made an ugly sound and walked away, turning in the door to snarl, "Welcome back, *slave.*"

You bastard. Her skin had turned cold and clammy, and as she filled the basket with the contents of the display window, her chest grew tighter and tighter, making it hard to breathe. Abandoning the pretense, she hurried toward the back of the store. As she passed, the two gray-haired customers looked at her as if they smelled week-old garbage.

At the counter, Maribelle was oblivious as she bantered with two children.

The back room was cool. Dark. It didn't help. *Oh God, oh God, oh God.* The tears started. Then her stomach heaved, and she ran for the bathroom.

Crying. Shaking. Throwing up.

Finally she rested her face against the wall. *Get up, Linda.* Her body wouldn't move. She watched a tiny spider in the corner. Working so hard on its web. The cleaning lady would probably destroy all its work.

That made her cry again.

Chapter Four

Sunday finally arrived. Linda had given herself the whole day off to enjoy. A day for bare feet, ripped jeans, and a Queen Latifah T-shirt. She hadn't been ready to face church, so she and the children had rescheduled their traditional after-church dinner for the evening. In the meantime, she planned to ignore the outside world and just...settle.

As she finished putting her lunch dishes into the dishwasher, she realized she was singing along with an old Carpenters' song on the radio, "I Need To Be in Love." She snorted. Wouldn't that just be a disaster, considering everything that had happened to her? Added to her past, she also had her *strange* desires...

Her jaw clenched. That horrible Dwayne. At least Lee had been polite, although the memory was still uncomfortable. Last fall after a couple of drinks, they'd gone to bed, and she'd asked for...more...trying to get him to bite, to spank. He'd been appalled.

Her mouth turned down. The mortification she'd felt with him had been the spur that sent her to a BDSM club. Like beads on a necklace, each event had led to the next and the next, until here she was. Postkidnapped. Kind of a mess. Trying to be normal.

She huffed a laugh, remembering the sting of Sam's hand hitting her bottom. Not exactly normal. Well, at least she was alive to whine about all her weird problems. And she was home, at last.

Sunlight streamed in through the big kitchen window, setting dust motes to dancing. Spirits lifting again, she sang the last line of the song into a pretend mic and finished with a quick spin before dropping the spatula into the rack. Yesterday at work had gone well. Her nightmares had decreased. She'd had a big bacon, tomato, and lettuce sandwich for lunch. *Yummy*. Slavery had taught her how important the tiny things in life were. A smile instead of a frown. Comfort foods rather than slop. Kind words. A warm hug could be more satisfying than the most intense orgasm—not that she'd gotten off recently.

Not since the night of the auction with Sam. A flush heated her cheeks. Damn the man.

Then again, maybe she should thank him. If it hadn't been for that night, she'd think nothing would ever arouse her again.

She shook her head. Somehow he'd simply overwhelmed her until all she'd been able to see or hear was him. His voice. His touch. The pain. And he'd driven her right to where he wanted her. Then humiliated her by making her orgasm. Her stomach clenched as she remembered the sleazy buyers leering at her. The slave next to her had stared, her face turning hard with a "how could you?" expression.

And Sam—she hadn't been able to read him at all. She sighed. She still couldn't. Considering the way she'd reacted to him at the Shadowlands, he hadn't lost his touch.

She wished she could say she responded sexually to any Dom, but that wouldn't be true. Sam had said they had *chemistry* between them. Then again, maybe it was just his lean, muscular body, sharp blue eyes, and aura of power that sparked her synapses into overdrive.

Or the way he talked... She put her hand over the flutter in her stomach. The man should have a license to kill for that voice. So deep and rough, like a gravel truck churning at the bottom of a chasm, with a flintlike edge that indicated he didn't take crap from anyone, especially a submissive.

She snorted. She'd normally have a fit if some guy called her "girl," but when Sam said it, every molecule in her body turned liquid. *Damn him.*

Wiping her hands on a towel, she tried to consider what her next task should be. Having her thoughts fall into a Sam rut couldn't be permitted. She couldn't afford anything...warped...in her life. In her children's lives.

Brenna and Charles had told her about the horrible time they'd suffered after she'd been kidnapped. How they'd panicked when no one could find her. They'd been terrified for her. And then reporters had hounded them, playing on their fears, coming up with all the worst scenarios.

How much worse would it be if the newspeople—or her children—learned she'd gone to a kink club?

But everything was returning to normal. The trials for the slavers were almost over. Her coworkers would forget her past. Her children could relax. She'd never, ever do anything to cause a sensation again.

She'd been Miss Boring and Respectable all her life, and being different had really not gone well.

After tossing the soiled towel in the laundry basket, she walked out the front door into the fresh air. She did that a lot—just to prove she could go outside when she wanted to. Typical ex-prisoner behavior.

In her yard, she inhaled slowly. Nothing smelled as good as the breeze off the ocean. The sky was a deep blue with puffy clouds white enough for a bleach commercial. Spring was coming, but this was the prettiest time of the year. The St. Augustine grass was crisp and bright. In a garish flash of color, a flock of feral parakeets settled onto the next-door lawn. She grinned at them.

The counselor had said her emotions would go up and down, but duh—that wasn't exactly news to anyone over twenty. One moment, a person celebrates a pregnancy, and the next, a father dies. A windfall of cash might be followed by a broken arm. *Learn to stand up. Learn to fall down.* Life's lessons didn't stop; they continued to the day of death.

And I'm alive. That was the important thing. Alive and free and... She stared at her house. To the right of the door, black words had been spray-painted over the pale blue wall: BURN IN HELL WHORE OF SATAN.

No. *No no no.* Her stomach roiled. Hand over her mouth, she ran for the house.

* * * *

Almost two hours later, she had sung every war song she knew as she scrubbed off the graffiti. Once finished, she frowned at the areas of lighter blue. Why in the world would someone do something like that? Whore of Satan. *Excuse me?*

Now that the words were gone, she could almost see the humor. It sounded like what her father—may he rest in peace—would roar during his pulpit-thumping sermons. *"And if you do not repent of your evil ways, then you will—"*

He'd considered the road to salvation to be extremely narrow. A *good* person needed faith, to do charitable works, to wear modest clothing, use respectful language, and observe proper behavior. Her sister, Wendy, had been cynical enough to ignore their parents' lectures, but Linda had never stopped trying to please them.

Her husband had been much like her father, but despite his conservative nature, at least Frederick had possessed a sense of humor.

A car door thudded, and as Linda turned, she heard, "Mom."

Her daughter was early. She plastered on a smile and dropped the brush behind the bushes. Thank goodness she'd finished eradicating the words from the wall. "Brenna!"

In a denim skirt and white tank top, Brenna ran across the lawn to give Linda a long hug. "Oh, Mom, I missed you so much."

"I missed you too, honey." Needing to stay strong for her baby, Linda blinked away tears and curved an arm around the girl. "Let's go have some tea. I made cookies for you and Charles."

Brenna grimaced. "Mo-om. As if I'm not fat enough."

"You certainly are not. You're lovely."

"As if." Hands waving in the air, Brenna led the way to the kitchen. "My ass is too big, my tits are like watermelons, and—"

Linda shook her head. Although an inch shorter than Linda's five feet seven, Brenna was at least thirty pounds lighter and nowhere near Linda's full figure. But over the years, Linda had learned to like having a curvy body. Brenna hadn't yet. "Sweetie, you have a beautiful figure, but you're never going to be tall and slender. It's not in our genes."

"Yeah, I know." Shoving her light brown hair behind her ears, she scowled. "Why couldn't I have inherited Dad's tall and skinny genes like Charles did?"

"Sorry. I didn't have a choice in that one." Linda spoke lightly, ignoring the feeling of rejection. "Have you seen Charles lately?"

"Not since we came over to make sure the house was okay."

"I appreciated you doing that."

Brenna shrugged away her mother's thanks. "You look good. Tan and like you've been living the high life at Aunt Wendy's."

Was that a hint of accusation in her words? Guilt tensed the muscles in Linda's chest. "I spent a lot of time in Wendy's garden." Yanking out the stubborn quack grass ferociously as if to kill the monsters that'd destroyed her life. Crying when the scent of blooming roses reminded her of her mother. Shaking and vomiting. The oddest things had affected her, like when her shovel had cut a worm in half. She'd gone into hysterics for half the day. "But it wasn't the high life."

"I'm sorry, Mom." Tears welled in her daughter's eyes. "I'm so glad you're back, but sometimes I just... I don't know why I said that."

"Oh, baby." Linda hugged her girl, trying to work past the hurt. Brenna wasn't cruel. "Do you remember when you ran away because I wouldn't let you go to a sleepover? You took your wagon with all your dolls in it."

Brenna choked on a laugh. "When I was in kindergarten?"

"Yes. For hours, we searched for you. You turned up at Myrtle's, playing with her grandchildren. We were so relieved. We hugged you and kissed you. But then—"

Brenna pulled away. "Daddy yelled at me. So did you. You guys never yelled, but…"

"That's right. But when you've been so scared, sometimes you react all over the person who scared you."

"Oh." After a moment's silence, she nodded. "Okay. I get it. I'll try not to take it out on you." Brenna wiped the tears from her eyes and attempted a frown. "But if I see you packing your dolls in the car, I'm going to yell."

"Fair enough." *Heavens, how did we make such beautiful children, Frederick?* "Want to help me get food on for supper? Charles should be here in a couple of hours, and I have the makings for a pot roast."

"Well, duh. Does a bear sh—" She caught her mother's warning look and adroitly substituted, "Poop in the woods? Can we add those little potatoes?"

"Well, duh."

Chapter Five

Sitting in his friend's great room, Sam took a long drink of beer. Raoul's home was a warm mix of Mediterranean and beach house. The patio doors stood open to let the sea breezes enter. With luck, the crisp air would unmuddle his brain.

Over a week had passed since the night at the Shadowlands when Linda had melted against him, given him everything he'd asked for, and then pushed him away. She wanted nothing to do with him.

He understood...somewhat. Didn't help his mood. He'd cleaned out the old stable, then started on the chicken house. Shoveling shit had suited his mood perfectly.

Yesterday the Internet alerts he'd set up on Linda's name had rewarded him with a newspaper article. After reading it—and stewing—he paid Raoul and Kim a visit. Maybe Raoul would know how to handle the situation. Damn the redhead for being so stubborn, and damn Sam for being an idiot. Damn him again for wanting a woman who hated the sight of him.

Only she didn't. Not from the way she'd responded at the Shadowlands.

"Sam?"

He looked up from his can of beer to see Raoul's pretty slave smiling at him from where she knelt beside her Master. With her black hair and striking blue eyes, she was pretty enough, but her spiritedness and caring nature were what had caught his friend. How someone so sweet had survived the slavers... Well, he knew another sweet woman who'd also survived.

"Yes, Kim?" The two women were very different. Kim created sparks and light wherever she went—and she'd livened up Raoul's life. Linda's personality was a steady fire, she had a compelling core of strength to draw upon, and she was as stubborn as a stump.

"Would you like some dessert?" Kim asked. "I made chocolate cake."

"In a bit. Have you spoken to Linda recently?"

"Not since she left. Her choice. She didn't want to be reminded of the past, at least as she settled in."

Yeah, that's what he'd been afraid of. He glanced at Raoul, who was stroking Kim's hair. "I'd like a favor."

"Of course," Raoul answered instantly. Although the man had the cynical practicality of an engineer who'd built an international company from scratch, his loyalty came with no strings attached.

"The Foggy Shores newspaper reported that Linda's house was spray-painted with something ugly." Although the tone of the article was pseudosweet, it had played up the gossip. Pissed Sam off thoroughly, and if the reporter had been in reach, the bastard would be spitting out teeth. Maybe his readers would enjoy that write-up as well.

Raoul's dark brown eyes filled with anger. "Has she not been through enough?" When Kim leaned against his thigh, he wrapped his arm around her, pulling her closer. "All of them suffered."

"Apparently someone doesn't think so." Sam rubbed his chin, a bad feeling growing inside him. He knew how bad homecomings could be. No, she wasn't a Vietnam vet, fresh from an unwinnable war, but death and cruelty weren't confined to battlegrounds. "Made me think, though. Kim had problems when she returned home, even with her mother to help. I don't think Linda has much support at all."

"Perhaps not." Raoul ran his fingers along the leather collar that Kim wore. "Would you call her now, gatita? So Sam might know whether to worry. Hopefully, we'll discover she is fine."

Sam met his gaze. Any Dom would be concerned about a submissive who'd been in his care. However, he didn't give a damn if Raoul figured out that Sam worried extra about Linda. "Appreciate it."

Kim brought a phone from the other room and punched in the number. A few seconds later, she said, "Linda, it's Kim. I called to see how you're doing."

The answer she got put a line between her brows. "You're fine? Honey, you don't sound all that good."

Sam scowled. Obviously Linda was damn well not *fine.*

"So what's it like to be home?"

All Sam could hear was a faint buzz.

Kim's mouth tightened. "That's bull. You don't have anything to do right now, and you're not getting off the phone so easy. You've been crying, haven't you? What's wrong?"

Sam growled, and Raoul sat forward.

The little slave rolled her eyes at them, but her frown was real. "Yes, I've been around Doms too long, and yes, I'm stubborn. So tell me what's going on."

Sam forced himself to sit back and not grab the phone. At least Kim was thoughtfully repeating bits of what Linda said.

Kim listened for a minute. "Spray-painted your house? What did it say?"

The answer made her eyes flash. "Sunday, Tuesday, and last night too? Linda, that's a little past persistent. Are the police doing anything?"

Anger surged through Sam so fiercely that he crushed the can in his hand. The bastard had struck three times in a week. What if he decided to escalate?

Raoul looked worried. He undoubtedly wanted to help. But his engineering company was swamped with work, and he was still behind from last fall when Kim had taken all his time.

"I don't care what you say. I'm sending you some help, one way or another." Kim's mouth flattened into a straight line.

As she wound up the phone call, Sam considered. Foggy Shores wasn't far from his house. He'd have to be home in the mornings to open the security gate when Nolan's crew arrived, but the neighbor's kid could handle the evening chores and reset the alarm. Everything else could wait. Didn't sound as if Linda could. "I'll go tomorrow," he told Raoul.

* * * *

A tapping noise wakened Linda. She tensed, expecting the Overseer's boot to slam into her ribs.

Nothing touched her.

Heart pounding, she cautiously opened her eyes and saw her own living room. *Home. I'm home.* Right. Worked all morning in the store. Indulged in a late-afternoon nap.

She jumped as the sound came again. Someone was knocking on the front door. *Someone* had scared her to death. She pursed her lips to slow her breathing. Where was a nice pistol when she needed one?

But when she cocked her thumb and aimed her finger at the door, her gun hand shook uncontrollably. Guess obtaining a real gun wouldn't work. Besides, her elderly postman would have a heart attack if bullets peppered the front stoop. It was probably him at the door now.

The knocking reverberated through her room, sounding a bit annoyed. The old guy had quite a fist on him.

Wiping the sweat from her face, Linda rose. "Coming." Her voice didn't reach past the end of the couch. "Coming!" After a few steps, her knees firmed up. She smoothed her sleeveless shirt and capris, attempted a smile, and opened the door.

No one was there.

She stepped outside to see a man in front of her house. "Sam?"

It really was him, in person, as if her dreams had conjured him out of thin air. The sunlight glinted off the gray strands in his collar-length hair. When he glanced at her, his pale eyes gleamed like light through clear blue glass.

He turned his attention back to the newest graffiti. *BITCH OF SATAN.* "Least the words are spelled right. Nice change from most," he said mildly and winked.

The half joke wasn't funny, yet it eased the fearful tenseness she'd had since discovering the ugly words. In fact, just his presence carried a sense of security with it. How did he do that?

As he walked closer, his shrewd gaze assessed her. "You look like hell, girl. Let's talk."

"But..."

"I don't do business on a doorstep." He grasped her upper arms, moved her so he could enter, and closed the door behind him. "Got something to drink? Water or tea or soda?"

"Of course." She was halfway to the kitchen before stopping. Boy, talk about automatic obedience. "Excuse me, but I don't recall inviting you here. How did you get my address?" Her hands tried to rub the chill from her arms. Had she found another kind of a stalker?

"Looked it up on the Internet." Her discomfort lightened when he sat down in an armchair, extended his long legs, and made himself at home. He obviously wasn't planning to jump on her. "Raoul couldn't come. I was available."

"I told Kim I didn't need help."

"And she told you she was sending help." He gave her a level stare. "Girl, you've been through enough grief. Let me help."

"But..." She scowled. If the cases had been reversed, she'd have sent someone to Kim. And from the tilt of Sam's jaw, arguing wouldn't get her anywhere. "Fine. Diet cola, Mountain Dew, or root beer?"

"Dew, thanks."

When she returned with his drink and a root beer for herself, he was studying her living room with the same intensity as he normally watched her. In jeans, worn brown boots, and a short-sleeved, button-up work shirt, he didn't seem as if interior decor would interest him.

She tilted her head. "What's so fascinating?"

"The colors. Brown, beige, off-white. Like you— warm but subdued." He took his drink from her and gestured toward the high windows. "Blinds up, lots of light. Not hiding." He pointed at the bright floral pillows and ran a finger over the silk-covered one at his feet, then patted the chair. "You like beauty but want comfort with it."

"Well." He was disconcertingly accurate.

The two acoustic guitars in the corner got an interested look. "Any chance you like country-western?"

"Among other things."

"We'll have to try plucking out a few tunes."

Since Charles moved out, she hadn't had anyone at home with whom to share music. She took a step toward the guitars and caught herself. *Don't be insane.* He hadn't driven to Foggy Shores to strum a guitar. "So you're here to help me?"

"One spray painting is a prank. More is a problem. You need some backup."

Just the word—backup—sent relief welling inside her. As tears prickled in her eyes, she busied herself with opening her root beer.

When she finally looked up, his hard blue eyes had softened. She hadn't hidden a thing. Odd how even the nastiest customers never realized what she thought of their behavior. But this man read her as accurately as if he had an instruction manual titled *How to Understand Linda.*

And he'd driven here to help her. "You...you don't have to. We're not even—" She stopped, realizing how rude that would sound.

He finished for her. "Friends. I know. I screwed up at the auction and made things more difficult for you. I owe you." Blunt. Rough. Devastatingly honest.

However, the past wasn't something he could fix. Not like this. She searched for a polite response. Settled on, "You were trying to help." And actually, he had. Otherwise, a real buyer would have whipped her. Hurt her. If only he'd stopped before...touching...her. Her face warmed, and she sipped against the uncomfortable twisting in her stomach. The mild bite of carbonation anchored her.

He looked as if he wanted to say something. Instead, he drank, swallow after swallow, his Adam's apple moving up and down, drawing her attention to his tanned, corded neck. The small hollow at the base was surrounded by muscles. She remembered the press of his body, a solid warm wall of flesh, and the room heated to match her face. What in the world was wrong with her?

"When does this happen? At night?"

She could almost feel a bed under her before realizing he was referring to the graffiti. She gave an involuntary snort. How could she possibly have lewd thoughts about this intimidating man? "Uh-huh."

"Anything else going on?" He glanced at the pile of newspapers on an end table. "Did you make the paper again today?"

"It's not important."

"Hogwash. Show me, Linda."

"Fine." Why did she feel as if she was going to cry? She walked across the room to where she'd put the ripped-out page on a bookshelf with the first, unable to destroy them, unable to look at them. "Here."

He took the paper. When he pulled a pair of reading glasses from his work-shirt pocket, she blinked. The glasses made him look...different. As if the jeans and rough behavior were a cover for the intelligent person beneath. After reading the article, he set the paper aside, and a tremor ran through her at the cold anger in his face.

"The reporter should be horsewhipped."

She took the paper from his lap and tossed it into the wastebasket. "It doesn't really matter. There's nothing you can do about it. I think you'd better go home."

He sipped his drink and watched her pace across the room.

She stopped. "Did you hear what I said?"

"I heard." He wasn't moving.

"Go home, Sam."

When she glared at him, he actually looked pleased. "Not much I can do about the reporter. Legally. But maybe your spray painter will show up tonight." He glanced over his shoulder at the hallway. "Got a place for me to sleep?"

She had to wonder if he raised cattle, because, oh boy, his expression was definitely a bullheaded one.

* * * *

Half an hour later, as Sam scrubbed and scraped the black paint off Linda's house, fury lashed his insides like a hailstorm. What kind of bastard picked on a woman—any woman—let alone one who had already suffered so much? He looked forward to getting his hands on the man. Be a pleasure to dispense a short, hard lesson in manners.

"Sam." She wore midcalf-length shorts—whatever they were called—and flip-flops. Her full breasts strained against her green top as she pulled her heavy red hair into a short tail. If her hair was a bit longer, he could wrap it around his fist. Less clothing would be good too. But no matter what she wore, she'd probably still warm his blood.

Scraper in hand, she joined him. "You really don't have to do this."

"'Course I do." The places where bare wood showed had obviously been written on before.

"Well, I appreciate it." She vigorously scrubbed at the black paint, and he noticed her freckled arms looked well toned.

Checking, he ran his hand over her upper arm and felt muscle beneath the soft padding.

She froze, staring up at him. "What are you doing?"

Why did he feel a magnetic pull every time he looked down into her big brown eyes? "You've put some muscle on. Been working out?" He kept his hand on her, feeling the slight quiver. Seeing nervousness replace fear.

"I-I was at my sister's house. In California." She pulled from his grasp and examined her arm as if she hadn't seen it before. "She has a huge garden."

"Gardens are good for mending."

She slanted him a disbelieving look. "Did you ever have anything to mend?"

His mouth tightened. But he'd finally got her talking. Backing away would silence her again. "'Nam."

"But..." She studied him. "You were old enough to be in Vietnam?"

"My recruiter cousin fudged the papers for me." Because his cuz had known about his stepfather's heavy hand. Pa had been a good man, but Ma hadn't chosen so well the second time.

"Dear God." She looked at him as if seeing the tall, lanky kid he'd been. Seeing him with a mother's eyes. "That wasn't right."

"Long time ago." At least he'd turned sixteen before his unit deployed. Nonetheless, he'd spent the next two years in hell. "The US pulled out when I hit eighteen."

"You were just a baby." Tears swam in her eyes, melting his memories.

"Nah. They don't call babies 'sergeant.'" He'd stayed in the army until his mother's and stepfather's deaths in a boating accident.

To erase Linda's tears, he cupped her chin. Her lips were soft. Sweet. And trembled slightly under his. When her hand pushed against his chest, he released her immediately. There would be other times.

"Where did you garden?" She sounded breathless, and he smothered a smile.

"Got some acres." Although his stepfather had sold off parts of his father's farm and run what was left into the ground, Sam had built it back up. Reacquired all the pieces and expanded as well. "And a vegetable garden." She had a faint dimple in her right cheek. He hadn't noticed it before.

"Kim said you had a place, but she didn't know if it was a ranch or a farm."

So she'd talked about him with others. When his lips tilted up, her face pinkened.

"Not much of a ranch with only a few horses and some cattle." He frowned as another brown patch of wood was exposed by the scrubbing. Looked like hell. After pulling out his cell, he punched in Nolan King's number.

"King."

"Davies. Friend's house got sprayed with graffiti. You got any of that special paint? Just need enough for the front."

"I don't have any at the moment. The shit expires fast. Got more ordered for a downtown job, though. You can have some when it comes in."

"That'll do." Closing the phone, Sam noticed Linda's confused expression. "Yeah?"

"Why not get something from the paint store?"

"They only have gloss coatings. With King's industrial stuff, the spray paint will run right off—won't even stick."

"Oh." Her eyes lit up, and she grinned at him. "I'd love to see the jerk's face if that happened."

He chuckled, pleased to have lifted her mood. In fact, it was disconcerting what he'd do to keep that light in her eyes.

But as he turned his attention back to the last letter on the wall, his anger ignited again. Probably wouldn't die down until he met the bastard artist up close and personal.

* * * *

Linda glanced at the kitchen table where Sam sat. The big, mean sadist had completed his assignment and neatly diced the vegetables. Should she be worried about how he got so skilled with a knife? "Very nice." After scooping them into a bowl, she dumped the contents into the meat sauce simmering on the stove.

His eyebrows went up.

"Yes, I know most people don't put veggies in their spaghetti sauce, but my children were fussy. I call it guerilla nutrition."

"Sneaky." His smile was as slow as his words. He didn't have a drawl exactly—he just took his time. And the smile didn't last long, but for a moment it totally transformed his face.

Not fair that he should look so appealing and comfortable in her kitchen. She spun back to the stove. After rinsing the noodles in the colander, she started creating the lasagna. It was a time-consuming dish, but she'd hoped to keep her hands busy and her mind occupied. Having Sam in her house was like inviting a grizzly bear in for a snack.

And yet having him here was incredibly reassuring. He knew who she was, what she'd been through, and he still...liked her. Or maybe not. Maybe he just felt guilty.

"Nice kitchen," he commented. His gaze shifted from the cream-colored pine cupboards to the dark blue walls to the golden marble countertops. He frowned as he studied the woven basket holding oranges, a tall coiled basket filled with wooden spoons, and the potted herbs inside colorful twined baskets. When he spotted the box of reeds on the kitchen shelves, he asked, "You do the baskets yourself?"

"Most of them." After setting a platter of cheese and crackers on the table, she pointed to a hand-sized plaited basket that held a variety of stones. The shape had odd bulges, and the weaving looked as if she'd been intoxicated. "I started when I was in high school."

"You've improved."

"Why, thank you." She grinned. "You know, you have a talent for being blunt without being quite rude." He gave her a contemplative stare as if he'd never had a woman tease him. Then again, who in their right mind would tease a sadist?

"Takes too much work to be rude." He nodded at a pile of baskets in a corner. "You planning something for those?"

She started the alternating layers of noodles, ricotta, mozzarella, and sauce. "I sell them at my store; otherwise I'd be buried in them. Hobbies are like zucchini—your friends and family can only absorb so much."

He snorted in agreement before loading a cracker with cheese. "Nicole quilts. Got one on every bed in the house. Couple hang on the walls."

Her hands stilled as a pang stabbed through her. Not...quite...pain. "Nicole?"

"My daughter."

She hadn't even considered that he'd have a family. He seemed to stand alone, like a cliff above the ocean. And yet what woman wouldn't want him? She stared down at the long casserole pan. "You're married?" Did he cheat on his wife?

With a creak of the chair, he rose to stand behind her. Ignoring the way she froze, he put his arm around her waist, holding her firmly against him. "I'm divorced." He huffed a laugh. "I'm a sadist, girl, not a cheater."

Even as relief streamed through her, she had to wonder how he could so easily say that. *"I'm a sadist."*

Chapter Six

What was that? Sam opened his eyes, frowning at the darkness in Linda's living room. For the previous three nights, he had slept on her couch. Although she'd offered a guest room, he had refused. In a back bedroom, he wouldn't hear a thing. He was here to catch the spray-painting bastard, not be comfortable.

He listened but heard only the hum of the refrigerator and slight ticking of the ceiling fan. The atmosphere of the house was cozy, clean without being obsessive, beautiful without being formal.

The first night, Linda had eventually relaxed after he'd talked her into playing guitar with him. Like Tanya Tucker, she had a low, rich voice that added a haunting quality to every song. He'd kept forgetting to play so he could listen.

The next evening, she'd let him pull her down beside him to watch a spy thriller. Warm body. Soft hips and shoulders. She had fit against his side as if she belonged there.

When she'd discovered he liked pie, he'd had homemade pie every night to go with her home-cooked meals. The woman was so grateful he was liable to put on twenty pounds.

Don't get attached to this one, Davies. He rubbed his chin, knowing it was already too late. She'd captivated him the moment he'd seen her, which seemed a mite odd. He wasn't some pimple-faced boy to fall for a girl on first sight, but he had. Maybe it was a sign of going senile?

Rustles. A *thump.* Sam rose. The sounds weren't from outside. He tracked the noise to Linda's bedroom and stopped outside, grinning. Was she playing with *toys*, having a good time?

Then he heard her whimper, her voice thin with fear. "No, no, please. Don't."

What the hell? Set to attack an intruder, Sam shoved the door open. A golden night-light revealed an empty room except for Linda thrashing on the bed in the throes of a nightmare. Hell, after what she'd endured, she probably had a lot of them. Her pale face gleamed with sweat. As her fingernails clawed the covers, his heart squeezed with pity.

He took a step forward and stopped. Which would she find more terrifying: a nightmare or Sam in her bedroom?

Probably him.

But his jaw clenched at the sounds of her fear. Scowling, he set a wooden chair a few feet from the bed, then sat and rested his elbows on his knees. A deep breath allowed him to calm his expression. The little sub didn't need to see an angry man at her bedside. "Linda. Linda, it's time to wake up."

Her movements stilled and then started again.

He deepened his voice to add a note of command. "Linda. Wake up now."

She gasped, and her eyes popped open. For a minute she lay as still as a petrified mouse. Then she turned her head slowly and looked around the room. Her muscles relaxed. Her gaze finally came to rest on him. "Sam?"

"Good guess." She hadn't panicked at the sight of him. Finest gift he'd had in a long time. "You had a nightmare."

"You woke me up?"

He nodded.

"Thank you." She sat up and pushed her damp hair out of her face. The covers pooled around her waist, and her breasts wobbled under the thin nightgown.

"Not a problem." He cursed silently at his hardening cock. She didn't need any reminders of what assholes men could be. Intending to leave, he stood, but her wide brown eyes were too vulnerable. Too haunted. "What's the matter, baby?" Moving slowly enough she could evade his touch, he ran his hand over her damp cheek.

Rather than pulling back, she leaned into his palm. The trust in the movement tightened his chest. "I'm still scared," she whispered. "I can feel them...the way they touched me. How it hurt." Her breath hitched.

Sam wasn't the one she feared. He sat on the bed, facing her, and pulled her into his arms so her head rested on his shoulder, her breasts against his chest. Closing his eyes, he treasured the chance to give her the comfort a man could offer.

Her hair always smelled of lavender with a hint of citrus—lime, maybe—and her gown was silky under his rough hands. All woman, this one. "You get a lot of nightmares?"

Her shoulders moved in a shrug, and she sighed, her breath a hint of warmth through his shirt. "They were getting better but increased again when I moved home."

Sam stiffened. "Does having me here make them worse?" He could always bunk in his truck if—

"*No.* No." Her forehead rubbed against his chest. "They were nastier when I was here alone. I feel safe around you." Her throaty laugh was rueful. "Isn't that the damnedest thing?"

No, because he'd protect her against the goddamned world if he had to. He stroked her back. Slowly. Silk over softness. "It's good. Now tell me why you were angry with me at the auction."

"I..." She tried to pull back, and he tightened his grip.

"No. Talk to me, girl." He doubted he'd share if he were in her position, but hell, that's why he got to be the Dom. "I got you off, and..."

"You're such a man." She huffed out a breath. "Women don't see things the same."

"Noticed that."

Damned if she didn't give a snorting laugh. "Okay, it's like this. They took everything from us. Clothes, speech. Took our b-bodies. All our choices. Our...humanity."

Our. Well if she found it easier to talk in generalities, he wouldn't correct her. "Go on."

She had her arms around him, and now her fingers dug into his back. Another connection. "All I—we—had left, all we could control were our thoughts. I stayed cold. Wouldn't give them the satisfaction of seeing they affected me."

He considered her strained voice. Rich buyers were egotistical assholes. A slave's lack of fear wouldn't go over well. "Didn't that make it worse for you?"

Her body tensed.

Yeah, it had gotten worse. He shut down the urge to slam his fist into something.

She whispered into his neck, "They got mad, especially the Overseer. But being frozen was the only way I could fight back. Then with you that night, I couldn't—"

"Hell. I took away your control and made you come."

Her head moved up and down on his shoulder. "In front of all of them. They were...watching." She shuddered. "The slave next to me... She looked at me like I'd betrayed her."

Damn. He'd known there was a reason she'd been so upset and angry, but it was worse than he'd figured. He'd undermined everything she'd fought to accomplish. Forced her own body to betray her. He was a damned fool. "I'm sorry, Linda. I wouldn't have...not if I'd realized."

Her breasts flattened on his chest as she pulled in a breath. "At first, I figured you made me get off for kicks. Just to prove you could."

A flicker of anger woke at the realization she'd lined him up with the assholes.

"But I know you better now. You didn't need to prove anything. You already knew what you could do to me. You even said as much." Her hands tightened on his back. "You thought you were doing me a favor, didn't you? Because you're a guy, and that's how men think about orgasms."

The sense of being forgiven was like stepping into the warmth of a Florida sun after being in dry air-conditioning. "I should have thought more carefully."

"It's okay. It wasn't a place where you had time to think."

"True." He closed his eyes, remembering the noise—crying and screaming. The auctioneer playing to the buyers' debased demands. The despair in the room had been a swamp, pulling him down. The stench of fear and sick lust had made it difficult to breathe, harder not to be sick. "It gave me nightmares too, girl."

WHAT A THING for a strong man to admit. Linda rolled her forehead against his shoulder. With a half laugh, he moved to lie flat on his back and pulled her down beside him. His muscles rippled as he arranged her so her cheek rested on his shoulder. His arms were iron bands around her, holding her closely, and the remnants of the nightmare melted in the warmth of his body.

How long had it been since she'd let herself be snuggled? Long before the kidnapping. Not with that jerk Dwayne—she'd just wanted him gone. And sweet as Lee was, he didn't cuddle.

This was…nice. She breathed in the clean fragrance of his shirt, and deeper, his masculine scent, and squirmed closer. But when she flung her left leg over his, she bumped into a hard erection. An appalled sound escaped her, and she tensed.

"Girl." The single chastising word somehow conveyed an entire speech of how he wouldn't do anything she didn't want and how guys get erections and she was being silly. All in one word.

A tiny laugh escaped her, because that was so…Sam. She'd seen the way he watched her, how he desired her, yet he never made her feel sleazy or dirty. Just…wanted. "Sam, I—"

"Go to sleep. Morning comes soon enough."

The hint of amusement and the stillness of his body eased the last of her worry, and she obeyed, letting the sense of safety tumble her into slumber.

* * * *

Sunlight through the curtains wakened her. He was gone, and she'd had her best sleep in months. The sheets still held his scent, and she pulled the pillow to her, breathing in all that was Sam. Feeling her body waken. Dampen. *Come alive.*

* * * *

That evening, Linda slipped into bed, the coolness of the sheets contrasting with her warm body. All day, she'd felt as if her body was playing a song like Pachelbel's "Canon"...and the melody with all its variations and repetitions was named *desire.*

When Sam had arrived that evening, the entire orchestra joined in.

And now she was ready. Surely she was.

After getting home from work, she'd taken a long bubble bath, then shaved her legs and underarms...and her pussy. She smiled, remembering her first awkward attempt at shaving down there—after her best friend had asked Linda if she intended to mourn her husband forever. That week, so long ago, she'd had her hair restyled, changed her makeup, bought brighter clothing, and...shaved. For the first time since Frederick's death, she had felt like a woman.

She certainly felt like a woman tonight. After Sam had arrived, Linda had fixed supper and scolded him for cutting the carrots too small. His swift grin had set up a beat low in her pelvis. When she'd talked him into playing guitar with her, the sight of his strong fingers wrapped around the neck of the guitar had mesmerized her. When he had picked out a scary movie, she'd agreed, wanting only a reason to burrow into him on the couch.

Every breath had held his scent of the crisp outdoors. Whole and right. And the buzz of awareness that said she was with a man—one she wanted—had never faded.

When the time grew late, he hadn't confused her with choices. Far too experienced in reading women—in reading her—he'd pulled her to her feet and told her to get ready for bed. That he'd be in soon.

Under the covers, she waited, worries swelling and clogging her throat until she couldn't swallow. The sheets were cool. Surely that's why she was shivering.

His footsteps were softer than normal. He'd removed his boots. As he entered the room, though, she saw he still wore his jeans. *Thank you, God.*

In silence, he pulled the covers back and settled beside her. Warm.

She snuggled against his side with a sigh.

He didn't move, letting her take things at her own speed. Letting her decide. The beauty of his patience made her eyes well with tears.

The knowledge that he wanted her sent a hum through her system. *I know him.* He'd touched her intimately at the auction. Again at the Shadowlands. *Hands calloused from work moving over her skin. His deep voice whispering in her ear.*

She wanted him, *oh yes*, but could she have sex with him without panicking? In San Diego, she'd thought she'd be celibate for…oh, a decade or so. At least. But that was before Sam had set desire simmering deep inside her.

But now what?

In grade school, she'd been so shy that reading aloud had terrified her, and if she stalled, her nervousness increased until she couldn't speak at all. So she would always volunteer to go first.

Now, even as she lay beside Sam, her anxiety was rising. Time to start while she still could. She pushed up onto one elbow.

In the dim light, his face was shadowy as his pale eyes studied her face. "Tell me what you want to do."

She took his hand from her shoulder and moved it to her breast. "I want to…to try."

He didn't even pretend to misunderstand her. "All right." His answer was immediate. Simple. "We're not playing now though. 'No' means no. 'Stop' means stop. Is that clear?"

Not playing, but you couldn't take the Dom out of the man. He was still setting the rules. Her lips quivered, then curved. "Yes, Sir."

His laugh was a rumbled chuckle before he kissed her. Oh, she remembered his lips. Firm and knowledgeable, but more gentle this time. As if he'd let her decide how fast and how far they'd go.

"Condoms?" he asked.

She rolled away, grabbed a packet from the bedside table, and returned to his arms before she lost her nerve.

As he pulled the condom from her clenched fingers, the war started inside her. How could she have asked him for sex? That was disgusting. Sleazy. Bad. She was bad.

When he kissed her, her body stiffened. He lifted his head, his lips an inch from hers. "Talk to me."

I want this. I don't. I shouldn't. "I don't want to...decide." She felt wrong. Dirty. Wanting to have sex was—

His eyes narrowed, and then he gripped her hair, holding her head immobile as he took her lips. Not cruelly, not like...them. *Them. The slavers.* Like an avalanche, memories swept over her, flattening her.

A nasty pinch on her thigh made her jerk. "Stay with me, girl." His growling voice was like sandpaper, scraping away the horrors, digging down to where her nerves were alive. "Say my name."

His unyielding expression set up a trembling in her belly that had nothing to do with fear. "Sam."

"Again." His left arm around her waist tightened as he closed his other hand on her breast. Cupping, kneading, tugging. His penetrating gaze stayed on her face, and his fingers closed on her nipple. And pinched...

When the pressure turned to pain, sensation streamed in a wave of light and heat straight to her core. "*Sam.*"

His lips curved in a ruthless smile. "Good that you respond to the reins." His hand moved to her other breast, no longer gentle but demanding. Yet...careful. Never with the careless brutality that the Overseer—

"Ow!" Her hip stung where he'd given it a mean pinch.

"When I want you to think, I'll tell you." And how could such an arrogant statement make her stomach drop? He took her lips again, and at the same time she felt him untying the lacing at the top of her nightgown, pushing it to her waist in a whisper of cool silk. His hand returned to her bare breasts. Calloused, abrasive...warm.

"I look forward to using clamps on these," he whispered in her ear, tugging and pinching. "They'll hurt like this." His fingernail dug into the tender flesh until she gasped at the burning pain. He bit her shoulder, adding a new sting to the ones bombarding her body.

Too much. One of the guards had... When they'd all... Hands and agony and... She shoved away frantically, gasping for air.

He released her immediately. But before she could escape, he gripped her shoulders and gave her a firm shake. "Look at me, girl."

That growl—it haunted her dreams and chased away nightmares. Her eyes popped open and met the blue fire of his. "Sam."

"That's right."

She was trembling hard enough to shake the bed as he sat up next to her. He gripped her, anchoring her with firmness, the levelness of his gaze holding her in safety.

Her heart rate slowed. "I'm sorry."

The sun lines around his eyes deepened. "You can control your body only so far. Stupid to blame anyone for a physical reaction."

And no matter how gruff his language, Sam was very far from a stupid person. But she felt dumb. "Why was it easier? At the auction."

Holding her shoulder with one hand, he ran his fingers through her hair, tugging slightly. "More than one reason. In a room of scumbags, Kim sent me to you. Right?"

She remembered the sense of relief when she'd seen Kim nod her approval at Sam. She'd figured Kim knew something she didn't. "And you didn't see me as a slave." The realization had been overwhelming. He'd seen a person, not an animal. After checking her restraints, he'd looked into her eyes. *"You still with me here, Linda?"* He'd even used her name.

"You trusted me, no matter how little." He continued playing with her hair. "But you were scared, and then I hurt you."

"I don't understand."

"Fight-or-flight revs up the nerves. So does pain. Means you felt more than normal. So after I'd whipped you, you were loaded with endorphins and in subspace. Turned your head right off." He cupped her face. "Baby, once you gave me your trust, you were a peach ready to be plucked, and there was nothing you could do about it."

"Oh." The explanation helped. "I still shouldn't have…" She still felt guilty for coming. Felt dirty.

"Do your eyes tear up when you peel an onion?"

"Huh?" What the heck? "Yes."

"That's your nerves reacting to chemicals. If you tell yourself not to cry when peeling onions, does that work?"

"No," she whispered. Nerves and chemicals. A person couldn't control those. She hadn't had a chance. The guilt of that orgasm wafted away along with the last of her anger at his actions.

"That's better." As he rubbed his cheek against hers, the rough stubble scraped her skin and sent a shiver through her. "But enough warnings. You think about anything but here and now, I'll spank you."

His bare hand would slap her bottom. He'd hurt her and… A shiver of need ran up her spine.

He laughed, actually laughed. "Why wait?" He rose. Grasping her around the waist, he pulled her out of the covers and bent her over the side of the bed.

"Sam!" Her face against the quilt muffled the words.

"Good. You remember my name." His hand gripped her nape, holding her down as he lifted her gown. Cool air washed over her skin. He rubbed her cheeks, massaged them. *Touching her.* "You have a beautiful ass. Just right."

With the first light spanks, blood felt as if it detoured from her heart straight to her clit.

He hit harder. Stinging increased into pain, and then he started to seriously spank her. Hard and even. *Slap, slap, slap.* It hurt. Tears filled her eyes, and her fingers fisted in the quilt. And then, within one breath and another, the magic happened. As each smack flowed inward, it transformed into glittering pleasure.

He stopped to rub her skin. The joy of his touch sheeted through her, deeper even than the throbbing of her bottom. As his fingers explored the wetness on her inner thighs, he growled in approval, erasing the ugly guilt inside her before it took hold.

Tortuously, he traced a finger over her labia and up to circle her clit, sending a burst of need through her.

"Wait," she whispered, trying to stand.

"No, missy. You don't run from pain…or desire."

Her breathing sped up. He didn't stop. Holding her in place, he continued touching her so very intimately. When he rolled her clit between his fingers, her whole body shook as the sensation blasted outward, burning past the last barrier. She moaned into the bedding.

"There's a good girl." His finger swirled her entrance before rubbing each side of her swollen nub and around the top in an inflexible, relentless pattern: side, side, top, side, side, top, until each sensitized part *anticipated* his touch. Pressure grew inside her as with every new cycle, he pressed harder, longer.

Her bottom arched up; her legs trembled. *More. More. Don't stop.*

He paused, his fingertip resting right on the very top of her clit.

Her breathing stopped, everything stopped, frozen right there at the edge. A high whine escaped.

His fingers tightened on her nape as if to remind her of his hold and to induce the rush of knowing she had no control. Then his finger moved: side, side, and on the top of her clit, it remained, hard and fast and merciless, rubbing over and over.

Everything inside her coalesced for one unending heartbeat...and the ball of sensation ignited. Brilliant pleasure seared outward through every cell in her body. *Oh God...*

Her hips were bucking, her fingernails tingling, and dear heavens, he started spanking her again, harder and faster. Another orgasm hit right on the tails of the first, plummeting her back into the joyous maelstrom.

Every slap on her bottom felt amazing, a flaring splendor. His powerful hand held her pinned, making her take everything he did.

Then he slid his hand between her legs and pushed two fingers up inside her.

Inside. They had—they had— Panic ripped through her, and she struggled.

"Linda." He pulled out, and his hand hit her bottom. Hard. The fiery blast shook her body. "Say my name."

"S-Sam." *Sam.* Clenching the blankets, she gasped and found the world held air.

"Better." His fingers entered her again, sliding easily. Shivers ran through her at his determined assault...and the swelling pleasure. As he set up a merciless rhythm, arousal spiraled up in her again.

He pulled out long enough to spank her more. As each sharply hot impact resounded deep in her core, her need twined and coiled into a thick ball of pressure. When his fingers thrust inside her again, slamming in so unexpectedly, the searing tension exploded into wave upon wave of sensation.

Gradually, he slowed, bringing her down, and she could feel how her insides clenched his thick fingers, trying to hold him in.

"God," she muttered and heard him laugh. Her thumping heart began to slow. She rolled her face against the quilt, almost appalled at the wonderful feeling inside her.

He pulled out slowly. With her wetness still on his fingers, he rubbed her bottom, making her groan at the exquisite burning. After caressing her nape, he released his hold.

She missed the warmth of his hand—and the sense of being held captive.

His rough voice was gentle as he asked, "You ready for my cock, missy?" He pushed her hair out of her face. "It will happen. We both know that. But it doesn't need to be tonight."

A cock. The slavers had... Pushing inside her and—

He swatted her bottom, and she yelped at the shock.

"Say my name."

"Sam." This time, the body over her, inside her, would be *his*. She'd dreamed of him. Her voice was hoarse as she answered. "Tonight. Now." Maybe she could even return to him some of the bliss he'd given her.

"All right."

She started to rise and was flattened by a hand between her shoulder blades.

"No. I like you there."

Her stomach tightened, and a shiver raced through her. Anticipation. Fear. Her eyes closed; her body tensed. She heard his belt buckle. A sliding sound. A zipper. The condom wrapper.

She tensed, waiting for him to push against her pussy to— Something smacked her bottom in a shocking eruption of pain.

"Aaaah!" That hurt like nothing she'd felt before. His hand flattened on her midback, shoving her into the mattress as he hit her again with...with his folded-over belt.

Leather hurt much more. *More, more, more.* The sharpness bit at her, wrapped around her, digging in with thickening tentacles of pleasure. As he continued, her brain went hazy and the bed dissolved beneath her, leaving her falling through the air. The blows slid right into a growing joy, and she wanted him to continue forever.

And then he pressed his cock against her, slid inside her. Filled her. The glorious stretching expanded outward from her core, even as the burning still sizzled on her skin, until she didn't know which feeling was which.

He was a solid, intimate presence inside her, keeping her centered as he drove into her, over and over.

The fog receded as his relentless strokes wakened her until she pushed back against each thrust, needing more.

His guttural laugh was as arousingly effective as the fingers he slid over her clit. Her entire lower half clenched as he teased her, hammered her, and drove her to the pinnacle.

There she balanced until each tiny movement felt like the ultimate of sensation. Everything inside her tightened. Her breathing stopped.

Then he seized hold of her burning, abused ass cheek, gripping hard. The searing blast shot inward, igniting her release—shoving her right off the cliff. "Ah, ah, ahhh."

"That a girl." With both hands, he gripped her hips, pounding into her, then pressing deep. Deep. Over the roaring of her pulse, she heard his rough, rumbling groan of satisfaction.

As her heart battered her ribs into mush and she gasped for air, she felt an unfamiliar peace touch her soul. *I made him happy.* His body was heavy, flattening her on the bed...and she wouldn't have moved for the world.

Eventually, he lifted up. When he ran his hand down her back and over her raw bottom, tingles sparked fitfully across her skin. "I'm pulling out, baby. Stay there."

He emptied her, leaving her limp and drained, and she'd have slid off the bed if he hadn't hoisted her higher on it. She heard his footsteps go, then return.

Without asking, he stripped her nightgown completely off, then took a place on the bed and pulled her into his arms.

His skin was slightly damp, and she rested her sweat-streaked cheek on his chest. "I had an orgasm," she said, her head still hazy.

"Several." With her ear against his chest, his laugh sounded like thunder in the distance.

The smell of sex in the room made her want to hide, yet Sam's scent was there. Not leather tonight, but hay and grass and the outdoors. And soap.

"You don't use cologne or aftershave?"

There was a pause as if he tried to follow her train of thought. Then he huffed a laugh. "Soap works well enough."

"Mmmm." With each breath, she felt as if she inhaled strength, and so she filled her lungs completely to get it all in.

SAM LISTENED TO Linda's breathing slow as she drifted into sleep. He stayed awake, simply enjoying the feel of her body against his, the limpness of a satisfied woman.

After an hour, her body stiffened, and her tears dampened his chest.

"Linda?"

She pushed against him, trying to sit up, but he held her in place. "If you need to cry, you do it here, girl." *Where I can watch over you.*

A sob broke off. "I don't... I was feeling fine."

"You said your emotions bounce around." He tensed. Had he caused this? Maybe she hadn't been ready.

As his concern grew, her tears continued. But these weren't the heaving sobs of emotional trauma; she cried almost silently.

"Linda, tell me what's wrong."

"Every-everything feels wrong."

After a minute, he realized he'd assumed the upheaval was from the past. But perhaps this was something more common. He tightened his arms around her and kissed the top of her head. "You know what subdrop is?"

Her head moved. *No.*

"Sometimes the endorphins that send you into a good place wear off. Leave you in a hole. Once you know what it feels like, it's not as bad." Or so the subs said. "Kinda like a kid after a party, buzzed on sugar, missing a nap. Nicole used to work her way into a tantrum and end up crying on my lap. Crashing as everything wore off. You're crashing, baby."

"Oh, wonderful. What's the cure?"

"Just this." He rubbed his hands up and down her back, letting her know she wasn't alone. That someone was there to watch over her. There wasn't much else he could do. Dammit.

"I'm glad you're here." She patted his shoulder, then took a shuddering breath. "And it was worth it. I had an orgasm."

Yeah, she was going to be fine. He stared up in the darkness, realizing he was smiling at how insufferably pleased she sounded.

Chapter Seven

Early the next day, behind the store counter, Linda was making lists of new merchandise to buy and possible craftspeople to consider. Two Canadian-sounding customers were browsing the quiet store. She took in their attire of shorts, tanks, and flip-flops. They were definitely from farther north.

In contrast, Linda wore a long-sleeved shirt and tan slacks. Opal, her clerk, was in an ankle-length denim dress, because—to Floridians—sixty degrees was on the chilly side.

As Opal dragged a box of tote bags across the floor, her kinky black hair bounced with each tug. She saw Linda watching, and her dark brown eyes brightened. "You look good today. Happier."

I had an orgasm. "I'm starting to settle back in." Had she looked that unhappy?

"I'm glad. It's nice to have you back. You'd think it would be good to have the boss gone, but it's not the same place without you."

As the young woman headed for the shelves, Linda felt as if she'd inhaled bubbles and was floating a couple of inches above the chair. The pressure in her chest was gone. That irritable itchy feeling was gone. Like a sandy beach, she'd been scoured clean, the ugly seaweed and junk swept away by the waves.

But was it only because she'd had an orgasm? Setting her chin in her palm, she doodled on the list. Drew a row of tulips.

Before she'd been kidnapped, a good night of sex had never resulted in such an uplift the next day. Her pen fashioned a rose...then an outline of Sam's big hand. Of course, no one—not even Frederick—had given her such amazing climaxes, but what if her mood wasn't due to sex at all? Hadn't she felt like this after Sam had flogged her in the Shadowlands? All open and free. Clean.

She frowned. The pressure inside her had built up again, hadn't it? She just hadn't noticed, what with all the other complications in her life.

But an experienced sadist might have noticed. Had Sam given her that spanking and strapping for more reasons than diverting her mind from the slavers? Her pen dug into the paper, sending jagged lightning toward the flowers. He always watched her so intently. Studied her. A belt took form on the paper and doubled over.

Yes, he'd known. And since he was a Dom down to his bootlaces, he'd given her what he figured she needed.

He'd been wrong, dammit. *I refuse to be a masochist.* She bit her lip, wondering if she was the one who was wrong. Maybe she *had* needed the pain. And possibly for longer than just the past few months. A sinking feeling made her lean against the counter. Possibly for a long, long time.

But she'd found other methods to handle the feelings. Eating foods spicy enough to make the children complain. Cleaning and doing yard work until her limbs trembled. Working out in the gym so long that every muscle in her body ached like a sore tooth. Her husband had called it *"having a mood on her"* and had attributed it to her being female.

Her lips quirked. A good spanking might have saved her all sorts of effort. But Frederick had never wanted to discuss sex. The few times she'd asked him for something different—a swat, some roughness, to hold her down— he'd been disgusted.

More customers came in, browsing the basket section. Actually, Frederick had been more than simply disgusted; he'd implied she had a mental problem. Her pen scribbled dark clouds along the edge of the paper. She'd never tried to talk about sex again.

But maybe she *was* mentally unstable. Dismay splattered over her happy mood like a cold rain. She'd told herself the flogging at the Shadowlands would be the last time. Insisted on it. But then she'd let Sam spank her. Whip her with his belt.

What had she been thinking? A normal person didn't visit BDSM clubs and definitely didn't let a man spank her. A little kink was one thing. *Needing* to be hurt was entirely different.

This had to stop. She wasn't going to let herself be a masochist.

But...what about Sam? She closed her eyes, remembering his hard kiss before he'd left her bed. If she continued to see him, he'd give her the pain she craved, and she'd never be able to stop. Like a drug dealer, he fed her addiction.

This must end. No matter how she felt about him, she couldn't keep sleeping with him. Not tonight. Not ever. The realization, the resolution, hurt something deep inside her.

"Miss?"

Linda pasted on a smile for the young woman. "That's a lovely piece." She rang up the sale of the carved candlestick and managed to chat with the Canadian and her friend.

As the two women walked out, Linda reached for her cell phone. Her hand shook. *Need to do this. Don't be a coward.* She punched in Sam's number.

"Davies." His dark, rasping voice sent her hormones bubbling into instant carbonation.

"It's Linda. I've been thinking. The graffiti guy seems to have stopped. I don't think you need to waste your time driving here every day." Even as she said it, her chest tightened.

Silence.

"Sam?"

"You saying you don't want to see me again?"

The disconcertingly blunt question stabbed through her, and she smothered an instinctive *no*. He deserved better than a stupid excuse. She was being cowardly. Tangling her fingers in her hair, she yanked. *Be honest.* "Sam, you mean a lot to me. And I really, really appreciate the time you've spent, helping me." *Holding me.* "We're friends, and I'll always be grateful." She closed her eyes, pulling in a slow breath. "God, I feel as if I've been using you. I didn't mean to."

"But..."

"But I don't want...want to do what we did. I can't be like that. I need to be normal." Her pen scribbled over the hand she'd drawn, blotting it out, each black line adding a fresh slice of hurt.

"*Normal.*"

Tears blurred her eyes at the disgust in his voice. "Yes."

"Girl, no one is normal. Even the ones who try to appear that way."

"That doesn't matter. This is—"

"I understand. All too well." He paused. "How about I come over and we talk?"

"There's no point." And he'd look at her with those perceptive blue eyes, say her name, and she'd cave. She would. A vise of guilt squeezed the breath from her. She'd do anything to keep from hurting Sam—anything but continue on the path they were going down.

"I see." Ice covered the gravel of his voice. "I think you're wrong, girl, but you'll find that out yourself."

"Yes. Then this is good-b—"

"Mebbe. Doesn't sound like you know what you're doing."

She did, didn't she? "But—"

He'd disconnected. *Well.* That was that. As she straightened, she looked down at her paper. Black scribbles had blotted out the flowers and the writing. After pulling in a steadying breath, she started a fresh list.

The afternoon dragged on and on and on. For the first time, she took no joy in her store, in the customers. *I want to go home.*

"Linda, sweetheart." She glanced up to see Lee halfway to the counter, his suit and tie a marked contrast to the casually dressed beachgoers. His sandy hair had been tousled by the wind, and he finger combed it as he grinned at her. The women customers gave him lingering looks.

Linda forced a smile. "What are you doing here?"

"I was in the area." Lee leaned over the counter to give her a quick kiss on the cheek. "Are you caught up yet? I want to take you out to dinner."

"I..."

"You know, you're an incredibly difficult woman to date."

"I'm not ready for...for anything, Lee." She bit her lip. "I know we were...intimate, but I don't—"

"No problem. We'll take it slow. Just dinner. Nothing else."

Here was the normal life she wanted. With a nice man. Months ago, when she'd sounded him out about kinky sex, he hadn't been interested at all, but he hadn't called her names as Dwayne had. Or implied she was mentally unstable like Frederick.

If she dated him, he'd keep her on the straight and narrow, and if she had to cope in other ways, she would. Hey, a ton of extra cleaning and exercising wouldn't be bad. "Then okay. I'd like that."

"I'll pick you up at seven."

Everything in her wanted to yell *no*. Let him in her house where memories of Sam would linger? She couldn't bear that. Not yet. "How about I meet you at the restaurant?"

* * * *

Now would this be considered stalking? Sam frowned. Seemed awfully close to it.

He'd been on the way to Linda's house, hoping she'd eased up and they could talk, when he'd spotted her car in a restaurant parking lot.

He shouldn't have turned in. Shouldn't have stopped. *Being a fool, Davies.*

As he followed the hostess across the restaurant, he spotted Linda sitting across from a man wearing a suit and tie. Damn, she was beautiful. She'd done that curling thing with her hair. Wore makeup to make her seal-brown eyes even bigger. Her light pink, silky top showed only a hint of cleavage.

The hostess moved past Linda and her goddamned date.

"Wait, miss," Sam said.

The waitress stopped.

"I'll sit there." He pointed to an empty table near the center of the room, a couple of tables from Linda's.

"But that's not—"

"Be appreciated."

"Uh." She gave him a flirtatious look. "Of course."

"Thank you." He ignored the chair she pulled out for him and chose one where he had a satisfying view of his quarry. *Acting like a stalker, Davies.* But the location was good. He couldn't hear their conversation, but she'd eventually catch sight of him. And then she would have a chance to see if she really wanted a normal life. A *normal* man.

If she was jumping into a relationship to flee from herself, that was just damn stupid. But if she seriously wanted Vanilla Boy, Sam would back off.

After ordering, he leaned back, sipped coffee, and enjoyed the view. Maybe some fools wouldn't consider her beautiful, but he thought she was stunning. And natural. After the years of Nancy's fake giggles and shrill hysterics, he appreciated Linda's open, full-bodied laughter.

Pissed him off that other men noticed as well.

And he resented the hell out of the fact that Vanilla Boy could make her laugh. Sam's jaw tightened. The man had no trouble keeping a conversation going; his words flowed like a flooding river.

If she wanted a talkative man, then she didn't want Sam.

Maybe she'd be happy with that bastard. If so...might as well leave. He lifted his hand for the waitress.

But Linda didn't appear sexually interested in the man. When Vanilla Boy reached across the table and took her hand, she displayed no reaction at all. Like she'd closed herself off.

Sam lowered his hand. She'd definitely reacted to him last night. He'd never felt a connection like that, as if he could smell her emotions as easily as he inhaled her scent. After what she'd been through, the trust she'd shown in him—letting him hold her, spank her, fuck her—had shaken him right to his bones.

Goddammit. He leaned back and settled in for the duration.

Eventually Linda's attention was diverted from the man by a family walking past. She glanced around the room. When her eyes met Sam's, her mouth dropped open. She stared at him blankly, then tore her gaze away. As she turned all her attention to her date, her jaw muscles were rigid.

Sam chuckled. She was obviously dying to glare at him but couldn't because the other guy would ask why.

Despite her desire to ignore him, her gaze kept flicking in his direction. He understood the feeling; he couldn't look away from her either. He saw that her cheeks and lips had turned a rose color; her eyes had taken on an added shine. Yeah, she definitely reacted sexually to Sam—as he did to her—as if being in the same room cranked the hormone level higher.

He tried not to stare at her as he ate his meal. Wasted money, since he might have been eating hay for all he tasted of the food. As he shoved the potatoes to one side, he frowned.

Was he being a fool? After all, they'd had sex a grand total of once.

Then again, although he'd dated Nancy a few times, the one time they'd screwed had convinced him to back away. His good sense hadn't been wrong, but by then it was too late. *"I'm on the pill"* wasn't the first of her lies but had the biggest impact. One that left him living in hell for over a decade—except for the bright light of his daughter. He could never regret the gift of Nicole.

So when it came to Linda, could his judgment be relied on? Well, he'd seen her at her worst. Seen her terrified. In pain. Angry with him. Even considering her panic attacks, she was one of the strongest people he knew.

No, he wasn't wrong about her.

After he finished eating, he leaned back, idly smacking his napkin against his palm, remembering the auction and how the dragon's tongue whip had flicked over her white skin. Her flinches, her groans, her arousal. Did she really want to live a life without that intensity? Feeling half-smothered?

THE RESTAURANT WAS way too hot, Linda thought as she gulped down her ice water. Across the table, Lee elaborated about next week's hotel conventions with a suggestion she drop off promotional material for the lobby information rack.

He was such a nice man. He always asked her opinion before deciding anything. He didn't try to boss her around. Shouldn't she be pleased that he treated her as an equal?

Her gaze flicked back to Sam. He'd dressed up—for him—in black jeans, black boots, a silver-buckled belt, and a burgundy western shirt with black snap pockets and piping. With his legs stretched out and crossed at the ankles, he looked like a man enjoying his coffee after a good meal. His muscled frame, hard face, and dangerous presence won interested looks from every woman in the place. Including her.

She wrenched her gaze away, managing to focus on Lee until she heard an odd rhythmic sound. What was that?

Idly watching a waiter clearing a nearby table, Sam was smacking the end of his linen napkin across his palm. *Slap, slap, slap.* It seemed an innocuous habit, as another man might tap his foot or play with his mustache; only this sounded and looked far too much like what he'd done to her in the dungeon. Or the bedroom.

Shifting, Linda licked lips that had gone dry, and the movement drew his attention. When his steady blue eyes met hers, she was suddenly, completely aroused.

A crease appeared in his cheek, and then he rose and walked out of the restaurant with the powerful saunter that was his alone.

"Linda?" Lee turned to follow her gaze. "What are you looking at?"

Chapter Eight

In the center of an empty corral, Sam helicoptered the bullwhip over his head and reversed. A *crack* split the air. Not bad. Never letting the whip settle, he threw again and again, working into a good rhythm.

After warming up, he moved to the target area. He'd needed something to take his mind off the redhead, and nothing required concentration like whip cracking. He had the scars to prove it.

Today he had spaghetti noodles to destroy. Poles to wrap and pull.

Eventually, as a treat to himself, he targeted cans of soda. The trick was to strike evenly enough to split the can in half. He hit the first can, and the spray fountained up. The bottom half of the can remained on the table, still filled with liquid.

"Show-off." The voice broke into his concentration.

With an amused snort, Sam stopped. Coiling the whip, he walked to where Nolan stood with his forearms resting on the top of the fence. "What's up?"

"Came to tell you we're done for the day."

Sam studied the beginnings of his new stable. The construction crew had accomplished a fair amount over the past week. "Getting there."

"Should have been built a decade ago. That old one's a fire trap."

"Wasn't needed before." Couldn't do it until his divorce. He could hardly subject construction workers to his wife's hysterics or the way she'd have hit them up for drug money.

Like she'd tried to shake him down for money yesterday. His mouth twisted with the foul taste that speaking to her left behind. He needed to warn Nicole that her mother was back in Tampa. "But breeding mares expect some amenities."

"Right." Nolan looked around. "Place looks good."

"Better." After the farm was safe from Nancy's destructive tantrums, he'd made much-needed improvements.

"Heard you did a scene with your buddy from the auction. You seeing her?"

Damn gossipy submissives. "No. She wants to be normal. Normal women don't hang out with sadists."

"From what Cullen said, she's as much a masochist as you are a sadist."

"Not if she can help it."

Nolan gave him a glance. "But she can't. Any more than Beth could help being submissive, and she sure as hell tried."

Sam nodded agreement. But people weren't logical.

At least Linda had forgiven him. And she had his phone number. Pushing her further would definitely be stalking. But, goddammit, not seeing her was like losing a wisdom tooth and constantly checking the empty socket. "Ball's in her corner." *For now.*

* * * *

"I see I've got some practicing to do," Linda said. Standing on the front lawn of the church in the early evening sunlight, she smiled at the gray-haired director of the choir.

"You'll catch up quickly." Mrs. Ritter riffled through a sheaf of sheet music. "It's good to have you back."

"I missed singing." And practice had been wonderful. But now, as the choir members mingled outside the church, her anxiety was creeping back.

"I saw the paper with the picture of your house," Mrs. Ritter said. "Has the creep been back?"

"No, thank goodness." Not for two weeks now—since the first night Sam had spent in her house, leaving his big truck parked at the curb. Perhaps the spray painter had seen Sam and decided to pursue less perilous canvases.

Apparently, Sam had decided to pursue less neurotic women. She hadn't seen him since the restaurant. Ignoring the hollow ache in her chest, she said, "I think the painter got bored."

"That's excellent news." Mrs. Ritter handed over selections of music, then frowned at a small group of women near the refreshments table. Their whispering abruptly stopped.

Linda stiffened. More gossip. Normal conversations were a low murmur, like background noise. But when people gossiped, their voices would lower and their glances would hit her like cold ocean spray as they checked to ensure she hadn't noticed and couldn't hear.

She didn't need to hear. One look at the group told her that the two women in their thirties had ruled her a slut. The two older women weren't judging.

I hate this. Even worse, she couldn't stop wondering if the obscenities on her house were done by someone she knew.

"The alto section will improve with you here. They've needed a stronger lead." The woman patted her shoulder. "Welcome back."

As Mrs. Ritter moved away, Linda stared after her. People were certainly unpredictable. She'd thought younger women would be the most accepting—and in her neighborhood they had been—but here, the older women were more open-minded. A couple of them in their sixties had even said their book club's selection last month was a popular BDSM romance. *Go figure.*

Really, almost everyone had welcomed her home. Yet somehow the few unfriendly gossips overshadowed the rest. She shook her head ruefully. Years ago she'd discovered Brenna and Charles might forget her compliments, but her critical comments lingered in their minds forever. Apparently, malicious remarks created the same imbalance.

Linda considered the clusters of people. Join one?

No, she'd braved enough for one day. Instead, she raised her voice. "I have to run. I'll see you all in a couple of days."

To a murmured chorus of farewells, she headed for her car with a sigh of relief. As she reached the street and her knotted muscles loosened, she glanced back. Normal people. Glasses and gray hair, housewives, secretaries, a lawyer, clerks, two businesswomen. Some retired, three in college. Not a monster among them, even though she often felt like Brenna's hamster the day Charles's puppy had cornered it.

Unable to face her too-quiet house, she drove to where the long city dock jutted out into the water. Just before dark, the pier held only an old man fishing. A pelican on a piling watched silently as Linda dropped onto a weathered bench.

The water was dark and calm. A light ocean breeze teased her hair and fluttered her clothing, blowing away the remnants of ugly gossip until she felt clean again. Her hand trembled when she tucked her hair behind her ear. As the days passed, leaving her house grew more difficult—not from fear of being kidnapped, although that hovered in the background—but from being around people. She felt as if everyone was judging her. *Getting paranoid much, honey?*

But worse—much more terrifying—was that she had started to feel distant, as if she'd raised walls and neglected to build doors in them. It was happening again. Her hands clenched as despair whipped around her like an unstoppable wind. It wasn't supposed to come back. *Dammit*, it wasn't supposed to ever come *back*.

She wanted that clear, open feeling that came from being with Sam...because he knew how to hurt her.

Whoever heard of craving a *sensation* rather than something like, say, chocolate or pizza? Of course, guys often complained if they didn't—how did one put it?—get their ashes hauled regularly. Marathoners got cranky if they were injured, saying things like *I need to run.*

I need pain. She shuddered. *No no no.*

A gull swooped past, its beady black eyes assessing her for potential food. "Not this time." Then again, in her pocket, she had a cookie from the refreshment table at practice. "Well, okay." She tossed a chunk onto the dock.

The gull landed with a light *thump* and waddled to the goodie. Suddenly, three more of the noisy birds appeared.

"Good grief." She tossed each a tidbit and scowled when the smallest gull was shoved aside. Bullies abounded, didn't they? Her next toss went directly under the little guy.

Birds and their pecking orders. Humans did the same thing. She sighed. Boy, did they. *Okay. Time to think*. Logically.

Basically, she had two, somewhat intertwined, problems going on.

The first was that her recent notoriety—being a slave—affected how she fit into life in Foggy Shores. That might eventually resolve, since hopefully, as the townspeople's memories faded, so would the gossip.

"Do I want to wait that long?"

Food finished, one by one, the gulls took to the sky, leaving only the sounds of water lapping at the pilings and the laughter of children playing on the beach. She'd been happy in this town. Her marriage had been a good one for the most part. When Frederick had died so unexpectedly in a car crash, the townspeople had been her support. Had helped her start her business. Here was where she'd raised Brenna and Charles.

She stared down at her hands. But now... The last of her close friends had moved away two years ago. *Stupid mobile society*. Her children had gone off to college. She had fewer ties; she could leave. Her home no longer felt like a refuge—she still saw the ugly words as if they'd never been scrubbed away. Her house would easily sell.

But my store? She loved her little beach store, loved being a businesswoman, loved supporting her fellow craftsmen. She didn't want to move her business. Her mouth tightened. And she darn well wasn't going to flee as if she'd done something wrong.

So the answer to problem number one? She'd wait it out.

She scrubbed the toe of her canvas shoe on the rough wood, realizing her second problem affected the first and vice versa. Gossip wouldn't be so unnerving if she was comfortable with herself.

Face it, she wasn't. At all. She closed her eyes and asked the question she'd been avoiding. Did needing to be hurt mean she was mentally unstable?

I don't know. She grimaced. It'd be easier to judge if she had more experience. But she'd been a virgin when she married Frederick, and she'd had very few lovers. Before Sam, she'd only mentioned her desires to three men—Dwayne, Frederick, and Lee. They'd all behaved as if she had a problem.

Then again, they were all...conservative...men. Should she use their opinions to measure herself? Perhaps not. She gave an unhappy laugh. Why hadn't she spent her time in that one BDSM club talking to people? Finding out what was normal, if there was such a thing.

As unhappiness welled up inside her, she blinked back tears. Why was it all so hard?

But her solution—ignoring her "problem"—wasn't working. At all. Somehow she had to find a way to come to terms with herself. *I need help. Advice.* The tears spilled over. *I need a hug so, so much.*

And with that, she had the answer. On her cell phone, she punched in a number. "Kim? Can I talk to you about something?"

* * * *

Filled with the scent of pizza, garlic, and olive oil, the small Italian restaurant was warm and cozy against the chill night. A cold front was moving in, temperatures were dropping, possibly down to freezing. Orange groves were on alert.

Linda followed Kim toward a small corner booth with only one occupant, a redhead with a vivid blue streak in her hair. She wore a blue, three-quarter-sleeved shirt to match and had blue-flowered wrist tattoos. Not a stodgy person, at least.

Kim motioned to her. "This is Gabi."

Linda smiled politely. Apparently the woman had volunteered to work with the FBI as a decoy in the Shadowlands. Successfully, since she'd been kidnapped by the Harvest Association. A snort threatened to escape. *Maybe this isn't the right person to talk to me about insanity.*

Gabi grinned. "Hi, Linda."

That voice. Mingled with memories of sobbing women, gentle orders from nurses in scrubs, and beeping medical machines was this lovely voice. "You were at the hospital." All the rescued slaves from the auction had been taken to one hospital for healing and counseling. Gabi had been with the counselors.

"I'm a victim specialist with the FBI and very happy to stay that way." Gabi gave a mock shiver. "Fieldwork is totally not my thing."

"But you did it for me, and I'll never forget it." Kim glanced at a single glass on the table. "Did you order?"

"You bet. Two large. One all meat, one pepperoni and black olive. There'll be plenty to take home."

"Good job. Raoul loves pizza. Linda, sit. I'll get us some drinks." She glanced at Gabi's drink, then at Linda. "Root beer, right?"

"Right." As Kim headed away, Linda slid into the other side of the booth, feeling less uncomfortable than she'd expected.

"I hear you have some questions and want to talk a bit."

Where to start? "Kim said you live with a Dom? You're submissive?"

"That's right. Marcus is one of the Masters of the Shadowlands. He used to handle the trainees there, which is how we met."

At the easy agreement, Linda released the breath she'd been holding. Obviously, she wouldn't shock this woman. *Maybe.* "I'm submissive too." She forced out the next words. "And a masochist." As she stared at the wavering wood of the booth, the buzzing in her ears blotted out the hum of conversation. She felt her hand being taken.

"Breathe, sweetie, before you pass out."

Linda pulled in a breath, and the room came back in focus. Sweat had beaded on her forehead. "Um. Sorry. I hadn't—"

Gabi's smile was sympathetic. "Hadn't said that aloud before? That must feel like one of those alcoholic programs. 'My name is Linda, and I'm a masochist.'"

Ouch. Yet the word had less impact this time. "Kind of. So does being a m-masochist mean I need some serious mental adjustment?"

"Well, let's see." Gabi leaned back. "Did being a slave turn you into a masochist?"

"No. In fact..." Linda's hands clenched. But she was already confiding, might as well go all the way. "I saw a woman Tasered outside a BDSM club. I tried to help and ended up kidnapped too." She swallowed. "Only, I'd just been in that club. So it feels like I got what I deserved. Like I—"

"Honey, that's bullshit." Gabi's brisk interruption made Linda blink. "Didn't your counselor tell you that?"

Linda stared at her hands. "I never—"

"You didn't share that with her, did you?" Gabi narrowed her eyes. "And a minute ago, you acted like you'd never said the word 'masochist' before. You didn't bring that up with her either?"

Linda shook her head.

"Oh boy. No wonder you're going around in circles." Gabi's brows drew together.

"Gabi, hello?" Kim thumped the drinks on the table and slid in beside Linda. "I wanted you to help, not frown at her."

"Well damn, how is a therapist supposed to help if she's left in the cold?" Gabi let out a long sigh before her lips twisted ruefully. "Then again, we're also supposed to push and get to the bottom of things. Yours obviously let you avoid a lot."

"Avoid what?" Kim asked.

"Avoid the things you worked through." Gabi patted Kim's hand. "Like how dirty you felt. And how you felt as if you deserved to be abused because you'd gone to a BDSM club."

Linda stared. "You too?"

"Kim got help with those feelings." Gabi's gaze settled on Linda. "So...you didn't tell your counselor because you think being into kink is wrong. Right? I mean, correct?"

Gabi was definitely a psychologist. Linda wanted to hide under the table, yet the understanding from both women kept her in her seat. "My husband and other...lovers...acted as if I'm unbalanced."

"Ah. Because you like pain. Crave it, probably. It makes sex better and—for some people—helps process their emotions." Gabi tapped her fingernails on the table. "You've got issues all right. First, the easiest one. You should realize that any assault leaves the victim thinking, 'What did I do wrong to cause that? If I'd only done something different, this wouldn't have happened.' A survivor will go over and over every detail leading up to the incident."

"Really?" Linda blinked.

Kim glanced over with a sheepish smile. "Oh yeah. Raoul said it's normal. Humans need to think we can affect fate and control our destiny. Maybe we can to an extent, but sometimes shit just happens."

Linda bit her lip. They were right. If she believed being kinky had led to the horrors she'd endured, then by being normal, she'd ensure that bad things wouldn't ever happen again. But if disasters occurred from simply being in the wrong place at the wrong time, then the universe held no certainties.

"Makes it scary, doesn't it?" Gabi patted her hand. "I went through a gang rape when I was a teen. I got past it, but the world never felt quite as safe again."

Gabi would have been younger than Brenna. Sadness mingled with pity as Linda turned her hand over and squeezed Gabi's. "I'm sorry."

Gabi squeezed back, not speaking. Letting Linda think.

After a moment, she pulled in a breath. Sometimes shit just happens. How logical. And freeing. *I didn't do anything bad to warrant being enslaved.* Something inside her loosened. Not completely. She'd have to work on believing that. But first, she needed to deal with the real reason she'd come. "And the other issue? Wanting pain?"

"Yes. Let's go over that." Gabi rummaged in her purse and pulled out two business cards. "I know counselors are supposed to be all enlightened, but we often have biases. S and M was taken off the mental disorders list. However, it still makes some psychologists uncomfortable." She handed over the cards. "I can't take you on as my patient, but these two are kink-friendly. And you need some help, sweetie."

"Right." Linda tucked the cards in her wallet. "S and M isn't a mental problem?"

"Uh-uh. Just another point in the wide sexual continuum. How you deal with it is what counts." Gabi leaned back. "Do you constantly need someone to hurt you? Does the craving affect your work or home life?"

"Not constantly, but I-I want it. Get cranky without it." Linda stared at her fingers and admitted, "I got really...needy...after the kidnapping."

"All the rescued women had problems afterward. That's not crazy. That's human. And if pain helps you get in touch with your inner self, then stress will increase your need for it." Gabi grinned. "Just like I'll eat an entire bag of potato chips when I'm frazzled."

"Oh." The next worry popped out before she could censor it. "But with sex. The guys thought I was unbalanced when I asked for something...different."

Kim flicked her fingers in annoyance. "The scum suckers didn't want to hear they're not gods in the bedroom or that you could possibly want anything other than what they did." She snickered. "Really, Linda, you should be ashamed, crushing their little egos."

Gabi snorted a laugh.

After a second, Linda's lips tipped up. That *was* rather how Frederick and Lee had acted. Insulted. And Dwayne had been seriously angry.

As if filled with helium, her spirits started to lift. "So I'm not mentally unbalanced? Don't need counseling?"

"You need counseling, but mainly to help you figure out how to deal with your needs." Gabi rolled her eyes. "Not to be *cured* of them."

Not crazy. Linda bit her lip, fighting back tears. She still had to choose whether or not to have BDSM in her life, but now the decision would be hers. Not one made from fear.

I'm not crazy. Maybe she should order champagne to go with the pizza.

Kim nudged her shoulder. "After we eat—and gossip for a while—you want to visit the Shadowlands?"

A thrill shot through her. Would Sam be there? Did she want to see him? *Duh.* Considering how his mere name made her insides quiver, that was a stupid question.

But should she see him? She still wasn't real comfortable with the idea of needing pain. But as Gabi said, if that was who she was, then she had to learn to deal with it. Stop trying to hide her head in the sand.

But I like sand. Still, avoidance hadn't done her any favors, now had it?

And yet, would Sam forgive her for how she'd run from him? There was only one way to find out. "Yes. Let's."

Chapter Nine

Dressed in black jeans and a black work shirt, Sam leaned against the bar and scowled at Z. "You got something you need me for?" He hadn't planned on visiting the Shadowlands. Not this weekend. Not until he could forget the last person under his lash and could stop seeing her everywhere.

Z hadn't said what he wanted, so Sam had brought in his bag. But he wasn't in the mood to do a teaching scene or whatever Z had in mind—not if he could escape it.

"Somehow, you've managed to evade your turn at supervising the trainees." Z gave him a faint smile. "This is Olivia's rotation, but her job schedule changed. Can you take her place?"

"Hell." He'd rather do a goddamned teaching scene. Sam's gaze took in the trainees who were flitting about the room. They were easy enough to spot, since they wore leather wrist cuffs decorated with colored ribbons, indicating their scene preferences. Red meant they were masochists. "I'd hoped you'd overlooked me. Or assigned someone permanently."

"Not a chance," Z said in a dry voice. "And I think the trainees benefit from having a variety of trainers. Their choice of a Dom might be more balanced."

Didn't look like he'd escape the chore. "Fine."

He didn't mind working with the trainees one-on-one, but as trainer, he'd also have to supervise, assign, punish, and set them up with either Doms or Masters who could widen their experiences. He frowned, considering the potential Tops. Not a good selection. Too many Masters didn't scene with anyone but their submissives. "We need more single Masters, Z."

Z nodded. "I agree. Suggestions?"

The title of Shadowlands Master—or Mistress—was bestowed by the membership during a voting process; however, Z nominated the candidates. "I think Holt might be ready."

"He would work out well. Galen Kouros and Vance Buchanan are members now, and they're undoubtedly at Master status." Z considered. "What do you think of Jacob?"

Sam frowned. "Thought he was in a relationship with Heather." Heather had been a trainee at one time.

"Their attachment didn't survive her acceptance of a job in Oregon."

"Guess that happens." A shame though. They'd looked good together.

"Indeed. He's back and helping out as a DM."

"He'd make a good Master."

"That's four. And Catherine is ready for a Mistress title." Z studied Sam. "You look tired."

Damn psychologist-Dom. Sam had grown exceedingly tired of therapists after his discharge and later with Nancy. Not that they'd done his addicted wife any good. Of course, she was the most manipulative person he'd ever met. *"I love you, Sam. If you loved me, you'd give me what I need."* His jaw set. Then he pushed the memories aside. "Early day. Nolan's crew starts at dawn."

"Hadn't you told me you always rise before dawn?" Z said with not a flicker of a changed expression.

Well, Sam wasn't much for evasions. Bluntness served him better. "Not your problem, Z. Leave off."

Z paused, then nodded. "Call me if I can help."

"Right." Sam slapped the bar. "I'll go terrify the trainees so I can sleep well tonight."

Z's grin flashed. "Considering Anne supervised them last month, scaring them will take some work."

"Hell." Mistress Anne was not only a sadist, but she had mind fucking down pat. Where Sam was straightforward, she was damned sneaky. And yet her male submissives—and she usually had more than one—worshipped the ground she walked on. Shaking his head, Sam moved down the bar to where Cullen was drawing a beer.

Cullen looked up with a grin. "Hey, buddy. Did Z drop the trainees in your lap?"

"Yep. Who are the first-shift barmaids?"

"Rainie, Dara, and Sally. Maxie's gone for a month or so. Uzuri and Tanner will take the last half of the night."

"Thanks." Sam strolled through the big room, automatically monitoring the scenes. When he spotted a male Dom preparing to take his sub bareback, Sam cleared his throat and nodded at the stand with condoms. Z didn't care how long a couple had been together; everybody suited up in the Shadowlands.

The Dom gave him a rueful look, then said to his partner, "Gotta dress for the party, boy. You stay right here." He gave the sub's balls a hard squeeze. "Hear me? Don't move."

Sam walked away, grinning at the sub's groan that started low and ended high. Nice range.

In the main room, he checked on Dara and Sally. They were doing well, not only keeping up with drink orders but also experienced enough to negotiate scenes for when they went off duty. Z deliberately made the trainees serve drinks. Some of them—well, not Dara or Sally—were shy, and barmaiding made it easy for them to meet the Doms.

In the dungeon room, a Domme was talking to Rainie. Pushing. The Domme wasn't...completely...out of line, but the trainee was too intimidated to give a firm no.

About five feet seven, Rainie probably weighed over two hundred pounds, and the younger Doms called her a BBW—a big, beautiful woman—which Sam considered a good description. A fairly new trainee, she was extremely popular.

She was dressed in blue boy shorts, a latex bra, and a wealth of tattoos. The red lotus flowers started at her ass and turned to blue water fountaining up her spine. More flower tats vined over her right shoulder, down her sternum to curl under her right breast. Her shoulder-length brown hair was highlighted with red and blonde streaks.

The trainee had a personality as colorful as her appearance. But she did intimidate easily.

"Whitney." Sam nodded to the Domme before turning his attention to Rainie. "Girl, Cullen needs you at the bar."

"Yes, Master Sam." Rainie cast him a look of relief before she disappeared from the dungeon room.

The Domme glared. "Sam, I—"

He crossed his arms over his chest. "She didn't say no, but some submissives won't. Read the body language. And you need to give them space to say if they don't want what you're offering."

"Shit." Whitney scowled. "What did I miss?"

"If you'd looked instead of pursuing, you'd have caught it," Sam said. "How close was she to you? Did she back away? Was she leaning forward or turning her side to you? Flirting with her hair or face...or crossing her arms defensively."

The Domme looked as if she'd like to put her fist through the wall. "Fuck, fuck, fuck. I really fucked it up." Tall and slender, she kept her black hair shorter than Sam's, and her delicate features concealed a mind as tough as her body. She'd make a fine Domme with a tad more experience.

"You did." Every Dominant in the world screwed up. The good ones admitted their mistakes and learned from them. "You'll be more careful next time."

"I will, and I'll apologize to the girl." She slapped his shoulder—one of the few people in the place who dared touch him. "Thanks for breaking in."

After nodding, he headed back to the bar to give Rainie a different lecture. Submissives, especially trainees, needed to be able to say no.

He snagged her as she walked toward the front of the room, having obviously traded places with Dara. Well, Dara definitely knew how to say no. "Rainie."

Her hazel eyes widened, and she took a step back. Hands in front. Clenched already. "Yes, Master Sam."

He sighed. Sometimes he enjoyed his "eat babies for breakfast" reputation, but sometimes it got old. Eventually the girl would discover that sadists tended to be politer than regular Doms—at least, when not in a scene. After all, if a sadist was nasty, then how would he get anyone to play with him? "Did you want a session with Whitney?"

She shook her head.

"Say it aloud, girl. Did you?"

"No," she whispered.

Might as well use his damned scary rep. If she could say no to him, she should be able to say it to anyone. "I can't hear you, missy," he snapped.

"No." Still a whisper.

Her wrist cuff included a yellow ribbon to show she liked mild pain. "Bend over the bar stool."

Her eyes widened, but after a second she obeyed.

When he forcefully slapped her boy-shorts-covered ass, she squeaked. He said, "Stand up."

Her face was red, more from embarrassment than from being hurt.

"Did you want to scene with the Domme?"

Her bottom lip quivered. "No." Still too faint.

"Until I hear a loud no from you, I'll continue." He gave her a heartless look. "This wouldn't be the first time I spanked someone for hours."

She gulped when he pointed to the stool, but bent obediently.

He delivered a swat hard enough to sting his palm, hard enough to make her yelp. When she stood, he asked, "Did you want to scene with the Domme?"

"No!"

Nice and loud. "Repeat that."

"No!"

"Do you want me to spank you again?"

"No!"

"Good." He looked upward. "Did the ceiling fall because you said no to a Dom?"

She blinked, and her mouth dropped open. "I guess not."

"Tell me the point of this lesson."

"I should have told her no."

"Right. Next time, say no with enough assertiveness that a Dom doesn't think you're saying yes." Sam tapped her cheek with his finger, pleased she didn't shy away. "Do better or next time I'll use a cane."

"Yes, Sir." She took a step away, then another. "Thank you, Sir, for the lesson."

He crossed his arms over his chest as she hurried away. She got halfway across the room before she reached around to rub her ass. He grinned.

WEARING A HALTER top and a short wraparound skirt, Linda sat between Gabi and Kim, watching Sam. As he'd delivered a hard swat to a tattooed submissive, she'd realized everything about the Dom was sexy—his severe expression, harsh face, square chin, corded wrists, lean muscles. Black tough-guy clothes, a big black belt, and boots. All that darkness made his ash-gray hair and pale eyes seem eerie. When he crossed his arms over his chest and watched the young woman flee, Linda gave a little sigh.

"What's up?" Kim eyed her and popped a tiny quiche in her mouth.

Just lusting after a man. Linda cleared her throat and went for a diversion. "Have you ever noticed what a guy's posture and demeanor say about him?"

"I'm not sure what you mean," Kim said.

"Well." Linda looked around, then nodded at the giant, craggy-faced bartender. "He moves like he'd not only fight hard, but he'd enjoy the heck out of it. A brawler."

Gabi snorted. "You got Master Cullen down. What about that one?" She nodded at a brutal-looking, darker Dom with a scarred face.

Linda studied him. No expression, but his eyes never stopped moving, and he stood as if... "Get in his way, and he'd flatten you without thinking twice. Then he'd step over your body without looking back."

"Damn, you got Master Nolan figured out too." Kim grinned.

"Working as a shopkeeper, you learn to read people quickly."

Gabi gave her a sly smile. "What about Master Sam?"

"I've met him, so it'd be cheating." Her lips curved up. "He wouldn't start a fight, wouldn't enjoy it, but wouldn't back down either. And he'd definitely finish the job."

Kim nodded. "That's him."

"Then he'd kick the guy, just to enjoy hearing him groan," Linda added.

Gabi choked on her drink, coughing hard enough to attract attention.

"Way to go, dummy. Cullen saw us," Kim hissed.

Gabi held up her hand, managed a breath, then wheezed, "Oh, please, as if Ben wouldn't have already called your Master? Didn't you tell Raoul we might visit the Shadowlands?"

Kim's eyes widened. "But...but Ben didn't tell on us before."

"After the last time we sneaked in, the guys undoubtedly had a chat with him." Gabi assumed a smug expression. "Which is why I asked permission."

Linda frowned, trying to catch up. Wasn't Ben the oversize security guard in the entry? "You're going to get in trouble? Just for being here?"

"Oh yeah." Kim glared at her friend. "You little brat."

"Hey, you guys. I heard you might come by." A short, buxom blonde with sea-green eyes dropped into a chair before smiling across the table. "You must be Linda. I'm Jessica." After swiping one of Gabi's pizza rolls, she popped the tidbit in her mouth. "Mmm."

"Have some more," Gabi said and pushed the plate over.

"Can't." Jessica's mouth turned down. "Z said when I wander around, I've been forgetting who I belong to." She patted her dark green corset. "He said he'd make sure I feel as if he's always got his arm around me...and pulled the strings so tight I can barely breathe."

"That's a new one." Kim looked worried. "Hopefully he won't share that trick with Raoul."

Belong to? Linda spotted the engagement ring on Jessica's hand. "You're engaged to Master Z?" *Are you insane?*

Jessica laughed. "He's not as scary in daily life." After a second, she amended, "Well, sometimes he's scarier."

"How did you know we might come here?" Kim asked.

"Let's see." Jessica squinted in thought. "Gabi called Marcus. When Marcus called Dan about some serial rapist, he mentioned Gabi's plans. Dan told Kari, and Kari told me, and I told Z."

"Drown it. Raoul's probably heard the news from at least three people." Kim tipped back her head to stare at the ceiling. "I am *doomed*."

Linda bit her lip, guilt dropping onto her shoulders. "Will you really get in trouble?"

"Not if I move fast. Time for preventative action." Kim whipped out her cell phone, turned it on, and hit speed dial. "Hey, Master? Gabi and I actually convinced Linda to visit Shadowlands. I didn't think she'd go for it. She's so stubborn." She winked at Linda. "But she agreed, so we're here, and I wanted to make sure you knew."

Through the phone, Raoul's voice was deep and smooth, although Linda couldn't make out what he was saying.

Kim winced. "Well, yes, we did plan to ask her if—" Pause. "No, I didn't think—" Pause. "Yes, but—" Pause. Kim's shoulders slumped. "Yes, Master." She turned the phone off.

"You're dead meat, girlfriend." Jessica shook her head with a suppressed giggle. "What's he going to do?"

"Don't know, but he sure wasn't pleased."

"I'm sorry," Linda said. "Maybe I can talk to him?"

"Nah, it would have happened sooner or later." Kim shrugged. "We're still kind of...defining...how much control he gets. He gives in on some things, me on others. But I got the feeling that being here without him isn't something he'll negotiate about, you know?"

"Well, he's incredibly possessive of you, so having you loose in a club full of hungry Doms?" Jessica snickered. "No, you're not going to win."

Linda glanced at Gabi to see if she agreed, but the counselor's attention was elsewhere. "Something wrong?"

"No. I'm just watching..." She pointed.

As Linda looked, her stomach got a weird "bottom dropping out" sensation. Near the bar, Sam had his hand curled around a black submissive's nape.

Linda clenched her jaw against the nasty shot of jealousy. *He's not mine. I turned him away.* Rationalization didn't help. *Darn the man.* "He's going to do a scene with her?"

Jessica shook her head. "No way. Uzuri doesn't even like light pain. No, I bet he *arranged* a scene for her."

Gabi looked over. "Why would he do that?"

"Oh, Z gave him the trainees tonight. Said Sam had avoided supervising them for long enough." She grinned. "Probably pissed that sadist off a bit, huh?"

Linda couldn't take her gaze from Sam. How many men would be comfortable guiding a woman by his grip on her neck? But he didn't look puffed up. Wasn't strutting. When they stopped, he kept a hand on her shoulder as he talked to a Dom in his thirties. He spoke to Uzuri, then the Dom again, for all the world as if he was arbitrating. When the Dom and Uzuri started conversing, Sam nodded and walked away.

In the movies, cowboys had a rolling gait, soldiers a predatory one. Sam's stride was somewhere between the two, like an ominous saunter.

What would happen when he noticed her? Her muscles tensed in anticipation. As her fingernails dug into her arm, the sting added to the sizzle under her skin, and she realized what she was doing. *The perversion of pain.* Her mouth tightened.

Gabi's gaze met hers. "Linda, if it's wrong to enjoy pain, does that mean I'm not supposed to like being tied up? Because I really do." Gabi gave her a smile of understanding.

Linda relaxed. Gabi was just as sweet as Kim was. And wasn't it odd that they both seemed so normal? A therapist. A biologist. "What do you do for a living, Jessica?"

"You're new, aren't you? Bet you're suffering from the 'ordinary people don't play like this syndrome.'" Jessica's eyes lit with laughter. "Try this on for size. I'm an accountant."

"No way."

"Oh yeah. Can't get stodgier." Considering, Jessica tapped her lips. "Kari's a schoolteacher; Andrea owns a cleaning business, Beth a landscaping biz. Sally's getting her master's degree, Uzuri over there is an executive in a department store, and Rainie manages a tow-truck chain."

Linda leaned back in disbelief. Regular jobs; regular people. And why not? Why should she think they'd be odd? She pulled in a breath, feeling like an idiot. How many times had she unthinkingly accepted her father's narrow-minded opinions as truth—in this case, that anyone wanting more than the missionary position must be creepy? "Thank you. That helps."

"Hey, we've all been at that place," Jessica said.

"Uh-oh, Linda." Gabi waggled her eyebrows. "You've been spotted by the man, Ms. Shopkeeper. Are you going to run?"

Even though her stomach suddenly felt as if she'd swallowed every butterfly in Florida, Linda assumed a haughty expression...and carefully didn't look around. "You children might run, but I'm too mature to give in to fear."

"You're so full of bullshit." Kim glanced over her shoulder. "Yep, the sadist has his eyes on you." She shivered. "Sorry, but he still scares me a little."

Like a hot spotlight centered upon her, his attention made her insides quiver. *Breathe. Look dignified. Relax.* When she unclenched her fingers, they were gooey—she'd totally squashed the pizza roll she'd picked up. With a huffed laugh, she wiped off her fingers. *Way to look indifferent, dummy.*

A glance at the others revealed Kim trying to smother her laughter and Gabi smiling encouragement.

Jessica gave her a covert thumbs-up. "Stay strong and make him work for it."

Why did she feel as if she'd dived off a mile-high cliff and was about to hit the water? With a final gulp of air, Linda turned her head.

Ice-blue eyes trapped her gaze. She realized she'd risen to her feet. *Heavens, how does he do that?* Even from a distance, she could see how suppressed laughter made his mouth quirk. He curved his index finger. *Come here.*

Well, this was what she wanted, wasn't it?

It's just a test. To see what was what. *Maybe.*

But as she walked up to him, the warmth in his gaze made her feel...beautiful.

Chapter Ten

Was she not the most beautiful woman in the club? Resting his hip on a bar stool, Sam watched Linda approach. Her brown eyes were wide, nervous, but not terrified. Her lower lip was caught between her teeth. He held out his hand, pleased when she didn't hesitate to give him hers. Soft skin, small bones. "Why are you here, girl?"

"I-I..." Her chin firmed. "I'm trying to decide if being...different...has a place in my life."

"*Different.*" Pissed him off the way she saw being unique as being wrong. "Are you talking about being a masochist? Or being a singer? Or a submissive? Or smarter than most? Or maybe being talented at basketry?"

Her spine straightened. "It's not a joke."

"I'm not joking." He curved his hand firmly around her nape as he'd done with Uzuri. Linda instinctively tried to take a step back. When his grip tightened, halting her, he enjoyed the hell out of the way she shivered.

Then he watched as she didn't move, yet silently, internally fought his control.

And he watched as she surrendered. To him.

When he leaned down and took her lips, not permitting her to withdraw, her mouth softened and opened.

My Linda. He pulled her between his legs and molded her so tightly against him that her full breasts flattened against his chest. Amazing how *different* one woman could feel from another. Why the hell did they all want to be alike? "Cut out all the *different* parts of yourself, and your personality will have the texture of mashed potatoes."

She blinked, then burst out laughing.

Damn, he liked her laugh. "What?"

"Just…aren't you a meat and potatoes sort of guy?"

Had him there. When she rubbed her forehead on his shoulder, he remembered how sweetly she'd snuggled against him in the night. She was a person who liked to touch.

She looked up at him, her eyes serious. "My dad was a fire-and-brimstone preacher, and my husband old-fashioned. My town is small and conservative. This isn't easy for me, but I'm trying."

"Good enough." He put his hand under her chin, feeling the softness of her flesh. Older, not tight and hard, and she was so goddamned appealing she could break his heart. He didn't require some eighteen-year-old to make his cock hard. He wanted a woman, one with lines in her face that said she'd done some living and had learned to cry. And to laugh.

A tiny trembling ran through her when she met his gaze, and the chemistry between them blazed up like dry wood in a wind. "Remember the safe word here?"

Her tongue touched her pink lips. "Red."

"Good." He ran his finger across her lower lip, circling her mouth with the wetness. "I'm glad you didn't wear a mask, girl. I like to see more than your body. Don't wear one again."

A tremor ran through her, and a glint of fear showed in her eyes before she whispered, "Yes, Sir."

Her trust sent warmth through him. "Good girl." So what area was available for a scene? Releasing Linda from his arms, he checked. The stocks were free or...the picture frame was empty. "Cullen."

The bartender looked over.

"Can you grab my bag?"

Cullen set a bottled mineral water in front of a Domme, then reached under the bar and brought out Sam's leather toy bag. "Have fun, you two."

"Thanks." Sam took a grip on Linda's nape again. "Come along, girl." As the heavy silk of her hair flowed over his fingers, he caught her clean lavender-and-tangy-citrus scent. Made him want to pick her up and rub her skin over his.

But he could wait.

He led her to a wooden structure built like an extra-tall and double-wide door frame. "Cullen calls this the picture frame because of the way it displays a submissive."

She eyed the chains and bolts studded around the inside of the frame, then glanced back toward the bar. "He's not as easygoing as he acts, is he?"

"Last submissive who annoyed him got strapped to the bar." With a bucket of ice cubes beside her for anyone that wanted to play. He grinned, remembering the sub's appalled shrieks.

He glanced down at his redhead. Might as well give her a few choices in the game—or let her think she was getting some. After setting his bag on a chair, Sam started unzipping the inside dividers. Opened the one for the toys. Clamps, yes. Gags or blindfold? No. Why deprive himself of hearing her screams, of seeing tears in her eyes? That section stayed closed.

After moving a rectangular tray table beside the chair, he told Linda, "Set out what's in the bag." He touched one end of the table. "The toys you'd most like me to use go here. Work your way to the other end and your least favorite toys. If something is a hard limit, leave it in the bag."

A sweet crease of worry appeared between her red-brown brows. "And you'll start at the good end and work your way through to the bad?"

"Nope." He stepped close enough that her breasts grazed his chest, and she had to tilt her head back to look up at him. "Just lets me know what will bother you and what won't. I choose what. And when."

"But—"

He smiled into her vulnerable eyes. "Trust me to know how much you can take, missy. And to push you to that point."

Even as the hint of anxiety appeared in her eyes, her nipples contracted to hard points.

As the beast inside him stirred and raised its head, he stepped back. "Get started."

While he worked on attaching chains to the proper bolts, he watched her pick and choose.

She put a thick cane midway, a lighter one closer to the good side. The heavy flogger was good; the one with knotted ends went to the bad side. His favorite short snake whip was considered. Put close to the bad end. Moved to the other side. Moved again. Was there anything more appetizing than a submissive's uncertainty? He'd definitely give her a taste of that whip, no matter where it ended up on the table.

When she pulled out the coiled six-footer, he said, "No, baby. There's not enough space in here to play with that one." She nodded and dropped it into the bag, coming out with a crop. A Wartenberg wheel. A vampire glove. Finally she finished.

After setting up the top restraints, Sam adjusted the lower chains so he could spread her legs. "Come here."

As she chewed her lower lip, he savored her hesitation, seeing her anticipation of the pain that would eventually take her to the height of pleasure, no matter how much the initial lash stung. His anticipation rose as well, since watching her ride that first bite of pain would give him an equally sized rush.

When she stood inside the picture frame, he untied her halter top and tossed it onto his bag. He was already hard, but the sight of her full breasts made his cock lengthen to serious discomfort, an interesting type of erotic ache. Pulling her into his arms, he ground his chest against her bare breasts, feeling her nipples contract back into stabbing points.

Her eyes were wide with nerves, and he could see the golden flecks that lightened the rich brown. Her lips were parted and inviting, so he fisted her hair, tipped her head back, and took her lips, demanding all he wanted from her mouth. At least for now. Damn but he'd missed kissing her and how she gave him everything, holding back nothing.

When he lifted his head, her fingers had dug into his back to hold him closer.

"I like the way you kiss, girl." His voice came out gruff.

She pinkened at the compliment. So sweet.

Time to push that giving nature of hers. He untied the side band of her skirt, tugging hard at the laces to drive home that she would soon be naked, without the most basic of defenses.

He tossed the skirt on his bag, followed by her panties. After using his boot to push her feet apart, he ran his hand between her legs. Not cruelly, simply a Dom's inspection that his submissive had kept herself groomed for his enjoyment.

His fingers met smooth, bare skin, already slick. Nice. Nothing there to cushion a blow. He rubbed his knuckles over her mound. "Good girl."

Although she was aroused and wet, her muscles tensed and her gaze dropped.

Gently, Davies. She'd been traumatized. Brutalized. Made into an object. He had to ride a path between dominance and abuse, and in her case, it was a goddamned narrow trail. So he enfolded her in his arms for a comforting hug and a reminder. "Your safe word is red. Do you remember?"

Her muscles relaxed, and she nodded.

"Good." He rubbed his chin on her smooth hair. "If I ask you how you're doing, green means keep going. Yellow means slow down, or that you can't take whatever I'm using on you at the time."

She nodded again.

He might also ask her who he was so she'd remember she wasn't with the bad guys. And hell, he simply liked the way she said his name as if he was goddamned John Wayne.

"All right." After fastening padded Velcro cuffs on her wrists, he snapped them to the overhead chains. The ankle cuffs and chains spread her legs wide apart. Then he tightened the arm restraints until her body was stretched nice and taut. Didn't want her to wiggle and spoil his aim. A shame he couldn't use his favorite single-tail, but Z rarely cordoned off space for the longer bullwhips.

Smiling into Linda's eyes, Sam flattened his hand over her exposed pussy, enjoying her startled response. Enjoying the increasing slickness coating his palm. "I've only given you pleasure here before. Tonight your pussy will get a sample of pain as well."

She swallowed so hard that he could hear the gulp.

Yep, this was going to be fun. As he kissed her, plunging his tongue deep, he cupped her ass with one hand and used his other hand to push his finger into her hot, wet cunt. Using the ball of his hand, he ground down on her clit as he thrust in and out. His tongue kept pace, driving her arousal higher. He could almost hear her endorphins start to dance.

He abandoned her pussy to rub her back firmly, letting the abrasiveness of his calloused palms rouse her tender skin. Another kiss and one more, simply for his enjoyment.

When he stepped back, her eyes held the gleam of a nicely aroused submissive.

After pulling the table of toys closer, he picked up a soft, wide-lashed flogger from the "good" side. Although a determined Dom could snap any flogger hard enough to hurt, this one was designed to be sensuous rather than painful. And he'd use it in that way. As he brushed the strands over her body, he studied the dark contrast of leather against her fair skin, the way her stomach muscles shivered, how her ass cheeks tried to draw away. Her pointing nipples grew tighter when he danced the tails over them.

Her breasts got a quick flick of the lash tips with enough of a sting to demonstrate he wasn't putting any part of her off limits this time.

Her gasp of shock was a hint of how much fun she'd give him tonight.

Working her up, he took the time to spank her gently, teasing her clit between each set of five, slapping lightly over her shoulders and thighs before returning to pinken her ass further. Her soft, dimpled ass. A squeeze made her hiss. Made him grin.

"Give me a color." Not as if he needed one. Her lips were open and rosy with excitement, eyes still clear. But they both needed to know she could speak.

"Green. I'm green."

He laughed. "Actually, girl, you're pink." Leaning into her body, he ran his hands up her arms to check the tightness of her cuffs. Checked her ankle cuffs as he stepped back. All good. "Now I'm going to turn your skin red."

The way her ass wiggled said she liked that.

This time he used a heavier flogger. Rotating his wrist, creating a figure eight, he slapped the falls up and down her outer thighs, ass cheeks, and upper back. A nice warm-up. Occasionally, he went lighter to sensitize her thighs, her stomach, and below her breasts, bringing the blood to the surface.

When he stopped, her eyes were fixed on him as if he were her lifeline. She was definitely aroused. Might as well have some more fun. He stepped close again, holding her nape in a hard grip, looking down at her. "Can you move at all, Linda?"

He almost grinned as she pulled at the restraints, learning that she couldn't. The knowledge of her helplessness made her pupils dilate. She licked her lips.

"See, I don't want you moving while I play with this." He picked up the Wartenberg wheel, which had been located near the middle of the table.

LINDA FELT AS if her skin was vibrating with anxiety. Heavens, was he really going to use that thing on her? It looked like a slender pizza cutter, only some insane person had replaced the smooth roller with spiky pins. Why couldn't he start with the gentle toys?

He smiled at her and lightly ran the thing over her stomach.

It tickled like a line of bugs crawling over her skin. As she tried to squirm away, he laughed, then moved to her back, using the wheel up and down the muscles along her spine, then down, pressing harder over her butt, drawing burning lines over her body. Her focus constricted as the wheel created a fine tapestry of pain. Over her stomach, upward to the tender undersides of her breasts, around her nipples. The tracks flamed through her, lassoing her with the wonderful bite. Her breasts grew heavier, and her nipples contracted as if trying to escape their fate.

When he paused, she looked down to see thin red lines on her pale skin. Despite the wheel's cutting sensation, she saw no blood. Her gaze lifted to the toy, to his hand, to his face...to his eyes. He was watching her intently, studying her responses.

A tremor started from her toes, working upward to her scalp. How could his single-minded attention be more arousing than the pain?

The sun lines at the corners of his eyes crinkled. Then the wheel circled the perimeter of her left areola, turned, and ran straight over the tip. The slash of pain was like he'd drawn a knife over her. She gasped, her back arching, pressing forward as the brilliant heat burst inward.

His rasping chuckle scraped over her nerves, arousing her in an entirely different way. "Love those tits, girl."

By the time he did her right nipple, her skin was on fire, sensitive and throbbing. After tossing the wheel onto the table, he cupped her breasts and firmly rubbed his calloused thumbs over the abused nipples.

Glorious, erotic rawness. Unsure if she hurt or felt wonderful, she whimpered.

Delight filled his eyes.

He switched to the palm-wide, leather-covered paddle, smacking her bottom over and over. The pain was—as Goldilocks said—just right. A lovely impact with not too much of a sting, and when he started hitting hard, the sensation reverberated straight through to her core. Her clit swelled and throbbed.

When he paused, she made a sound and pulled at her restraints in protest. *Don't stop.*

He stepped in front of her, his face filling her vision. His grip on her hair pulled her head back, and he kissed her gently, luring her into responding before turning rough. Wet. Removing control from her in a way that took her willpower as well.

Her eyelids were heavy, but she couldn't look away from his hard face—the dent in his square chin, lines around his eyes, strong nose. A five o'clock shadow darkened his jawline.

His firm lips quirked as she stared at him. "Like the paddle on your ass, do you? How about other places?"

He moved behind her, and light slaps ran down the backs of her thighs, then around to the fronts. To the insides. Stinging followed in the wake. Up and down and back up, arousal blossoming as the strikes approached the open area between her legs. Her whole body tensed with need. With fear...

Without speaking, he swatted the narrow paddle three times right on top of her labia and clit.

Oh God! The fireball turned into shockingly exquisite pleasure. She went up on tiptoes, hovering at the edge of release. The noise she made... She'd never heard that sound before.

The paddle dropped onto the table, and his wide hand covered her throbbing pussy. Heat on top of heat. "Almost went over, little girl." His skilled fingers slid across her burning tissues in a purely erotic caress.

One digit circled her unbearably swollen clit. Moved down. As he slowly, slowly pushed a finger inside her, his keen blue eyes held hers trapped. She stared helplessly, unable to speak, only feel, as he pressed deeper. Fully in, he rubbed his thumb over her clit until her hips arched forward.

His laugh rumbled like the bass drum in an orchestra. "Soon enough, missy. First, I want to make you suffer." His voice dropped. "Hear you scream." The pale fire of his gaze held hers as he pressed down on her clit, making the swollen tissue hurt. Throb.

"Sam," she whispered, and his eyes crinkled.

When he picked up the short two-tailed whip thing from the very end of the "bad" side of the table, her hands closed into fists. She hadn't liked its looks before and liked it less now.

Slowly, repetitively, he lashed up and down her bottom, and the horrid stinging made her flinch and try to escape. Tears sprang to her eyes. Overflowed. *Hurts.*

When he stopped, she pulled in a shuddering breath. His beard-scratchy face rubbed against her wet cheek as he murmured, "Figured you wouldn't like the quirt."

The intense afterburn shimmered over her skin as if she'd slid headlong into a hot springs. She pushed the question out: "Why then?"

"Because I like seeing you squirm. And cry." Gently, he kissed the tears from her cheeks. His voice dropped to a low, merciless rumble. "Because when you know that I can—and will—make you take more than you wanted, even when it hurts, you slide far deeper."

Her body shook as she stared at the resolve—and satisfaction—in his face. The truth dug into her with pinpoint claws, because he was right. She wanted that ruthless part of him. With him, she wouldn't have to beg for more, because he'd force her to where the sharp edge between pain and pleasure slipped away, and he'd keep her there, where her soul was bared to him.

As he read her surrender, his lips curved in a hard, hard smile.

When he released her from his gaze, she managed to draw in a breath.

After donning the furry glove she'd tossed on the "good" end of the table, he stroked her shoulder with the back of the glove. Fuzzy and soothing, yet her skin was so incredibly sensitive, she felt every tiny, soft strand. Her eyes half closed as he caressed her whole body.

"Like the glove?" The amusement in his voice pulled her eyes back open. "You didn't really check it out, though." He turned his glove-covered hand over and slid it, palm side down, across her collarbone to the top of her breast.

She sucked in a hard breath of air at the scritchy-scratchy feeling. When he lifted his hand, she saw the fur had concealed thumbtack-like points.

Alternating between the innocent fur side and the evil palm side, he glided over the tender places left by the quirt and the flogger. As her stomach muscles flinched, he pressed harder. "Don't move, girl."

"Mmm." She should move, do something, but as the glove created swaths of sparkling pain all over her body, she was sliding down, down, down into her happy place. Into the shadow world where decisions were made by someone else. Where her body wasn't really hers. Where the hurting and the yearning wove together into a basket that held her safely inside.

The glove spiraled up her inner thighs and, before she could tense, covered her pussy. A million spiky points pressed into her labia, ricocheting through her clit. God, she needed to come. Every cell in her body throbbed with burgeoning need, sharp and sweet, and she heard a long, husky moan. Hers.

The deep rumble was Sam's laugh. "There's a good girl." Something pinched her chin, and she dragged her eyes open to see Sam's icy ones. "Give me a color, Linda."

Color? Oh, there was supposed to be a color. One to keep going. Her mind floated like foam on rolling waves. Continue or stop. *Must continue.* Like a stoplight. "Green. More. Green."

He snorted. Then his lips touched hers in a gentle kiss. "For a little while, then."

Something slapped against her bottom, and it hurt—maybe it hurt. She couldn't even tell anymore as the molten sensation flowed through her. Caning. He was caning her, mostly on her bottom, light taps on her thighs, flicking at intervals between her legs hard enough to make her cry out. Hard enough to make her shake with need.

The wonderful edgy pattering continued on and on until her body felt so full of sensation that she was rocking. Humming. Her tipped-up lips tasted of the salt from her tears.

"I think you're done, missy." His voice splashed like rain into her warm pool of bliss. "I'm letting you loose."

"More. Green. More."

He chuckled, and his rough voice shivered over her, far sweeter than the whip. "You're past the point where you can decide. No more."

Coolness ringed her ankles when the cuffs came off. His fingers traced over her clit, circling, sending her to the edge, before he drew her legs together over the throbbing tissue.

Her whimper of protest got a laugh. He hooked an arm around her as he reached up to her wrists. Her shoulders seemed to groan—or was that her?—as her arms lowered.

"There we go," he said. Her head bounced off the clouds as he lifted her up into his arms, but he was warm and solid and so very safe. Her eyes closed again...or had she opened them at all?

"Ask Peggy to clean up for me, please."

Was he talking to her? She rubbed her cheek against him, listening to the low reverberation of sound in his chest. His musky fragrance sent need washing in hot waves over her.

A voice murmured.

"The toys go into a plastic bag. It all goes behind the bar."

"Yes, Sir," someone answered.

"Thanks, Tanner."

He was walking. Carrying her. The noise from the clubroom was a lovely song of torment and joy. She tried to lift her head, to see what was happening. A railing. Stairs. They were going upstairs.

Okay.

When a door shut, she opened her eyes again.

One of those sawhorse things was in the center of the room. Sam deposited her, stomach down, along the length of the padded surface, moving her until her forearms and knees rested on lower supports on each side. The cold leather on her burning skin sent a chill through her.

Slow and sure, he positioned her breasts so they dangled free.

"Sam." She blinked, unsure if she wanted—

He pinched her nipples, making her jolt. The carnal pain seared through her system, throwing her back into the clouds. Making him laugh.

As his hands moved over her roughly, harsh on her abused skin, the wonderfully hurtful caresses made her moan and squirm with need. "Please, Sam, I want—"

"I know, baby. And you're going to get that." He chuckled. "I want to hear you scream a little first."

Her mind told her body to tense, but the anticipation of more was...wonderful. "More. Want more."

"Yes. But this will be different. Let's see how you like a clamp."

She didn't like clamps, did she? She tried to shake her head, but her cheek rested on the cushion and hadn't moved.

He patted her hand. "I'm not going to restrain your arms, baby. Just your ass." He tugged her body down toward the end of the horse so her butt stuck out. Something pressed into her left calf—a strap—then the right. Another one chilled the skin on her lower back, and she realized she couldn't move her bottom at all. The sensation of being so exposed, so...ready...sent more need sizzling across her pussy. *Want. Please, want.*

He massaged her stinging ass cheeks, then smacked each one hard, and like coals with fresh tinder, the glow under her skin flamed up, searing through her in every color of the rainbow. Her moan shuddered inside her ribs before escaping.

Cold drizzled between her ass cheeks, making her squirm, and then he pressed something hard against her asshole. She instinctively tightened. Slowly he worked the plug through the rim of muscle, ruthlessly pushing in until her nerves sparkled like fireworks in the night. Confused, she tried to move, to escape, and couldn't. Her bottom was held right there for his use.

Her hands opened and closed convulsively as she realized he'd do exactly what he wanted. Her arousal expanded like a balloon. *Need to come. Oh, need to come.*

When the anal plug plopped into place, throbbing and burning, she whimpered at the jagged onslaught of fresh pleasure.

She heard his belt, then the crinkle of a condom wrapper, and his grating laugh. "Now for the part that you'll hate—and will really enjoy."

What? The pulsing sense of need eroded her thoughts and tied her tongue.

His hands slid over her bottom, down her inner thighs. And then his fingers settled on her clit, pinching hard enough that she screamed and tried to buck.

The urgent coil in her lower belly tightened and grew.

His fingers released her. Then something else locked onto her clit, tighter and tighter, as if tiny teeth were gnawing on her. The exquisite bite was shocking, overwhelming, and everything inside her exploded. *Oh God!* Her body spasmed, tried to move...couldn't...and the waves of sensation spread outward through her body, filling her mind.

Before she could recover, she felt his finger opening her labia. His thick cock pressed against her entrance, pushed inside, stretching her ferociously. *Too much.* As the tidal wave of ecstasy swept her away, she screamed.

LINDA'S SCREAM ALMOST sent Sam over the edge. The sound of a woman screaming and coming at the same time was the finest of wines, filling his soul. As her cunt convulsed around him in an unstoppable orgasm, her body shook like she'd break into pieces.

He gave her a few seconds to adapt to his entry, then pulled back and thrust in harder. Faster. Damned if she didn't keep spasming around him. Couldn't complain about that.

She finally sagged against the sawhorse, gasping for breath as if he'd held her underwater.

She was incredibly wet, and by God, he wanted to see her come again. He changed to a gentle sliding in and out as he ran his hands over her reddened back, savoring her moan. He'd never had someone more fun to play with. To hurt. To fuck.

He kept his thrusts slow enough to maintain control until she stirred. As her eyes blinked open, he ran his hands over the backs of her thighs. When his fingers encountered the tiny raised lines, he knew she'd get a fine burst of pain. As if in agreement, her cunt clenched around him, and he grinned. He could fuck her for years and never tire of it.

Mercilessly, he massaged her ass, pleased at the light welting, even more pleased at how she wiggled when the tender skin was further abused. As she started to pant, he tugged on the anal plug, adding new sensations. Overloading her system.

When he leaned forward, his cock rammed in deeper, right up against her cervix, and he heard her sharp inhalation, her attempt to squirm away. But the low back strap kept her right where he liked her, kept her feeling just what he wanted her to feel.

With his chest against her back, he reached around to palm her swaying breasts. Gorgeous breasts, heavy and large enough to fill his hands. He massaged them, tugged at them.

Her nipples were already sore from the wheel, the vampire glove, even a few hits from the quirt. When he pinched hard, her body stiffened, and her low shriek made him laugh. The way she tightened around his cock reaffirmed she was hardwired for pain, and those sensitive breasts made a direct circuit to her pussy. As he played with them, her breasts swelled, increasing his pleasure.

Increasing hers. She gave a sweet moan and slid deeper into subspace.

"That's my girl." He pounded into her hard enough to make the sawhorse rock. As he shoved her toward coming again, her cunt clamped down and tested his control.

Her breathing quickened, the sound mingling with her moans as he teased her nipples. *Goddamn.* His jaw clenched. His straining cock felt as if it would split; his balls seemed as if they'd been compressed between boards. Almost there—both of them.

Reaching around, he removed the clamp from her clit and could almost hear blood rush back into the abused nub. He drank in how her wailing scream filled the room, how her neck arched to lift her head, how her core clenched and spasmed around him as her orgasm hit her like a pile driver.

He gripped her hair, pulling as he released control and drove into her fast and hard. His balls were boiling, and the heat poured out of them and through his cock in bone-jolting jerks as he came and came and came.

God. Damn. With an effort, he released her hair and buried his face in the scented silkiness, content to stay just where he was—buried as deep as a man could go.

Chapter Eleven

Seated at a chair near a suspension scene, Aaron watched the little brunette trainee clean off a nearby table. Quite amusing how Sally—wasn't that her name?—never looked at him if she could help it. Not since he'd slapped her face for speaking up during a scene.

Her horror had been delightful—her tears even more so.

But everything had gone to hell after that. Z's mouthy sub had charged in, which meant Z had gotten involved. Truly a mess. At least the trainee had admitted she hadn't specified no slapping. When she said she'd been too shocked to safe word, he'd almost laughed. What was the point of slapping someone if you didn't shock her?

But it had pissed him off when Z monitored him closely for a time afterward. That was the slut's fault. He motioned to her. "You. Come here."

Her jaw tightened. Didn't it just break his heart that the trainee bitch had to acknowledge a Dom, even one she hated?

She approached, although he almost laughed at the ample space she left between them. "Yes, Sir."

"Bring me a..." He frowned, remembering he'd already had his two drinks. Cullen kept careful track. "Bring me a mineral water."

"Right away, Sir."

"Wait." When he raised his hand and she flinched, he laughed. "Remember our scene, do you? I enjoyed it."

Her whole body turned statue still, and an angry flush lit her cheeks. But, oh, too bad for her, the trainee couldn't yell at a Dom. Couldn't do shit.

"Maybe I'll ask for you again." He massaged his hand, enjoying how warily she watched him.

She clenched her tray so hard her knuckles turned white, but her voice stayed polite. Cold. "I'm afraid that would be a waste of your time...Sir."

The slut had a backbone. And he couldn't prod her further without chancing Z's attention. He flicked his fingers at her. "Go."

Her posture displayed a cock-hardening mix of anger and fear as she walked away. He shook his head, regretting that the Harvest Association hadn't picked her up. She'd have been perfect for the "rebellious slave" themed auction. Unfortunately, she'd gone to visit relatives before the contractor could kidnap her.

Truly a shame. He'd have loved to break the insolent bitch. Easy-peasy. Force her mouth open with a spider gag and let everyone face fuck her until only whimpers came out. Wouldn't take long before that cocky walk would turn to a slink, showing her fear of attracting any attention.

But that opportunity was gone. The Harvest Association wouldn't expand back into the southern quadrant for quite some time, if ever. Stinking FBI.

However, the northeast quadrant was in operation, and the Harvest Association took *vindictive* to new levels. The two asshole agents leading the investigation might well come to regret their actions.

Something to look forward to.

Turning, Aaron eyed the unoccupied submissives near the bar. His need wasn't urgent since he'd indulged in a whore last night. When he'd flashed a wad of money, the foolish woman had climbed right into his car. Poor safety awareness on her part. A shame she'd never learn any better.

She hadn't been a bad fuck. After getting off, he'd played with her, hurting her with his fists, then his knife. He'd been furious when she got quiet, like she'd mentally retreated. But no—she'd been dead. No stamina. Truly, the older slaves were more fun.

Damn Davies for latching on to the redheaded slut.

Then again, she'd undoubtedly be around. Without Davies. Her hair would look good in his drawer. Maybe he'd tie it up with a black ribbon for contrast.

For now...Aaron studied the submissives again. Perhaps the sharp-nosed slut with dark hair would serve his tastes.

* * * *

Linda blinked. *Dark*. Had she gone blind? She tried to work up some concern, but at the moment, her body felt...awesome. So replete that her insides throbbed with satisfaction. Her ass was tender, her clit ached, and her skin sizzled with delicious pain. With each breath she took, her breasts rubbed against soft fabric. Warmth radiated into her from... *Oh*.

She was on Sam's lap, his powerful arms holding her firmly to his chest. A blanket had been wrapped around her, and her face was buried in the hollow of his neck.

She considered lifting her head, but that seemed like too much effort.

"You back with me, baby?" The rumble of his voice was delicious.

When she wiggled, the scrape of his rough jeans on her tender, bare bottom was like sitting on white-hot coals. She jumped to her feet.

He yanked her back down. "Stay put."

Ow, ow, ow. "Sadist." But already the burn was sliding into a sweet throb.

He snorted. "That supposed to be an insult?" His calloused hand stroked down her bare back, making her hiss at the wash of wonderful pain, and he laughed again before reaching for something. A bottle. "Drink some of this."

The strawberry-flavored sports drink poured into her parched mouth like a river of coolness. "Mmm." She sipped more, glorying in the taste and all the bright sensations—the feel of Sam's warm body, how her skin burned in places, ached in others, the sound of his heartbeat, and music from outside the room. Everything. The comfort of being held—cuddled—made her want to cry and burrow even closer. She'd never felt so close to another human being, as if a ribbon of awareness cycled from him to her.

At a discreet tap on the door, she reluctantly lifted her head. The time for their special world must be over since she saw Raoul in the hallway. "There's a window in the door."

Sam rose and set her in the chair. "Someone's always on duty up here. Z doesn't take chances with his submissives."

She frowned. Surely someone didn't stand at the window all the time. "So if I'd yelled red?"

"Audio is handled by computer. He's got some odd software that can pick out words and distress—though the distress category gets a lot of false positives." Sam winked. "Seems that to a computer, an orgasm sounds like a heart attack."

He stepped outside. The men's voices drifted in through the open doorway.

Pulling the blanket higher, Linda watched. How come men looked so...edible...in the morning when women looked like hell? With a frown, she tried to smooth out what was probably the worst case of bedhead in all the world.

Sam glanced back at her, and his eyes lit with laughter. "I like the rumpled look...since I made you that way. It's a turn-on."

Oh. Well. Far be it from her to deny a man his little diversions. Then again...

When she kept finger combing her hair, his lips quirked. "Raoul and Kim are leaving. Do you want to go with them, or—"

"Oh, heavens!" Where were her brains? How could she possibly have forgotten she'd arrived with people? "Tell him I'm sorry! I'll be right there."

Her clothes were folded on top of Sam's toy bag. She donned her halter top and skirt, inhaling hard when the fabric encountered sore skin. Memory after memory of how her skin had gotten that way sent heat flushing through her until her face probably glowed. *I want to stay.*

Leaning against the door frame as he talked with Raoul, Sam wasn't bothering to conceal his enjoyment. Once she was dressed, he walked over and pulled her into a hug. "If you stay, we could move to one of the rooms with a bed. I'd like to run my hands over you and hear those noises before I took you again." He squeezed her welted bottom, making her moan. He rumbled a laugh. "That's a good sound."

As the sultry burn washed through her, every drop of blood pooled in her lower half and set up an urgent need. She wanted it all again. The pain. His demands. Him taking her. She rested her forehead against him, trying to burrow closer. To hang on forever. "I'm opening the store tomorrow. I have to go."

"All right." She felt him kiss the top of her head.

When Linda stepped into the hallway, Raoul was leaning against the railing. His dark gaze swept over her in a slow perusal before his lips curled in an easy smile. "You look as if you had a good time."

After all the things Sam had done to her, how could she possibly have a blush left? But she did.

Beside her, Sam ran a knuckle down her cheek, obviously enjoying the color show. "If you get depressed or weepy, you tell Raoul or you call me. Clear?"

A definite order. Sometimes that military background of his popped right out, didn't it? "Okay, Sarge. Got it." Oh, bad mouth. And if he slapped her butt right now, she'd melt into a puddle at his feet.

He stilled, gave her an assessing look from ice-blue eyes, then snorted. "You look so sweet, but you got some brat in there." He tugged on her hair, and Lord help her, even her scalp was sore. She didn't make any noise, but his eyes crinkled with what he must have seen in her face. "Want me to come by tomorrow?"

Her heart lifted. *Yes yes yes.* Then she felt a twinge of guilt. He was always driving to her house. That didn't seem fair. "I can come to your place instead."

The laughter disappeared from his eyes, as did any trace of softness. "Ah—"

She took a step back, realizing he'd never invited her over. Never even talked about his farm. Because he didn't want her there? "Oh. Never mind." The inside of her chest suddenly hurt worse than her back and bottom. Did he think she'd contaminate his home?

Sam reached out, but she stepped away.

"Linda."

No laugh, no apology. All she heard in that one word was reluctance. Regret. He really didn't want her at his house.

The Overseer's voice slid into her head. *"You're a slut. A fuck hole. That's all you are."* She swallowed. She'd thought Sam liked her...liked her for more than... The cold wind of reality ripped any lingering warmth away, leaving her exposed and chilled. Trembling.

"I really need to go." She took two steps to Raoul, hoping, still hoping, that Sam would react.

But it was Kim's Master who put an arm around her. "Come, chiquita."

When he gently pulled her to his side, she blinked back tears. Had there ever been such a nice man? "Thank you," she whispered, burying her face against his chest.

"Shhh," he whispered into her hair. He lifted his head. "My friend, you are a fool."

Sam didn't answer.

As Raoul guided her down the hallway to where Kim waited, no footsteps sounded behind them. Eyes blurry with tears, Linda looked back. Sam was gripping the railing. His head was bowed.

He didn't come after her.

*   *   *   *

Nolan's construction crew took Sundays off, which suited Sam just fine. He was irritable enough without the noise of construction—had been irritable ever since he shoved both boots in his mouth with Linda. Hell, his boots hadn't gone in his mouth; instead they'd trampled all over an innocent submissive.

You're a bastard, Davies. He'd picked up the phone several times, intending to apologize and to...to do what? What did he want to happen between them?

Tilting back on his porch chair, feet up on the railing, he drank coffee and watched the cold, gray world come to life. From the chicken pen, the rooster announced dawn. In the pastures, the cattle and horses trailed down toward the pond. Connagher was doing perimeter patrol, lifting his leg in some preset canine pattern to mark his territory. With no field hands today, the orange groves were quiet.

Chores or not, he couldn't summon the energy to start moving. Caffeine hadn't helped his energy level. Time hadn't helped his guilt.

The pain in Linda's eyes had stabbed right through him. Made him realize how badly he'd screwed up. He hadn't thought, just reacted. The idea of a woman in his home—after the war zone it had been during his marriage—had paralyzed him completely. Seemed that four years of quiet hadn't erased the bitterness and memories.

He wanted Linda—*hell, yes*—but for what? A play partner? An occasional fuck buddy? The thought thinned his mouth. She deserved better. He had plenty of play partners and fuck buddies. She meant more. The feel of her around his cock was fantastic; the feel of her in his arms, warm and soft, was even better. The hollow of her neck smelled faintly of lavender.

Closing his eyes, he shook his head. *Got it bad.* He could remember every laugh line on her face and see how her freckles faded into the pure white of her breasts. He liked how unexpected things would catch her fancy and her laughter would escape, so surprisingly full-bodied that he'd grin every time.

She hummed when she cooked. Sang when she scrubbed. She wore her music as another woman would wear jewelry.

She was fucking brave. And smart. Fun to talk with. Cute with her grumpiness in the mornings.

If she lived here, they'd... Yeah, that right there was the problem. He liked being single. Compared to the alternative he'd experienced, he could live with occasional loneliness.

He glanced over his shoulder at the small window he'd replaced after Nancy's door-slamming tantrum had shattered the antique glass. For a year after the divorce, it seemed like her screams and vitriol had continued to echo off the walls. He and Nicole had moved around the place like shell-shocked survivors. Then they'd slowly redecorated the entire house. Breakables had worked their way back in.

How could he bring someone into this carefully crafted peace? Even briefly?

Hell, he hadn't even known Linda that long.

Like Nancy. Three dates and she'd turned up pregnant. He'd had no clue about her messed-up welfare family or her drug habit.

Then again, he'd spent long hours in Linda's home, enjoying her company. He'd scened with her, bared her body and her soul. And sure as hell he'd been a Dom long enough to know when a submissive was lying.

Linda was exactly who she'd shown herself to be: a courageous, warmhearted survivor.

His mouth twisted. He was the scarred survivor of a fucked-up marriage, and he'd hurt her badly. Maybe she was better off without him.

* * * *

Linda's store was a heaven-sent distraction. She needed to stay busy because her spirits took a dive whenever she thought of Sam...or the previous weekend...or the times with him before that. She'd thought they had more between them than just floggings and sex. She'd thought they'd...connected.

Guess not.

Scowling, she set another basket on the shelf, angling it so the subtle design showed.

With Sam, she'd felt safe. Safe enough to let go, to let pain transform into pleasure, to let herself slide into her happy place. His strength, his voice, even his brutal honesty was reassuring. So was the way he'd hold her afterward with surprisingly tender hands, caring for her as if she...meant...something.

Yeah, I meant a lot to him. As long as I stayed away from his home.

As tears burned her eyes, she set two more baskets—small bright ones—on each side of the first.

Still, no matter how it ended, knowing him had been worth it. And last weekend had been wonderful. She'd learned that other women accepted and openly enjoyed their BDSM lifestyles. And what a relief it had been to acknowledge her own need to be hurt and dominated. She smiled slightly. Her bookaholic friends "needed" to read or they got irritable, and she felt that way about pain. Since that was her "thing," she'd better acknowledge it.

And she'd better not date men who thought unconventional meant sick.

Darn it. It wasn't fair that the one man who accepted her—no, who really *liked* her other side—didn't want more. Her lips quivered. She'd wanted to give him all of herself.

She couldn't even hate him. *Well, not much.* He'd been gentle with her, slept in her house to protect her, cared for her after their scenes. He wasn't a bastard, although she'd called him a few nasty names off and on all week. He just didn't see what they had together as a...relationship.

Obviously, she'd read more into his actions than he'd intended. Gritting her teeth, she shoved the Overseer's voice away. *I'm not a slut.*

She gave her head a firm shake. Yes, it was a pity that her little jar of hopes got knocked over, but how long was she going to whine about it? A year or two?

Do your job and be a shopkeeper.

A few minutes later, as she set the last basket on the shelf, she heard, "Hey, Mom."

Turning, she saw her son walking through the store, and her spirits lifted. "Charles, how nice. What are you doing here?"

"I wanted to give you something." His brown eyes warmed with happiness as he handed her a grocery sack.

"Well." She opened the sack. It was filled with... "Sweet grass?"

"Yeah. I was over at the coast and saw dunes of it. It's the right kind?"

"Oh, it's lovely. It'll make the prettiest baskets."

He rocked back and forth, hands in his pockets, pleased as punch with his surprise. How many bouquets of flowers, sheet music, books, and pottery had her generous-spirited son gifted her with over the years? Even as a toddler, he'd brought home pretty rocks for Mommy. They were still on the kitchen table, warming her heart whenever she saw them.

"Thank you, honey. This is wonderful."

He grinned, gave her a quick squeeze, and kissed her cheek. "I've got a class in an hour. Love you."

"Love you, sweetie."

As Charles trotted out of the store, an elderly customer approached the counter, beaming. "What a nice boy."

"Yes." Linda's heart expanded with pride. "He really is."

A quick sale later, the woman left, her newly purchased tote sagging from the addition of a diet soda and an assortment of Belgian chocolates and truffles. Someone really liked her fancy chocolates.

As the customer stepped onto the boardwalk, a man stepped back to let her pass. *Lee.* Linda watched him walk into the store, his expression open. Friendly. Not a fancy chocolate person. No, he was a plain milk chocolate bar. Straightforward. No surprises. Liked by everyone.

She looked away. Sam would be dark chocolate with almonds and sea salt. Complex. Not overly sweet. Not to everyone's taste. But having experienced Sam made it difficult to return to everyday chocolate.

As Lee walked up to the counter, Linda smiled at him. "Hi there."

"You look beautiful today." He grinned. "I came by to see if you wanted to go to a movie tonight. We can check the listings and find something we both like."

"You pull out one of those chick romances, and I'll beat your butt, missy." The memory of Sam's grating warning made her throat tighten. When she'd tossed *Dirty Dancing* into his lap, she'd learned in a painful way that he didn't make idle threats. *That's over, Linda. Move on.*

"I don't think..." She took his hand. The knowledge that her decision would hurt him pressed a heavy weight onto her shoulders. But she wouldn't lead him on as Sam had done with her. Lee deserved honesty. "This isn't going to work, Lee. I like edgy sex, and you don't."

But he'd been kind. During her awkward attempt at discussing it with him, he'd tried so carefully to hide his disapproval.

His expression was that of a man whose terrier had nipped him. "Linda, I—"

"Neither of us is wrong." *Thank you, Gabi. I know that now.* "But we have different desires and needs." She pulled in a breath, hoping she wouldn't lose him as a friend. "I think we should call this quits."

He stood silently for a minute as if hoping she'd change her mind. "Well. We might have found a way to compromise, but...rumor has it you're seeing someone. I guess he's giving you what you like." Lee squeezed her fingers and pulled back. "If it doesn't work out, I hope you'll give me another chance."

"I'm sorry," she whispered.

"Me too." Brows drawn together in unhappiness, he turned and walked out of the store.

She sighed. Only Lee could have handled an awkward situation so smoothly, but she still felt like scum for hurting him.

"Hey, hey, hey. Don't look like that went very well."

Linda pulled her gaze from the empty door to see Dwayne by the wall, his purple and green shirt clashing with the colorful paintings. What had he heard? How could she have been so indiscreet as to have an intimate talk in her own store? *Dumb.*

Even dumber to have discussed anything in front of a reporter. Ignoring him, she walked to the other side of the store and started restocking shelves.

He followed. "Are you having a difficult time adjusting? Going from being a slave to a normal person?" *Slave.* He said it as if he liked the taste of the word.

Her skin crawled. *Note to self—never date a reporter.* "If you're not going to buy anything, please leave."

"Did your business fall off when people realized what you are...were?" He casually leaned against the wall shelves, his gaze as avid as a dog looking at raw meat. "You know, I heard a rumor about a place you visited before your kidnapping. Disturbing stuff."

Her skin went cold, and she could actually feel the blood leave her face. Even knowing her reaction confirmed his rumor, she couldn't stop herself. "Get out. You're not welcome in my store." She pointed to the door.

His expression darkened. "You'd do better to talk to me. Give me something juicy, and maybe I won't use that other information."

"Get. Out."

"Fine." He paused in the door to look back. "You're gonna be sorry." He stalked out, bumping against the coffee shop owner who'd stopped on the boardwalk.

Oh, God. As Linda's knees started to buckle, she grabbed the shelf. Two totes fell onto the floor, flattened like roadkill.

"My heavens, he threatened you!" With an appalled expression, Betty entered the shop. "'You're gonna be sorry.' That's a threat."

"Yes." Her energy leaked away, leaving exhaustion behind. Would this never end? "But he wouldn't be the first reporter to print nasty things." *About slaves. About me.*

"What an awful man." Betty set her hands on her hips. "I'm going to talk to Curtis about the quality of staff he employs." Giving a huff of fury, she marched out.

Linda stared after her. Brassy red hair with graying roots, round face, quick temper, the owner of the coffee shop was as sweet as her pastries. However, if the newspaper revealed Linda had visited a BDSM club before being kidnapped, Betty's sweetness might quickly change.

Odd, wasn't it? As a slave, she'd thought rescue would end all her problems. *Guess not.* Mouth flattening, she straightened her shoulders. It was a nightmare, but all nightmares eventually ended, right? She just had to hang in there. *I'm strong. I am.*

Chapter Twelve

Sam scowled at the cars lining the curb in Linda's cul-de-sac and ended up parking several houses down. As he walked down the sidewalk, he saw the red and yellow balloons dotting the yard next door. Children were laughing, yelling, whooping. Sounded like someone was having a birthday party. His jaw tightened as he remembered the one time he'd given a party for Nicole.

An hour before the party, Nancy had gone to town to fetch the cake. After demanding a refund, she'd used the money to buy drugs. Oxycodone. She'd returned midparty, higher than a kite, foulmouthed and out of control. He'd had to ask another child's mother to supervise as he kept his wife out of the room. Had to turn the music up to drown out her yelling and cursing. Had to call the parents to pick up their children early. A major clusterfuck.

Nicole had refused any more parties. So each birthday, he'd taken her and her buddies to a children's pizza place or a skating rink or a water park. They'd never told Nancy.

Had to wonder if Nicole would have found it easier to have a consistently abusive mother rather than one who was loving at intervals, but viciously destructive the rest of the time? Why the hell couldn't he have made her life easier?

When he reached Linda's, he spotted new white blotches on the house. He scowled. The asshole had marked up her house again. Because Sam hadn't been around. Looked like he was letting everyone down.

As he tapped on the door, he felt his muscles tighten. Would she still be pissed off? Or worse, hurt?

The door opened. "Sam!" Happiness lit her eyes. Then her expression turned flat. "Go away." She started to close the door.

Hell. He stuck his foot in the door. "I'm sorry."

"Get your boot out." She shoved on the door and glared.

Stubborn woman. He pushed the door open far enough for his shoulders. Far enough that he could bracket her face with his hands and compel her to actually see him. Her eyes looked haunted. His chest squeezed. "Linda, I'm sorry."

"Apology accepted. Now go."

Despite his remorse, he had to laugh. "That's not forgiveness, girl. Is that hypocrisy what you taught your children?"

His insult struck home, but she didn't retreat. "So I'm a bad example. I didn't teach them to be fuck toys either."

He slapped the door hard enough to make his palm sting. "You're no goddamned fuck toy!" He pulled in a breath. *Stow it, Davies.* "You are undoubtedly the strongest woman I know."

Surprise weakened her posture.

"Don't you want to hear me grovel?"

She leaned her head against the edge of the door and closed her eyes. A second passed. Another.

The sound of her shuddering breath shook him. If she started to cry, she would break his heart.

Finally, she looked at him, then nodded. "All right. Come on in."

AS SAM WALKED past her, the chill winter air slipped in the door after him. Linda shook her head. How in the world had he managed to change her mind? She didn't have anything to say to him; there was nothing between them except pain and sex.

As if to refute that, he gathered her into a warm, nonsexual hug. "Even if you don't want to"—he snorted—"be my fuck toy, can we be friends?"

Friends? Why did his work shirts have to smell like sunshine? She rested her cheek on the well-worn fabric, thinking of all the times he'd held her. Talked to her. He'd helped her scrape her house. Had cooked her breakfast. Demanded an old Clint Eastwood movie as payback for her Katharine Hepburn one. Played guitar with her and then for her as she wove a new basket. Somehow, in those few days, he'd sneaked right past her defenses. *Yes, friends.* "I'm sorry I was rude."

He rubbed his chin on the top of her head. "I like knowing you can fight back."

Me too. And more than fight back. Darned if she'd let him get away with only an apology. "Are you going to explain?"

The muscles under her cheek turned rigid. "Yes."

Just the one word. But it was enough to tell her he had a reason for not wanting her to see his home—one that made him uncomfortable. He didn't want to tell her.

Although Frederick hadn't had a problem talking about anything and everything, Charles had been a taciturn teenager. So she'd treat Sam as she did Charles. "Come and help me get supper ready." Kitchens were designed for sharing more than food.

She settled Sam on a stool at the big island and assigned him to putting together a salad. When she put a glass of wine in front of him, he gave her a surprised look.

"No beer, sorry." Her lips twitched as she glanced at the sink where she'd dumped the contents of the three bottles of beer he'd left in her refrigerator.

His gaze followed hers, and laughter lit his eyes. "You got a nasty temper there, missy." He took a sip of wine.

After a second of thought, she abandoned her original plan of a supper of tomato soup and crackers. Potatoes went into the oven. She browned pork chops, poured cream of mushroom soup over them, and tucked them in to bake as well.

"Salad's done," Sam said. The tightness had left his face, and he'd finished his wine. She poured him more and some for herself.

After putting crackers and cheese on a platter, she sat beside him. "What's at your house that you don't want me to see?"

"Like dead wives stored in closets?" When a corner of his mouth curved up with amusement, her breath caught. He had such a hard face that his sense of humor tended to catch her by surprise.

"Yeah, like that." Following techniques learned from raising teenagers, Linda turned her attention to the cheese and crackers.

"She's not dead."

"Your ex-wife?"

"Right." He put a piece of cheese on a cracker and simply held it. Stared at it. "She was—is—a drug addict. Made life hell." He rubbed his jaw. "I haven't taken a woman there since. When you..." He paused.

"Women don't go home with you? Ever?"

"No." His mouth tightened.

Heavens. She stared at him. That must have been one nasty marriage. Considering how many whips Sam owned, his wife was lucky to have survived. Then again, she'd come to realize that although he might be a sadist— or *because* he was one—he held to stronger rules of conduct than most "normal" guys. "I can't imagine what you went through. So it wasn't about me at all?"

"No." He turned his hand over and squeezed her fingers. "Just me being a goddamned idiot. You're welcome to come out to the farm, Linda."

A simple, sincere invitation. Her heart did a flip-flop. *I'm in trouble, all right.* But what would it hurt to see where this would go? She leaned her cheek against his rough-skinned hand as the warmth in her heart blossomed. "I'd like to see your place someday."

"It's spring. There'll soon be babies—chicks, calves, foals, goslings." He tugged her hair. "You'll enjoy it."

"Because I'm a mother?" She huffed a laugh and added as a joke, "Are fuck toys supposed to be into babies?"

His bark of a laugh was a reward. "Girl, you're as maternal as they come." The warmth in his gaze said he found that side of her nature attractive. Found *her* attractive.

The glow of that disappeared when he yanked her to her feet. "Time you learned not to call yourself names."

Her mouth dropped open. "But..."

"No buts. No excuses. No more." His grip was daunting, his uncompromising expression even more so.

She had a feeling that even begging wasn't going to save her poor bottom.

* * * *

A noise roused Linda. Was her next-door neighbor working on his house again? So early? *I am not getting up yet.* Unless... She rolled over and disappointingly found no one to rouse. Darn early risers.

The pounding started up again. *Phooey.* As she tried to burrow into the bedding, various hurts came to life. The sheet scraped over her sore back and bottom. Her breasts were tender from the wonderfully ouchy clamps Sam had used. As her lips curved at the memory, her nipples tightened into peaks that made the ache even worse.

She wiggled her butt on the bed to increase the burn there, enjoying both the memory and the wakening flame inside her.

Makeup sex with a sadist was amazing.

More pounding. Could that be her door? *Not fair. I haven't even had breakfast yet.* Grumpily, she slipped out of bed and picked up her robe. The children planned to visit next weekend, so it wouldn't be them. Had she paid the paperboy yet? Probably some door-to-door salesman.

She heard the door open.

"Who the hell are you?" Charles's voice.

Oh no. Oh bad. Frantically, she dropped her robe and yanked on jeans, a bra, and a T-shirt. *Please let Sam be dressed.* She hurried out.

Sam was dressed. *Thank you, God.* In the middle of the living room, both her children stared at him as if the man was the devil come to life.

Busted. Her lips quirked. Moms weren't supposed to have sex, obviously. She'd always tried to be discreet the few times a man had spent the night, but honestly, she had a right to her own life. Her children were adults, after all—or so they kept informing her. "What are you two doing here?

They turned to her. Brenna's face was white. Flushed with anger, Charles glared at her. "No, the question is what were *you* doing?" He slapped a newspaper down on the coffee table.

She glanced at it. In a huge font, the headline read: SEX SLAVE VISITED FETISH CLUB. The letters started to dance up and down as a swarm of bees buzzed in her head. Her knees buckled.

Sam caught her with a steely arm around her waist. "Easy, girl. Sit."

As he helped her into a chair, she wanted to cling— needed to. Instead she put her hands in her lap. The buzzing didn't let up.

"That said"—Charles pointed to the paper—"you-you went to a BDSM club. Where they whip people. Perverts chain up women. You fucking brought the kidnapping on yourself." She'd never seen him wear such a look of disgust, and he was looking at her.

Perverts. An invisible hand ringed Linda's throat, squeezing her words back, keeping them inside. "I'm not—"*Not dirty, not filthy, not a pervert. Am I?* Just last night, she'd let Sam hurt her. Had liked it.

Brenna had tears in her eyes. "Everyone in my dorm saw the newspaper. Were whispering about...you.

They know you're my mother." Her voice got louder. "You put us through all that because you went out trolling for sex? Everyone's going to think I'm a slut."

"I didn't—" How could she explain the difference?

"Your mother was the victim," Sam snapped. "Don't treat her like—"

"Who the fuck are you?" Charles's color heightened as he looked at Sam, then her.

She glanced at Sam. Dressed but unshaven. And her cheeks and neck were undoubtedly reddened from the beard stubble. Her lips swollen.

"I saw pictures from the club. Women being whipped." Brenna stared at Linda as if she'd turned into something hideous. "How could you go to a place like that?"

"Yeah, whipping. For real." Charles's jaw jutted out, and he took a step toward Sam. "So you some big bad sadist? Didn't think we'd know those words, huh, Mom? Isn't the fucking Internet great?" He widened his stance as he glared at Sam. "You a sadist? Huh?"

A whirlpool of misery was pulling Linda in.

Sam dismissed her son as if he were a two-year-old having a tantrum. "Not your business, boy."

"Yeah, that's what I figured."

Damn you, Sam. With that answer, he might as well have said yes.

As her children stared at Sam, Linda lowered her head. Her hands trembled. Abrasions from the rope Sam had used on her wrists showed below the shirtsleeves. She pulled in a breath and lost it again because her children were looking at her. As if she were a freak.

"I feel sick," Brenna said.

"Yeah." Charles's lips curled up. "You're just a—"

"Don't finish that." Sam's voice was a threatening growl.

Charles took a hasty step back.

Her heart seemed to crack within her chest. *They don't know—don't understand.* At their age, a parent's vulnerability would be treated with scorn. She'd seen how cruel children could be.

But not mine. Not until now.

Linda rose, surprised the floor held her even though the world had shattered. Her eyes blurred with tears as she looked at her daughter. Once she'd been so little and her mommy had been the only one who could comfort her. So many memories. *Walking and rocking her for hours when she had croup, singing lullabies after a nightmare, picking just the right cartoon Band-Aid for a scraped knee.*

Her lips trembled as she turned to her son. How many hours had she sat with him in her lap? *His cheeks flushed with fever, head on her shoulder, sucking his thumb as they watched* The Lion King *for the hundredth time.* Now he looked at her as if he'd never seen her before.

Maybe she hadn't seen them before either. "Go."

"What?" Charles said.

"Get out." Linda pointed to the door. "All of you. I don't want any of you in my house."

"But—" Brenna took a step forward.

Linda felt sobs welling up, and sheer rage drove them back. She turned her gaze to Sam, who'd as much as admitted he was a sadist. "You too. Out."

He frowned, glanced at her children, then simply walked out the door.

She turned her attention to her self-righteous children. They'd never even been spanked, let alone beaten. Not been whipped. Or raped. Or called names like "slut" and "whore." Never gone hungry. And somehow grown up without any compassion whatsoever.

She'd thought she was a good mother, but she'd failed. "Get out. I don't want you in my house."

Charles turned white. "Mom?"

"Get. Out!" The first tear spilled over as she watched them leave. More tears followed as she stumbled to the door, locked it, and sagged against it. *Why. Oh God, why?*

She should never have returned. Should have gone far away. Should have died instead of Holly. Burying her face in her arms, she cried.

* * * *

Hours later, Linda walked into her store. Gail's first grandchild was being baptized, and Linda had agreed to let her clerk off early.

If not for that, she might not have left her house at all, especially after reading the newspaper. Dwayne had interviewed a person who'd watched Linda being flogged in the BDSM club the night she was abducted. The slanted wording implied that in being kidnapped, she'd gotten what was coming to her.

No wonder her children had been upset. But the way they'd behaved? As she forced tears back, the hole in her heart gushed agony with every beat. But she'd survive. Slavery had taught her how to do that. She'd learned how to keep putting one foot in front of the other, no matter what happened. Survival didn't mean she didn't hurt; it only meant she was alive.

"Good, you're here!" Her clerk looked up, and her smile wavered slightly. She'd obviously read the paper.

"I'm here," Linda said. *The dirty slut has arrived.* Here was one more person who thought she was scum. "Get on to that baptism before you're late." Maybe she should ask if Gail would be back tomorrow, but she couldn't take another blow. Not today.

"Been steady business all day." Gail's voice drifted from the back room as she retrieved her purse. She reappeared, a tall, slim woman slightly older than Linda. She started to walk past, then shook her head. "Honey, I've never seen anyone look so in need of a hug." She wrapped her arms around Linda and squeezed, then stepped back.

"I...I did need that. Thank you."

"Nah." The gray-green eyes hardened. "My Cindy was assaulted when she was sixteen. The scumbag's lawyer tried to make it sound like she'd asked for it, and thank God, the prosecutor flattened him good. But I got a good education in warped thinking. So maybe you like your sex on the kinky side, but that's not asking for rape any more than Cindy's wearing sexy clothes. That's how I see it. Now buck up." She gave Linda a firm nod and strode out of the store.

Linda stared after her. "Well." She'd misread Gail's expression completely. Had she been retreating from people without needing to?

On the drive to the store, she'd wondered again if she even wanted to stay in the town. But she loved her beach shop, loved the gulls strutting along the boardwalk, the quiet sound of the waves, and the chattering of the tourists. Loved the way their sunburned faces brightened at seeing the unique handcrafted souvenirs. She'd worked too hard to get the store going. She and the children had painted the walls. A friend had designed the sign. Her craftspeople relied on her to sell their goods.

Her chin rose. This was her place, and she wouldn't give anyone—especially Dwayne—the satisfaction of knowing they'd driven her out. *I'm staying.*

That afternoon, she bent her efforts to being the most welcoming shopkeeper on the beachfront and was so successful that it was closing time before she realized it.

After locking the door and shutting off the lights, she pulled her cell phone out and stared at it. *Call the children?*

The longing to hear their voices, to *fix* the problem, shook her. Her finger hovered over the keypad, then moved away.

No. They were wrong. No matter how comforting, calling them would demonstrate that they could get away with such behavior.

They already felt they knew all the answers.

Speaking of answers, why had Sam answered the way he had? Why did he have to confirm all their suspicions? As bitter anger welled inside her, impossible to set aside, she pulled out her car keys.

Chapter Thirteen

Twilight cast shadows over the yard as Sam closed the chickens in their coop for the night. The day had been cloudy, and the evening temperature was in the fifties. After buttoning his denim jacket, he checked his cell phone—no call from Linda. *Goddammit*. All day, he'd expected her to call.

He still didn't know if he should have left the house. Right then, he'd figured she needed time and space to sort things out with the kids. Having him there sure hadn't helped anything. But what if she'd held firm and kicked the kids out as well? She'd have been alone...after being eviscerated by the brats.

His mouth tightened. Time and space be damned. He'd call her when he got back to the house.

After a quick visual search, he spotted Connagher in the pasture, pouncing on something in the grass. "You coming, dog?"

Abandoning the chase, the mountain cur scrambled over the post-and-rail fence, his golden-red fur glinting with the last rays of the sun. His tongue lolled out as he trotted across the yard, ears pricked up to report in. *Yes, sir, field mice won't be bothering you this evening.*

"Good job." Sam stopped long enough to give him a good rib scratching before heading down the long drive to lock up and turn on the security system.

The front gate screeched. Sam's jaw clenched. If that was his ex coming in, he was going to... He heard the car move forward, then another screech as the gate was closed. No, not his ex. Nancy never closed anything behind her.

"Stay with me," he told Conn as the dog quivered with eagerness to chase the intruder off their land. Protective little bastard. Sam's father had bred mountain curs, but he'd liked how the dark-brindled dogs could disappear in the night. Liked seeing them scare people. As a child, Sam had experienced his share of frights.

Conn's reddish fur was a damn sight easier to spot.

As a familiar-looking Toyota sped up the drive, Sam's spirits rose. Looked like he wouldn't have to call her after all.

The car pulled in adjacent to Sam's truck at the side of the house.

"Heel," he said to Conn. He strode forward, the dog a step behind, and opened the door for her. Her scent drifted out, and he had to wonder if lavender would now give him a hard-on every time he smelled it. "Come to visit?"

She slid out of the car, slammed the door, and then shoved him back a pace. "What do you think?" If her voice had been a whip, it would have drawn blood.

Conn growled, and even as Sam snapped, "Shut it," Linda glared at the dog. "Go sit."

With a whine—attacked by two pack leaders at once—Conn put his ass on the ground.

Sam eyed Linda. The redhead's temper didn't fire up quickly, but damn, she was cute when she got angry. He set his hand on the car roof and leaned in, deliberately invading her space. "You're pissed off at me."

"Well, isn't that observant?" The sarcasm was thick even before she added, "Have you considered suing your brains for nonsupport?"

Now that sounded just like Gabi. Sam barely managed to smother a laugh. No wonder Marcus enjoyed his little submissive so much. "Explain."

"You said...you told Charles, 'None of your business.'" She scowled. "You might just as well have said yes. So yeah, thanks for helping out."

Ah. His temper started to rise, and he shut it down. She'd had a crappy day and wanted to take it out on him. Not fair, but still good she trusted him enough to do that. Even better that she gave enough of a damn to be angry with him. But she was out of line. "Linda." Risking another shove, he cupped her chin. "You really want a man who'd lie? Does that set a good example for your kids?"

She froze as if he'd slapped her, and tried to turn her face away.

Not going to happen. His fingers tightened, and he watched her anger fade.

"You're right." Her voice was barely audible above the sighing of the dogwood trees lining the drive. She closed her eyes and sagged against the car.

He waited.

"I'm sorry. I don't know what I was thinking, coming here to give you grief for being honest."

Such big brown eyes. She was a heartbreaker. He gathered her in. "You needed someone, and you can't yell at the children—not more than you did already."

She winced. "I can't believe I kicked them out of my house."

So she'd held to her course. Strong woman. "Good. They were brats."

She stiffened for a second, then sighed. "They were. But they're usually good kids."

"Then they'll come around."

"Maybe not. Not after this." Her breathing hitched.

"Nah. Right now, they're mad. It hit them where they're vulnerable—the opinion of their friends."

"I know the feeling," she said under her breath.

Hell. Her kids wouldn't have been the only ones to read that goddamned paper. He gripped her arms. "Are people giving you a rough time?"

LINDA STARED UP into Sam's lean, weathered face. His blue eyes blazed. He should have been furious with the way she'd attacked him, but only now was he showing anger. Protective, wasn't he?

Her mouth tilted up as she remembered her afternoon. "Some. Some were snoopy, some rude. But quite a few were angry on my behalf." She'd collected more hugs that had almost reduced her to crying again. Odd how disconcerting kindness could be.

"Hard day. C'mere." His arms came around her, and he engulfed her in warmth again.

As the cooling air brought the scents of the pasture and barn, she heard the low flap of bats catching insects in the air and the rustle of a breeze through the leaves. A cow mooed. She closed her eyes, knowing she could happily spend an eternity in his arms. Who'd ever think the tough rancher could give such fantastic hugs? With a sigh of regret, she pulled back. "I'm sorry to have bothered you. I'll get out of your hair now."

He leaned his hip against the car door. "Nope. You're here. Now you stay."

"You didn't... I didn't mean to just barge in."

He gave her a hard look. "Be quiet. You're staying."

Her unhappiness drifted back a few feet. Being with Sam would be nice. Her house was empty. Silent. "I... Okay."

"Good answer."

"How about I cook you dinner to make up for my being an idiot?" What kind of extra-special dessert could she concoct for him?

"Works for me." He nodded at the dog. "That's Connagher. Conn"—he slapped Linda's leg—"this is Linda. Linda. Linda."

The dog rose, sniffed her leg, and wagged its tail.

Sam glanced at Linda. "He keeps track of people. Comes in handy when I want to find a field hand." He tugged on the dog's ears. "Now, say hello to Linda."

The dog barked once, then gave her a canine grin. She bent to pet him. Interesting appearance. Medium-short, rough fur, stocky body, ears that drooped at the tip. His frame was smaller than a lab's but similar. "What kind of dog is this?"

"Basic hound. Called a mountain cur." He ruffled the fur on the dog's neck affectionately. "They're working and hunting dogs. Helped settle the Appalachians."

"Huh." She smiled as she straightened. Conn was like Sam: hard body, no frills, no particular charm, but tough enough to do whatever he had to do.

Sam put his hand on the small of her back, a circle of warmth in the cooling night, and guided her around the side of the house. In the front, the drive made a circle, enclosing a splashing fountain and landscaping plants. Through the twilight, she could see the shapes of farm buildings. Farther out, white fencing divided up dark pastures and ended at a line of trees.

The white, two-story farmhouse was probably mid-last century but well kept. A wide porch held a hanging swing and Adirondack chairs. He took her up the steps, across the porch, and through a heavy front door with an arched stained-glass window.

In the small entry, he helped her off with her white wool coat and hung it up. As he tossed his jean jacket onto a hook, then pulled off his boots, she had to shake her head. As a teen, she'd adored cowboy movies. Sam Davies was like a fantasy come true.

When he jerked his chin toward her high heels, she removed them before following him into the family room.

"Oh, this is nice." An interior wall had been removed, letting the huge room flow into the dining area. The pale cream paneling lightened the heaviness of the brown suede sectional couch and chairs. A dark hardwood floor gleamed under a faded Oriental carpet. The entire room was designed for comfort, right down to the small fire crackling in the massive stone fireplace on the right.

When Conn flopped down on the hearth with a sigh as if he'd battled all day, Linda grinned.

Sam ran his hand up her back. "You've had dogs?"

"Oh, always, until... Well, the last one died a few months ago." Her heart wrenched. "He was old. And it was good that he didn't...he wasn't..." Wasn't there to be left alone after she'd been abducted.

Sam squeezed her shoulder in wordless comfort, then left her to walk into the kitchen.

Unsure what to do, she curled into a corner of the oversize couch. "I can't stay long."

"Don't you have tomorrow off?" He reappeared with a glass of wine for her and a beer for himself.

"Um." She took a tiny sip of wine, pleased he'd paid attention to her schedule. But she couldn't stay...could she?

He dropped down beside her and put his arm along the back of the couch. Just as when they watched movies at her place, his fingers curled over her shoulder, pulling her closer. "Relax. You don't have anything or anyone to worry about here."

No neighbors, no spray painter, no newspapers or rude reporters. Paradise. She took a bigger drink. "I don't want to make you uncomfortable. I feel as if I pushed my way in."

"If I didn't want you here, I'd say so."

Bluntly instruct someone to go home? Yes, he'd probably do just that. She stared at him.

"What?" He curled her hair around his finger.

"I just realized how honest you are. Even to the point of being rude."

"What's the point in lying?"

Note to self: never ask this man if a dress makes me look fat. But such honesty was oddly freeing. She could relax, knowing she really was welcome. And she'd never have to wonder if he had agreed to something just to be nice.

His hand curved over her shoulder, and he frowned. "You're knotted up."

"Bad day."

"I'll trade you back rubs."

A back rub? She really could use one.

"Hang on a minute." He walked out of the room, returning with a jar of coconut oil.

"You had a bad day too?"

"Not like yours. Got in a hay delivery, and the bales are heavy." His eyes crinkled. "I'm not as young as I used to be."

"I've heard that happens." All too soon. At least redheads didn't go gray as quickly as brunettes. Her sister had colored her hair for over a decade now.

Sam motioned to Conn. "Move, dog."

With a disgruntled look, Conn trotted off to lie in the entryway.

Sam tossed a quilt from the back of the couch onto the floor, then pulled Linda to her feet. Efficiently, he stripped off her blouse and bra, taking a moment to fondle her.

Arousal speared downward so quickly she made a sound. Who knew that standing in a room half-naked and having her breasts handled could be so hot?

Smiling, he gave her a slow, thorough kiss. "You're goddamned tempting, you know. Especially these." Her breasts sat comfortably cupped in his palms.

She liked her body, but compliments like that made her feel all warm and fuzzy. After taking another kiss, he pushed her to lie facedown on the quilt.

On his knees, he straddled her, resting his jean-covered butt on hers. After warming the oil, he started off with long, easy strokes up and down her back. Her eyes slid shut as his greased hands moved over her shoulders. "Ooooohhhh. More."

He huffed a laugh and continued. When she'd melted right into the blanket, his fingers started to massage each muscle, one by one, working their way up her back. When he reached her tight shoulders, he traced around a taut place. His thumb came down on the knot...and kept pressing harder. She squeaked as the hurting grew.

"Breathe through it, girl."

Ow, ow, ow. More of his weight settled on her butt, pinning her to the blanket. She fought for a breath, took another slower one, before his thumb lifted. As blood rushed into the area with a flood of warmth, she realized the knot was gone. But still... She glared over her shoulder. "That hurt."

He winked. "Best part of giving a massage."

Damn sadist.

He found three more places to torture her with, but by the time he was through, she was incredibly relaxed and turned on as well. Whenever he forced her to take pain—more than she wanted—it had the same effect as if she'd swallowed an instant arousal pill.

Before she could move, he reached under her, unzipped her slacks, and dragged them and her thong right off.

"Hey!"

"I prefer my masseuses to be naked." He stripped off his shirt, set her to one side, and took her place on the quilt.

She could only laugh and take a perch on his very hard ass. After the coconut oil warmed and liquefied in her palm, she rubbed it over his back. Heavens, just look at him. Broad shoulders, lean musculature, and a tan that showed he sometimes didn't wear a shirt outside. After massaging his shoulders, she worked her way down. To make any impression in his rock-hard flesh, she had to really work at it. *Massage, the newest aerobic exercise.* When she reached his low spine, the muscles on each side were like concrete. "Here's where it hurts, huh?"

"Yep. Push as hard as you can."

She edged her bottom back, put all her weight on her palms, and pressed slowly upward. His pleased rumble made her glow inside. She repeated the movement, over and over, but all too soon, her arms tired.

"Up you go, girl," he said, obviously feeling her weakening strokes.

She rose.

He followed and stretched. "Much better. You're good at that, missy."

The compliment warmed her. "Thank you. You too."

With a light laugh, he pulled her forward, rubbing his chest on her breasts and taking her lips in a hard, hard kiss.

"Now for the more enjoyable part." He pointed to the quilt. "Lie down."

"More?" She gave him a puzzled look, then dropped to her knees.

"Uh-uh. On your back."

Feeling uncomfortably exposed in the bright firelight, she complied. But how come she was naked and he got to keep his pants on?

As his gaze wandered over her, he smiled, probably enjoying her flush as much as her nakedness. But when he said, "You're a beautiful woman," the temptation to smack him one disappeared.

He straddled her again, planting himself on her upper thighs, and scooped up more coconut oil. First, he worked on the small muscles in front of her shoulders, in the hollow under her collarbones, and her upper arms. She hadn't realized those areas could get so tense until he'd turned those muscles to happy noodles.

Then his eyes grew half-lidded when his hands started to oil her breasts. He massaged the underlying pectoral muscles and started to play. With his gaze on her face, he pulled at her nipples, then pinched lightly. Harder. He rolled each peak between his thumb and forefinger, increasing the pressure until she made a sound.

"Hurts?"

"Yes, darn you."

"Good." He squeezed harder.

As the pain grew and heat bloomed in her core, she moaned.

Delight lit his eyes. He didn't stop.

"That's too hard." She reached up to push him away.

"Did I hear your safe word?" He grabbed her wrists, set them above her head, and anchored them in his fist, then continued torturing her breasts with his other hand.

His grip was too tight, hurting her, and he was pinching her nipples too hard. When she started to squirm—half with pain, half with arousal—he only laughed, continuing until her breasts felt incredibly swollen and throbbed.

As he rose to his feet, he gave her a stern look. "Don't move from where I put you."

Needing to rub the ache, she lowered her arms, and received a stinging slap on one breast. *Ow ow ow.* Tears filled her eyes as she hastily put her arms back in place.

His eyebrows lifted. "Safe word?"

Pain was rolling through her, yet...despite her tears, she loved it. Her body flamed with arousal. The very roughness he showed her created shivers deep in her belly.

His lips quirked. "Guess not." He stripped out of his remaining clothes, and she was mesmerized by how the firelight flickered over his body. He had the tight, flat butt and great legs of a horseman. His shoulders rippled with muscle—from lifting hay bales? He sure didn't get his physique from a gym. It was a treat to see him in the light.

His cock was fully erect and seemed just like the rest of Sam—straight, solid, potent. Veins curved around the rigid shaft, inviting a tongue to trace them. Her fingers twitched, wanting to touch.

He pulled her legs apart and knelt between them. After positioning square cushions on each side of her hips, he bent and pressed her knees to the pillows, opening her to his gaze. With his hands on her thighs to keep her in place, he looked down, studying her private areas with a slight smile.

Maybe all this light wasn't so wonderful. He was embarrassing the heck out of her, and she squirmed in response.

His grip tightened on her knees. "Stay put."

She froze obediently, but his frown continued. After a second, he took two coasters from the end table and balanced one on each knee. "If one of these falls because you move, I'll whip that pretty pussy."

"What?"

"Yeah." A crease deepened in his cheek as he ran a finger from her knee down to her groin, making her muscles quiver. He nodded to a wooden crate beside the couch. "I just finished making a short, softer flogger. A coaster hits the ground, and I get to try it out."

"You wouldn't." She really, really remembered the paddle he'd used. But a flogger?

"Oh, I would." He slid down until his mouth hovered over her, and his breath wafted against her mound. "I like blindfolds on submissives, but I think you might not enjoy that."

After being a slave? "No, Sir."

"Then you'll blindfold yourself." He lifted his chin, his voice darkening. "Put an arm over your eyes, girl."

A shiver ran through her, but she closed her eyes and buried her face in the angle of her elbow.

"That'll do." He didn't move. Didn't speak. Gave her nothing to listen to.

In the silent room with only the sounds of the crackling fire—and her pulse in her ears—she waited. With each second, the air grew thicker, her skin more sensitive. Her nipples had bunched so tightly that they throbbed with each beat of her heart. "Sam?"

"No talking, moaning, screaming. Use your safe word if you need it. Otherwise no noise. Got it?"

Afraid to say anything, she stayed silent, and his chuckle was low and definitely sadistic.

But despite—because of?—his rules, she felt liberated. During sex, she always worried she wasn't responsive enough, that she should moan or wiggle or talk more. But Sam had removed that worry. She wasn't to do *anything*.

His hands curved under her bottom, the palms hard, the thumbs stroking in the crease between her hip and pussy.

Her instinctive jump made the coasters wobble, and she stilled immediately. *Don't move.* When he squeezed her ass cheeks mercilessly, his strength was frightening—and shockingly erotic. He shifted his weight and pulled back, leaving her buttocks aching.

Don't move. Don't speak. Her thoughts fragmented until only anticipation remained. When his breath warmed her flesh, her stomach muscles tightened.

He licked up and over her pussy, and as his velvety, wet tongue curled around her clit, she barely smothered a whimper. She was so, so ready. He focused there, licking and teasing, until every slide of his tongue brought her closer. Heat streamed through her, hotter than the warmth from the fireplace.

SAM LIFTED HIS head to study Linda, pleased at how quickly she'd reached the state he wanted her in. Her gorgeous tits rose and fell, showing how close she was to panting. Almost there.

But he damned well wanted to try out his flogger on her pussy, which meant she needed to move. And she wasn't. Determined little woman.

He needed to shut her brain right down without really hurting her. That would be cheating. So he'd drive her a tad higher, make that orgasm shake her good—and knock the coasters off. Slowly, he stroked a finger up and down between her slick folds, then pressed his middle finger inside. She contracted around him in a way that showed she was completely on board with his plan. He pumped her, fast, slow, then added another finger, feeling her stretch around him. His dick tightened to fucking discomfort. He wanted to take her, but damned if he didn't need to torture her a bit.

Her hips started to rise, but she regained control.

Circle the outside of her cunt. Plunge in hard and hear her strained inhalation. Feel her thigh muscles grow tighter. See the shininess appear on her upper lip as she breaks into a sweat. Holding his fingers deep inside her, he growled, "Don't move, girl."

At the hard order, her cunt clenched around him, and he grinned. Goddamn, he loved playing with submissives. Propped on an elbow, he reached up and grabbed a nipple, pinching hard, rolling hard, hearing her almost silent whine. With his arm resting on her soft stomach, he licked over her clit again and felt her begin to quiver.

Would she be able to maintain when he got her off? He looked up. The coasters perched on her knees were shaking with her tiny movements. *Nope.*

Abandoning her breast, he thrust in and out of her pussy. Two fingers, then three, then one, then three. Her clit was so engorged it strained up toward his flicking tongue.

He backed off, lifted his head, and removed his fingers.

Yep, that was a definite whine, no matter how soft. Her jaw was clenched. She held herself rigid as her arousal faded.

He waited...waited...then licked hard over her clit, over and over, bringing her back up. Very, very slowly, he slid his fingers back into her cunt. Her panting had changed to gasps. Goddamn, this was fun.

Her face was flushed, and he regretted not being able to watch her eyes. But she needed to work through some of the lingering triggers left by the slavers. He'd take his time, not push her too fast, but eventually, she'd be clear of their crap.

He gave her clit a break as he curved his fingers to find her G-spot. Ah, not far inside the entrance, and roughed up with plumpness. She didn't react with his first rub or the second, so he increased the pressure, massaging firmly, and her cunt jerked tightly around him as if startled awake.

He kept stroking, added small licks at erratic intervals to her clit, and heard her breathing turn erratic as well.

Close. Very close. Time for a break. He stopped everything and pulled his fingers out. Her frustration built visibly as he counted her breaths. One...five...fifteen. On twenty, he rammed two fingers in, rubbing her G-spot hard and fast.

Her back arched, and she let out a squeak before smothering it. A coaster wobbled and slid off her knee, hitting the quilt with a soft thump. Her whimper held both despair...and anticipation.

Satisfaction sizzled through him. The little masochist wanted to know what his whip felt like, and he was definitely of a mind to show her. "Damn, missy, looks like you get that pussy flogged."

He set the coaster back on her knee. "Keep still and I'll give you only five. Lose another coaster, it'll be more." The husky sound of her fear did his sadist's heart good. He took the miniflogger from the crate and gave her pussy a light flick.

Both coasters fell off.

THE EXQUISITE AGONY burst over her like a wave of flames. *Oh my God.* Linda shook, unsure when the pain had turned to pleasure—unsure if it had. She realized her knees were clamped together, and she'd also uncovered her eyes. Gasping for air, she stared up at Sam.

He was grinning, an evil grin that let her know he wasn't about to stop. And his enjoyment was horribly erotic.

But if he hit her with that thing again, she'd die.

He studied her for a minute, then shook his head. "A bit too much for you just yet." He pulled something else out of the crate. "I'll use this instead. Since you got more than five coming."

The whimper that escaped her was humiliating. The crease in his cheek deepened.

He held a narrow rectangle of reinforced leather. She started to panic at how much it looked like a belt, but then realized it seemed to have the thickness and texture of a tripled piece of suede. Soft?

"Legs open, girl."

Dear sweet heaven. It took an effort to open herself back up and rest her knees on the thick pillows.

He bent and ran his fingers over her pussy, making her wiggle. "Not too bad. You're just pink."

Oh well, that's nice. Although she bit back the words, the sun lines at the corners of his eyes deepened.

He straightened, and then the suede slashed down, hitting her left labia. The blast of sensation made her gasp, then moan as it flared into bliss.

"Better." He watched her for a second, and she could feel sweat on her neck. Everything inside her tightened as he forced her to wait.

He let fly with five more swats, alternating to the right and left of her clit, the last landing directly on top.

The world flashed red as shocking, thick pleasure scalded her whole pussy. "Aaah!" Her clit seemed to expand as the pressure boiled higher and higher.

Shoving her legs open with his feet—when had she moved them?—he whipped the strap against her right inner thigh, then her left, hard enough that the burn shook her.

Before she could move, he went down on one knee. Using his fingers, he scissored her labia open, and with his hand, he administered three more stinging swats directly to her clit.

Everything inside her surged upward, the pain knotting into hard pleasure, shoving her so, so close. Tears streamed from her eyes, and she hurt, and it was wonderful, but she couldn't...couldn't get there.

He didn't move, studying her face, her clenched hands, her breathing. His satisfaction with her response was obvious.

"Please," she whispered, hating herself. Needing more. Hating that she couldn't keep the word back.

His brows drew together, and his warm, calloused hands massaged her thighs. Gently. "Linda, don't be ashamed to ask your Dom to let you come. It's what he wants." His deep, focused eyes met hers, held hers. His voice was rough with the truth he wanted her to absorb.

Then he bent his head and closed his mouth over her clit. His tongue, hot and flat, rubbed over the still-stinging flesh, and the feeling was indescribable as everything inside her tightened. Tightened again.

With a rumble of enjoyment, he closed his lips around her and sucked hard, hard, hard, even as he plunged two fingers inside her. One thrust, two.

Her breathing halted completely as the avalanche struck. Unstoppable, it ripped everything free, hit bottom, and exploded into brilliance. Ecstasy tore upward through her, and electricity sheeted across every brain cell she owned.

My sweet heavens. She hauled in a shaky breath. Even as her body jerked with tiny aftershocks, he rubbed his cock against her entrance...and pressed in. He was much thicker than his fingers, and her labia were so swollen that the sliding scrape of his entry sent her into a long, rolling orgasm again.

His laugh was deep, more gravelly than normal, and his eyes gleamed into hers. "I'm going to take you hard, girl. Are you ready?"

She nodded. Braced on one hand, he captured her wrists with the other and set them above her head. Again. Her shoulders twinged, not in a good way. *Getting decrepit, Linda.*

After studying her for a long moment, he pulled her arms down. "This time, keep your arms around me."

She couldn't ask for anything finer than being allowed to touch him. As her palms traced out the hills and valleys of his hard back muscles, the knowledge of his strength made her bones go soft.

He started slowly, pulling almost all the way out before slamming into her. The shock wave set off little convulsions again. As he went faster, his face grew tighter and the cords stood out on his neck.

His gaze met hers, his eyes hot. "More." Bracing himself on one arm, he put his elbow under her knee and lifted her leg up. The next thrust was far deeper.

As he hammered into her, the erotically satisfying feeling of being positioned for his use swept through her. *Take me as you want.*

He rested his forehead against hers, his body stiffened with release, and his groan was low and rumbling and beautiful.

She pulled him closer, cherishing the knowledge of pleasing him. She wanted to give him everything. Her eyes closed for a moment. God, God, she shouldn't—couldn't—fall for this man.

He released her leg and gathered her close, cuddling her to him in that disconcertingly tender way he had. When he rubbed his cheek against hers, his face softer than she'd ever seen it, she knew she was in trouble.

Chapter Fourteen

The next morning, Sam wakened to the sound of a woman singing. Ice circled his spine, and his jaws clenched so tightly his teeth ground together. *Nancy.* How had she gotten in?

He rolled out of bed, his feet hitting the floor with a thump. In the bathroom. He yanked open the door. "How the hell did you get—"

By the counter, the naked woman spun, turned white, and backed up until she hit the wall. One hand clutched a towel to her chest. Big brown eyes, red hair.

He'd just scared the crap out of Linda.

Wake up, Davies, you idiot. He sagged against the door frame. "Hell. Sorry."

As color returned to her face, she wrapped the dark blue bath towel around her. "What was that all about?" Soft voice. Firm. Expecting an answer. There was a downside to involvement with an intelligent, older woman.

"I woke up and heard singing." He stopped. There was no way to explain.

"You don't like the blues?"

"Thought you were someone else." He couldn't go further.

Her mouth opened in a silent *oh*. "Your ex-wife." After securing her towel more firmly, she moved closer and rested her hand on his chest. Brave woman—her breathing was still fast. He'd scared her badly. "She liked to sing?"

The memories of Nancy singing were...ugly, and his face tightened, but Linda's soft hand stayed warm against his skin. "Sometimes." Whenever she was high.

"Why would that bother you so much?" Her brows together, she waited, expecting more.

Why? The short bursts of memories clawed at his gut. How Nancy sang as she shattered Nicole's soccer trophies. Danced while throwing his grandfather's carvings into the fireplace. She hadn't sung for happiness, just destruction. He needed to explain, to erase Linda's unhappiness, but his jaw was clamped shut.

His silence hurt her, and her soft lips trembled before she stepped back. "Oh, Sam." She shook her head. "She must have given you a horrible time, and I'm sorry. But I can't stop singing. It's part of who I am."

It was. Music followed her everywhere. He liked that about her. "Don't stop."

"Can you tell me—"

He shook his head. *Not going to talk about Nancy. Never.*

The little mama came out. "You should talk to me." She crossed her arms over her gorgeous breasts. "We need to discuss this."

"Don't think so." As he forced his muscles to relax, he smiled slowly. Seems he had a bossy masochist trapped in his bathroom. Looked like a fine way to improve his mood. "I figure you owe me for starting my day off so badly."

"I owe *you?*"

He set her hand on his shoulder. Watching her closely, he bent and slid his fingers down her inner thigh, finding a small welt from the night before. He pressed lightly, enough to hurt. More than that—enough to bring back her memories of how it had happened.

Her pupils dilated, her fingers on his bare shoulder curved, pulling him closer, as if needing more contact with his skin.

That he could do. He gathered her in, shoving her towel down in the process so her breasts rubbed against his chest. Her nipples jutted out, two points of extra pressure. "I haven't had my shower yet," he murmured in her ear. If he turned the water to ice-cold and held her under it, would she scream? "You can help me."

"Aren't you just a generous guy?" Pink washed into her face as he pressed his erection against her soft lower pelvis. "I'm not—"

A car horn sounded.

Now? Sam grunted in exasperation.

She glanced over her shoulder at the slightly open window. "Who is that?"

"Construction crew. Building a new stable." His arms tightened. "Goddammit."

His annoyance lessened at the sound of her husky laugh. She patted his cheek. "You're just having a heck of a morning, aren't you?"

* * * *

Linda shifted her weight, smiling as the saddle creaked under her. The soft sounds of hooves on the dirt trail and the rattle of bridles spelled peace in the quiet afternoon. As the trees thinned, the late afternoon sun warmed her shoulders. It had been a lovely day.

After Sam had returned from opening his gate, he'd cooked her a breakfast of French toast and sausage. Unhealthy carbs and unhealthy fat. When she'd informed him that nothing in the entire meal was good for him, he'd only laughed. Unshaven, rumpled, heavy-eyed from sex and lack of sleep, the man was too sexy for words, even at the breakfast table.

And in the full light of day? On a dappled gelding, he led the way down the trail. Face it, the man was too sexy, period, and definitely outclassed a stodgy widow in her forties. He might be older than she was, but aside from his gray hair, he sure didn't show it.

Must be all the work he did on his place. The horseback tour had led from a huge garden to acres of citrus groves to pastureland for his horses and cattle. The lushly overgrown creekside trail made a sweet finish to the ride.

As the trail opened up, Sam nudged his horse into a trot, and her horse followed suit. *Ouch.* Either she'd have to get better at riding, or Sam better stop walloping her bottom and other places that met a saddle. Gritting her teeth, she pulled her horse to a walk.

After a minute, Sam glanced over his shoulder. Then his slow grin appeared. "Bit sore, missy?"

When she glared at him, he laughed…but waited for her to catch up and stayed at a walking pace. The noise of construction soon filled the air as they neared the house and barns.

In the corral, Sam dismounted and tied his horse to the fence.

"We could have gone longer," she protested as she swung down.

When he squeezed her tender bottom and she stiffened, he shook his head. "I like giving you pain, like making you hurt, but not this way. Don't want you crippled."

The man took her breath with his candidness. "Do you tell *everyone* you're a sadist?"

He kissed the top of her head. "Don't particularly care if people know, but I don't talk about it." He gave her a direct look. "Most people don't talk about their private business—like what they did in bed the night before. Why would sadists be any different?"

"Well. Guess that was a dumb question."

He ran his finger down her cheek. "Got yourself quite a pack of worries, don't you?"

As they walked out of the corral, Connagher trotted over. He'd been with them for most of the ride, then disappeared at the creek.

Sam ruffled the hair on the dog's neck. "Anything to report?"

Conn wagged his tail as if in answer.

Linda tried to stifle her laugh and failed, getting her a raised eyebrow. "You really do sound like a sergeant sometimes."

He snorted. "Been decades, girl."

Maybe. But habits picked up as a teenager—or under stress—tended to endure. "Right. So, Sarge, did your four-footed soldier find anything interesting?"

"I like it when masochists get impertinent, you know."

How could he create that curling of heat with just a few words and a look?

"Davies." A skinny construction guy came around the corner of the stable. "Got a minute? The boss wants to check with you about the wiring."

Sam hesitated, and Linda patted his arm. "I should be getting back anyway."

"You're spending the night."

Her heart wanted to flutter, and she told it no. "Ah. Fine. Then I'll just look around for a bit, okay?"

He ran his hand down her arm and nodded. "Won't be long."

* * * *

Once their talk was concluded, Sam walked with Nolan King to where the contractor had parked. The last of the crew had just driven through the gates, returning the farm to quiet.

"That's a pretty woman you got." Nolan opened his truck door and paused. "She give up on being *normal*?"

"Getting there."

King grinned, then swung into his truck.

After locking the front gate, Sam unsaddled the horses and turned them loose. Immediate tasks finished, he looked around. No redhead in sight. Had she gone up to the house? He whistled for Conn.

After a minute, the dog tore across the south pasture, ducked under the fence, and stopped in front of Sam.

"Good boy." Sam tossed him a dog treat from his pocket. "Find Linda. *Linda.*" Conn usually needed longer to associate a name with a scent, but he'd strongly taken to the redhead. "Find Linda."

A short bark indicated agreement. The dog did a quick circle of the corral, caught the trail, and headed off, bouncing in happiness at performing his favorite task.

Sam followed. Looked as if Linda had visited the chickens, checked the pasture, circled the construction, and headed down to the small pond. Partway there, Conn lifted his nose, caught her scent in the air, and gave his triumphant bay of *I found her.*

She was sitting on the bank of the pond, watching the ducks and an egret in the shallows. Her hair glinted red in the sun, and her cheeks were sunburned from their ride; he'd need to take care of that. When Conn charged up to her and knocked her backward with his enthusiastic greeting, she simply laughed.

The woman laughed in the same way she climaxed—nothing held back, open and delighted. A man could fall for that laugh. *Hell.*

She tilted her head back, and the dimple in her cheek appeared. "You found me."

"Conn did." Sam dropped down beside her, close enough to tell he liked the scent of his soap on her.

"When you said he kept track of people, I didn't realize you meant he'd hunt for them."

"Nicole taught him to play hide-and-seek. I took it from there. Working dogs need challenges, or they get into trouble."

Linda scratched Conn's neck in a way that would earn his lifelong devotion. "He's pretty proud of himself."

"Yep." Sam ran his knuckles over her cheek, pink from the sun. "Been meaning to ask—you on the pill?"

"An implant." Her mouth twisted. "A gift of the slavers, but I decided to leave it in place."

Damn but he disliked raising ugly memories, but these were questions that needed to be asked. Should have done it before. "As a member of the Shadowlands, I get tested regularly." And he knew that over the past few months, the ex-slaves had been checked often.

Her eyes narrowed. Then she caught where he was heading. Her lips tilted up. "You want to skip the condoms?"

"Hell, yes."

Her laugh let him relax. Then she tilted her head. "As long as you're not...with...anyone else, I'm okay with that."

"Same goes, missy." He traced her lips before giving her a level look. "I don't share."

He received the same look back. Damn, he liked this woman. "We're on the same page, then."

"Good enough. So there's time before I need to start evening chores. You have anything you'd like to see or do?" He tugged on a lock of her hair. "I know what I'd prefer"—he smiled as her face flushed—"but you might need to walk tomorrow." And, from the way she'd been shifting in the saddle, he knew how sore she was going to be.

"Oh." The disappointment in her voice and her involuntary wiggle told him she'd be willing anyway.

He pulled her hair, dragging her until she was on her back in the soft grass. Enthusiasm should be rewarded.

Chapter Fifteen

The cold morning breeze off the Gulf whipped around Sam as he followed Linda into her beachfront store. After yesterday, she was walking a bit stiffly, but although he'd seen her wince off and on, she'd smiled each time. Probably enjoying the memory of how the soreness had occurred.

His first impression of her store was cheerful clutter, but on closer examination he could see she'd arranged the merchandise to lure a customer in. On one side, two middle-aged women browsed the landscape paintings. A young couple was checking out the stoneware.

Sam glanced around. Something seemed missing. *Ah.* "No shot glasses with palm trees or 'Florida' on the side?"

"'Fraid not. There are plenty of other stores selling the usual souvenirs." She grinned. "My cousin collected stuff when she traveled, tiny spoons and shot glasses, and a few years later, she got tired of dusting and gave everything to Goodwill. Tourists should have vacation mementos that are useful as well as fun."

He tucked his arm around her. "Fine job." The place even smelled good, reminding him of pumpkin pie. They passed a shelf of candles, then a chest-high wrought-iron candelabrum. He stopped. Be nice to get something for Z and Jessica's wedding.

The people by the stoneware were looking around for assistance. Sam gave Linda a quick, hard kiss. "Go help your customers. I'm going to buy a candelabra. See you tonight."

"I..." She glanced at the couple. "Okay. But next time is my place."

"Works for me." As she went to answer questions, Sam hauled his present-to-be to the front. Heavy bastard. The nicely dressed clerk gave him a cheerful greeting. Appeared Linda selected her employees as carefully as she did her merchandise. As the clerk rang up the sale and arranged to package and send the gift, Sam listened to the chatter in the store.

Linda was giving the young couple a briefing on the various potters' backgrounds.

On the left, the older women were gossiping.

Hearing Linda's name, he straightened.

The plump one was whispering, "...she...a slave. I heard she..."

"Then she asked for it, didn't she?" The brassy-haired one drew herself up, looking as self-righteous as a nun.

Sam's jaw clenched. If Linda overheard crap like that, no wonder she got frazzled. And her children had shoveled more shit onto the pile.

"...got what she deserved."

He felt a muscle twitch in his cheek. Ripping a person down in her own place? Judging without the facts? And worst of all, for a woman...

He accepted his receipt from the clerk, nodded at her, and then followed the two old biddies out of the store. Their mean-spirited whispers sounded like snakes slithering through the grass.

"Ladies."

They turned, faces pleasant.

"Could be wrong about that. In my book, a lady doesn't bad-mouth someone. Especially a woman who already suffered enough."

They looked shocked. The brassy one drew herself up again. "How dare—"

"You really figure *any* woman asks to be abused?"

The plump one's face reddened.

"Yeah. What I thought." He barely bit back an offer to show them what a whipping felt like. But his face— Dom and sadist—must have spoken for him, since they tripped over each other backing away.

As he stalked to his truck, they scurried off in the other direction. Hell. He probably hadn't done Linda any favors, but *goddamn.*

He shook his head and started his truck. Then turned it off. Linda's children had bleated out the same crap, and the brats still hadn't called to apologize. When she'd checked her phone this morning, he could see their betrayal was eating at her.

Long as he was on a roll, he might as well enjoy himself.

* * * *

Linda leaned back in the booth of the small sandwich shop and smiled at Andrea, Beth, and Jessica. Their lunch was almost over, and she'd finally learned what had brought the three women to Foggy Shores. They were determined to get Linda to attend Jessica's bachelorette party. "I'm not really part of your group," Linda said, fighting a losing battle.

Jessica wasn't taking no for an answer. Then again, Master Z wouldn't fall for a pushover.

Andrea wasn't any weakling either. The bartender's submissive had a slight Hispanic accent, was a couple of inches taller than Linda, and was darned determined.

Although soft-spoken and quiet, Beth was just as stubborn. Lean and fit with dark auburn hair and turquoise eyes, she ran a landscaping business and was probably used to getting her own way. Except maybe with her Dom, who apparently was Sam's construction contractor.

"Being with Sam makes you part of the group. All the trainees and the Masters' submissives are coming." Andrea shoved her curly, butterscotch-colored hair behind her ears. "Not any Masters, of course, and not the Mistresses either."

"Mistresses are female," Linda noted. "Why not them?"

"The Shadowlands Masters and Mistresses stick together. They'd report back." Andrea grinned. "I sure don't want Cullen finding out what I do at a bachelorette party, right?"

Remembering the antics at parties she'd attended, Linda could only nod. "Probably not."

"Mistress Anne's Joey was tempted, but he didn't want to be the only guy." Beth's lips curved. "Besides, any party with Gabi and Sally will be insane, and he didn't want to get in trouble with Anne."

Linda ran through the people she'd met at the Shadowlands. "I don't think I know her."

"Oh, you'd remember. She's as scary a sadist as Sam." Jessica gave a fake shiver and then grinned at Beth's chiding look. "Oh, please. The man's terrifying. I'm sure Linda's noticed."

Oh, had she. She still carried some bruises. Linda widened her eyes in confusion. "But Sam is just a sweetie. How could you say that?" And actually, the past couple of days had been wonderful. She'd forgotten what it felt like to have someone *there*. Just to watch television or talk with while having a glass of wine. Someone to cuddle against in bed.

Jessica shook her head in admiration. "You're so full of it." Turning sideways, she stole a french fry from Andrea.

"Why didn't you just order some?" Andrea asked.

"Didn't want to gain weight before my wedding. And everybody knows stolen food has no calories."

"Good point." Laughing, Andrea pushed her plate into the center of the table to share. "So, Linda, does Master Sam scare you?"

"Ah. Sometimes." Linda eyed the plate. *No calories?* After taking a fry, she tried to explain further. "It's a good scary when we're playing. I know he'll push, and that's a bit frightening, but"—she pressed her hand over the quiver low in her belly—"exciting too."

The smiles of understanding she got made her relax. They really did get it.

"Good word, 'exciting,'" Jessica agreed.

"But when he's mad?" Linda continued. "He gets this cold...dangerous...look. Sure, I know he'd never hurt me—not in anger—but my body isn't hearing logic."

"Oh, God, that's how I feel when Nolan's angry," Beth said. "And I want to hide under the bed, only he sees that and really gets mad, because he hates it when he scares me, even though my reaction's just instinct."

"Exactly." Linda tilted her head. "Were you one of the kidnapped women?"

"No. I had an abusive husband," Beth said.

Jessica glanced at Linda. "He was a real psycho sadist. Makes you appreciate how careful and controlled ours are."

"Ours?"

"The Doms in the Shadowlands." Jessica leaned back with a sigh. "I'm so full I'll probably fall asleep at my computer."

"Yeah, exciting life, playing with numbers." Andrea grinned. "I've got a couple more places to clean this afternoon, so I'd better get moving."

"I have fruit trees to plant." Beth looked at Linda. "This weekend...it'll be really, really fun."

Fun with a bunch of women who were submissive like her yet assertive as all get-out. "I'd love to join you."

* * * *

Near suppertime, Sam walked into a small diner near the University of South Florida and saw Linda's children had shown up. Probably not because they wanted to cooperate with his instructions, but because they needed someone to fight with.

If they took him on, he'd have to figure they hadn't inherited their mother's brains.

A half-full iced tea sat in front of the girl, a can of Pepsi in front of the boy. Looked as if they'd been there awhile.

When he slid into the booth across from them, the girl startled. The boy managed to suppress his reaction...somewhat.

Sam leaned back and studied them. They had their mother's rich brown eyes. Brenna had Linda's figure. Charles had her nose and determined chin. His anger increased. Her own blood was destroying her. Refusing to speak with her. Calling her names.

As his silence continued, Brenna shifted uneasily in her seat.

Charles's mouth was tight; his fingers around the can were white-knuckled. "You wanted to speak to us, right?"

"I did. Your mother talks about you, you know. She's proud of you."

Charles answered. "Yeah, well we're not proud of her, the—"

"If I bust your jaw, she'll be pissed off at me," Sam said mildly. "I'm a sadist. I'd enjoy seeing you suck your meals through a straw." Actually, it would bother the hell out of him.

The boy turned white. When the girl started to slide out, Sam set his boot on the seat beside her, blocking her escape. "Let's be polite here. I'll have my say. You do the same. We'll be done." He nailed her with a look that made most people cower.

She cringed, then raised her chin. "Go on, then." Like her mama, the girl had guts.

"Smart girl. First, let me see if I got my facts right. Your dad died when you were little. Your mom ran the store to make money, raised you both, and used his life insurance money to pay for your tuitions. She covers your rent every month." He set his gaze on the boy. "She works hard for you. What do you do for her, besides calling her names?"

Charles scowled harder as if to cover up his guilt. "We help her with stuff at the house. Yard work."

"We watched the house while she was gone," Brenna offered. Her frown said she saw the imbalance.

A waitress walked up. "What can I get you folks?"

"Come back in ten minutes," Sam growled.

With a gulp, she retreated.

Yeah, he might still be a tad angry. So were the children. In fact, Brenna's expression was a duplicate of Nicole's when she was pissed off at him. His daughter wasn't a brat, and these two didn't seem like brats either. But if they weren't and considering what Linda went through, why the hell were they acting like this?

From ignorance? He rubbed his jaw. How much did they know of what she'd been through? Many of the trials had been conducted in closed courtroom sessions. The violently graphic details—especially for the victims who'd lived—had been withheld from the press. "What did your mother tell you about what happened to her?"

"We read the papers. We know." Charles turned a dark red. "We didn't talk about it."

Hell. She'd kill him for clueing her kids in. "You understand she was raped."

Brenna's chin lifted. "But she likes—"

He slapped the table, shutting her up. "There's a *goddamn* difference between kinky games with someone you like and..." *Don't yell at them, Davies.* "If I strip you, dump you in the slums, and let every lowlife there take a turn, that's *rape*...and that's what your mother endured."

Both kids turned white.

"Your mama has scars on her back. Not from fun, but from a bastard ripping the skin open with a whip."

Brenna's breath hitched; Charles was silent.

"She befriended a girl your age, Brenna." He gave them an even look. "You know your mom. She's a mother to everybody, right?"

The kids nodded.

"The girl was sold and then beaten to death." His belly still turned over at the thought. "Your mom cries for her. She testified against the man and came out of the courtroom as shocky as if she'd had her guts ripped out." *Dammit, Linda, you should have shared some of this.*

"We didn't know," Charles whispered.

Sam snorted. "Your mother protected you all her life. She wanted to be strong for you."

"She went to Aunt Wendy's. And she looked horrible when she left." Brenna glanced at Charles. "But then we thought it was, like, a vacation. Only it wasn't, was it? She said it wasn't." Her hand covered her mouth. "I-I didn't believe her."

When he'd pushed, Linda had grudgingly shared some with him. "She had panic attacks. Was throwing up a few times a day. Screaming her way out of nightmares. Going through counseling. Hysterical one day, depressed and suicidal the next. Hell of a vacation."

"Oh, Mommy..." When Brenna burst into tears, Sam forgave her. But the little bastard hadn't said a word, was staring out the window.

Sam's hand fisted, and then he saw tears rolling down the kid's cheek. He'd clenched his jaw...and his chin was quivering. Macho boy had a tender heart, after all.

Job almost done. Wrap it up. "So. Your mama might like sex with a side dish of kink, but doesn't mean she asked for any of that." He rose. Add a threat if they gave her any more trouble? No, they looked shell-shocked. "Call her. She's had enough grief. Doesn't need it from the ones who are *supposed* to love her."

When they both flinched, he slapped the table in satisfaction and walked away.

As he strode down the street, he pondered his next problem. How was he going to keep Linda from killing him when she learned he'd given her children a come-to-Jesus talk?

Chapter Sixteen

Linda parked her car in the small parking area at the side of Sam's house and got out, disappointed his truck wasn't there.

After greeting her with a quick lick of her fingers, Connagher returned to his front porch perch. Sam had said the dog "supervised" from there.

The construction crew was still working on the stable. Leaving her purse in the car, Linda wandered over to watch. They were amazing—like a choreographed musical with the dancers wearing jeans and T-shirts. Piece by piece, she could see the building coming together.

"You must be Linda." A rough voice came from behind her.

She spun. A huge, dark-faced, scarred man loomed far too close, and she stumbled back. *Run!* Even as she recognized him as one of the construction crew, the icy fear refused to abate, forcing her to retreat another step. She couldn't think—

"I'm Nolan. Saw you at the club." He stood with Sam's quiet patience. His face even held the same "panic if you need to, I'll wait" expression.

The club? Of course. The subs at the Shadowlands had pointed him out. Her heart slowed to a mild gallop as she realized this was the Dom she'd said would step over a person's body without looking back. Up close, he was even more intimidating. "I'm sorry. You startled me and I—"*Was afraid you were a slaver.* Um, not a polite thing to say.

"I'm not one of the bad guys, although my wife might disagree at times." His grin came and went so fast she wasn't sure she'd seen it. "Beth said she was going to have lunch with you today."

Just shoot me now. Beth had even said her husband was the contractor here. Linda smiled and held out her hand. "It's nice to meet you."

He shook her hand gently. Like Sam, he seemed very aware of his strength.

And like Sam, he didn't feel obligated to hold up his side of a conversation. At a loss, she said, "So you belong to Beth?"

The corner of his mouth turned up. "I see it as the other way around."

Linda felt herself turn red. The guy was a Dom. *Duh, Linda.*

To her relief, Sam pulled his truck in beside her car and got out.

Her heart lifted higher as each of his long strides brought him closer.

"I didn't expect you this soon," he said. She had a moment of worry that he wasn't happy to see her before he yanked her onto her toes for a kiss. Hard hands, demanding lips.

Her body slid into meltdown.

After tucking her against his side, he gave his dog a quick pat and greeted Nolan. "How's it going?"

Nolan's gaze touched her. He looked as if he was almost smiling before he answered Sam, "Ahead of schedule." He checked his watch and turned to yell at his crew, "Day's over. Finish up."

The cheers made the horses in the pasture trot to the far end.

Nolan turned back to tell Sam. "Left your paint in the old barn." After nodding to Linda, he rejoined his gang.

She shook her head. A woman who'd been abused married to that scary-looking man. Beth was braver than she looked.

Sam curved his hand over her hip. "I'd like a beer, a meal, and sex...not in that order."

When his grip increased to the point of pain, she gasped, feeling everything shiver and loosen inside. "Well, I—"

His eyes crinkled. "Yeah, we could go straight to sex."

Her heart acquired the same *rat-tat* rhythm as the nail gun. "I suppose."

"Suppose?" He yanked her head back, holding her easily so she stared up into his light eyes. "Try again, missy. You might start begging now."

Beg? Never. Ever. A nasty buzz like a million bees stung the insides of her head. *"Slut, you want food? Beg for it."* As coldness shot through her, she struggled against his grip.

Sam released her hair instantly. His other hand lay lightly on her shoulder. Not gripping. Palm open. Warm. "Linda. Settle." His level, patient eyes caught hers.

As the buzzing in her head decreased and died away, she shuddered.

"Well." He put one finger under her chin and tilted her head up. "Bad reaction. What set you off?"

The lack of emotion in his voice helped dispel the last of her fear and fury and even smoothed away some of her embarrassment at overreacting. "I...don't like the word. *Beg.*"

His eyebrows, a shade darker than his steel-gray hair, lifted in inquiry. "Why?"

"The Overseer"—the slaver Kim called a scum sucker—"made us beg for everything. To eat. To use the bathroom. To stand up. Sit down. For light."

Sam growled. "And if you didn't beg, he'd hurt you. If you did, it would never be enough."

He knew. Understood. She closed her eyes and nodded.

He gathered her into his arms, rocked her back and forth. "Rough time, girl."

She melted into him. He didn't have a smooth tongue, but the comfort he offered was unsurpassed anywhere. His left palm kept her firmly against him; his other hand massaged the muscles on each side of her spine, loosening the knots.

"That's not a good trigger word to have, though." He pulled back and cupped her cheek. "I'll work on getting you past that."

"I..." *Lovely.* "Do all Doms try to fix things?"

The lines fanning out from the corners of his eyes deepened. "Yep."

With a huff of exasperation, she walked with him to the house. In pickups and cars, the construction workers were streaming down the drive. The one at the end gave a *honk-honk*, and then quiet settled over the farm.

Conn stopped them for a minute to gather pets, then loped toward the pasture.

Linda glanced at Sam. "What's he up to?"

"He was on guard while the construction crew was here. Now he'll make sure no varmints invaded since his morning patrol."

Linda laughed when the dog turned to look at them, as if to say the house was in their care now.

"So what did you do today?" Linda asked as Sam led the way into the kitchen. She nodded when he pulled out a bottle of wine.

He poured her a glass. "Financial chores—bank, accountant. Had a chat with a couple of people, looked at some new equipment, ordered more grain." He grabbed a beer for himself and drew her out to the front porch to join him on the swing.

"Busy man." He had so many balls in the air, it was a wonder he could keep track. And she'd thought running a store was tricky...and thinking of that made her remember basketry. "Oops. I left a basket I wanted to finish out in the car. And my purse."

He walked to her car with her and carried in the oversize tote of basketry supplies.

After setting her purse near the door, she pulled her cell out. The display showed texts and voice mails from Brenna and Charles. She sucked in a startled breath. So many messages. Had something happened? Why'd she been so stupid as to leave her phone in the car?

"Got a problem?"

She glanced at Sam. "My children called. Lots of calls." Her hand shook as she hit Brenna's speed-dial number.

"Mom. Mommy. I'm sorry. God, I'm so sorry." Her daughter was crying, almost incoherent. "We didn't mean it. We shouldn't—"

"Mom, I'm sorry." Charles had apparently grabbed Brenna's phone, and he didn't sound any better.

"What?" What had they done? Burned her house down? "Charles, whatever you did, I forgive you, but what did you do?"

"Jesus, the way we talked to you. What we said. We didn't realize." Her big, strong son sounded as if he was in tears.

She looked at Sam, terror rising inside her. "They're almost hysterical. What—"

Sam plucked the phone from her limp fingers and said into it, "A man makes his apologies in person. Got a piece of paper?" He paused, then gave his address. "A half hour? Good." He tossed the phone into her open purse before giving her a nod. "They'll come here. I need a shower."

Mouth open, she stared after him. Her children had tried to apologize for the way they'd talked to her. Had been crying. And Sam hadn't been surprised; his dark gray eyebrows hadn't even lifted. As she sank into a chair, she heard the shower come on. Sam had given orders to Charles, and her obstinate son had taken them.

After a moment of weighing the facts, suspicion wove into knowledge. Sam had *expected* them to call. Could they have called him earlier? No, they didn't know his last name.

But Master Sam Davies certainly wouldn't have had any trouble finding her children. What had he done?

SAM LET THE hot water massage the tightness out of his shoulders and counted minutes in his head.

He'd made it to three minutes when the shower door was flung open.

Mama Bear had left the cave. He tried to avert his face before she noticed his amusement, but didn't succeed.

Hands on hips, Linda glared at him. "What did you do to my children?" Even as furious as she was, her voice was still controlled. No shrieking, no hysterics. She was one fine woman. Then she slapped his shoulder. "You tell me. Now!"

He gave her a quick scan. She'd dressed for the farm in a V-neck T-shirt and jeans and left her shoes in the entry as he liked. Good enough. "As the sadist in this relationship, I do the slapping." He grabbed the front of her shirt and yanked her into the shower.

She was soaked in seconds. Nice scream. Set all the hair on his body tingling.

"You aren't allowed to hit me." He ripped her T-shirt at the neck and drew it downward, pinning her arms against her sides.

"You-you-you bastard!"

"If you figure to sit and stew until they show, think again." As she struggled, he unzipped her jeans and shoved them and her underwear down to hobble her ankles.

"Dammit, let me go."

"Nope." He dug his fingers into the last remaining welts on her ass, pulling her against him. With an unbreakable grip on her nape, he held her for his kiss, taking and taking until she went limp against him. Until she kissed him back.

Goddamn, the woman could kiss. As he hardened, he rubbed his dick against her and felt her resistance melt. *My woman.* Reluctantly, he released her lips and lifted his head. "Cooperate and we finish fast. Otherwise your children will have to wait on the porch while you're busy in here."

Her eyes widened. "You wouldn't."

"Try me." Her pants pinned her legs together, and he had to work to push his hand between her thighs. But there he found her wet and ready. She trembled when he stroked over her pussy. She heated up fast. For him. The knowledge was a bone-deep satisfaction.

He circled her clit, pushed inside her entrance, then circled again. *Fast, Davies. Remember?* He wanted to linger and play until she screamed his name in frustration, but with a resigned sigh, he pulled her T-shirt up and off, then her bra. Hand between her shoulder blades, he bent her over, then positioned her hands on the corner shower seat. "Keep them there."

"Sam. My children will—"

When he slapped her ass in reprimand—and to please himself—the sound echoed beautifully in the big tile shower. How many years had it been since he'd fucked a woman in a bathroom?

As the water beat on her ass, her bent-over position showed a hint of her glistening pussy, more of her anus. *Nice.* Even nicer, she stayed in place, and her face showed only arousal.

He rubbed the sting from her ass, pulled her labia open, and pushed his cock in an inch. Not roughly—she was still too emotionally fragile for that—but firmly. Had to be careful, but her wetness and low moan of pleasure said he was on the right path.

She was hotter than the shower, wetter, and tight enough to make him struggle for control. He pulled out halfway. When he thrust in all the way, the zing went straight to his balls.

Her ass tilted up slightly; she wanted more. Goddamn, she was cute.

He bent over her back. As his dick pressed deeper, she squirmed, taking him to the hilt. Burying his face in her lavender-citrus-scented hair, he reached around and cupped her breasts. Soft as anything he'd found in his life. He kneaded them and pinched her nipples hard enough to have her whimpering and trying to pull away. But his chest pressed down on her, his dick impaled her; she wasn't going anywhere. Fucking nice. Her hot, slick cunt tightened each time he tugged on her breasts.

As the pain fed her arousal, her hips started to wiggle. He yanked her hair, pulling her head up as he drove into her. "Give me more."

Her moan was like food for a starving man.

She certainly wasn't thinking about anything but him. And he was going to push her hard enough that when her children arrived, she'd be glowing. So any guilt they tried to lay on her would slide off.

He coated his fingers with cream rinse and with the next thrust of his cock, he breached her asshole with a finger.

She gave a strangled gasp and attempted to straighten.

He leaned forward and gripped her shoulder, holding her down. "Stay put, missy." But he paused to check her response. Combining rough sex and anal sex might trigger some bad memories. "We at green?"

As a fine trembling shook her body, her head bowed. Her whisper was barely loud enough to be heard over the water. "Green."

He smiled. Not only did taking it in the ass wake up every nerve down there, but it was also the pinnacle of surrender. Linda was giving him her submission.

So beautiful and loving and responsive—she warmed his heart. He ran his hand over her back. "Good girl. Now stay there." Spreading his legs for balance, he thrust his cock in deep, pulled back, and slid his finger into her ass. Alternating each until he could almost feel the humming in her body. He added another finger in her asshole, heard her breathing catch. "Someday, you'll take my cock there."

When a tremor shook her body, he grinned.

But time to head for the finish line. "Don't move." As she braced her arms on the corner seat, he reached around her with his free hand and fingered her clit, then hammered into her pussy and thrust his fingers into her ass. Deliberately overloading her senses, he drove her hard, not easing up at all.

He could feel her legs shaking. Then her cunt tightened around his cock, her ass around his fingers. Her clit was fully unhooded, begging for more. Almost there.

Her neck arched, her body froze, and she came with a high wail that echoed off the tiles and made him grin.

As her pussy squeezed around his cock, he released his control and let her cunt suck him dry. With a low groan, he wrapped an arm around her waist, holding her up.

Although he could have stayed right there, buried deep, he felt her knees threatening to buckle. With a sigh of regret, he pulled out. After putting her on the seat, he washed up.

He grasped her jeans, still around her ankles. "Lift your legs."

She lifted one pretty leg, then the other. As he pulled her to her feet, she muttered, "You're such a jerk."

Hard to get offended when her voice was still husky from panting and coming. Still...no chance at punishing a little submissive should be overlooked. "For that, I'm going to spank you later," he whispered in her ear.

She stiffened, making him grin. And the redhead would get off on being spanked—he'd see to it. He pulled her closer, feeling her softness all along his front.

Some people played in the bath with rubber ducks. Damn fools. Nothing was better than a flushed, trembling woman, scented with satisfaction.

After pushing her under the spray, he scrubbed her, making her dance as he played with her pussy and cleaned her tender little asshole.

Might be fun to see how sore she was there later tonight.

After he pulled on clean jeans and a work shirt, he helped her dry off, then gave her a set of sweats that would fit almost anyone. Ugly but adequate. Before she could complain, he warned, "Better hurry. Your half hour is almost up."

As she glared, he smothered a laugh and prudently left.

Did she realize he enjoyed pissing her off, just to see that cute expression on her face?

After checking the parking area, he knew the kids hadn't arrived yet. Soon though. He considered the next hour or so and shook his head ruefully. Be a rough evening. Lots of waterworks.

Might be smart to plan a distraction. He rubbed his chin. Maybe Nicole would like to join them.

* * * *

Linda rose from the porch swing as her children ran up to the house. They were all right, no bandages, no limping, no scars. But they looked...awkward. Unsure.

Old memories flowed through her. *Charles squealing with laughter when he'd taken his first step and landed on his diapered bottom. Brenna's perpetually scabbed knees. Their bickering when Charles climbed a tree and Brenna couldn't. Their angelic faces when asleep.* Her eyes blurred with tears. God, she loved them.

"Mommy." Brenna flung herself into Linda's arms.

Charles wrapped his arms around both of them. His cheek against her temple was wet, and Brenna was sobbing. What in the world had Sam said to them?

But now, now, she reveled in having her children back, in holding her girl, in trying to hug Charles and, as always, being shocked that he was taller than she was. Her babies had grown up, and she should treat them like adults. Talk over the problem. "Let's sit down, guys," she said to Brenna, then squeezed Charles's hand.

As she took a seat on the swing, she noticed the end table held an iced tea, a root beer, and a Pepsi. *Sam.* But how did he know the children's preferences? She glanced around and saw him strolling toward the barn with

Connagher trailing along. Were sadists supposed to be so tactful?

Brenna joined her on the swing, and Charles pulled a chair so close their knees touched.

"Now, tell me what's going on." Linda strove for an even voice, knowing that only Sam's nonchalance—and shower diversion—had prevented her from fretting herself sick.

Brenna's eyelids were red and swollen. "Your friend, he said..." She choked, and tears ran down her face.

Linda turned to Charles.

His hands were in fists on his knees. "He told us what you went through. Mom, we didn't know. We would never... We didn't know!"

Sam, that rat bastard. She sighed. Sam wouldn't have exaggerated or lied. He would have given them only the truth. "I see."

"You should have told us." Brenna had a death grip on Linda's hand and now gave it a shake. "Why didn't you tell us how horrible it was?"

"I..." Linda blinked back her own tears. Having her babies so upset made her chest hurt. "I didn't want... It was hard enough on you, just hearing I'd been kidnapped. You didn't need more."

"You tried to spare us, and so we dumped all over you." Charles gave a half laugh and opened her root beer. His hand trembled as he handed her the can, then gave Brenna her iced tea. "Your friend is pretty protective."

"I'm sorry. Sam shouldn't have—"

"He should." Charles's lips firmed. "Thank God, he did."

Brenna leaned against Linda. "We needed to know, Mommy."

Brenna hadn't called her Mommy in years. Linda felt a tear escape. Somehow, she had a feeling she'd never have the heart to yell at Sam for interfering.

"Can you forgive us?" Charles had never lacked the courage to admit his mistakes. "Forgive me?"

Brenna snorted, snuggling closer. "She already did, dummy."

"I did." Linda slid a few inches over on the swing, making room for her boy on her other side. Three was crowded...but wonderful.

* * * *

Sam did his evening chores early since he'd have company for supper. Be odd to have a full table. When his father had been alive, neighbors, friends, and relatives had often stayed for a meal. His stepfather had changed all that.

After a glance at Linda and the kids on the front porch, he and Conn swung around and used the back door.

Potatoes and chicken went in the oven to bake. Hopefully the kids weren't vegetarian, but he put together a big green salad just in case.

Through the open front door came only murmuring. No wailing. No shouting. Good sign.

Even as Conn gave a happy bark and charged out the screen door, Sam heard tires on the drive. Nicole must have arrived. After grabbing a beer, he stepped out onto the porch. All three on the swing showed signs of a fair amount of tears, and goddamn, he hated seeing

Linda upset. If she cried from a flogging or spanking, that was acceptable—even enjoyable—but this was a stab in the gut.

Yet the three were pressed together as close as they could get. All better, as Nicole would say. Now they needed time to get back to normal. He gave the kids a firm stare. "You'll stay for supper. My daughter will join us."

Linda gave him a startled look, then dimpled as her children nodded agreement.

Good enough. He leaned against the side porch railing and watched Nicole jump out of her Volkswagen Beetle. Back when he was young, most Bugs were splashed with paint in varying designs. Guess he should be grateful hers was merely bright yellow. She wore her usual jeans and layered tank tops, and—he sighed—she'd dyed her short hair black. *Women.* No man could understand them.

She trotted up and gave him a fierce hug. "Good timing, Dad. I didn't have a thing in the fridge, and I'm starving. What's for supper?"

He hugged her back, his pride in her as uncontrolled as a wildfire. Tough. Smart. Compassionate. How'd he gotten so lucky? Arm around her, he turned toward the others. "Linda, this is my daughter, Nicole. Those are Linda's kids, Charles and Brenna." He waited until they finished with the polite greetings. "Nicole, give Charles and Brenna a tour while Linda and I finish cooking. Figure forty-five minutes."

"Sounds good." She went up on her tiptoes and whispered, "Bad Daddy. What did you *do* to them?"

He choked down a laugh as Nicole waved the other two toward the yard, saying, "What do you want to see first?"

As the three headed down the steps, Charles asked her, "Aren't you in my sociology class? Mondays at ten?"

"I *knew* I'd seen you before. What's your major?"

Sam shook his head. Amazing how well kids could rebound. After setting his beer on the end table, he joined Linda on the swing. When he put his arm around her and pulled her closer, she sighed and snuggled in. A worry drained away; she wasn't furious with him. "All made up?"

"We are." She gave him a glare, although her puffy eyes and tear streaks removed the power. "What did you tell them, Sam?"

"Just the truth." He tucked a lock of hair behind her ear and pulled her closer for a slow kiss. "I can understand why you didn't share with them, but not knowing caused a rift between you."

"Yes." She yanked his hair lightly. "I should wallop you for making them cry, but thank you." Her breath hitched. "God, Sam, thank you. I have my babies back."

He understood her relief. He and Nicole had gone through a few ugly battles. Felt like a hole in the heart when she was mad at him.

They rocked for a while as the children stopped at the fountain in the front yard circle to admire the koi, then headed for the pasture behind the stable. The horses, ever greedy, trotted to the fence for handouts. Above the orchards, puffy clouds broke up the blue of the sky. The cooling air held the scent of the ocean mixed with the pastures. Next to him, Linda smelled of his soap, and he liked it, possessive bastard that he was.

"Come and set the table for me," he said eventually and hauled her to her feet.

"Five of us," Linda said. As he pulled out the chicken and potatoes, she added a leaf to the table and found place settings.

The thumping of feet and laughter came through the screen door as the kids stopped on the porch to finish their drinks. Nicole's clear voice drifted in. "Dad, kinky? Oh, somebody said something once, but *ew*... Thinking of my father having sex makes me want to bleach my brain, right?"

Linda snorted and flashed him a grin.

"Goes both ways. Don't like thinking of Nicole with some asshole," Sam muttered. "When she started dating, I hung a bullwhip by the door. Just in case..."

And why the hell should that make Linda bust out laughing?

* * * *

After a long, cheerful supper, Linda's children gave her warm hugs and followed Nicole out to the cars. Back to their lives.

As Linda strummed Sam's guitar, her eyes welled with tears...again. The possibility of losing her babies had shaken her more than she'd ever want to admit. *Bless Sam.*

At her smothered sob, he glanced up and, seeing her tears, shook his head in reproof. But he didn't speak, just continued braiding leather in an intricate pattern around a whipstock. His very silence wove a spell of peace in the room.

And as she watched the sureness of his lean fingers, she felt a flush of heat from her toes to her fingers. She remembered all too well those hard hands on her body. Wanted his hands on her again. Honestly, she was turning into a nympho.

At my age. How funny—both of them had adult children. She smiled and switched to fingerpicking an old ballad. Sam had a lovely daughter. Intelligent, friendly, and quirky with outrageous opinions on everything, ranging from Tampa politics to earthworms. Sam had merely listened with laughter in his eyes. He never said anything openly affectionate to his girl, nothing like the "I love you's" that she and her children had exchanged, but now and then, he'd wrap an arm around the girl's waist and give her a squeeze or ruffle her spiky black hair. The love was there.

Nicole's comment about not wanting to know about her father's sex life had been...interesting. Then again, Sam had said he didn't bring women home. Not that he ever explained any more about that. Or anything. She frowned down at the strings of the guitar. Was that reticence who Sam was, or was there another reason? Sometimes, it would be so much easier to talk things over if she really *knew* him.

When he met her eyes, she realized she'd been staring at him. He gave her a half smile. "Let me put this away, and we can watch a show if you want."

"Okay."

After nudging Conn over so he could rise, Sam walked out of the room.

Linda returned the guitar to its rack and curled into a corner of the couch, trying to muster up her courage. With no fire in the fireplace, the room seemed to have chilled. She considered pulling out her basketry. Her fingers needed something to do.

Big hands closed around hers. "What's bothering you, girl?" Seated on the oversize leather ottoman, Sam studied her face.

She cleared her throat. "About today."

He waited.

Darn him, it would help if he prompted her or something. "I-I appreciate what you did. To get my children back. I guess I won't kill you for interfering."

His lips quirked. "Guess I can sleep easy tonight."

Hitting him now would be unwise. "About the shower. I wanted to..." There was no easy way to talk about this. How did other submissives manage?

His eyes grew intense. "Just spit it out."

"I'm submissive."

"Yes."

"But I can't be that way except..."

"Do it now, slut."

"Present yourself to the buyer, slut."

She bit her lip as nausea roiled inside her.

He made a noise in the back of his throat, then plucked her from the couch and sat with her in his lap. "Sam!"

His left arm curved around her shoulders, holding her against his chest. With his right hand, he tilted her head up, brushing his thumb over her chin. "See if you can talk easier like this," he said.

She curled her fingers around his forearm. He'd derailed her thoughts. "I can't figure it out."

"Figure what out, baby?"

She stared into his eyes. Sometimes, the pale blue of his eyes had a darker rim. "The...they kept us under control. All the time. And now, now, I can't let you do that. Because of them. I need to know—to agree to—"

"To give up your power," he suggested softly.

"Yes. And when you yanked me into the shower, I..." She dredged up all the honesty she could find, opening herself. "I liked it. I did. But it scared me too, because if you tell me to do some slavey thing, something I really don't want to do, I'm not sure I'd refuse. I sometimes don't know if I obey you because they...conditioned...me or because I want to."

"Go on."

Her throat tightened with frustration. She couldn't explain because she didn't really understand it herself. "I just want limits on when...when you order me around." Her breathing hitched.

"Shhh." He tucked her head against his shoulder, letting her get herself back under control. Not driving her to expose more, to bare her soul.

Her breathing steadied.

"Between a Dom and sub, most things are negotiable." He pushed her hair out of her face. "I have certain requirements. I want to be in control when it comes to sex." He considered and added, "I like demanding sex when I want it, but I can give in there."

She raised her head. "You didn't exactly back off earlier."

"No." He traced his finger down her jaw. "That was my next point. Making you kneel or strip or do menial labor? Not interested. But if it comes to your well-being, I'm not flexible." His square jaw hardened. "This afternoon, I wasn't about to let you fret yourself sick."

Oh. Her gaze traced down the strong line of his neck to his right shoulder. The shirtsleeve covered the rocklike bulge of his biceps and was rolled up over his thick forearm. He had the strength to enforce anything he wanted. Like he had this afternoon.

But she hadn't felt dirty when he'd dragged her into the shower, maybe because he'd said why he was forcing her to cooperate. *"If you figure to worry until they show, think again."* It hadn't been an arbitrary act. "Maybe that will work," she whispered. "If there's a reason. More than you just want to...to..."

"Flaunt my control over you?" he finished in a dry voice.

"Yes." She looked up with butterflies in her stomach. He didn't look upset, just thoughtful.

"Then we'll limit power exchanges to this: I control everything dealing with sex...or pain. You always have a safe word. Timing is negotiable unless I step in for your safety or health."

Really? She felt as if she'd been braced against a hard wind that had just disappeared, leaving her falling forward. Looking him in the eyes, she agreed. "Yes." In a lower voice, she added, "Thank you."

"You're welcome." He traced his finger around her mouth. "I should warn you, though. I'll find other methods to get my way."

She stiffened. "Like?"

"Like it's your turn to pick the movie. But if it has a romance in it, I'm going to play with the pussy whip as well as spank your ass."

Oh heavens. She couldn't keep from squirming at the memory of that whip. She wanted—didn't want—wanted that intense torment again. And the most sadistic part was now she couldn't decide whether to pick a romance or not.

From the evil glint in his ice-colored eyes, he'd deliberately left her with that dilemma.

Chapter Seventeen

On Saturday, Linda, trying to remember everyone's names, brought up the rear of the women piling out of the bachelorette party limousine. She'd already met Andrea, Jessica, Kim, Gabi, and Beth. Kari was the submissive of another Shadowlands Master. Sally, Uzuri, Rainie, and Dara were trainees—submissives who didn't have a Dom but wanted to learn more about the lifestyle.

None of the women were her age, but the common interest of BDSM had bridged the gap. A couple of glasses of champagne hadn't hurt the bonding either.

She'd decided the women were all crazy. On the ride over, they'd told stories of what *not* to do to a Dom and other mistakes they'd made. Like the night a tired Uzuri had downed two coffees before a scene. After the poor Dom spent ages on the bondage and suspension, she'd had to beg for a bathroom break. Or Gabi, who'd gotten mad at Marcus and used his favorite canes as fireplace kindling.

Just the idea of doing that with one of Sam's toys was...appalling. Oh, she might enjoy the look on his face for all of a few seconds, but then...the wrath of God would come crashing down on her.

Why did that sound so tempting?

Linda followed the group into the nightclub. Rather than the Shadowland's medieval atmosphere, this place's decor was grungy harshness. Concrete floor, black brick walls, red-hued paintings. Metal everywhere, from bar stools to aluminum siding behind the bar to twisted metal railings leading to the second floor. "Interesting," Linda said. "Jessica likes this kind of place?"

"No. We're here because the club advertised it has BDSM equipment." Gabi hooked an arm with hers.

"You brought Shadowlands submissives to a different club?"

Gabi grinned. "We couldn't exactly get falling down drunk in Z's club, now could we?"

"Good point." In fact, doing anything wild and crazy under Master Z's nose would be sheer insanity. "Are we dressed up like Dommes to keep from getting hit on as submissives?"

Beth heard the comment and turned. "Nah. We just wanted to give Jessica one last chance to switch to the dominant side." Beth unzipped the biker jacket she wore, revealing a black bustier and black vinyl pants. "Besides, Dommes have the coolest clothes."

Linda grinned. "True." She wore all black as well. Her skinny black jeans almost disappeared under the impact of high vinyl boots and her skintight, long-sleeved latex shirt. She'd unzipped the front low enough that most guys wouldn't see past the cleavage.

"I used to wear clothes like this, right up until my first night as a trainee." Andrea tried to look pitiful—not easy for someone who reminded Linda of Wonder Woman. "Cullen was the trainer, and he said a sub couldn't wear more clothes than the Dom. The *cabrón* made me strip right in the center of the club."

"Ouch." Linda frowned, recalling the giant bartender with his booming laugh. "And I thought he seemed so easygoing."

"He is...right until he slides into Demon Dom mode." Andrea grinned. "Don't tell him, but I go all melty inside when he does."

"I know the feeling," Linda muttered. When Sam got that look in his eyes—the one that said she'd better do exactly what he ordered—her bones turned squishy. "It's nice to know I'm not the only one."

"Kim's creating us a spot," announced Sally. "Come on, Mistresses." Although not that tall, the brunette wore such a red latex T-shirt that she stood out like Rudolph, the reindeer. They followed her through the crowd at the entrance, past the bar, along the side of the dance floor, and up some stairs.

When Linda looked around, she saw a balcony ran around the perimeter of the second floor. From there, people were watching the dancing and the randomly scattered short St. Andrew's crosses, spanking benches, and stocks.

"Over here," Kim called as she industriously shoved chairs, couches, and coffee tables into a disorganized cluster near the railing. "Ladies. Here's our little bit of heaven for the evening." She dropped into a chair by the railing.

The rest of the group happily spread out.

"Sit with me." Jessica pulled Linda down next to her on a long couch, then nodded to her left. "Look at them. Aren't they a study in contrasts?"

Linda had to laugh. Dara had a pale complexion with blonde, spiky hair and wore black leathers. Next to her was Uzuri, with black skin, braided hair, and a dark red catsuit. Obviously hearing the comment, Uzuri grinned over her shoulder. "We're going to find us a boy and beat his white ass for a while."

Sprawled in an armchair, Rainie snickered. "I don't know about Dara, but Mistress U, I bet you've never been on the handle side of a flogger."

"Maybe not." Uzuri's beaded hair clattered as she tossed her head. "But we look so fine he won't notice anything else." She knocked her fist against Dara's.

Giggling, Jessica rose. "Thank you all! This is just great and so much more fun that what I thought it would be."

"Oh, we're just getting started, Mistress Jessica," Gabi said. "Rainie, did you bring your stuff?"

"You bet." Rainie grinned. A big woman, she'd refused to try to squirm her way into latex or leather pants, but wore a fluorescent blue vinyl dress, fingerless gloves with small spikes on the back, and a coiled whip on her studded belt. A vine tattoo ran from her shoulder to disappear between her breasts. "The chauffeur agreed he'd haul it up here for us. That's what Sally's watching for."

Stuff? Linda wondered.

Jessica's mouth dropped open. "You wouldn't. Here, in a public place?"

"It was Sally's idea, so Jessica would have fun toys for her honeymoon," Rainie said. "Besides, it's supposed to be a BDSM club, right? Shouldn't be anything they've never seen before."

"Oh God." Jessica's champagne-fueled giggles increased. "Sally, you're insane."

Sally glanced back with the "I'm so innocent" look of a dedicated troublemaker, then leaned over the railing and yelled, "Hey, Chauffeur!"

Uzuri added her voice. "Up here, Limo Man!"

A minute later, the lanky chauffeur hauled two heavy-duty suitcases up the stairs.

"He's earned himself a huge tip," Kim muttered.

The man set the suitcases on the two coffee tables, gave the gathering a slight bow, and left without saying a word.

"All right, Mistresses, here you go." Rainie opened the cases with a flourish.

Linda's mouth dropped open. Foam padding lined one suitcase and had been cut out to hold...dildos. Vibrators. She turned her head. The other case held colorful spray bottles and tubes, a couple of crops, a few cuffs, blindfolds... She stared at Rainie. "You have suitcases of sex toys?"

The trainee laughed so hard her breasts jiggled. "I spend all day surrounded by men. Hosting these parties lets me hang out with women." She raised her voice. "Check it out, ladies. I set it up, so if you decide you just have to own something tonight, I can do that."

As Sally, Uzuri, and Dara whooped and converged on the toys, Linda sagged back in her couch. "I need a drink."

Before the words were out of her mouth, Gabi thumped two pitchers down. "Margaritas, anyone?"

The evening passed in a blur of gossip, intriguing tidbits of life at home with a Dom, playing the Domme game that Gabi and Sally had invented, and checking out Rainie's stock of toys. By the time the first pitchers were gone, half the places in the suitcases were empty. Clever

Rainie had brought along brown paper bags to hold their purchases.

It had only taken two margaritas before Linda caved in. A vibrator for the G-spot. How could she resist? And then she won a prize she never intended to use but no one would trade with her. She'd definitely make sure Sam never saw that one.

Frowning, Kari sank onto the couch next to Linda and dubiously examined her own prize. A cock ring.

"Problems?" Rainie asked.

"Aside from talking Dan into letting me near his guy parts with this?" Kari looked over ruefully. "The main problem is finding the energy. Zane is teething, Dan is putting in overtime because of some creepy rapist, and all too often I'd rather sleep than mess around."

Remembering the sleep-deprived, zombie world of new motherhood, Linda patted her hand. "Once Zane is older, you'll catch up on sleep. And if you want a babysitter so you can...play...out of hearing range, well, I love babies."

Kari hugged Linda. "You're so nice. Thank you. We'll take you up on that." She fingered the cock ring and grinned. "I'm dying to see Dan's face when I pull this out—let alone when I try to get it on him."

Dan was the cop, wasn't he? Gorgeous but awfully stern looking. Poor Kari. Linda smothered a laugh, trying to imagine talking Sam into cooperating.

"Kari, it's time for the next competition," Kim called.

"Right." Kari checked the clipboard on the end table. "Linda and Jessica, your attention, please." Sweet-faced Kari sounded exactly like the schoolteacher she was.

"Yes, Mistress." Jessica saluted. "Our assignment?"

Kari handed each of them a paddle. "Go downstairs, find a man, get him to bend over, then give him three good swats."

Linda stared. "Seriously?"

"The first to swat wins." From her chair by the railing, Kim raised her glass in a toast. "But the loser still has to paddle a guy, or else you'll receive the swats from us up here."

Jessica scowled. "How come Andrea and Dara got off easy? Getting a guy to unzip and show if he's wearing tighty-whities or boxers isn't that difficult."

"Luck of the draw, girlfriend," Gabi said, no sympathy in her voice. "Go."

As Linda stood, she could feel the alcohol buzzing in her veins. Champagne, then...margaritas. *Note to self: slow down on the consumption.* She glanced at Jessica, who was in the same condition. Not...quite...drunk. "We can do this."

Jessica gave her a shoulder bump. "You bet."

At the top step, Linda paused.

Jessica stopped behind her. "What's wrong?"

"Nothing. I'm summoning my inner Domme."

"I don't think I have one of those, inner or outer. I'm an accountant. I don't boss people around. Well, unless they're missing paperwork."

"There you go." Linda grinned. "Ever had someone dump a shoebox of receipts on your desk just before tax day?"

Jessica's expression changed completely. "Oh, have I." Her mouth firmed and her back straightened as they walked down the steps. "How about you?"

"Any mother who's survived teenagers has developed some Domme." Linda reached for a memory to put her in the right frame of mind. Maybe Charles's sixteenth birthday party when she'd discovered a boy had smuggled in a bottle of tequila. Yeah, she'd definitely gone Domme all over that youngster's head. *Maintain that attitude.*

They reached the bottom of the stairs.

"Here we go," Jessica muttered.

"May the best woman win," Linda said. She headed to the left; Jessica went right.

Men lined the bar, watching the dance floor, checking out the women. Very few were her age, but for her assignment, a younger man would be easier.

Not the one in a suit. Not the skinny lad who looked barely twenty-one. Not the jock. Not...

When an older man's gaze swept over her, then focused sharply, she got a bit of the squirmy little mouse feeling that Sam's Dom look could induce. Could the guy tell she was submissive?

And wouldn't Sam have a fit if he saw her in Domme gear, wielding a paddle?

With a huff of amusement, she turned away to check the nearby tables. Not the obnoxious drunk. Not the geek. Then she saw a candidate standing at a tall table. His gaze lingered on her tight shirt, well enhanced with cleavage. *Mistress L for Lethal, that's me.*

He looked midtwenties. A trim mustache. Light brown frohawk. Jeans and an All American Rejects T-shirt.

Wish me luck; I'm going in. She approached his table. "What's your name, *boy*?"

His eyes widened. "Jeremy." He swallowed as she stepped into his space. "You look...wow."

"Yes, I do." She gave him an assured head tilt. "I want you to bend over."

He stared into her eyes as if mesmerized. "What?" She could actually see him shiver.

"Present that pretty ass to me, boy." Her voice took on a familiar-sounding growl. *Don't think about Sam.* "Now."

To her surprise, he did just that. *Seriously?* Without letting herself hesitate, she swatted him. One. Two. The third got a grunt from him. Cheers came from the bar, and Linda heard screams and applause from her crew above.

"What a good boy." Trying not to burst into laughter, she waited for him to straighten, gave him a firm kiss on the lips, then started to walk away.

"No, no. *Wait.*" He was following her.

What in the world? She stopped.

He held his hand out. "Kneel—am I supposed to kneel? Can I give you my number? Will you call me? Please?"

Oh, dear heavens, someone just found his inner submissive. She patted his cheek. "I'm afraid I'm taken, sweetie. But I'm sure you can find a nice Mistress."

From the look in his eyes, he'd be doing just that. She knew the feeling. Pretending to be a Top left her craving Sam's dominance.

On the stairs, she spotted Jessica near the dance floor, trying to convince a man to bend over. When Linda wiggled her hips in a victory dance, the little blonde sent her a sizzling glare.

The women on the balcony greeted her with laughter and high fives. Dara slapped her back, and Rainie handed her a prize of lubricant, saying, "Gabi said you should have this flavor."

"Orange?" Linda took it. *Why orange?*

On the couch, Kim hadn't stopped laughing. She finally hauled in a breath and pointed at Linda. "Your expression when that puppy tried to follow you?"

Shaking her head, Linda sank down next to her. "I felt guilty, leading the poor baby on." She picked up her drink and took a couple of good swallows, savoring the underlying bite of tequila. "It was amazing he couldn't tell I was pretending. Bet a Dom would see right through the act." Sam would have.

"When I met Dan, I told him I wasn't submissive." In the adjacent chair, Kari wrinkled her nose. "He laughed at me."

"It's nice when a guy sees who you are." Sally leaned back against the railing. "When I'm dating vanilla guys, I feel like I have to pretend to be someone I'm not. Gets to me."

"Yeah," Linda said under her breath. Letting Lee go had been the right decision.

And Sam? Sam definitely saw her for who she was...and liked her that way.

* * * *

The chauffeur was hauling people home in two batches. The ones who wanted an early night left on the first run. The last few remained, waiting for the chauffer to return for them. Linda, Sally, Jessica, Gabi, and Kim. After getting more margaritas—strawberry, this time—

they'd pushed the two couches over to the railing so they could crowd together and watch the dance floor.

Sitting between Gabi and Kim, Linda sipped her tangy, sweet drink. How many had she had now? She felt nicely blurry and very happy. It was wonderful to be with women again. *I miss my girlfriends.*

"You lost touch?" Gabi asked softly.

Realizing she'd spoken the thought, Linda frowned at the glass in her hand. *Definitely over your limit, girl.* She set her drink on the railing. "I had two BFFs, but one moved to Oregon, the other to California. You know how it is when you meet someone who just clicks? We clicked."

Gabi tilted her head toward Kim. "We met in college, and then no matter how long between visits, we could just take up where we'd left off. I feel that way about this crew now." She patted Linda's arm. "And that includes you."

Warmth filled Linda as she realized Gabi meant it. Sally and Jessica on the other couch were both nodding in agreement.

Then Jessica gave an annoyed sniff. "Only I'm going to hold a grudge because you beat me at Domming."

"After you and Z have children, you'll be able to intimidate anyone." Linda grinned. "Trust me."

"Look at that guy." Kim pointed. A man with a beer belly, weak chin, and pompous expression strutted across the dance floor. "The creep has been doing that 'Oh dear, the floor's so crowded. Did I rub against your tit?' maneuver. I'm going to rank him at the TNTC level, maybe midway."

"Rating men is so shallow. You should be ashamed." Linda tsk-tsked at Kim. Besides, Kim had the ranking wrong—someone who groped women should be at the bottom level.

"Sally and Rainie invented it," Kim pseudowhined, sounding so much like Brenna in a pout that Linda laughed.

Jessica pointed a finger at Linda. "Hypocat...hypercrat...hypo...hell with it, you faker. I heard you give that cutie a 'tie me up, baby rating'."

"A TMUB? Really?" Kim popped upright, spilling her drink as she craned her neck. "Where?"

Gabi snickered. "You are so drunk. Raoul's going to have a fit."

"Nah." Kim held up her sack. "I'll just show him my new toys."

"You're such a sneaky brat." Gabi opened her sack and peered inside. "I don't remember what I got...except that I won a gag. Marcus is *never* going to see that one."

A second later, they were all checking their bags.

"Aw, poor baby," Sally said to her bag. "Do you want to come out and play?"

Jessica was giggling. "Mine does."

As Linda leaned forward to speak to Jessica, she noticed a balding man on the ground floor staring up, eyes bulging.

Linda followed his gaze, and her mouth dropped open.

Jessica was bouncing her oversize cock-like vibrator along the railing toward where Sally was moving her vibrator in circles.

"You two. What are you doing?" Linda sputtered.

"Hey," Jessica said with a grin. "It's a rabbit. It wants to hop."

"Mine's searching for the G-spot. It knows there's one around here somewhere." Sally crossed her eyes. "I've been with guys like that."

"How 'bout the ones who couldn't find your clit if it bit them?" Gabi asked.

"You are so—" Jessica's rabbit hopped, missed the railing. She fumbled, secured it before it fell.

Giggling uncontrollably, they all stared down at where it would have landed...on the balding man.

He leered at them and cupped his crotch.

"Ew. I wouldn't have him. Not *even* after a bottle of tequila." Jessica shoved her poor rabbit back into the bag.

"That's pretty harsh." The "not even" rating was the lowest of all. Linda considered, then saw the guy licking his lips, rubbing his pelvis vigorously. "Well, maybe not."

Kim looked down at the floor, and her nose wrinkled. "Not even if he had a cock piercing."

After putting her vibe into her bag, Sally said, "Not even if he killed a palmetto bug for me."

"Ouch," Linda said. "But you'd think there'd be a better class of male in this establishment." She looked around hopefully. "A few older ones—you know—for my enjoyment? I haven't spotted an AYW-ID yet, and I wanted one for my record."

Gabi studied her glass. "I'm so trashed I can't remember what an AYW-ID is."

"Anything you want," Sally started, and Jessica sang along for the last part, "I'll do. AYW-ID."

"Oh. Right." Gabi took the last swallow of her drink. "I knew that."

Linda gave up checking the dance floor. Maybe, like cream, the better guys rose to the top. She turned her attention to the balcony on the far wall. The waiter over there wasn't bad. He was serving a skinny young man who didn't look old enough to be in a bar. Past that table was a group of men seated in a cluster of chairs. They looked older. She tried to focus.

The one on the left looked over. Pale eyes in a darkly tanned face met her gaze...*trapped* her gaze. Knocked the bottom out of her stomach and her drink out of her hand onto her boot. *Sam.* "AYW-ID," she whispered. "AYW-ID."

"Really? You found a hottie?" Gabi half stood, froze, and fell back onto the couch, moaning. "Marcus is over there. They're all over there." She pulled her policeman's leather jacket closed.

"Seriously?" Jessica scrambled to her feet.

"Oh, God, they're staring at us." Kim balanced herself on the couch. "You think we could go out the back?"

Jessica's hands were over her mouth, trying to stop her laughter. "Girl, you can't even stand up."

"Damn chauffeur should have picked us up sooner." Gabi scowled. Then her eyes widened. "How long do you suppose they were there?"

Linda risked a quick glance. "However long, they're headed over here now." Exhilaration bubbled in her blood. *Sam is here.*

"Here! Noooo, Z mustn't see these." Jessica frantically shoved her wealth of toys in her oversize bag.

"The gag! And I didn't bring a purse." Gabi staggered over to the couch, dumped her sack of toys, and tried to force them into her jacket pockets. A bright red ball gag hit the floor and bounced under the couch. She dropped to her knees with a painful-sounding thud and tried to retrieve it.

"Can't even stand? Now that's downright pitiful." The deep voice was as slow as the Mississippi and held a faint Southern drawl. The man's sharp blue eyes were several shades darker than Sam's.

Gabi's head jerked up, eyes wide.

Linda tilted her head. Would this be Gabi's Marcus?

"Have to agree. Better get them home." Sam tucked his thumbs under his belt, drawing her attention to where his long sleeves had been rolled up, revealing his muscled forearms and powerful hands. She knew how those hands felt on her body. And those fingers sure didn't have any trouble finding her clit—or G-spot either.

Jessica shoved her blonde hair behind her shoulders. "Hey. You don't get a say in this. It's my bacher...balorette...bachette... It's my party."

Master Z put his hand on Jessica's shoulder and then tilted her head up. "Kitten, you make an adorable drunk."

She beamed at him. "I do?"

"Indeed." He hooked her purse on her shoulder, scooped her up in his arms, and headed for the stairs. "Let's see how good you are at drunken sex."

"*Sumisa.*" Raoul pulled Kim to her feet and caught her as she tipped sideways.

"I've got bribes to get out of trouble." She held up her bag.

"Planning ahead, are you?" When he lifted her into his arms, she buried her face against his shoulder.

Linda gave a sigh of envy. The Masters were so sweet. Sam was too. She smiled at him before noticing his stern expression. His arms were crossed over his chest.

Oh boy, she was going to catch hell. A thrill ran through her at the thought. What would he do?

Lips quirking, Marcus took Gabi's newly retrieved ball gag from her hand. After studying it for a second, he tried to tuck it into her jacket pocket and found the pockets full. "You've been busy, sugar."

"I..." She batted her eyelashes at him, slipping the gag from his fingers. "Guess we'd better go, huh?"

"I do believe that would be wise." With an arm around her waist, he tried to help her down the stairs.

Halfway down, she staggered.

Laughing, Marcus bent over and picked her up. As he straightened, Gabi flung the hated ball gag over the railing. It bounced along the floor and hit an older man's foot.

Linda exchanged a look with Sally, and they both burst into laughter.

The chauffeur passed Marcus and Gabi on the stairs. He nodded at Sam, then gave Linda and Sally a concerned look. "Where are the others?"

"Their Mas—um, friends took them home," Sally said. The laughter faded from her face, leaving a vulnerable sadness behind. "Wish I was so lucky."

"Oh, sweetie." Linda wrapped her arms around the young woman. "You'll find your special one. You will."

Blinking wet eyes, Sally squeezed her back.

Feeling luckier than she could say, Linda held the young woman and looked up at Sam. He was watching them, his expression gentle.

After a minute, Sally pulled in a slow breath. When she lifted her head, her usual vivaciousness was back. "Well, until I find the perfect one, let the good times roll." She gave the chauffeur a wicked grin. "Let's go, Jeeves. I'm your only passenger, so I expect awesome service."

"Yes, miss." With the hauteur of an English butler, he gave a slight bow and offered his arm when she staggered slightly.

As the two walked toward the stairs, Linda realized with a jolt that she was the last one left. *Uh-oh.* She turned her head.

Sam was watching her. His gaze ran slowly over her Domme outfit, and then his lips curved in a hard smile. "Did you give some submissive a thrill, Mistress Red?"

After a second, she remembered the young man. She laughed, laughed again, and said triumphantly, "I did."

Sam's brows drew together. "What? What did you do?"

"Just paddled his butt."

Sam growled, the sound as low as any wolf.

Oops. She eyed him worriedly. "Are you upset?"

His face went unreadable as if he'd frozen his emotions.

Worry slid into her veins like cold grease. Why didn't he answer? "Sam. I didn't... It was just a game. Really." Remembering the outcome of the game, she started to grin. "I beat Jessica and won a toy."

After a long second, his eyes filled with amusement, and he barked a laugh. "You're sloshed, missy. Time to go home."

With an easy swing, he pulled her to her feet, then wrapped an arm around her as he guided her toward the stairs. She only tripped twice...well, maybe three times...and dropped her sack once before he huffed a laugh and swung her into his arms.

She gave a happy sigh. *Okay, admit it, I was jealous of the others getting carried.*

Outside, Sam set her on her feet beside his truck. Linda's ears rang in the quiet night. A car moved past with a glare of lights and a wash of gas fumes. As she tried to read Sam's expression, she realized she was seeing two of him. She blinked. Heavens, she couldn't handle one Sam; two might make her heart stop. She giggled.

"That's a pretty sound. You don't laugh enough, girl." He pulled open the truck door.

She grinned at him. "I'm happy. Cuz I'm with an AYW-ID."

She felt him kiss the top of her head before he lifted her onto the passenger seat. Once behind the wheel, he asked, "What the hell is an AYW-ID?"

"It's when you look at a man and think, 'Anything you want, I'll do.'"

"Is that right?" He turned on the engine, then nodded at the brown paper bag clutched in her hands. "In that case, tell me what's in the sack?"

Oh, heavens. "Nothing interesting."

Chapter Eighteen

Standing in his bedroom, Sam smothered a grin. Linda was seated in the center of his king-size bed. Naked. As she'd tried to remove her skintight latex shirt, he'd discovered she knew a fair number of interesting curses.

When she looked up at him, her big brown eyes held more than a hint of anxiety. But although some of the alcohol had worn off, she still wasn't completely sober, and he didn't beat on drunken masochists. He needed her either capable of using her safe word or for her body language to not be muddled.

Didn't mean he wouldn't have a good time though. He'd spent part of the afternoon adding chains to the frame of his bed. Rope would have been easier, but nothing beat the clinking of chains when a submissive yanked on them. *Yeah.*

"We're going to play now?" She looked up at him. "You don't mind that I'm on the drunken side?"

"Nope." He liked seeing her like this, relaxed. A little giggly. No haunting worries visible in those eyes— none but what he put there. He winked at her. "I intend to enjoy the hell out of it."

He buckled her into leather wrist and ankle cuffs. Maybe he'd leave them on. Nice easy access in the morning.

After shoving a thick foam wedge under her ass, he chained her arms to the upper posts, leaving her legs free.

"Sam." She took a gulping breath as she tested the restraints.

"Chains and bedposts. Just call me old-fashioned." He curved his hand under her jaw and kissed her, not viciously but rougher than normal. Giving her a hint at what would be coming.

The way her breathing sped up was damned appealing.

He put a tweezers clamp on her left nipple, tightening until she whined, then backing off quite a bit since her sensitivity might be impaired. After doing the left, he stopped to kiss her and remind her who he was. Being intoxicated could let old fears surface. She needed to see *him*, hear *him*.

"Are you going to hurt me?" she whispered, her expression half-worried, half-eager.

"Not much." Mostly when the clamps came off. But she wouldn't be thinking about pain by then. He picked up his handmade cunt-spreader setup. "Spread your legs, girl."

Her eyes widened at the clamps dangling from the two Velcro straps. "What are those?"

Under his stare, she slowly moved her legs apart.

When he dropped the straps next to her hip, she caught on to where he intended to put those clamps.

He smothered a grin when she started to bring her legs together to cover her vulnerable pussy bits.

"No," he growled.

She stopped, legs still apart. When he traced a finger over her inner thigh, she shivered. Damn, but she had delicate skin. Soft. So white he knew the sun's rays had never touched it.

For his own enjoyment, he teased her for a while until she was pleasingly wet and squirming. Then he wrapped a wide strap around each upper thigh as high as he could get. Out of her sight, he plugged in his favorite toy and set it conveniently at hand on the floor.

"Let's see what you got tonight." He picked up the brown paper bag she'd forgotten in the truck.

Her face turned a satisfying red, then outraged. "Leave that bag alone!"

"Nope." Once he had a look at what she'd bought, he'd know what to do about her legs. He pulled out a tiny bottle. Orange-flavored lubricant? He snorted, remembering Gabi's surprise when she'd given him a blowjob and discovered he'd used an orange-flavored condom.

After tossing it onto the bed, he found the next toy. A long, thin vibrator that curved upward to a flat, ribbed tip. He studied it a minute, then realized the shape was designed to reach the G-spot. *Perfect.* He gave her an amused look. "You were busy at that party, weren't you?"

She was so fair-skinned that her blush reached a bright red. "Those are my toys. Not yours."

"I don't intend to use them on me, missy."

The last thing in the bag was... He grinned. No wonder she'd worried.

Her eyes widened when he held it up. "You wouldn't."

The anal plug was also a vibrator. Even had batteries already installed. "It's bigger than I'd have chosen for you."

Her voice came out nicely higher than normal. "I didn't choose it. It was a prize. And it's huge."

"It'll fit...with a little work."

The chains clanked as she yanked on them. Trying not to laugh, he figured out the scenario and what to do with her legs. Hell, this was going to be fun.

HE WOULDN'T REALLY stick that thing up her butt, would he? Linda pulled on the restraints, wanting to put her hands over her vulnerable asshole.

The clamps on her breasts were throbbing with a growing heat. But...what about those straps around her thighs? Did he really intend to use those horrible-looking clamps on her pussy? She saw him squirt lube on the anal plug, and her voice came out sounding strangled. "*Sam.*"

To her surprise, he set it down.

She let out a sigh of relief. He wasn't going to—

He picked up a chain fastened to the headboard, then lifted her left leg. A snick connected her ankle cuff and the chain. Her leg was raised, pointing toward her head. Elevated by the wedge pillow, her bottom now tilted upward. "What are you doing?"

"Now, missy, you know the answer to that." The cool calculation in his eyes made her quake. She was still fuzzy-minded from the alcohol; he definitely was not. He bent her right knee and chained that ankle to the side of the bed, then squeezed her thigh. Just the strength in his powerful hand sent a tremor through her. "Don't want you to kick at me when I do this."

This? When she saw him pick up the anal plug, she realized he'd positioned her legs so he could easily reach her asshole. "You bastard. I don't want any anal stuff."

"Safe word is red, girl." His eyes narrowed. "You call me any more names, and I'll gag you."

She choked the next curse back, almost strangling herself, and it was a good thing that he'd chained her other leg, since she'd have definitely kicked him.

He studied her, waiting to see if she'd safe word. Then one corner of his mouth tipped up.

Safe word, you fool. But her apprehension was balanced by anticipation; she wanted everything he'd do to her. Wanted his hands on her. Didn't want anything to stop. But that plug... Her inner voice was whining up a storm and got louder when she felt him push the plug against her anus.

Every muscle on her backside tightened in denial.

His icy eyes met hers. "I have bigger plugs. If I have to work hard to put one in, I might as well use one that will make you yell." His palm hit her bottom with a resounding slap.

Like fireworks, the stinging sparkled into beauty. The buzzing alcohol in her veins made it even better. A sigh escaped as the feeling faded.

"Relax and push out, or I'll see how big of a plug you can take." His expression was...amused. He enjoyed making her anxious. He'd like making her yell. A quiver ran through her that held more need than fear. Gritting her teeth, she complied.

"That a girl." His gravelly laugh raised goose bumps on her arms. He started to work the plug in, pushing, easing out, pushing.

It felt so depraved, so sinfully carnal, having him see her, touch her in such a private place. And as he played with her, his deep, focused gaze wandered from her face and down her body to where his hand pushed the plug against her anus.

Her nipples tried to peak, making the clamps pinch harder. Her voice came out shaky. "Please. Just...just put it in."

"Safer for you if I go slow and stretch you out." His eyes gleamed. "Besides, I like drawing it out."

Her attempt to kick him earned her a swat on her ass.

The burn expanded into a sharp pleasure, quickening her breathing.

He continued. Each advance of the plug stretched and burned, reaching a disconcerting, erotic tightness. Then it plopped into place.

She closed her eyes and squirmed, feeling as if it were pushing all the way to her tonsils. Too full, too much.

"Look at me, girl."

Her eyes met his merciless ones. "I'm going to fuck you while that's in your ass."

Oh God. He was so big. With the plug... Terror and lust made her shiver.

A crease appeared in his cheek, but the way he brushed his knuckles over her cheek was heart-stoppingly tender.

After he unrestrained the leg chained to the headboard, he clipped it to a chain on the edge of the bed. When he finished, her arms were still restrained over her head, her knees were raised, and her ankles pulled toward the sides of the mattress. The high wedge tilted her crotch embarrassingly high in the air...and rubbed on the plug. She tried to lift up. Didn't work.

He settled between her knees. "Been looking forward to tasting you all night."

Her face flushed even as her bones went limp.

He bent forward and ran his tongue over her pussy before his lips closed around her clit. She'd already been aroused from everything he'd done, and she gasped as an inferno lit inside her. His tongue flickered over the top of her clit. Then he sucked, licked, sucked. Her insides coiled, and as she clenched, the plug set off odd sensations, sending her higher. The pressure built and suddenly, without warning, she came.

So quick. As she recovered her breath, she frowned. All that work for a fast orgasm?

Expecting him to let her loose, she realized he was adjusting the Velcro strap on her right thigh. He picked up one of the clamps that dangled from thick twine. Oh, heck, she'd forgotten that thing. Her legs involuntarily tried to close and got nowhere.

Something bit like teeth on her right labia and kept biting. "Ow!"

He'd put the clamp on her down *there*. Another clamp went on next to the first. Her back arched as the stinging expanded, billowing upward through her body, changing into liquid heat.

One more. And then he started on the left labia.

Her entire pussy was a river of pain, filled with an unstoppable current of pleasure, taking her out of herself. Leaving her adrift like a paddleless canoe.

Leaving her in Sam's control. As her eyes met his, she let go and let herself be swept away.

After a minute—hours, years—she felt a tugging down there. She lifted her head.

He was tightening the thick twine between the clamps and the thigh straps, pulling her labia open to expose her entrance and clit. A cool wash of air brushed over normally hidden places and contrasted with the burn of the clamps circling them.

"Like those, do you?" He was studying her reactions, his gaze moving again from her face to her breasts, her hands, her body. His eyes were the same blue as in the hottest part of a flame. "Say my name, Linda."

"Sam." Her voice was breathless but clear enough to gain a smile.

"Good girl."

How could she need his approval so much? Want it and work for it? But she did.

He slid the small dildo-vibrator inside her vagina, angling it, and set it to a low hum. The vibrations didn't feel like anything special...until he leaned down and licked over her clit.

Oh mercy. With the touch of his tongue, the nub felt as if it were being teased from two sides. As it swelled, she felt as if its size was doubling or even tripling.

Sam tormented her clit, circling up and over, forcing Linda back into arousal as if she'd never come a few minutes before. Her body's attempt to move, to tighten, pulled on the labia clamps. The burst of pain soared right into sheer bliss with not a second between.

As she shuddered, her hips strained to lift to his mouth. The sensations came too fast to process, shoving her up and up until her body contracted like a fist as the fireworks of an orgasm shot upward, then sparkled through every cell inside her. *So magnificent.*

As she floated down to earth, she felt the bed under her, the aching in her nipples and labia. She opened her eyes. "Heavens, that was…" She frowned at the laughter in his eyes as he turned off the vibrator. "What are you planning?"

"Just more of the same, missy. Nothing special."

More? She'd come twice in only a few minutes, and her heart still hammered. "I don't think so."

He leaned forward between her knees to lick her breasts and nibble on the compressed peaks before pushing her breasts together.

As the teeth of the clamps dug into her areolae, she groaned. He continued.

By the time he finished, a freeway of electricity sizzled up and down between her pussy and her breasts, and heat wafted upward from her skin as if her blood was boiling inside her veins.

He sat back on his heels, studied her for a second, and grinned. "Ready for another round?"

She was. How could she want more?

Nodding as if she'd answered, he flipped the G-spot vibrator to a setting that created a roller coaster, up and down, of vibrations.

When his mouth closed on her clit, she jumped. Too much, too sensitive.

Ignoring her squirming attempts to evade his tongue, he mercilessly worked her up, rubbing the sides. Toying with her.

The restraints held her limbs still, the wedge tilted her up. Clamps on her pussy held her so open. Every step he'd taken had left her more exposed, positioned right where he could force her to come for his own enjoyment. The bone-deep knowledge that he was playing with her, doing just as he wanted, sent her arousal spiraling out of control. "Sam," she whispered.

He lifted his head, meeting her gaze, the demand in his expression perfectly clear. *Give me everything.*

The breath she pulled in shuddered through her, feeling as if it cracked something deep inside her.

His diamond-blue gaze warmed. Leaning down, he took her clit between his lips and sucked on the tip as hard as he did on her breasts.

"Aaaaaah!" Her back arched, held, held, as the orgasm blasted through her without finesse, without mercy. Her arms tugged on the chains. Then she went limp. A fine sweat covered her body, chilling her as it cooled.

Sitting back, he flicked the vibrator off. His hands were warm as he stroked her hips. "Pretty Linda." His gaze ran over her as he smiled.

Her pulse was roaring in her head, and each heaving breath pulled on the clamps. The alcohol was definitely gone.

He pulled his shirt off. Such broad shoulders. A muscular chest with a six-pack that a twenty-year-old would envy. All man. And with an erection that bulged his jeans. Why wasn't he inside her? Satisfying his own need.

She swallowed against a dry throat. "Can I... Will you let me please you?" Everything in her wanted to give him the same joy he gave her. Making him happy satisfied her in ways she'd never be able to describe. "It's your turn, honey. I've had enough." Trying to entice him, she licked her lips.

"Not yet." His eyes held hers. "I'll tell you when you've come enough." He played with the vibrator settings, choosing one with a continuous heavy buzz.

She could feel it, enjoy it, but her body was finished and not reacting. "I'm pretty sure that's it for me, Sam. Let me—"

"Pretty sure it's not." He lifted a...thing...from the floor. A giant vibrator with a mushroom head the size of a girl's fist.

After turning it on, he pressed the head lightly between the labia clamps and against her exposed clit.

"Sam!" The vibrations were so intense her clit felt zapped by jolts of electricity.

As he rolled it back and forth, everything in her clenched and, like a flash fire, exploded into a brutal orgasm. Her scream echoed off the walls.

He turned everything off.

She felt as if her body was sinking into the mattress. Perspiration had wet the hair at her temples and behind her neck. "I'm done. Really."

"Nope."

He did it again. She came.

And again. She came. *Oh God.* She groaned as she roused from the last orgasm. How could something feel so good that her whole body ached? Her voice came out a moan. "Can't. No m-more left."

His eyes held an evil satisfaction as he studied her trembling body. "I think there is."

She tried to move, to escape, and couldn't. The restraints held her open to anything he wanted to do, whether getting her off or hurting her. The knowledge set up a separate pulse of desire, a low chant saying, *Use me, take me, do what you will.*

Damn, damn sadist...and Dom. His hard lips curved as he watched her futile attempts, head tilted as if he could hear the yielding voice inside her. Yes, he'd make her take until he decided to stop.

Why did knowing that set her insides fluttering with more than anxiety? The part of her that was still thinking protested, "Sam, really."

He reached between her legs, and the anal plug sprang to life with wicked vibrations. Every nerve between her butt cheeks blasted awake, an entirely new region of sensation. Her thigh muscles trembled as her need for more, for *something*, grew to unbearable.

When he pressed the vibrator to her clit, it ignited an explosion that ripped her right from the world as she came in long, almost painful rolls of pleasure.

After a while, she could hear herself sucking in air. She blinked and tried to focus. Sweat had drenched her body, trickling under her breasts and arms. "Please. No more."

"Safe word?" he reminded her.

A shiver ran through her. She wanted...wanted whatever he did.

A crease appeared in his cheek as he set the vibrator on the bed and switched off the anal plug. "Think I'm ready to fuck you now, girl."

An uncontrollable tremor rolled through her body. When his eyes gleamed, her insides quivered even more. "No," she whispered, just to hear herself protest...and to watch him ignore it.

Smoothly, he slid the G-spot vibrator out of her and set it to one side. When he opened his jeans, she swallowed. His cock was far bigger than the thin vibrator, and he hadn't removed the anal plug. He pressed the tip of his shaft against her entrance. With the labia clamps on, nothing blocked his way. Balanced on one arm, he worked in with incremental thrusts.

Everything felt too, too tight. Her body was stretched out, her arms chained. She couldn't move, no matter what he did, and she felt her excitement increase at the knowledge. "You don't fit."

His smile was...sadistic. "You'll take me to the hilt, missy. Even if it hurts." He gave her a level, implacable gaze that shot lust straight to her core. "Especially if it hurts."

As he stared down into her eyes, openly savoring her discomfort, currents of excitement sizzled through her.

Slowly, inevitably, he impaled her, continuing until his groin rubbed against the labia clamps. The glorious heat from the pinching soon engulfed the throbbing at her entrance.

He reached under her to start the anal plug again. With him filling her so completely, the vibrations shook through her whole lower half, and she gasped at the overwhelming sensations pulsing through her.

"Damned tight." He kissed her, driving his tongue into her mouth as ferociously as he started pounding his cock into her body.

He thrust in and out, filling her pussy, emptying her. The multitude of input—vibrators, clamps, his mouth, his cock—rang through her like a tolling bell, confusing her, driving her up again.

Every slick slide of his cock preceded the feeling of being filled to discomfort. His weight was heavy on her hips. She breathed in the clean outdoors scent of him as he kissed her deeply, making her feel thoroughly possessed. Restrained, pressed down, filled everywhere. The shivery knowledge was like bubbles racing through her.

She felt his body start to tighten. Oh yes. She loved feeling him come, seeing the satisfaction on his face. Nothing compared to making this man happy.

"One more," he said.

"What?"

Without answering, he lifted up slightly and removed her left breast clamp. After a second of almost relief, the agony of blood rushing into the abused flesh made her arch and suck in air. Insidious pleasure wove tendrils between the pain until she wasn't sure what she felt. Her insides clenched down against his thickness, against the vibrations of the anal plug, and she shot into arousal and need as if a rocket had gone off.

"There's a good girl." He stared into her eyes as he slid his cock out, and then he removed the other clamp.

She felt every little prong pull away from her nipple. The shocking influx of blood turned to the most exquisite pulsing, and her body clenched again. The anal plug vibrated, but she was empty...

Laughing under his breath, he slammed his cock home. Her back tried to arch against his heavy weight as her entire body filled with searing, scalding pleasure, filled and overflowed, cascading into an unstoppable climax. *Oh God*. Wave after wave of sensation rushed through her until her hair and fingers zinged with the orgasm.

Heaven help me; I'm going to die just from a climax. She tried to glare at him, but even her eyelids felt limp. And he was still hard inside her, moving in and out slowly. The realization sent a shudder through her.

"Honey. Not coming?" Her words sounded slurred.

"I will." His gravelly chuckle was soft against her ear. "When you get off again."

Her body had died. For sure, this time. "Not happening." Regret at disappointing him made her breath hitch. "I'm sorry."

The creases at the corners of his eyes deepened, and the look he gave her tugged at her heart. "Don't worry, girl." He nipped her chin, then rubbed his chest against her oversensitive nipples, sending pain zinging down to her clit. Her insides tightened around him and the plug. Somehow, without dislodging himself, he sat back onto his knees, withdrawing until his cock was barely inside her.

Cool air wafted over her damp skin, and her nipples tightened again, increasing the burn. The delight.

He ran a finger over her sensitive clit, making her jump, and she clenched again. His smile showed his enjoyment at controlling her responses...and that he knew exactly what he was doing to her. "Oh, I think you've got another orgasm in there," he said, and his laugh held a cruel, wonderful edge that took her breath away.

Her pulse felt like a throbbing in her lower half. He wouldn't—he couldn't make her come again. She'd die.

She yanked on her arm restraints. "Not again. Please, I can't take it again."

"You can."

Every sensitive bit on her body felt raw with sensation, like she was getting a continuous delicious whipping. "It's too much," she whispered.

His eyes lit. "Then this will top you off." Still on his knees, he held her gaze as he reached down...and pulled off a labia clamp. She had only a moment to realize what he'd done before he slammed his cock in. Hard. Deep. Pain blasted through her as blood churned back into her labia. Then it all zipped into an unholy pleasure. Her pussy tightened around his slick cock, feeling so, so good.

He picked up the huge vibrator and touched her clit.

The vibrations blasted straight to her core, impacting the pulsations from the plug in her ass. She shuddered at the flood of sensations.

He pulled his shaft out and lifted the vibrator away.

She managed to pull in a breath.

Until he removed another labial clamp and rammed his thick cock in. The vibrator went back onto her clit.

Before, just before she could come, he pulled his cock back. The vibrator up.

She was panting.

The next clamp came off...and the cycle started again. Again and again and again.

She broke, exploding so hard that her hips bucked in protest, every muscle seized into rigidity. Like a volcano, heat erupted into sheer ecstasy, searing through every nerve.

He'd dropped forward onto one arm. His sandpaper laugh scraped in her ear as he pounded into her, deep and deeper, until his cock jerked, adding to the unending vibrations inside her. He came, long and long. As his fingers twined with hers, he kissed her with a rumbling groan of satisfaction that added to her own. She'd pleased him.

Ever so gradually, the waves inside her receded. The ringing in her ears faded. She was still panting, unsure if she'd ever achieve a normal breath again. Her heart felt like when Charles had learned to drum, hammering the house with erratic noise. When she managed to open her eyes, Sam was staring down at her, his face as gentle as she'd ever seen it.

After giving her a light kiss, he took a deep breath that rubbed his chest against her incredibly sensitive nipples and made her moan.

Slowly, he pulled out. When the anal vibrator switched off and was removed, her body could only twitch.

One by one, he unfastened the chains from her legs and arms. When he pulled her arms down, she groaned and gritted her teeth. Sore joints were not a good pain.

"Easy." As his powerful hands massaged the ache from her shoulders, her body felt as if it was oozing down into the bed, drenched in satiation. Her emotions felt the same way. He was being so careful with her. Evil sadist had turned to lover.

"Hurt too much anywhere?" His fingers trailed over her body, his warm gaze checking for any damage. "Tell me, baby."

"Uhh-uhhh. Fine."

"Good." With gentle, unwavering hands, he rolled her onto her side and curled behind her. His legs tangled with hers; his chest warmed her back. "Sleep, girl," he growled in her ear.

When she'd been a child, an elderly neighbor's dog had growled at her constantly. She'd been terrified until the owner explained the noise was Bruno's way of talking. Light growls, low growls, chompy growls. Even happy growls. She'd discovered that the local bullies never appeared when Bruno walked her to school…growling the entire way.

He'd sounded just like Sam.

Chapter Nineteen

On a worn-smooth wooden pew, Linda sat in the church waiting for the ceremony to begin. She'd been disappointed when Sam had called to tell her to go on to Jessica and Z's wedding without him. Nonetheless, she was delighted to be present.

How could anyone not love the ritual when a couple formally began their life together? For that one moment, no second thoughts were allowed to intrude. Even the air in the church seemed filled with joyful anticipation.

She smiled. She'd been so young when she and Frederick had married. If she'd waited to gain a bit more experience, perhaps she'd have made a wiser choice. But then she wouldn't have Brenna and Charles. And really, her marriage had been more happy than sad.

A gurgle of laughter came from beside her. Having defeated the other submissives, Sally cuddled Zane, Kari's adorable baby. He was having a wonderful time tugging on her long hair. Tanner, the male trainee, had squeezed closer, obviously awaiting his chance to snatch the baby for himself.

The rest of the row was filled with all the single Shadowlands submissives who weren't serving as bridesmaids. The club had shown up in force, filling the church with the wonderful diversity of the membership—

not only a range of ethnicities, but also the wide variety of sexual, gender, and relationship choices.

Obviously, Z wasn't ashamed of his friends. Linda shook her head. Once they married, would Z and Jessica still manage to balance the BDSM side of their lives with the vanilla world?

* * * *

In the bridal suite, Jessica looked at herself in the mirror. Thank God, Gabi was an expert with makeup. Jessica's hands had been shaking so hard that she'd have ended up with mascara everywhere...and probably have poked her eye out with the wand. "I'm getting married," she told herself.

Her bridesmaids burst into laughter, and Andrea added, "No. Really?"

Jessica turned on the chair. Damn, she loved these women—the submissives of the Shadowlands Masters. It had seemed so appropriate that their groomsmen and bridesmaids would be the attached couples in the Masters. Kari and Dan, Beth and Nolan, Andrea and Cullen, Gabi and Marcus, Kim and Raoul. She gave them a watery smile.

Beth set her hands on her hips. "Don't you start that crying business. Gabi already put her makeup kit away."

"No, Ma'am. I won't, Ma'am." Jessica grinned at Beth. "You were such a cute Mistress at the party. What did Nolan say when he saw you all Dommed up?"

"He said I was cute too. But then he wanted to see if I could dominate him. As if." The slender redhead rubbed her bottom. "Don't ever let Z get one of those evil stick things. That *thwap* really hurts."

As everyone laughed, Jessica heard Z outside the bridal room. Even after two years, she still got quivers when she heard his deep voice.

In the hallway, her mother said something that sounded like a protest.

Z answered firmly. "This is a tradition also." Ignoring the sputtering response, he walked past her mother and Aunt Eunice into the room and set a large gift bag on the floor. When he spotted Jessica, still in her underwear, his eyes warmed. "You're absolutely lovely, kitten."

Under his gaze... She felt beautiful.

He glanced at the women. "Give us a few minutes, please." No matter how politely phrased, it was a command from a Dom to a group of submissives.

Without a word, they disappeared into the hallway where her mother was having a whisperfest with Eunice.

What in the world was going on? "Zachary?"

"Try again." His eyes had turned a dark gray that melted her insides.

"Master?"

The corners of his eyes crinkled—the best reward she'd ever found. He rested his hands on her shoulders. "We decided you'd receive your submissive collar in the wedding ceremony instead of a separate one. Since we're not in a formal Master/slave relationship, that seemed right."

She nodded. They'd had a long discussion about how to integrate everything.

"But I decided I want more."

"More?"

He lifted her to her feet. His faint smile and the glint in his eyes sent a tremor deep into her bones. "You're mine, Jessica. My submissive. My wife. And the ceremony makes the spouse role more important than the submissive." He opened the bag he'd brought into the room and took out a...

"A corset?" A new one of pure white lace and satin that would go from her breasts to her hips and as beautiful in its own way as her wedding dress.

"Indeed." His gaze darkened. "Strip, please."

Her mouth dropped open. "Now?"

At the slight rise of his chin, she hurriedly pulled off her silky bra and thong.

"Hands up." As he wrapped the corset around her, she frowned at the perfect fit. "Where did you get this?"

"Your wedding gown seamstress used your other corset as a guide and changed your wedding dress accordingly."

No wonder the woman had that odd gleam in her eyes during the last fitting.

Z laced up the corset far more quickly than any man should. With a darkly wicked chuckle, he said, "Brace yourself, little one."

She felt tugging and more tugging as the corset tightened. And tightened. "I can't breathe."

"Give it a minute." He patted her bottom. "Move around the room."

As she walked, the corset loosened or maybe her insides were being squashed up against her lungs.

After a couple of minutes, he horrified her by tightening the laces until she could only squeak. With firm hands, he turned her around to face him, and his face held the stern, caring expression that had dropped her heart at his feet on the first night they'd met. "The way you look at me... I love you, Jessica."

To gain his approval, she would let him lace her to the width of a beanpole.

His gaze heated. Then he shook his head. "Ravishing the bride before the wedding would be bad form." A crease appeared in his cheek as he ran his finger along the top of the corset where her breasts were pressed upward into X-rated exposure. "Hopefully the tailor calculated correctly, or you'll give the preacher a heart attack."

The warmth of his fingers seared her skin, slid deep inside her.

"I'm looking forward to freeing these pretty breasts and then taking you. Hard. And easy. And slow. And fast. All night."

She closed her eyes as her insides turned to lava, and she dampened. Where was that thong, by the way? She'd definitely need to wear—

"No underwear, Jessica."

What? Her eyes opened to meet her Master's steel-gray gaze. "But—"

"As you walk down the aisle to me—and for the rest of the evening—you'll feel the tightness of the corset that I laced you into," he said, his voice deeper, authority resonating with every word. "You'll feel the control I have over you. Over your body...and your life." He brushed her lips with his, leaving her wanting more. "The collar I'll put on you will be the outward symbol that you're mine. But as with all power exchanges, the real truth is buried deep within, just as this symbol of my control is hidden from the world under your dress. Do you understand?"

As if something had slid into place, she felt...right. Balanced. Even if he wasn't beside her, he still exerted his control. "I love you, Master."

* * * *

Due to a downed fence and scattered cattle, Sam had told Linda to go to the wedding without him since he'd be late. He came in the church's side door and took a seat at the end of the third row as quietly as possible. Looked like he'd arrived in good time. A shame he'd missed seeing the bride come down the aisle though.

Stretching out his legs, he watched as the ceremony proceeded with both dignity and warmth, quite typical of Z yet with some of Jessica's exuberance.

The Dom had done well in selecting his mate. Had gone slow after meeting her. Sam knew Z hadn't wanted to push his lover into a commitment, especially since he was older. But she was thirty, and a woman usually knew her own mind by then. Jessica might be submissive, but she assuredly had her own strong opinions.

As the couple exchanged rings to the usual vows, the bride radiated happiness.

Sam sighed, feeling on the older side. Jessica had been delightful as she ventured into the club, into the lifestyle, and into a relationship. Although they'd started with playing in the bedroom, Z's dominance had slowly extended outward. They hadn't ended up with a Master/slave relationship, but the D/s dynamic was definitely part of their everyday lives.

He had to admit to feeling some envy.

His ex-wife had regarded BDSM with loathing, and he'd never tried to change her mind. But in the Shadowlands, he saw what he'd missed as the couples worked out what fit them. Some had gone from Master/slave to a limited power exchange; some went the other way.

As he glanced across the aisle, his gaze fell on the row of submissives who weren't bridesmaids. All were beaming, some in tears. Why did women cry at these things? Uzuri, Dara, and Rainie sat in a line. Sally was bouncing Kari's baby on her knee, while Tanner diverted the boy with the BDSM symbol on his keychain. Next to Sally was... Sam straightened.

Linda. Like a typical female, she'd primped up. Rather than the heavy makeup she'd worn at the bachelorette party, today she'd gone for quiet and classy. Her hair had grown long enough for her to pull it back in some complicated braid. Her dark green dress hugged her curves and made her skin glow.

He wished she were sitting beside him.

In front of the altar, Cullen handed Z a glittering strand—a necklace—and Sam blinked in surprise. Z planned to collar Jessica in front of vanilla guests? That took balls.

"This chain of links is a symbol of the events that drew us together." As Z held up a choker of diamond-encrusted links, his lips quirked. "From a car in a ditch to you rescuing women and me rescuing you."

Sam heard suppressed laughter at the reminder of how Jessica would charge in if she felt another submissive was in trouble.

Jessica gazed up at Z, and her voice was soft but steady. "Since I don't have any jewelry handy"—she gave him a teasing look—"I offer you the gift of myself: heart, mind, body, and soul. I trust you"—everyone in the lifestyle heard the unspoken *Master*—"and I'll wear your gift with joy." Jessica's need to offer all of herself was obvious to every Dom in the room and one of the most beautiful things Sam had ever seen.

When she pulled up her hair and bent her neck, Z fastened on the necklace. He lifted her chin. "Kitten, I vow to be worthy of the trust you've given me. I'll protect you, push you to grow, and cherish you with all my heart."

Z drew her into his arms, and his voice was only audible to the people in the first few rows as he murmured into her hair, "Mine."

Even as Sam felt his eyes sting, amusement trickled through him. Apparently, he wouldn't be teasing the ladies about their tears after all.

* * * *

Linda decided the Florida weather had cooperated wonderfully with the wedding, and sunny skies reigned above Z's private gardens behind the Shadowlands. With a backdrop of purple fountain grass, a five-person band was playing oldies for the guests at tables dotting the green lawn. Linda hummed along, pleased with the selection of tunes. Thank goodness the happy couple hadn't gone for the edgy techno music played in the Shadowlands.

The area was filling with people. Only the couple's friends and family had attended the wedding, but the reception included business associates and hometown guests as well as all the Shadowlands members.

She shook her head, feeling at a loss. The ceremony had been lovely, and when they'd given each other D/s vows disguised as a gift of jewelry, her heart had squeezed.

It still did, because she wanted that kind of relationship for herself and Sam. The time with him, each time with him, seemed to get more serious. He demanded more from her, and she gave it. So, so willingly. The desire to offer him...everything...was terrifying.

He cared for her. She knew it, even if he didn't speak the words. But could she give him what he wanted? Needed? He helped her scrape her house, stood up for her, and held her when she cried. He hurt her. He made love to her. What did she do for him?

He obviously liked her companionship. But she wanted to give him more than a dinner partner or someone to watch movies with. She wanted to support him. And the more she grew to care for him, the more she wanted to offer. But he was so darned self-sufficient.

Frederick had always brought home his problems. By sharing them with her, he might not have found answers, but his burden was lightened. It had been a gift she could offer. But Sam didn't talk about his concerns. In fact, very little seemed to bother him. And she wanted not only the closeness of sharing worries, but also the joy of being able to help. To comfort and support.

Her chest tightened. Over the past couple of weeks, she'd realized she had an insecurity, something new since her kidnapping. Another one, dammit. But she couldn't ignore the fact that she wanted Sam to *talk* to her. No one could possibly be more supportive than he was, yet sometimes she needed the actual words. Needed to hear what he felt about her, about their relationship.

Any woman would want to know how she fitted into a man's life—and she'd want that no matter what—but she had to admit that the twisting of his silence into something ominous came from her own misgivings. Not his. The slavers had made her feel as if she were an animal. Just an object to fuck. And yes, this was her own screwed-up remnant of that experience, but...it was bothering her.

Linda shook her head, trying to turn her thoughts to something more cheerful.

On the lanai, the bride's mother and aunt and a horde of women from her small town directed the catering crew, who were still setting food and drink on linen-covered tables. Z smiled at the women, making a gesture that he was leaving them in charge, before returning to the informal reception line.

Linda turned in a circle, marveling at the setting. Jessica had chosen blue and white for her colors, and somehow Z's garden matched, from the lanai's hanging pots that spilled over with white alyssum to blue-purple hyacinths and snowflake blooms in the flower gardens. Amazing.

"Hey, Linda." Wearing a deep red, ruched satin sheath with a plunging neckline, Sally crossed the lawn.

Linda grinned. "I really like that gown—and your versatility. I've seen you in braids and a schoolgirl uniform, then dressed as a Domme for the bachelorette party, and now you look incredibly sophisticated."

Sally gave her a mischievous grin. "I get bored easily." In much the way that Linda had, she looked back and forth from the nearby cluster of bridesmaids to the matching gardens. "Beth did good."

"She did all this?"

"Yeah. Z was one of her first big clients, and she busted her butt to make the Shadowlands and his private gardens special. Before, the place was pretty, but all formal. Squares and straight lines."

"I'd say she paid him back for his trust," Linda murmured. She'd never seen anything so luxuriant. Even without moving, she glimpsed curving garden paths, splashing fountains, more flower beds, and small, intimate nooks. "It's like a fantasy garden."

Overhearing, Beth turned from the bridesmaids and beamed. "Exactly what I was trying to achieve." She walked over. "But don't tell Z, okay? *Fantasy* sounds far too feminine."

As Sally giggled, Linda choked on a laugh. "Got it."

"Nolan and I had our wedding here," Beth said. "It's nice to see it used that way again."

Linda followed Beth's gaze to her husband. She still had trouble believing the slender redhead had married the cruel-looking man. But while Jessica was saying her vows, Beth had blown a kiss at Nolan, and his cold black eyes had warmed, his face softened.

I envy her.

Linda's marriage to Frederick had been stable, but he hadn't accepted who she was. To see these loving Dominant/submissive relationships was heartening.

And attending the reception had certain other benefits. "I must say, the gardens are lovely, but the human scenery is also rather fine." Her gaze wandered to the lanai where the Masters were talking. How the black tuxedoes could make the men look even bigger, she didn't understand.

Standing with the groomsmen, Sam wore a classic cut, dark gray suit with a white dress shirt and a silver-gray tie that matched his hair. Did the man have to look so dangerously sexy in every darn thing he wore?

"You must be looking at Sam." Snickering, Beth mimicked wiping drool off her chin. "That's the way I reacted when I first saw Nolan in a suit."

Linda's cheeks warmed. But...wow. The tailoring was superb, showing off his broad shoulders and flat stomach. She had a craving to undress him like a gift-wrapped present. Push his jacket open. Undo the shirt buttons. Run her finger down the deep line between his pectoral muscles. His eyes would light with amusement as if lit by the sun. Maybe he'd grip her hair, firmly push her to her knees, and direct her to free his cock. She'd take him in her mouth. Maybe he'd give her that look she'd never seen him use on anyone else—the one that softened his hard features and made his mouth curve just the slightest bit.

God, she loved the man. *Love?* She pressed a hand over the stuttering heart that had betrayed her into acting like an idiot in a romance novel. Love between Mr. Sadistic Rancher and Ms. Conservative Businesswoman. Right. How would a relationship between them even work? She still hadn't figured out how to balance her life as it was.

Then again, love was love. It didn't exactly conform to a person's schedule. Her lips curved. *Love.* Terrifying, yet what a wonderful gift.

Her eyebrows rose when a woman walked up to the Masters and took Sam's hand. Just like that. Sam's smile flashed. When he touched the woman's cheek, almost affectionately, Linda felt the bottom of her stomach drop.

Cold crept up her spine, and then she forced it down. There were lots of Shadowlands people here, and she knew...had seen him play with other women.

I don't want him to do that. But at the pond, he'd stated they wouldn't share. Her chest loosened, letting her breathe. She watched him. The woman might want more—*he's mine, darn you*—but that touch was all Sam had given her. And she wasn't getting his "special" smile.

"You look funny. Are you all right?" Sally asked.

Linda jumped. She'd forgotten she wasn't alone. Beth had returned to the bridesmaids' group, but Sally remained. "I'm okay. Just saw something that unsettled me a bit."

"Oh, I know that feeling," Sally muttered. She glanced around the open area, crowded with friends and family, then nodded to a cluster of Shadowlands members. "I've played with a lot of those guys. Usually had fun. But now and then, you get a Dom who's a real dickhead."

"Really?" Linda frowned. Raoul had made the place sound so safe. "In the Shadowlands?"

Sally scowled. "Master Z tries, but jerks still get in. Like one guy who just wanted blowjobs. He'd do what a sub wanted, but he wasn't interested in Domming—just getting off. Or some will do whatever they want if you haven't been real clear what you'll allow." She nodded at a lean man in a black suit. "That one slapped me. I hadn't put it on my hard limits, but Doms usually start out light in the first scene, you know?"

Linda studied the guy. Long nose, thin lips, sandy hair. He didn't look cruel, but she'd learned from the slavers that a man's appearance didn't always indicate what lay beneath. "What happened?"

"Jessica saw me crying and busted in." Sally grinned. "She got in trouble for not calling a dungeon monitor, but Z stopped the scene." She nodded at a younger, dark-haired Dom. "That one wanted his buddy to join our scene. Hey, I like threesomes but not with total strangers."

Linda shook her head. Maybe she'd have enjoyed threesomes if she were younger. Amusement bubbled up. Younger and less of a stick-in-the-mud. But she was, and she didn't want anyone but Sam touching her. "I can see how you'd get upset."

"Yeah. Then there was a really unnerving guy who—"

"Just one guy? Not two?" When a big man stepped up behind Sally and ran his hands down her arms, Linda recognized Vance Buchanan, one of the FBI agents who'd attended the trial. "You must be talking about me, pet. I'm going to tell Galen that he's so boring you didn't even mention him."

Sally spun and glared at the fair-skinned man. "I wasn't talking about either of you."

He had a hearty laugh. "You will be, sweetie. You will be." He smiled at Linda, then strolled over to his partner, a shorter man with an olive complexion. After a brief conversation, Galen turned to regard Sally with eyes as dark as his hair.

When Sally stiffened, the man grinned.

"I'd have to say they do seem to unsettle you." Linda smothered a laugh.

Although Galen had resumed talking to Vance, Sally continued to stare at them. "Those two. They've got tag teaming down to a science. And they make me feel stupid. I *never* feel stupid. I need a drink."

As Sally managed the impressive feat of stomping away in stilettos, Linda chuckled, then found an empty table to watch Z lead Jessica out for the first dance. They looked so perfect together that a sigh escaped.

A young man nearby grinned. "What's it about weddings that makes chicks all gushy?"

Linda huffed a laugh. He had black hair, brown eyes, and was about the same age as Charles. Her son would say exactly the same thing. "We're suckers for romance." She held her hand out. "I'm Linda, a friend of Jessica's."

"Richard." As they shook hands, he nodded to Z. "His son." He nudged the young man beside him. "This is my brother, Eric."

"Nice to meet you. They make a lovely couple," Linda said, hoping she wasn't putting her foot in it. She'd seen Charles's wariness with Sam. Young men could be very territorial.

"Yeah." Eric shook his head. "I didn't think so at first, and Mom was pissed off. But before Jessica, he used to look kinda sad. Cold." The two boys exchanged a look.

"You couldn't pay me enough to be a shrink to messed-up kids," Richard said. "He needed her."

Eric nodded. "She makes him happy."

Linda leaned back in her chair, brows pulling together. Jessica made Z happy; he needed her. *I want Sam to need me like that.*

As the newlyweds circled the grassy space, Z's expression when he looked down into Jessica's face showed so much love that Linda's eyes burned. *Could I make Sam that happy?*

The need to see him, to talk with him pulled at her, and she rose. Other dancers were flooding onto the grassy dance space. Gabi was scolding Marcus about something—at least until he yanked her up onto her tiptoes and kissed her so thoroughly that she sagged wordlessly against him. He grinned at Raoul, who had

Kim on his arm, and Raoul laughed. Kim wore a gorgeous sparkling choker—a symbolic collar. Someday, when she was ready, Raoul would attach a tiny padlock and keep the key.

Z's sons had fallen into an argument about the upcoming basketball game. Linda nodded to them before making her way toward the lanai. Around her, conversations hummed, broken occasionally by Cullen's hearty laughter and giggles from the trainees, whom Sally had joined.

When Linda reached the lanai, she saw Sam on the far side of the Shadowlands Masters. Did she really want to squeeze her way through a bunch of men? Would Sam even want to see her when he was with the guys?

As she hesitated, something...a sound, a word, a voice...sent an icy hand of uneasiness up her spine. Her grandmother would have called it someone stepping on her grave. She took a step back, another, then headed the opposite direction. Kari would let her hold the baby.

Before she'd reached the scattered tables, an arm curved around her waist, stopping her. "You look good."

Wasn't it odd how Sam's rough voice could smooth any discomfort away? Except perhaps the uneasiness he gave her just by being himself. "You too. Who knew you could wear a suit so well?"

He snorted. "Rather be in jeans, but this is better than the tux Nolan made me wear at his wedding."

Oh boy, the thought of him in a tux was lust inducing.

Sam's arm was firmly around her waist as he strolled with her. The feeling of being part of a couple again was wonderful.

Off to one side, an older couple stood and watched the dancing. When the white-haired man's eyes met hers, he smiled and raised his voice. "Sam. Introduce us."

Sam's grin flashed. Without waiting for her to agree, he guided her forward, his big hand a warm spot at the hollow of her back. "Martha, this is Linda." He glanced at Linda. "The ugly one is Gerald."

The wrinkles that softened her face couldn't hide Martha's dimples. "It's nice to finally meet you. We noticed you with Sam the other night."

The other night?

"At the club," Gerald offered, obviously noticing her confusion.

Them? "You're... You do..."

Martha's laugh sounded like...like Linda's mother's. "Yes, we do. We've been married for decades, and he's been my Master for almost that long."

"Decades?" Kinksters for most of their life?

Gerald gave a wheezing laugh. "We met when I wrote her a ticket for speeding, married soon after. Then we discovered the fun stuff about a decade after that."

Linda's mouth dropped open. "How in the world did you hear about BDSM? I mean, you were married. Did he take you to a club or something?"

"Oh my, no. Clubs like the Shadowlands were impossible to find, and heterosexuals weren't welcome at most." Wrinkles curved around the old woman's smile. "A friend gave me *The Story of O.*" She tsk-tsked. "The hero showed appallingly insensitive behavior at times, but the story was fascinating. When I told Gerald, he made me read him my favorite parts."

"She blushed with every page." Gerald kissed his wife's fingertips. "We experimented. Found a few people to answer questions."

"We were delighted when Zachary opened his club. It's pleasant knowing others in the lifestyle." Martha patted Sam's arm. "Do bring her to dinner sometime." Her eyes danced. "I make a mean pot roast."

"I'd love that." *Jumping right into this relationship, aren't you, girl?* She looked away and took a slow breath. She was old enough to know that loving someone didn't mean you could live with him, after all. But everything in her wanted to go full speed ahead.

As Martha and Gerald responded to a hail from another older couple, Linda looked up at Sam. "I should be going now. I have some accounting to do."

"Nope." He pulled her toward the grassy dance area. "Happens I like waltzing. None of that other crap. And I got a craving to feel your beautiful tits against me. In public." One eyebrow rose. "Especially with what you're wearing. Got panties on under that?"

Her face warmed, and she glanced around to make sure no one was close. "Of course I do."

"Since it's a vanilla function, I can't order you not to wear them." He mercilessly pulled her against him, closer than he should for a waltz. He had a lead as strong as his attitude, and the realization gave her a quiver of appreciation.

He leaned down to murmur in her ear. "But if I find you in briefs at the Shadowlands, I'll rip them off and whip whatever parts they covered."

Despite the cool, high-sixties weather, heat blasted into Linda as if the weather had turned to a muggy July day. To hide her face, she pressed her forehead against his shoulder.

With a rumbled laugh, he said, "Goddamned pants weren't tailored for a hard dick. We're dancing till I'm presentable...or I'll drag you into the gardens and take care of the problem in a different way."

"Shhh. I can't believe you talk like this."

"Mmmmh. And I can see you're upset." As he spun them in a circle, he rubbed his chest against her breasts and, even through the clothing, could undoubtedly feel how her nipples had spiked.

God, I love you. But even as she pressed closer, she knew it wasn't something he was ready to hear. Considering his past marriage, he might never be ready.

And considering how screwed up she still was? Going slowly made far too much sense.

Chapter Twenty

In the Shadowlands, Sam leaned against the bar, keeping an eye on the door. No Linda yet. His gut was coiled like a rattlesnake about to strike. Over the past couple of weeks, she'd been out of town on buying trips to restock her store. The two times she'd returned, he'd been tied up with the construction, the groves, planting.

Was she pulling away? He snorted. Men often stepped back from a relationship after a wedding, but not women. Wouldn't that be fucked-up?

He wasn't comfortable with how much he missed talking with her. He missed her sweet body against him in bed. Missed hearing her laugh. She'd given him her cell phone number, but damn. He wasn't the type to talk on a phone.

"Sam." Wearing the gold-trimmed vest of a dungeon monitor, Jake strolled up. "Z asked if you wanted to monitor the Gardens tonight."

Linda had said she'd try to make it tonight. "Not this time."

"Here go, boys." Cullen handed Jake a bottled water and thumped one down in front of Sam before moving up the bar to mix a drink from the fancy-ass liquors.

"Thanks, Cullen," Jake called. He opened the bottle and regarded Sam quizzically. "Never seen you play in the Capture Gardens."

"Never will." Sam studied the man. A shame it hadn't worked out with Heather. "Served in 'Nam. I can understand the rape fantasy. Seeing it in real life left a bad taste."

Jake lowered the bottle without drinking. "I get that. Saw the aftermath a time or two." He paused for a moment, then said slowly, "You monitor the Gardens a lot."

Sam shrugged. Fantasy was fine, but there wouldn't be any *real* rapes happening on his watch.

As if Sam had spoken, Jake frowned. "Got it." After sucking his water down, he checked his watch. "I'll keep an eye on the Games for you tonight."

Good man. As the Dom strolled away, Sam watched Linda appear in the door. *And there she is.* The tightness in his shoulders relaxed.

Her black dress was midthigh—too long—but the way it clung to her ample curves left him in a forgiving mood. She was barefoot too, so Ben hadn't approved whatever shoes she'd hoped to wear. She made it a few steps into the clubroom before the noise stopped her.

Sam grinned. Z and Jessica had returned from their honeymoon. The club had been closed for the two weeks they were gone, and now everyone was in a celebratory mood.

The music was an upbeat Lacuna Coil, making the scenes lighter than normal. The Mistress caning her blonde sub danced a few steps between each strike. Over at a suspension scene, the Dom had set the submissive to swinging in time with the music.

Linda took it in, picking up the atmosphere immediately. She bounced a little herself. To Sam's satisfaction, when she spotted him, she headed over immediately.

When he caught her lavender-and-lime scent, he hardened. As he roused to the darker side of the Shadowlands, the beast inside him rose at the approach of its prey. A sadist's toy.

Her pupils dilated at the look he gave her. Under her silky black top, her nipples contracted into hard spikes.

Good. Someone wanted to play. Curving his fingers around her nape, he cupped her breast with his other hand. When his thumb circled a nipple, he saw the tension mount inside her. Damn, but he'd missed her. "I'd order you a drink, but I'd rather hurt you first."

She looked shocked. Then red streaked her cheeks.

He kissed her lightly and whispered against her mouth, "See you cry."

Her lips quivered under his.

"Hear you scream."

"Oh, heavens." Her voice was as husky as if she'd already gifted him with a few screams.

He fisted her hair, keeping her in place, then tightened his fingers on one nipple, firmly enough to hear her suck in air. As he watched, he could see how the pain slid into her like a caress.

Arousal lit her eyes and darkened her lips.

"Let's go." He led her through the main room, down the hallway, and into the colder, crueler dungeon room. Manacles and shackles were embedded in the rock walls. Chains hung from the dark ceiling beams. A queen's throne near the back held a Mistress with a slave worshipping her feet. Whimpering came from a submissive on the bondage table who had a dominant couple taking turns with wax play. A thin male sub strapped in the leather sling groaned as his Dom fucked him hard.

Sam put his arm around Linda and pulled her close, studying her face. Anxiety and arousal, but no fear. She'd come a long way in trusting him. He picked a free area and yanked on the chains dangling from a heavy beam. Sturdy. Z was as careful as any Dom he'd met, but checking equipment was a habit. No submissive would suffer harm he didn't intend to give her.

Linda's gaze focused on the chain, and she jumped when he ordered, "Strip and kneel."

Her sweet compliance made him smile.

"Good girl." He really did like the submissive-masochists. And he intended to test her surrender, to push it a step further.

Her melting brown eyes showed both trepidation and need. It had been over two weeks since they'd played, since he'd hurt her. They'd both enjoy tonight.

He bent and fastened well-padded leather wrist cuffs on her with panic snaps attached to the D-rings.

Her eyes went wide, and she started to shiver. Just the way he liked his subs. Pain was meat and potatoes, but anxiety added the dessert. "Up, girl."

She rose, moving into position slowly. Odd how a masochist craved pain yet wanted to avoid it.

He clipped her wrist cuffs to a place on the chain that would keep her steady but not up on tiptoes. Not only because she didn't have a younger woman's supple joints, but also because he wanted her able to wiggle her ass this time. A Velcro strap around her ankles kept her legs together and limited other mobility. Her breathing had sped up, and he took a minute to stroke her smooth back. She had the prettiest dimples on each side of her low spine. Her legs were tanned, but her ass remained a seductive white that begged for stripes.

"Relax, missy. This won't hurt much."

She snorted. "'This won't hurt much' from a sadist is as believable as hearing a root canal is just a little uncomfortable."

"You're right." He grinned and slapped her ass, leaving red handprints on the white canvas. And because he enjoyed the sound of his palm hitting skin and her sharp inhalations, he spanked her even longer. After a bit, her muscles loosened and her ass pushed back for each swat. His cock hardened, wanting to satisfy her unspoken request, but he'd wait until she was breathing in the stinging like incense.

When her skin glowed a rosy red, he decided to up her arousal. Some masochists were a straight line—pain alone. Some liked a base of pain and sex, and he loved to drive both sides of that triangle right to a peak at the top.

After pulling a stool over to her side, he donned a glove and lubed the fingers. With a hand on her belly to keep her still, he forced his slick his fingers between her ass cheeks.

"Noooooo." Even her whining was beautifully musical.

Trying not to laugh, he pressed one finger against her anus, breached the rim of muscle, and slid in.

Her back arched in unspoken protest as she gasped.

"We're just getting started, you know." He emphasized the statement by sliding his free hand up to give each breast a hard squeeze. Even as she hissed a protest, her ass cheeks clenched on his hand, making him grin. He added another finger. Damn, she was tight. His dick was uncomfortable inside his leather pants.

When he moved his hand from her breasts down to her pussy, she was as slick as any Dom could want. Still seated on the round stool, he pinned her legs between his knees. Watching her face, he set his thumb over her clit and thrust two fingers into her cunt. Her asshole clenched in response around his other fingers. Circling her clit, he alternated finger thrusts between her cunt and asshole until he heard her breathing change, until he felt her leg muscles tighten as she approached orgasm.

The perfect time to add in more pain.

When he slid his fingers out, she groaned in frustration.

After disposing of the glove, Sam took a kiss, playing with her nipples at the same time. When he lifted his head, her eyes were closed, her cheeks flushed. Beautiful Linda.

Wrapping an arm around her waist, he bent and swatted her ass. Her body tensed—no, she wasn't in subspace yet. The beast in him loved this point, when she still felt the pain a moment before the pleasure. She was almost to the shift, after which every blow would feel good.

As guttural Lesiëm chants came from the dungeon's speakers, Sam spanked her ass in time with the music. Undoubtedly, each swat vibrated that tender little asshole he'd just stretched.

When a few people came into the dungeon to stand by the wall and watch, Linda noticed and flushed.

Sam grasped her chin, turning her head toward him. "Attention on me."

"Yes, Sir." Her eyes focused on him. Only him.

"That's right, girl." He ran his knuckles gently down her cheek. A submissive's need to please could often override any other instinct, and Linda was deeply submissive.

And ready for more. Her breasts were puckered nicely, her cheeks flushed, lips reddened. Damn, she was pretty.

He picked up the cane from his bag and started on her ass. Eventually, he'd move around to her breasts for some fun.

SOMETIME LATER, AS Linda slid back into reality, her skin swam with lingering sensations. Her breasts ached with the most delicious burn from the light caning followed by the crop. As if in balance, her back, bottom, and upper thighs felt scalded with sublime pleasure.

Everything had felt so *good*. Her head sagged against her upraised arm; her mind as hazy as if filled with fragrant smoke that made curling tendrils in the empty space.

Time had passed. Maybe a lot. She'd gotten off twice and still wanted more. More pain, more touches. *More, more, more.* But Sam had said no—said she'd had enough. And now he flicked the crop up and down her back in mere touches of velvety pleasure rather than a conflagration. He was bringing her up slowly, barely cracking the window to reality. He was so careful of her.

And she loved him so much.

Her body throbbed, but now she could feel how the air was slightly cool against her legs. How her shoulders were starting to ache. The heavy sound of a flogger came from her right. People were talking somewhere in a low hum of conversation. She tried to raise her head and gave it up as a lost effort. Didn't seem to matter. Everything was so comfortable. Her blood sang through her veins with lovely little surges; air flowed in and out of her lungs. What a nicely working body.

"Linda?"

"Mmmm?"

Sam made that low snorty chuckle. "You're still off in space."

She started to close her eyes—realized they'd already closed—and instead tipped her head, hoping he'd make that growly sound—the one that squeezed her spine, hand over hand, right down to her core.

Instead, she heard other voices from the observers. A tenor, a baritone, a woman's contralto. Then a higher tenor with an odd...scratchy sound.

Goose bumps broke out on her body as her chest tightened. *That voice.* Her hands fisted as the stench of the slave cages swept over her. *Her own body stinking of urine and fear, women sobbing and screaming, and—*

"Goddamn." Hard hands closed on her shoulders, a body pressed against her, and she cringed, shook her head, trying to get the fog to lift. "No. No." Her lips were numb, her words slurred.

"Open your eyes."

The rough command swept through her, lifting the pressure on her chest so she could take a breath. Many, many breaths. The air was too heavy to fill her lungs.

"Eyes on me." Fingers gripped her chin, lifted her head.

Eyes. Hers were scrunched shut. She forced them open and stared into the blazing blue fire of Sam's gaze. As her knees buckled, her weight dropped painfully onto her restrained arms. She jerked at them, needing to be free. *Get away. Run.*

"Easy, girl." His powerful arm closed around her waist, holding her up. With his other hand, he used the quick release to free her left wrist, then the right.

"I'll get her ankles, Sam." A woman's voice. Worried.

Chills ran up Linda's spine, spreading to fill her until she shuddered. A blast of heat swept over her skin, followed by more ice. She couldn't stop shaking.

The world spun as Sam lifted her into his arms. "Look at me, Linda. Just at me," he growled. Lights flickered to the sides as if she were in a car moving through a fog-filled landscape. Lost in a blurry world.

But his arms were around her, his chest solid against her side. A tremor shook her so horribly she moaned, and the fear-filled sound of her own voice shocked her.

Somewhere darker, quieter, he sat down.

He said something incomprehensible, yet the senseless growling smoothed the terrified knots in her head. Something wrapped around her. Warm. Fuzzy. Sam shifted, pulling it securely around her.

Naked. She'd been naked. Now she wasn't. She blinked, expecting to see a ballroom filled with buyers and slaves. Her gaze focused on a pedestal planter filled with ferns. Another held begonias. The tiny blooms were like stars in the dark foliage. Life in the darkness. No one was screaming. The police had shouted and—no, that wasn't here.

She wasn't at the slave auction.

Men were talking. Her brows drew together as she tried to understand the words.

"What happened? She didn't seem anywhere close to a panic attack." A voice like the most expensive of dark chocolates. Familiar.

"Hit some trigger, but damned if I know what." The subterranean rumble through the chest under her ear. She could listen to him forever. "Never had a sub panic at the *end* of a scene. She'd been totally in subspace, and I was bringing her down."

"That is odd. May I speak to her?"

"Do it. She's back with us."

She felt a brush of something on her hair. Sam was rubbing his chin on the top of her head in the most comforting of gestures, the one that said, *I got you.*

The other man's voice lowered. "Linda, I feel you listening. Can you look at me?"

Why did her eyes keep closing? Sam's arm was across her waist, his fingers holding her hip. She curled her fingers around his forearm—*stay here*—and forced her eyes open. Saw nothing except skin. Her face was pressed against his chest. *Don't want to move. Don't want to see.*

"C'mon, baby. Head up." His voice was deeper. Rougher. She'd worried him. *Love him. Don't want to worry him.*

She dug her fingernails into his skin so no one could snatch her away, then lifted her head. He held her tighter as if to reinforce she was safe. She turned her head.

Master Z was on one knee, both forearms on his thigh as he waited for her. "That's a good girl." His smile was faint, his gaze dark gray. Someone else she'd worried.

"I'm sorry." Her throat felt as if it had rusted from years of disuse. "It's your coming-home celebration. I didn't mean—"

Sam made a gruff sound of disbelief, but his arms didn't loosen.

As long as he held her, she didn't care how many noises he made. Her body was waking, starting to feel everything he'd done. The burgeoning fear made her skin feel as if a scrub brush had scraped her raw.

"You're more important." Z's voice was low, patient. He didn't move. She'd lured a kitten from under her porch in just that way. Fuzzy, soft kitten. "You had a panic attack," Z said. "Can you tell me what happened?"

Did he think Sam had done something wrong? "Not Sam. He didn't do—"

"Not Samuel," he agreed. "Or you wouldn't cling to him like that." His gaze dropped to where her fingers were clenched around Sam's arm.

She must be hurting him. She couldn't make her fingers loosen. A whimper slid out of her.

"Shhh." Sam's whisper ruffled her hair. "Hang on all you want, girl."

"Did you see something that frightened you?" Master Z asked.

"My eyes were closed," she said as Sam muttered, "Her eyes were closed."

"Feel something that brought back memories?"

She pulled in a breath. Right before she'd panicked, she'd felt the tiny flickers of the crop, like a light touch after an orgasm, just enough to keep it going. He was good at giving pain. Giving orgasms too. The corners of her lips tilted up as she brought her attention back to Z.

"You're feeling better." He was smiling slightly. "So not anything Sam did."

"Did you smell something?" Sam's voice was as soft as a gravel truck could get.

Think, Linda. She tilted her head, remembering the feel of the whip, then the smells of the dungeon. A mineral scent along with the fragrance of leather and a hint of the cleanser. "No."

"That leaves sound," Z said. "Tell me what you heard, Linda."

The whip flicking. "Music. Gregorian chants. People talking. They were watching." She moved her shoulders. "But that didn't bother me." Nice voices. Talking. *A tenor, a baritone, a woman's contralto. A higher tenor with an...odd scratchy sound.* Her breath caught as if someone had stomped on her chest.

Sam's arms squeezed the last of the air from her. "Got you, Linda. You're safe."

Her eyes had scrunched closed again. *I've heard that tenor before.* She forced her eyes open.

Master Z held her gaze. "Tell us."

"He was here. Someone...someone from..." She forced the word past her lips. "A slaver. I know his laugh. His voice."

Sam growled under his breath.

Master Z's eyes turned almost black. "What does he look like?"

Over and over, she tried to put a face with the voice. Nothing. She was disappointing Sam. Tears stung her eyes. "I'm sorry. I'm sorry."

Sam's arm moved, even with her holding it, as he tilted her face up to look at her. "Sorry for what, baby?"

"I don't know his face," she whispered. "I never..."

They stayed silent.

"In the cages. We were in cages for a while. And when people came, I kept my eyes closed. Trying to make them go away." *Make everything all go away.*

"Closed your eyes, huh?" Sam huffed an actual laugh. "Bet you hid under the covers as a little girl like Nicole did." He wasn't mad. Wasn't blaming her. In fact, his hand slid from her chin to cup her cheek as he tucked her back against his chest.

She let out a sigh, feeling her body melt into him. Warm. Safe.

"Linda," Z asked, "are you sure you heard someone from when you were imprisoned? Could the voice just be similar?"

"I'm sure."

Silence. She felt the owner of the Shadowlands study her and realized her eyes were shut again.

"Talk later, Z," Sam said. "I took her deep. She's going to drop hard."

The rustle of clothes. She didn't want to open her eyes. Maybe the bad ones would all go away. Only they never had before. Closing her eyes hadn't worked. Hadn't saved her. Nothing had. She felt tears spill from her eyes to roll down her cheeks.

"Linda. Look at me." When she opened her eyes, Z was looking down at her with a gentle expression.

"Samuel and I are proud of you, little one. You did well."
He squeezed her shoulder and left, his gait smooth and
silent.

A knot loosened inside her but didn't halt the
sadness, a thick ocean fog through the streets of her
mind, covering her world in gray. Sad, sad gray. *Is that
where Holly is? Buried in gray?*

A sob made her breathing stumble. Then another.

Sam rumbled something, and after a second she
realized what he'd said. "Cry, girl. I won't let go. Cry."

Burying her head in his shoulder, she did.

* * * *

To see the redheaded ex-slave have a panic attack
had been quite diverting. As the spotter strolled toward
the unattached submissives' area, he smiled.

Even more satisfying was seeing the Dom's scene
crash and burn. Such a pity, *Master* Sam. The asshole.
Although Davies could wield a whip well, he always
stopped too soon. Didn't break the submissives, didn't
force them to grovel. And afterward, he treated the sluts
like pampered babies.

Disgusting. Aaron's jaw clenched. Stupid slaves
would kneel and beg Davies for a flogging. Some of them
were ones who'd turned Aaron down when he'd invited
them to play. *I'm far more of a Master than he'll ever be.
I've fucked more women, hurt more women.*

Killed more women.

He smoothed his hair down as satisfaction filled
him. Yes, he'd had a fine time recently. He'd been smart
to continue using prostitutes. They were sleazy,
but...nicely simple. Flash some money, pick one up, deal

with her how he pleased. Leave the body in a ditch and take his money back. Yes, he had to be cautious about leaving evidence, but at least he had no Harvest Association Overseer to placate over damaged—or dead— merchandise.

And for a pleasant treat between kills, he used the Shadowlands.

As he neared the bar, he noticed the side door was ajar. Z must have opened the Capture Gardens. Now that promised to be fun. Perhaps a bit risky, since Z and the Masters kept a close eye on the proceedings. But there were ways around that.

As he approached the unattached submissives, he surveyed the offerings. Two of them he'd played with before. *No.* Not in a mood to exert himself unduly, he also rejected the most athletic-looking women. He'd save his energy for roughing up his prey. And fucking her. Up the ass would suit his mood tonight.

A tattooed one caught his eye. Nice. But then he saw the trainee cuffs on her wrists. Not a good choice. Z kept a close eye on the trainees. All the Masters did.

Ah, perhaps that brunette. She couldn't be more than midtwenties. He preferred older slaves, but for what he had in mind in the Gardens, an inexperienced submissive would be best. He stalked into the sitting area, gave them all an impersonal, cold stare, and watched them react to his dominance. "I'm looking for some sport in the Capture Gardens," he said.

Three of the submissives, including his choice, showed interest. He held his hand out to her. "Would you care to play the game?"

She jumped to her feet. "Sure."

Noticing a slut he'd used before shaking her head *no* toward the girl, he smoothly moved the girl away. "Do you have a safe word?"

"I use red." The girl tried to look confident.

He almost laughed. "Red will be fine." Wasn't it a shame she wouldn't be able to yell with his hand over her mouth? And he could tell that when he broke the insecure sub down and scared her enough, she wouldn't return to the Shadowlands. Wouldn't tell a soul.

Chapter Twenty-One

Sam scowled as he watched Linda drive down his farm lane toward the front gate. Goddamned stubborn woman. She sure as hell hadn't slept long enough but still dragged herself out of bed to sing in a church service. Wouldn't even wait for him to get the gate for her.

His mood lightened as he remembered how she'd snarled at him. Her grumpy morning face was damn cute.

And he'd see her later. Z had called already this morning. He'd arranged a late-afternoon meeting today with her, the Feds, and the other Masters. Just what she needed. More stress in her life. At least, she'd agreed to let him pick her up at her home after work and drive her to the Shadowlands for the meeting.

With a snap of his fingers for Conn, he headed down the drive. Since the construction crew took Sundays off, he'd lock the gate before heading to the orchards.

Halfway down the lane, Conn let out an "incoming" bark as a car turned in. The vehicle was an ancient two-door with dings and dents all over the bumper. One headlight gone. Blonde at the wheel. *Hell.* Even before he saw her face, he knew, and his gut felt as if he'd swallowed glass.

Without thinking—just to keep her from his house—he stepped into the center of the drive, forcing her to stop if she didn't want to run him over. Muscles tense, he prepared to jump out of the way if she was too drugged out to notice an obstacle.

She stopped.

His fury grew, and he yanked open her door. Conn growled.

She gave him a beseeching look. "Sam. Darling. I know you didn't want—"

"Get the hell off my land." She wasn't high but strung out instead. Face sweaty. Hands shaking. His jaw tightened. No matter how often he'd seen her like this, it still grated. No one—ex-wife or not—should do that to herself.

He smothered the maddening need to fix her. Year after year, he'd tried that. Programs, clinics, therapy, detoxing wards. The minute she was released, she'd return to shooting poison into her veins.

"I need a little help, darling. To buy food."

Right. Any cash would go straight into a smack buy. "Been through this, Nancy. No money. You aren't gone when I reach the house, I call the cops."

"You fucking bastard." Her mask of niceness slipped, and mean replaced it. "I put up with you for years, gave you a child. You can't even spare me a few bucks?"

"You get money from the trustee every month. You get no more." Their divorce had been ugly, but the evidence of her drug use and toxic behavior had disgusted the judge. She hadn't been awarded alimony. Nonetheless, she was Nicole's mother. He'd hired a trustee to pay for a room and groceries, and to deal with her. Because he couldn't.

Seeing her—each and every time—left him frozen inside. It would take a few days before he even wanted to see people again.

"Asshole," she hissed like the viper she'd turned out to be. "I loved you."

"Only when you wanted something from me." His mouth twisted at the foul taste.

"I love you, Sam. Darling, I owe Stevie a thousand dollars. Can you give it to me?"

"I love you, Sam. Oh, darling, I broke my laptop. Will you buy me a new one?"

Broken, hell. She'd hocked that laptop for drug money. Although he'd canceled her credit cards and stopped handing her cash, he'd been slow to realize she was selling things off. She'd even pawned some of Nicole's toys. "You wouldn't know love if it bit you in the ass." As ice wrapped around him, he welcomed the way it blunted his rage. His memories.

"Fine. I'll go to Nicole."

"You bother Nicole, I cut off your monthly money, and you get nothing. Get out of here." He slammed her door shut and stepped away.

Two minutes later, as her car squealed down the road, he locked the gate and flipped on the security alarm. After the second time she'd broken into the house, he'd shelled out for the fancy-ass system.

For a minute, many minutes, he stood, unable to move. Her car was no longer in sight, but her presence lingered like a rotting carcass, casting a stench over the farm.

Leaning on the gate, he felt as hollowed out as if she'd gutted him. His energy, his emotions were drained. Turning, he looked up toward the farm buildings. The sky showed clouds rolling in. The temperature was probably dropping, although he was already cold to the bone.

Got chores to do. He couldn't seem to move.

With a whine, Conn pawed at Sam's boot.

Sam shook his head, knowing he should reassure the dog. Couldn't. Moving slowly, he started the long walk up the drive.

* * * *

As the wintery sunlight came through the windshield of Sam's truck, he drove toward the Shadowlands. Linda sat quietly in the passenger seat.

Hours after Nancy's visit, he still felt...off. Cold, inside and out. Like parts of him had been ripped away, leaving a husk behind.

After a few attempts to talk that had fallen flat, Linda had remained silent. He glanced over at her.

She was watching him. "Are you okay, Sam?"

Why the hell did she ask him that? "Yeah."

"I don't believe you." Her brows drew together. "Is it because of last night? Because our scene went from wonderful to horrible?"

His gut twisted. He was a Dom. If anything went wrong in a scene, it was his fault. For a second, he thought about explaining, but the blackness roiling through his head eroded the words into dust. "I'm fine."

Her huff wasn't a happy one. "I wish you'd tell me what's wrong. Can't you talk to me?"

Talk? From a distance, the windows of Z's manor glinted. "Nothing to say."

Her fingers pleated the bottom of her shirt. "You let me cry, get me to dump all over you, but won't share what's bothering you." She gave him an unhappy look. "Contrary to popular belief, a Dom isn't a bulletproof superman. I want to help when you feel bad, Sam."

"No need."

She pulled back as if he'd slapped her.

He should apologize. Take her hand. But ropes had been wrapped around his soul. His hands tightened on the steering wheel, and he turned into the drive to the Shadowlands. Beneath the tall palms that lined the road, the flower beds seemed garishly bright in the gray light.

* * * *

As Linda walked beside Sam through the side gate in the privacy fence, she tried to ignore the ache in her chest.

Although he was hurting, apparently she wasn't someone he felt he could lean on or share with.

Last night, she'd been so happy to see him. Her heart had actually lifted, bounced, danced. And he'd comforted her so sweetly after that horrible scene.

Today he was terrifyingly distant. The lines bracketing his mouth were deeper, his eyes a colder blue. He was suffering, and she wanted to help. A shiver ran through her as her stupid insecurities flared up. He didn't need her. Didn't need anything from her.

Without speaking, he held the side gate open for her, and they crossed the yard to the back lanai. The decorations from the wedding were gone, but the landscaping was still stunningly beautiful. People were scattered in chairs and couches in the screen-covered outdoor room. After a second, Linda recognized the two

Mistresses, Olivia and Anne, whom Rainie had pointed out during the wedding ceremony. All of the Shadowlands Masters—Dan, Nolan, Cullen, Marcus, and Raoul—were present. Z sat at a long iron-and-oak table beside Vance and Galen. The two FBI agents headed the task force concentrating on the Harvest Association.

In jeans and a pink scoop-neck T-shirt, Jessica was serving soft drinks to the guests. Her "collar" sparkled in the sunlight almost as much as she did. She saw them and set the drinks down. "Linda!"

Pushing her worries back, Linda abandoned Sam to receive an enthusiastic hug from the short blonde. "Welcome home. Did you have a good honeymoon?"

"Awesome. Mostly." After a glance over her shoulder at Master Z, her voice dropped. "When we got to the chalet, I gave him the toys I bought from Rainie. A present, right? But the bastard used them all that night. Every. Single. One."

Remembering the number of items Jessica had purchased, Linda bit the inside of her cheek to keep from laughing.

"Yeah." Jessica narrowed her eyes. "You know how some Doms don't let you get off until they say? It's much, much worse when they won't let you stop. Seriously."

Like what Sam had done to her after the bachelorette party? "I know *exactly* what you mean, and all I can say is that I'm really happy I didn't buy half the things you did."

Jessica busted out laughing so hard that everyone looked at them. "Damn Doms."

Linda's spirits lifted. How lovely to hear laughter.

Smiling, Z shook his head and said to Marcus, "I thought two weeks away from your little brat would be good for her."

"Doesn't look like it," Nolan said. "You've got your work cut out for you."

"Indeed," Z said.

"Work? He calls me work?" Jessica said under her breath. She glared at Nolan. Then her eyes sliced to Linda, and she whispered, "That Dom needs a lesson. Let's work on corrupting Beth."

Linda choked on a laugh.

Z raised his voice. "I asked Galen and Vance to give us a rundown on what's happening. Then perhaps Linda can talk with us."

He'd want her to talk about that voice. About the slavers. Of course, she'd known the plan. Sickness rose in her belly.

Even as Z stood, concern on his face, Jessica tugged her to a chair. "Sit before you fall."

"Thank you." A shadow fell across her face. She looked up. Sam had taken a position next to her, arms crossed over his chest. The tightness under her breastbone eased slightly, then came back as she realized he wasn't even looking at her. He stood there with a remote expression as if he were watching a boring television show. Not involved at all. *Why? Why, Sam?* Unable to help herself, she put her hand on his hip.

He shifted away.

She looked down, blinking hard. After a minute, she realized Jessica had sat beside her. Had taken her hand.

After squeezing Jessica's hand in gratitude, Linda concentrated on the discussion.

Galen had been talking, his intensity a distinct contrast to his more laid-back partner. But both held the unmistakable aura of authority.

"We've eliminated the Harvest Association in three of the four quadrants," Galen said. "The last one is the most entrenched and will be the most difficult."

"Linda, I wanted to update you." Vance's blue eyes met hers. "The murderer you helped convict lasted three days in the penitentiary, then was shivved during a prison yard fight. He didn't make it."

She stared at him, unable to process the information.

After a moment of silence, Marcus sighed. "I do believe that sounds like a fitting end. May God have mercy on his soul."

Someday, someday she hoped she'd feel the same. Maybe then, she'd know she was healed. She pulled in a slow breath. *Be at peace, Holly. He won't hurt anyone else.*

Vance continued, enumerating other convictions. Then he glanced at Raoul. "A while back, we recovered a slave from Greville's estate."

Greville. Linda's mouth compressed. He'd been Kim's owner and had stabbed her. Almost killed her.

Raoul straightened. "Greville bought a slave after Kim?"

"I'm afraid so. I don't know if you want to share this with Kim, but the girl was totally closed up. Not talking. Almost catatonic." Galen's lips tightened. "She came out of it soon after I told her Greville was dead, that another slave had killed him."

"I thank you for the news," Raoul said. "Mi gatita might find it helps the guilt she carries for his death."

Poor Kim. But thinking of the lives the slavers had ruined, Linda couldn't keep from shuddering. Unable to help herself, she glanced over at Sam. He was watching her, but he didn't move closer.

"We're still trying to locate all the missing women," Vance said. "Not many of the slavers are willing to cooperate."

"Those fucktards," Anne growled. "Let me have a turn with them, and they'll beg to tell you everything."

As laughter broke out, Linda glanced inquisitively at Jessica.

Jessica leaned over and whispered, "Remember, she's a sadist." Her eyebrows waggled. "And she loves cock-and-ball torture."

Oh. Ow. But wouldn't that be a wonderful kind of justice?

"Now that you're caught up, let's talk about the spotter in the Shadowlands," Vance said.

Was he talking about the person whose voice she'd heard? "What's that?"

"Since the association targets women in the lifestyle, BDSM clubs are prime hunting grounds," Galen said. "The spotter chooses which women should be kidnapped."

Linda shivered.

"You arrested the Overseer," Olivia said. "He worked with the spotter. Can't he identify him?"

"He didn't know the spotter's name, just had an e-mail address and phone number." Vance's jaw hardened. "The description the Overseer gave us fits half the men in the club, and since he's blind, he can't ID the bastard."

"You picked up a lot of the association personnel. None of them can help?" Cullen asked.

"The association hires a different person for each part of a kidnapping," Galen said. "A spotter to pick the women, an investigator to choose the most vulnerable, one for the kidnapping, others to 'warehouse' the victims until the auction. One person in that chain knows very little about the others."

Vance nodded at Sam and Raoul. "Without you two, this quadrant would still be in operation."

"But the bastard who targeted Shadowlands submissives remains." Z's voice was low, but the fury was plain.

"Surprising you couldn't pick him out, psychologist-mind reader that you are," Cullen said.

Linda thought Cullen was joking, but no one laughed.

"I wondered that myself," Z said. "But a Dom considering a submissive for a scene has the same emotions as the spotter—lust and acquisitiveness. I doubt there's any guilt present."

Galen took a sip of his drink. "You're right. Human traffickers feel women are meant to be slaves."

Yes, Linda thought. The slavers had made her feel as if she were nothing. She unclenched her hands. *Stay focused.* "So last night I probably heard the man who targeted Gabi and Jessica for kidnapping?"

No wonder Z was so furious.

"The rat bastard," Jessica muttered. "If I find him, I'll help Anne crush his widdle dick."

Linda snickered.

"You find something funny about this?" Nolan growled in disbelief.

"It's just"—Linda swallowed down more laughter—"if he picked Jessica and Gabi for a *rebellious* slave auction, he's got a really good eye."

After a second, Jessica burst into giggles. No one else even smiled.

Galen stared at the two of them, laughing like fools, before commenting to Z, "Women really are the tougher sex."

"Indeed." Z picked up Jessica and sat down with her in his lap. "Silence, pet. Let's keep going."

"Z said you'd heard the man during your captivity. Do you remember when?" Vance asked Linda.

Her amusement disappeared, and she tried to steady her breathing. "It would have to be before the first auction. On the boat. I-I had my eyes closed. Didn't look at anything."

Galen tilted his head. "Why only then?"

The temperature in the garden seemed to drop, and she wrapped her arms around herself, wishing Sam would hold her the way Z was holding Jessica. But today...today he wasn't the man she knew. "They stored us belowdecks in k-kennels."

Galen nodded. "We impounded a boat like that." His level gaze met hers, silently saying, *It can't hurt you now.*

The tightness around her chest loosened a little. "On the boat, select buyers came to look at us. I-I felt like an animal. In a cage. Being stared at. I'd curl up on the floor and close my eyes." She pulled in a breath. "The man I heard in the Shadowlands was in a group arguing the merits of older or younger slaves."

Vance frowned. "Z said you were sure that was the man, so he must have a pretty distinctive voice. Can you describe it?"

She cocked her head to listen to the memory. Her nausea increased. "Tenor. Thin and slightly metallic."

Everyone stared at her.

"What?" she asked.

Marcus smiled. "That won't help to find him, darlin'. Tell us, how is his voice different from a normal one?"

"There are no normal voices. Everybody is different."

"Are they now?" Galen gave her an odd look. "If we blindfolded you, would you be able to tell our voices apart."

She nodded, feeling like a freak.

"An auditory person," Z murmured. "Do you sing?"

She nodded again.

"Dropped out getting her BA in music," Sam said. "Sings in a choir—was director for a while. Has a piano and a guitar."

She looked up at him. He might be staring out at the gardens, but apparently he was listening. Her feeling of loss lightened slightly. "My son tries to fake me out on the phone by assuming different voices. He never wins." She stopped, searching for a word that didn't exist. "The resonance? Timbre? The pattern is the same whether baritone or soprano."

"I have the attendance records from last night, but almost the entire membership was there," Z said grimly.

"Line up all the members and Linda listens to them?" Olivia suggested.

"Getting them there at one time would be difficult, even without the members who were present from out of the area," Z said. "And unfortunately, contact information isn't always current."

"If the spotter caught a whisper of a lineup, he'd disappear." Galen turned to Linda. "Can you spend time at the Shadowlands? Just to listen?" Galen asked. "Then if you can't pick him out that way, we'll try rounding them up."

"I... Yes. I can." The thought made her feel sick.

"No." Sam growled, speaking for the first time. "You won't."

She stiffened. "That's not your choice." Memories swamped her. Sickened her. *I decide when you piss. When you eat. Who you fuck.* The Overseer's hand lashing across her face, the pain as he slapped her over and over. *"Don't think, slut. Just obey."* She swallowed against rising bile and tried to straighten her shoulders. She was free. No one could order her around. Never again.

Galen frowned at Sam and then gave her an intense look. "It could be dangerous. Despite the arrests of his companions, the spotter is bold enough—and needy enough—to return to the Shadowlands. He'd react badly to the threat of exposure."

Vance nodded. "The club won't be open until next Friday. You think this over."

A chill of fear raised the hairs on Linda's nape. "I'll let you know."

She'd had enough. Although none of the rest appeared ready to leave, she turned to Sam. "Can you take me home?"

* * * *

Sam pulled up in front of Linda's house after a trip as silent as the one to the Shadowlands. He needed to talk to her, to convince her to stay away from the Shadowlands.

He didn't speak.

"Thanks for the ride." Linda slid out of the truck and closed the door.

Hell. Watching her walk up the sidewalk, he spotted white blotches on the house. More paint had been scrubbed away. The spray painter had hit again. Anger lit a low burn in his gut.

He got out of the truck. "Wait."

She came back down the sidewalk. "Yes?" Her voice was tight. The afternoon had been hard on her.

He hadn't been any help. Guilt and worry started to erode the ice inside him. "Got your paint. King's antigraffiti stuff. I stopped by the paint store, and they matched your blue."

"Really?" Her eyes brightened. "No more coming home to nasty words? Best news all day." She grabbed him around the waist and hugged him hard. "God, I love you, Sam."

He froze.

"I love you, Sam. Can I have some money?"

"If you loved me, you'd give me money."

He had no control over the way his body turned stiff or how he pulled away.

Her big brown eyes searched his face as she drew in a breath. "Maybe I rushed my fences, but Sam, I know you feel something for me even if you don't say the words."

He fought against the thickness in his throat. The ice in his gut.

"Sam." Her voice came out pleading. "I don't know what's wrong. Is it something I did?"

"No."

"Then. I-I need to know." She bit her lip, blinking hard. "I thought... Is that what today was—you pulling away?"

She looked vulnerable. Hurt. "Linda, I—" His lips were stiff. He knew his face must be cold.

"*They* looked at me like that," she whispered.

He never wanted her to feel like that. "I'm sorry."

Regret darkened her eyes, and she backed up.

Pain filled him as he realized she'd taken his words for a good-bye rather than an apology.

"I'll miss you," she whispered. She turned and—not running, no, not Linda—walked steadily into her house and closed the door.

* * * *

Feeling as stunned as after his first mortar-shelling barrage in 'Nam, Sam drove through the tiny beach town. His jaw was clenched so hard his teeth made a grinding sound. What had he done?

A black animal ran right in front of his truck, and Sam stomped on the brakes. With a shriek, the truck skidded to a halt, rocking back and forth. The stench of burned rubber wafted through the open window as the scrawny mutt skittered under a hole in a fence.

He'd almost killed a dog with his goddamned inattention. As stupid as driving drunk.

After parking at the curb, he headed toward the beach a few blocks away. A yellow-haired boy ran past him, chased by a smaller girl.

When a woman pulling weeds looked up and stiffened, Sam knew he must look bad. He'd visited Michigan once in the winter. Froze his face so bad that his lips didn't want to move. Felt like that now.

Felt like that with Linda.

At the edge of the beach, Sam put a foot up on the low railing, leaned on his knee, and watched the rough waves splash against the sand. Dark clouds had covered the sky, and the palms lining the sidewalk bowed against the bitter wind. The whole damn world felt cold.

Over and over today, Linda had needed him, and he'd stood silent. Unmoving.

And now... *"God, I love you, Sam."* He scrubbed his face as if he could erase the memory of the hurt in her eyes when he hadn't spoken. Years of being a Dom meant he could see when his words—or lack of them—did damage.

He'd known. But couldn't reach out. Couldn't speak. She'd been damned brave today, and he hadn't told her that. Hadn't told her how proud he was of her.

What kind of a bastard got involved with a woman and didn't help her when she needed him? Got so twisted into knots that he couldn't even tell her how he felt? Or take her hand when she looked lost?

He straightened, looking up into the ugly sky as the first drops of rain hit. Linda deserved someone who'd be there for her.

That someone wasn't him. He rubbed the tight spot in his chest, then headed back to his truck.

As he climbed in his truck, he remembered the paint cans in the back and the white blotches on her house. He'd taken that task on himself, and it wasn't finished. Once that was done...

* * * *

Linda hadn't been able to cry or eat or even think. Her emotions felt battered, as if someone had taken a baseball bat to them. The television had bothered her. She'd turned it off. She'd tried reading and then stared at one page for half an hour. The basket she started was a misshapen disaster. Finally she went to bed and stared at the ceiling.

She'd think tomorrow. *Me and Scarlett O'Hara—we know how to handle life. You bet.*

A man shouted.

Linda jolted upright in bed, realizing she must have finally drifted off. The red display on her clock said four a.m., and her room was dark. Quiet. Unlike all the noise outside. What in the world?

"Fucking son of a bitch, let me go!" The man's voice was high-pitched but familiar.

The low growl in response was instantaneously recognizable. Sam.

Linda yanked on her robe. Her heart was pounding crazily. Really, this wasn't a good way for an ex-slave to wake up. *I need a dog.*

She pulled Frederick's ancient golf club from under the bed and ran into the living room.

A hammering on the door burst like a bomb into the quiet house.

With a tight grip on her weapon, Linda cracked the door. "What's going on?"

Sam stood on her doorstep. She started to smile, then saw the man sprawled at his feet, squirming like a worm. His wrists were restrained behind his back with handcuffs.

When he tried to sit up, Sam flattened him with a boot on his back. "Annoy me, asshole, and I'll break your spine just to enjoy the crunch." He glanced at Linda, eyes colder than she'd ever seen. "Feels like cracking ice cubes with your teeth."

"Good to know." She swallowed, remembering the sound from something much, much more horrible.

Sam's gaze softened. "Sorry, girl." He thumped the man with his boot, getting a pained oomph. "This is your graffiti artist."

"Seriously?" When the man looked up at her, her jaw dropped. "Dwayne?" Dwayne had been painting filth on her house?

"Know him?"

"Yes!" She took in his nod. "You're not surprised?"

"Too persistent. Too nasty. Doubted he was a stranger."

Dwayne glared at her. "Let me go, or I'll sue the fucking crap out of you. I was just walking by when this..."

Sam put weight on the man's back, and Dwayne squeaked. "Idiot," Sam muttered. "No gloves. Your prints will be all over the cans out there."

Dwayne's eyes widened.

"Why, Dwayne?" Linda tightened her belt against the chill night. The rain had swept through, leaving the air fresh except for the scent of paint. "What did I do that you'd hate me this much?"

Silence. Sweat broke out on the reporter's brow as he continued to struggle.

"Talk to her, boy." Sam dropped his voice into a Dom's low threat. "Or you'll scream for me."

Dwayne stared up at Sam like a mouse confronting a hawk. After a minute, he managed to pull his gaze away and say to Linda, "Why? We fucked, and it was good, but then you dump me and go to a sleazy club. You're a whore."

"Watch the language, boy." When Sam fisted his hair and yanked, Dwayne shrieked like a girl. His cheek was mashed into the step, one brown eye staring up at her.

"You wrote filth on my house because I didn't want to date you?" That didn't make sense. Dwayne wasn't that energetic, which was why he worked for the small Foggy Shores newspaper...although he was always talking about getting his big break by writing a prizewinning article.

Oh heavens, that was it. Fury flamed inside her. "You just wanted more stories for the paper. The graffiti kept the gossip alive." She heard something outside but couldn't get past her anger.

"Like anyone would believe you," Dwayne muttered. "You're a slut. A nothing in this town. And everybody knows it."

"You painted that crap on her house to get a goddamned story?" Sam's voice rose.

"Hell, yeah. Sex slaves? Everybody reads that shit." Dwayne smirked. "A shame you can't prove fuck all."

"I think that admission will work in court," a man said.

Linda's head jerked up. Officer Joe Blount stood just outside the circle of light. Another uniformed policeman was hurrying up the sidewalk.

Sam nodded to the men. "Caught him spray-painting her house. Paint cans are there. Probably have his fingerprints. You can match his shoes to the tracks in the mud."

"Ward, see to collecting evidence, would you?" Officer Blount glanced at Sam. "I'd like you to come down to the station to make a report."

"No problem." Sam jerked his chin toward Linda. "She just woke up when I pounded on her door."

Joe gave her a sympathetic smile. The gray-haired cop had taken her complaints before. "You'll press charges, right?"

"I will," she said firmly, ignoring Dwayne's incoherent protest.

"Then stop by in the morning. No need for us all to lose sleep."

Finally realizing his life was spinning down the drain, Dwayne started struggling again. "Hey, I want a lawyer. I want—"

"All in good time." Joe bent and traced a finger over the smooth silver curves of the handcuffs on Dwayne. He glanced up at Sam. "Nice cuffs you got there, buddy."

Sam silently handed him the key.

After switching the cuffs, Joe pulled a paper from his pocket and read from it. "You have the right..."

Linda turned toward Sam. He'd been guarding her. He did care for her. "Thank you." She took a step toward him. "Sam..."

He shook his head and stepped away from her. "No. You're better off without me." His eyes were pale ice, his face cold. "Have a good life, Linda." He strode down the sidewalk.

Taking her heart with him.

Chapter Twenty-Two

I don't need him. I don't. Linda bent her head and fingerpicked a melody in minor, the sound plaintive in the early dawn. Earlier she'd tried to play lighthearted songs, but her guitar wanted to mourn.

The scent of the freesias drifted through the air, reminding her of Jessica and Z's wedding. They were so happy together. She'd bet that Z talked to Jessica, shared his feelings. His past.

Sam hadn't. But why?

Maybe because she wasn't important enough in his life.

Why did she keep stewing over it? Linda shook her head. She didn't know what had happened, what she'd done wrong, but he wasn't a man who said what he didn't mean. Their relationship—if that's what it had been—was over. He'd said so.

She frowned. She'd just watched him walk away from her.

At one time, she might have argued with him, but the cold look in his eyes had paralyzed her. It had been too close to how the slavers had looked at her. And after being treated like an animal, a nothing that didn't deserve answers, she hadn't been able to say...anything. Her fingers clenched, turning the C-minor chord into ugliness. She flattened her hand over the strings, muting the sound.

That was what the human traffickers had done to her. Muted her as if her voice shouldn't be heard in the world.

But they hadn't succeeded. No, she was here in her own home, outside in the sweet air, seeing the stars disappearing in the dawn sky.

Nonetheless they'd changed her, made her more vulnerable. Her breathing hitched for a moment as she remembered Sam's tough, weathered face, his strong hands, his heavy-lidded eyes when he planned to take her. Such a stern man, yet his eyes would unexpectedly light with amusement.

For a moment she wanted him with everything inside her.

She shook her head and changed to a new song. If her guitar wanted to mourn, then she should allow it. Over the years, she'd learned that her guitar always spoke truth—the truth in her heart. Her fingers slid into Joan Baez's sad "Diamonds and Rust."

"Yes, Sam, I did love you...oh so dearly," she whispered. *But you didn't love me.*

It hurt—God, it did. Her chest felt agonizingly hollow, a grave that hadn't been filled in. The first tear dropped onto the slick face of her guitar with a tapping sound. Another followed.

* * * *

When Linda walked into the coffee shop, the three customers in the room went silent. Their attention on her felt like sandpaper against raw skin. SueAnn, a woman from church who always acted as if Linda had cooties, sat with Patsy, a clerk from two shops down, and a stylish middle-aged woman.

Linda's body stiffened as if chilled in the freezer. Patsy was just a gossip, but SueAnn could be hateful. Ignoring them, she gave Betty her order, glanced at the pastries, then shrugged. No appetite today. Again. Heck of a way to diet.

"How are you doing, Linda?" SueAnn asked, her voice even sweeter than her overly sugared desserts at potlucks.

"I'm fine." Her lips felt stiff as if reluctant to form the words. Hadn't Sam said just that to her? *"I'm fine."* Hadn't his face looked as frozen as hers was now as he spoke the same lie? "How are you?"

"Oh, good, good. But didn't I hear that you and Lee broke up?" SueAnn's face was alight with vindictive interest, and Linda remembered Lee had said SueAnn made a pass at him. "Does your new boyfriend like all the...special things...you learned when you were...away?"

I am not in the mood for this. Linda planted her feet. As she'd come to acceptance with herself, she realized almost everyone in town had been supportive. There'd only been a few—like Dwayne—who behaved like gossipy, spiteful teenage girls. She'd tried to ignore them; obviously that wasn't working.

She wished she could flatten the woman the way Sam had stomped on Dwayne. But no. Besides, SueAnn's weapons were words. So be it. Linda gave the woman a toothy smile. "Oh, most men like variety." Her voice came out even and pleasant. "Bless your heart, SueAnn. Maybe if you'd expanded your repertoire to something besides the missionary position, your ex wouldn't have tried to fuck every female in town."

As SueAnn went bug-eyed, Linda moved to the end of the counter, hoping her coffee was ready. But Betty had disappeared, and whoops of laughter came from the back room. Linda bit the inside of her cheek, half-appalled at what she'd said. Mostly okay with it.

She heard chairs scrape and the door open as SueAnn and crew fled from the battlefield. *What a shame.* Linda glanced over her shoulder and blinked.

The stylish woman remained at the table. "I'm Meredith Blake, the new owner of the swimsuit store." She rose and shook hands with Linda. "That was the prettiest smackdown I've seen since I left Boston."

"Wasn't it though?" Flushed with laughter, Betty stood in the door of the back room. "Good to see you getting back to normal."

Linda's mouth dropped open. "I'm not—"

"Oh, you're a polite woman, never said you weren't. The look in your eye told people not to push you. But you've been slinking around here since you returned." Betty's grin widened as she handed Linda her coffee. "On the house. Welcome home, child."

A few minutes later, Linda settled onto her favorite beachside picnic table and toed off her high heels. It was a cheerful day with a bright sun and a breeze strong enough to fling tiny grains of sand at Linda's ankles and bare feet.

Along the boardwalk, tourists were window-shopping. Down on the beach, a toddler charged straight into the water, screaming in delight when a wave splashed up and over his stomach. His brother, a year or so older, held his mother's hand, not wanting to get close at all.

An elderly couple—probably snowbirds from Canada—walked barefoot, letting the water roll over their ankles. Others stayed out of reach of the waves.

Linda always chose to get her feet wet. Which would Sam do—water or stay dry? *Water.* But probably he'd growl at her for having to take off his boots. Her lips quirked. Actually, he'd probably throw her in, then follow—just to be contrary.

And he'd undoubtedly sit out here with her, drinking coffee. Sam always took the time to look at the world. How often had they sat on his porch to watch a sunset or a dawn?

Darn it, every other thought was about the stubborn man. With her elbows on the table, she rested her chin on her hands. *I love him.*

He didn't want me.

That was so strange, though, the way he'd changed. Her brows drew together. When she'd left him the morning after the disastrous scene, he'd not been cold. In fact, he'd teased her that she owed him for using his shoulder to cry on.

She'd been grumpy. Precoffee, not a good time. When she'd grumbled at him in bed, he'd rolled her over, spanked her bottom until she was blind with arousal, and indulged in a blazing quickie. Then he hadn't wanted her to go to work. Had wanted her to spend the day with him. He hadn't acted as if he wanted to pull away. To rethink their relationship.

Hours later, he'd been as warm as an ice cube.

She took a sip of coffee and smiled at the realization that Betty had added extra chocolate. Sam was thoughtful like that. Every time they'd been together, he'd cared for her. Protected her. He'd backed off if she was afraid. Pushed her when she wasn't. He cared.

Yet he'd made it obvious that he was done with her. *"You're better off without me."* He never lied. She frowned. But what kind of a statement was that, anyway? As if he didn't think he was good for her?

Her eyes narrowed, remembering how frozen he'd seemed. Not like himself at all. In fact, a normal Sam would simply say he'd decided not to continue the relationship. He'd be nice, but...blunt. Sam didn't pull his punches.

And she couldn't see him getting all frozen up over making that kind of decision.

But on Sunday, his expression had been like hers just now in the coffee shop. All cold and pulled in against being hurt. Defenses up.

Why would he behave like that with her? She had never hurt him. Maybe someone else had? It wasn't as if the man gave much personal information. It would be easier to figure him out if he had.

But...from the hints she'd picked up of his past, maybe he didn't know how to give, not without help. When she'd pushed him or kept him busy with food, she could get answers out of him. Only tidbits, but that was a lot for him.

Did that matter though? She pulled in a breath, remembering how she'd taken a chance. Told him she loved him. And he'd hurt her. Even now, her chest squeezed, tightening enough to affect her ability to breath.

Did she want someone who could change into a different person like that?

She stared at her hands. How many times had he held hers to calm her, support her? Was she being a coward now?

A relationship was a learning experience. She'd had to learn to trust him before she shared about her past. Maybe it would take more to get past Sam's defenses. Her lips pursed as she remembered how he'd withdrawn when she said she'd visit his place. Because he didn't have women out there, not since his divorce.

If she hadn't caused his withdrawal, perhaps something else had. Maybe something from the past.

Idly rotating the cup, she considered. She'd never been a quitter, and she'd essentially done just that. He'd said she was better off without him, and she'd caved in and hadn't fought at all. She deserved—no, they deserved—more of a fight. Then, if it didn't work, at least she'd know she tried.

So how to go about this? Drive up to his farm? Her insides curled into a ball at the thought of confronting Sam. The cold Sam.

Maybe that was asking too much of herself. She'd rather find somewhere that her presence would open a dialogue. Somewhere he'd have to see her. Maybe want her. She could be like a ripe apple, dangling almost in his reach.

A moment of doubt struck. What if he really didn't want her anymore? It was possible. It was a risk. She stared at the ocean. The child who'd been afraid of the waves was splashing his brother, both of them giggling, drenched head to foot.

Life was full of challenges.

And Sam was worth the risk. What they had together was worth the risk.

She tapped her fingers on the rough wood of the picnic table before straightening her shoulders. She had a task to do for the Feds. Maybe she could accomplish two goals simultaneously. Down two birds with one stone.

Ignoring the stares of the people around her, she laughed aloud and felt her heart lighten. Maybe this wouldn't work, but she'd darn well try. *God, please let him be at the Shadowlands when I am.*

Her jaw firmed. She'd teach that man to talk to her instead of shutting himself away.

She started to stand, then sat down slowly. Before she could begin the battle to win Sam, she had another issue to deal with. And she was in a pissy enough mood to want to kick some butt. Time for a quick change and then a drive.

* * * *

Half an hour later, after a call to Gabi's Master Marcus, she parked in front of the small brick newspaper building. Crossing the parking lot, she realized she was singing "Eye of the Tiger" under her breath. *Yeah, just you wait. I'm on my way.* The air coming off the Gulf was sharp and salty, like a brisk slap in the face.

She tugged her suit jacket straight. One severely cut black suit, one dark, dark red—aggressive—silk shirt. No cleavage. Hair pulled back. Gold stud earrings and watch.

The look obviously worked, since when she strode into the building, the receptionist took her right into the owner/editor's office. Curtis Bentley rose as she entered and shook her hand.

"What can I do for you, Ms. Madison? Are you here about the secretarial opening?"

"No." As they both sat, she gave him a small smile. "I'm not sure if you recognize my name. My house has been spray-painted several times with foul language. Your paper has run at least three articles about the problem. More articles about my history. Quite sensational articles."

His eyes widened, and he straightened. "Ah, I'm sure the facts were correctly reported."

"Oh, the facts were correct. However, the sexual innuendoes could be construed as libelous, especially since I'd broken off dating the reporter and he resented the fact."

Mr. Bentley's back got straighter. "I'm sure that wasn't rele—"

"I believe the law frowns upon a newspaper that commits a crime in order to increase sales."

"I don't understand what you're talking about."

Of course not. Dwayne had been the one who checked the police blotter for arrests. Probably no one had since. "Your reporter, Dwayne Cowper, has been spray-painting my home with words like 'Filthy slut, Burn in hell.' Both for revenge and for a good story."

Mr. Bentley rose. "I don't believe that for a minute."

She rose as well. "Believe it. He was caught in the act. And told us his motivation. 'Us' includes the police." She fixed the man with a cold, cold look. "I'm afraid a jury would find it appalling that a victim of a crime is victimized by a newspaper trying to increase sales."

"Now wait. I had no idea the man—"

"Perhaps. My lawyer will be happy to discuss both criminal and civil charges with you, I'm sure." She marched out of the office, imagining Dwayne's career squishing to mush with each click of her heel.

If only her battle for Sam could be won as easily.

Chapter Twenty-Three

The night was dark and cold as Sam strode past the few cars in the parking lot toward the Shadowlands. The black wrought-iron sconces on the stone mansion walls gave off an ominous, flickering light that matched his grim mood.

For the last few days, all he could think about was the hurt in Linda's eyes. Dammit, he wanted her back, but how could he put her through this kind of crap again? Any reminders of Nancy—let alone visits—had an adverse effect on his mood, but he sure as hell hadn't realized how that mood could affect others.

And every time he thought about trying to explain, his throat turned dry as Death Valley.

He couldn't tell her. Wasn't good for her. Best to leave things the way they were or he'd end up hurting her over and over.

Being in the Shadowlands wasn't going to be easy. He scowled. Damn Z for calling at the last minute to tell Sam that he needed to supervise the trainees tonight.

They'd probably already be lining up.

* * * *

Linda knelt in the cold entryway in the line of trainees. The subs knew why she was here, and she could feel their silent support.

Sally leaned her shoulder against Linda's and whispered, "I changed my mind. This is totally not a good idea. What if the watcher guy figures out you're trying to ID him?"

Wow, way to bring her worst fear right out into the open. "Guess I better not jump up and yell, 'Here he is! It's the bad guy.'"

Sally sputtered, then said, "We'll all be here for you. But don't you go anywhere isolated."

In the clubroom? Fat chance. "You're quite the mother hen, aren't you?"

"Jessica's not here, so I figure it's my job."

I always thought that was my job. It was nice to be worried about. "Thank you. So what happens now with the trainees?"

"Master Cullen inspects us and gives us our assignments. Half of us are barmaids, and the other half are free to play. Then we switch off." She lowered her voice. "As long as you're polite, Master Cullen isn't too fussy. Not like some of the others who care about what we wear too."

"What—"

Sam walked into the entry.

The air clogged in Linda's throat. She hadn't seen him since he'd handed Dwayne over to the police. Since he'd said she'd be better off without him.

I want him to be here. Remember? But her resolve drained away, right into the wood floor. Not wanting him to see her nervousness, she dropped her gaze, but the glimpse of him was burned into her brain.

He always looked bigger in his Shadowlands gear. Rather than a vest, he wore a black suede shirt with the sleeves rolled up, showing his darkly tanned, powerful arms. His black leather pants fit like skin over his muscular thighs.

His boots stopped in front of the line. "I'm the trainer tonight," he said. His sandpapery voice sent a zing of need down her spine. Darn the man.

"As soon as I—*goddammit*."

One quick glance told her exactly whose presence had drawn that growl out of him. Apparently Master Z hadn't mentioned that she'd joined the trainees.

That darn owner. He could have warned her that Sam would be supervising tonight. Anxiety made quivers in her chest as she stared at the floor. He'd be her trainer. She gripped her thighs to hide the trembling of her fingers.

After an interminable time, he walked around the trainees. He stopped in front of one. "Dara, did Ben approve your boots?"

Linda looked up through her eyelashes. She knew the big security guard decided if a submissive's footwear was seductive enough. Otherwise the sub had to go barefoot.

"No." Dara's voice was resentful. Understandable, since her red and black boots were perfect for her Goth outfit of a shredded red T-shirt, a tiny red vinyl skirt, a studded black belt, black jewelry, and thick black eyeliner. "I just... I need the boots for this look."

Linda glanced at Ben. The guard's battered face held only worry.

"Is that your choice to make, girl?" Sam didn't look angry, just stern. Why did that expression always make her limbs go weak?

Tough Dara actually bowed her head. "No, Sir." When the trainee had been dressing, Linda had seen she was a female whose happiness depended on wearing the perfect outfit with the right accessories. Was Sam going to ruin her night?

Sam studied her for a minute. "After you apologize to Ben, you have a choice. Take the boots off or take ten from his belt and wear the boots."

Linda looked down, trying not to grin. For one of the others trainees, Sam's offer might have been a make-or-break deal. But Dara liked a fair amount of pain.

"The belt, please, Sir."

Sam nodded toward Ben. Dara scrambled to the guard and knelt. Poor Ben. He looked torn between laughter and embarrassment. The guy was good to everyone, especially the submissives, but he wasn't into kink at all.

"I'm sorry, Ben," Dara said with obvious remorse.

"It's all right, Dara." He glanced at Sam. "An apology's good enough for me."

Dara started to rise.

"Not good enough for me," Sam growled. "Stay there, girl, pull up your skirt, and present your ass. Ben, give me your belt."

Both of them looked shocked. Then Ben yanked his belt from his jeans, handed it to Sam, and pushed his chair away. Dara assumed the position.

A couple of Doms stopped at the desk, waiting for Ben to check them off the attendance list...and to enjoy the show.

Without speaking, Sam doubled over the belt and struck. No wrist action, just a flat slap of the leather against Dara's bottom without any warm-up.

Dara flinched, and her hands clenched as Sam continued. *Slap, slap, slap.* Linda counted silently. At nine, Dara squeaked. At an even ten, Sam straightened. "Up."

Dara knelt up, tears in her eyes.

"Do you like getting punished in the entry?" Sam asked.

Dara shook her head.

"You figure Ben enjoyed watching you being hurt?"

Linda's jaw dropped. Everyone's attention turned to the guard.

Ben's face was pale, his jaw tight.

Dara looked horrified. "I'm sorry, Ben." Her voice shook.

Before Ben could speak, Sam said, "You're serving drinks first shift, Dara, in the dungeon. You got off easy, girl, because the boots are cute." His lips quirked before he gave her a flat stare. "Don't push your luck a second time." He jerked his chin in the direction of the door, and she fled.

Taking a baby wipe from the basket on Ben's desk, Sam cleaned off the man's belt and handed it back. He gave the younger man the same harsh stare. "The trainees are here to hook up with a Dom, Ben. You do them no favors if you let them get away with crap."

Ben nodded.

Linda realized her hands were wrapped around her waist. The way Sam had punished Dara was frightening; nonetheless...*I want that.* Wanted it and didn't. Her stomach felt fluttery, her chest tight. The punishment had been too similar to that of the slavers yet...different. Sam had given Dara a choice, taking into account not only what she owed to Ben, but also her need to wear her *cute* boots.

His dry sense of humor popped up at the oddest times.

Sam checked over the others, assigned them, and dismissed them, until only Linda was left. *Lovely.*

He motioned with his fingers for her to stand. She rose, keeping her gaze on the floor.

When he lifted her chin, his calloused hand was warm and familiar, as if the feel of him was lodged in her soul. "I don't want you to do this, Linda."

She saw the crease between his brows, the tenseness in his face. Oh, he cared, the stubborn, closed-off cretin. "Nobody tells me what I can do. Not now."

After studying her for a long moment, he repeated, "*Not now?*"

He really didn't understand. "When I was younger, if I'd known about any of this, I might have wanted a full-time D/s relationship—maybe—but that changed when I was kidnapped." His hand smelled of soap with the faintest trace of horses. She wanted to kiss his palm. She forced herself to stand still.

His face had grown cold and remote, the moment of concern gone as if it had never happened, and the loss hurt her.

Her words spilled out. "You look at me now like *they* did—like I'm not human. God, they probably showed more feeling to their dogs."

Sam stiffened as if she'd struck him. His hand dropped.

Oh, she hadn't meant to say that. To attack him. "I'm sorry. That's how I feel, but that wasn't what I meant to say."

"Try again, then," he said evenly.

She swallowed and chose her words carefully. "You and I talked about this before. It's about taking orders. The slavers dictated everything—shower, grooming, food, even bathroom times. Knowing we were...programmed...to obey scares me." She pulled in a breath and met his gaze. "I like being submissive. But I need to choose when I hand over control. And the rest of the time, I have to own myself. Make my own choices. Especially decisions on what risks I'll take. I'm not *merchandise*."

Of course he'd have a problem with seeing her in danger. Had she ever met anyone more protective? His face wasn't expressionless now; she could actually see his need to keep her safe warring with his desire to give her what she required for herself.

Finally he stepped back. "First shift, you barmaid in the main room. We'll discuss the second shift when the time comes."

Her eyes closed briefly in relief, even as her fingers chilled and fear started to rise. "Thank you, Sam."

His chin lifted toward the door, silently telling her to go.

She headed for the door, forcing her feet forward rather than running back to him, throwing herself into his arms, and begging him to keep her safe.

She didn't look back. No, not at all. Because if he saw how terrified she was, he'd never let her through the door.

* * * *

"You look at me now like they did...showed more feeling to their dogs." Sam walked through the Shadowlands as Linda's words swirled through his memory. Painfully.

The club was coming to life. Cullen and Andrea were setting up the bar. At the sound system, Z was choosing the music for the evening.

Sam shook his head. It was a crying shame Z would play country-western music only on the rare western-theme nights.

Sam stepped up to the bar. "Got a water back there?"

Andrea's whiskey-colored hair blanketed her shoulders as she brought him a bottle. She set it on the bar top. "You don't look so great. Are you feeling all right?"

Cullen's sub was almost as observant as her Dom. "Long week. And Z saddled me with the trainees again, damn him."

Andrea grinned and looked past Sam. "Hear that, Master Z?"

"Oddly enough, the trainees say they enjoy having you as a trainer." Z moved from behind Sam to take a seat on a bar stool. He gave Sam a long look. "Andrea is right. You don't look up to par."

Andrea turned at a call from Cullen and moved away.

"I fear I didn't get a chance to warn you," Z said. "I added another trainee to see how she'll work out."

Sam gave him a sour look. "I noticed. How'd that happen?"

"Perhaps submissives shouldn't be allowed to fraternize."

Sam snorted. "Good luck. What's that got to do with Linda?"

"They discussed the spotter."

Sam's hand tightened on the bottle of water until the plastic crackled. "Jessica talked to them?"

"No. Linda did. Then Sally suggested a trainee position so Linda could meet all the members without being obvious."

"That's hogwash."

"My first reaction. She's been through too much already." Z leaned one elbow on the bar, turning toward Sam. "Buchanan and Kouros found it an excellent idea. And she agreed."

"Why is she so determined?" Sam remembered her panic during the scene last week. She'd scared the crap out of him.

"Mixture of reasons." Z rubbed his temple as if his head hurt. "A bit of healthy payback motivation. I enjoyed that. Wanting to fight past her fears." He sighed. "Mostly to protect the others."

"That damned maternal instinct," Sam muttered.

"Indeed." Z stared across the bar at nothing. "Kim once mentioned how important Linda was to her and the other slaves. Apparently she mothered them all."

Dammit.

"What happened between you two?" Z asked.

Sam gave him a cold look.

"Normally, your relationship wouldn't be my business, no. But she's now a trainee."

And the Shadowlands owner stood as Master to the trainees. Sam drank some water, his throat desert dry. "She wanted more than I can give." Wanted him to love her. Worse, to be able to say it.

"Yes? You have money enough to support a woman. You're obviously adequate with both sex and scenes— submissives beg for your attention. You're smart, careful, controlled." Z tapped his fingers on the bar. "What aren't you giving her?"

Sam stared at him.

Z's lips twitched. "That says it all. You're not talking to her?"

Goddamned psychologist. Sam thumped the bottle of water onto the bar top. "That's not who I am, dammit."

Z studied him as if he were a submissive. "You never told your mother that you loved her?"

"Of course I did." Every bedtime. When leaving the house. Whenever she'd said it to him, and she had often. The words had come easily enough. *"Love you, Mom."*

"When you were young, did you tell your girlfriend your concerns about school? Making ends meet?" Z waited for an answer.

Sam frowned, trying to remember. In the military. Complaining about a hard-ass lieutenant—one who reminded him of his stepfather. As a civilian, attending college at night. Telling...Tammy—that was her name— about how he worried over his grades. "Guess I did."

"How about your daughter? Do you discuss your worries about the farm? Or tell her what she means to you?"

Sam opened his mouth. Closed it. How long had it been since he'd said anything like that to her?

Z straightened. "At one time, you were that kind of a person. Now you're not. To me, that says you changed because of some experience."

Sam frowned, knowledge getting a good clamp on his guts. He'd experienced *Nancy.*

"Think about it. Figure out if you want that experience to determine the rest of your life." Z took a few steps away before glancing back with a slight smile. "Be nice to the trainees, please. There's a new one tonight, and she's nervous."

Goddammit.

After stewing at the bar for far too long, Sam headed through the room to check on his trainees. He stopped near the back to watch old Gerald strapping his wife to a whipping post. At least seventy, Martha was what Sam would consider a lightweight masochist. But pain fulfilled something in her, both in her submission to Gerald and erotically.

Once Martha was restrained, Gerald swatted her ass with a narrow paddle, watching her as if she were a *Playboy* bunny. After a few blows, he leaned down and tucked a stray lock of gray hair behind her ear. He was speaking softly.

But Sam could hear him.

"I love you, Martha mine. Love seeing you wiggle. Love seeing you pant. Love you, period."

The look in her eyes was...indescribable.

Sam walked away. That's what Linda wanted. That baring of the soul. Emotions. Z hit the nail right on the head. Damn Nancy for messing with his mind. Damn himself for letting her and retreating so far he couldn't give Linda what she needed. So far that she compared him to a slaver.

Near the end of the room, Sam saw a Dom considering some of the paddles hanging on the wall. Z didn't bother with artwork—not when he had toys to display. Maybe Sam should decorate his walls that way too. He frowned, remembering the painting that used to hang over the mantel—one of the farmhouse when it was first built.

Nancy had destroyed it in a tantrum. With the talent of a manipulator, she'd destroyed anything they loved. Sometimes just objects, other times nonphysical prizes—memories and emotions. Whatever she discovered about a person, she later used as a weapon. He'd learned to keep everything to himself.

Sam's throat tightened. How had that affected his little girl? After a minute, he realized Nicole had bottled up her emotions, but just with her mother. She still talked with others, laughed, showed how she felt. Nicole pushed away only Nancy.

Sam had locked all the doors with himself inside. Nicole was stronger than he was.

"Sam?" A light touch on his arm. "I mean, Master Sam?"

He straightened and looked down. Linda.

"Are you all right?" Concern filled her gentle eyes. For him. He'd been rude to her, had pulled away, and she still worried about him. The woman hadn't a clue how special she was. Or what she meant to him. His fault.

"Linda—"

"I don't know what you're thinking about, but stop." Her expression showed only sweetness as she put her arms around him. "I love you, Sam. It's okay if you don't feel the same, but honey, I do love you."

Warmth spread through him, dissolving the ice that had started to grow. He put his arms around her and pulled her closer. She didn't know what she was offering. She shouldn't love a person so messed up.

"Figure out if you want that experience to determine the rest of your life." Did he let Nancy win, or did he fight? He swallowed. "I told you that my ex-wife is a drug addict. She always needed drugs, and she'd use anything I told her as ammunition to get what she wanted. I stopped sharing."

Linda didn't look up, just tightened her grip.

His mouth flattened. "Nancy came to the farm last Sunday. That's why—" Hell, how did people do this? He couldn't. He pulled her closer, not wanting to let her go. But he must. "I'm sorry. I'm not good for you, girl." He gently set her from him and walked—fled—toward the dungeon.

LINDA SAGGED AGAINST the back of a couch, staring after Sam. She'd said she loved him—and he'd hugged her as if it meant something to him. And he'd apologized and shared. His ex sounded purely horrible.

He'd held her before pushing her away. Her lips curved. He'd said one thing—his hug had said another.

"Whoa, what was all that about?" Sally slipped an arm around her and leaned her hip on the couch. "He sure didn't look happy with you."

Linda shook her head. "He told me something about his ex. She sounds like a real bitch."

"Seriously? He never talks about his wife. Or much of anything else, come to think of it."

But he'd opened up for her, cracked his wall of silence. *I love you, Sam, and I see you're trying. Don't give up—we can do this.* "He's definitely confusing me." She huffed a sigh. "But I can't think about it now. Time to get to work." She had a slaver to find.

"I'm on the other side of the room," Sally said, "but I'll try to keep an eye on you."

Linda gave her a squeeze. "Thanks." And Sam would watch over her. She never doubted that for a second.

* * * *

See who was now a trainee. The spotter pretended to watch a girl-on-girl scene as he studied the redheaded ex-slave. Quite interesting that she'd become one of Z's trainees. He could see her getting involved with a Dom—after all, the Association "harvested" women in the lifestyle. But the trainee duties seemed rather beneath her.

He wasn't complaining though. Now he'd have a chance to enjoy her. A pale- redhead whose skin would mark up beautifully. He liked seeing the results of his efforts.

He also preferred the older women, who were less brittle than the young ones, more adaptable, with a stronger core.

And he loved breaking masochists. If they were terrified enough or the pain was the type they hated, he could keep them out of subspace. Hurt them in ways that made them scream.

He was uncomfortably hard as the redhead walked past the bar. Unfortunately, since she was a new trainee, he'd get no chance at her tonight. But eventually? Most definitely.

Maybe he could talk her into meeting him somewhere. He needed some relief. His kills had been discovered, and the reporters were having a field day announcing a serial killer who chopped off his victim's hair. And that the women were all prostitutes. Last night in the red-light district, he'd spotted four plainclothes officers. Even worse, the whores weren't getting into cars.

As he watched her talk with people, he frowned. Her demeanor seemed...off. After greeting a Dom, she'd tilt her head as if listening intently and the man would get a careful study. Her attitude wasn't that of a submissive looking for a master.

Uneasiness made him stiffen as she walked past. Her gaze flickered over him. When her body language didn't change, he relaxed. She didn't recognize him.

She would though.

He'd enjoy reminding her of where they'd "met." Right before he started on her with his knife.

Chapter Twenty-Four

Later that evening, Sam released the first shift of
trainees and put the second shift to work as barmaids.
After matching Dara and Sally with Doms who fit their
interests, he saw Linda moving toward the bar.

She walked past the two FBI agents who were—
apparently—arguing the merits of a female president,
and set her tray of empties in front of Cullen.

"Thank you, pet," the bartender said. As he tugged
her hair, she gave that low, open laugh that always lifted
Sam's spirits.

Damn, he'd missed her.

A Dom seated at the bar chatted with her and ran
his hand down her bare upper arm. Her back muscles
tightened. She didn't like the guy's touch.

Sam stalked over. "Trainee. Come with me."

She glanced over her shoulder, and her eyes
widened. "Yes, Sir." To Sam's satisfaction, she obeyed
instantly, pulling away from the Dom.

Sam closed his hand around her nape, enjoying the
shiver she gave at his touch, then guided her to a quieter
place in the room. "You got any idea of what you want to
do now, girl?"

She frowned. "What do you mean?"

"It's my job to see that you meet Doms and explore the areas you're interested in." Z, with typical thoroughness, had made Linda complete the trainee paperwork, including a limits list. Earlier, Sam had checked the file and noted activities they hadn't tried.

"But I'm not here to, uh, explore."

"I know." He moved forward, past her personal boundary and into intimate space. Another inch and her gorgeous breasts would rub against his chest. Or his rapidly hardening cock would nudge her lower stomach.

Rather than stepping back, she made an infinitesimal movement toward him.

Oh, hell yeah, she still wanted him. "Part of the night is saved for a trainee to gain experience, and it will look odd if you don't. Got anyone in mind you want to play with?"

"Play with...someone?" She pulled in a breath. "Of course. I-I knew that." He watched as she recovered. "I can do that. I did the first time I came here, didn't I?"

So damned brave. He might have called her bluff, but she wasn't in a good place to be teased. His hand moved of its own accord and cupped her cheek. "Linda, it's your choice. Would you rather play with me?"

The answer showed so clearly in her beautiful brown eyes that he didn't need her to speak. Although the hesitation before she said, "Yes. If you wouldn't mind," felt like an insult.

For the insult, he answered, "No problem. Part of the job."

At the flicker of hurt in her face, he cursed himself and curved his hands on each side of her neck, letting his thumbs stroke her jawline. "More than that, girl." He pushed past the bottleneck on his words and continued. "I'd like to play with you. I always have." *Always will.*

Tears gleamed in her eyes before she blinked them back. "Okay. Okay then. Now what?"

Tough little woman. Too damn tough and brave for her own good. "Are you up for a full scene? Pain, bondage, sex?"

She bit her lip, and he could read her too easily. Her head said no, but the rest of her wanted him. The relief that she hadn't given up on them shook him.

When she nodded, he couldn't keep from moving closer. From kissing her. He'd missed the pleasure of taking her mouth. "It's a good night for role-playing."

She looked intrigued. "Like what?"

Like a scene he'd planned a while back. Her speech in the entry about being programmed had shoved it to the top of the list. "A reversal of the businessman-secretary role-play. A game within a game."

Her brows drew together.

"I give you tasks and ask questions. You must answer honestly. But I also want you to act out. Be a brat. Be rude. Do the tasks badly. When you do, you'll get rewarded by being punished in a way we'll both like. However, if you're quiet and well-behaved, I'll make you do things you won't find appealing."

Her mouth dropped open. "What's the point of that?"

"I'll explain later. Maybe." Would she figure it out? He rubbed her cheek with his knuckles, enjoying the softness. "Upstairs in the Purple Room, Z keeps fetish and costume wear. Put on secretarial clothing. No underwear. Hair up off your neck. Glasses. Bring me a suit coat when you come down. Extra-large. I'll see you in the office-theme room in ten minutes."

She simply stood, staring at him.

He put a low snap in his voice. "Move, girl."

* * * *

Wow, she really felt like a secretary. As she crossed the club and walked down the theme-room hallway, a few members grinned, recognizing the stereotypical look. Her black skirt hugged her butt more closely than she liked, but the white silk blouse she might have bought for herself. Without a bra, her nipples made dark points under the thin material. But the black reading glasses—without lenses—were great.

The hall contained people observing scenes through the large windows. The medical room was across from the office room, and she glanced in, then winced. A Domme was inserting needles in a straight line down one side of her submissive's muscular back. The man flinched with each puncture, but from his expression, he was in a happy place.

Linda felt envious. Not of the piercing—heavens, no. But the subspace. She felt as if centuries had passed since she'd played with Sam.

As she opened the door, she saw him and felt that inexplicable bounce of her heart. He waited beside a fancy oak desk in a room fashioned to look like an office. A tall filing cabinet stood against one wall. A chair sat in front of the desk. A couch and coffee table were near the far wall.

After donning the suit coat she'd fetched, he gave her an approving smile. "Miss Madison, I'm Sam Davies, the CEO of Pain International." He held his hand out.

"Ah." *Right. Get with the program.* She shook his hand. "I'm pleased to meet you."

"Take a seat. We'll get right to the interview."

Interview? She blinked, then shrugged and took the hardwood chair in front of the massive oak desk. At least she wouldn't have to pretend to take notes in shorthand.

After seating himself behind the desk, Sam opened a red folder and actually donned his reading glasses to peruse the contents. He was so, so sexy with glasses.

He nodded to himself as he read. When he frowned at another paper, her hands turned clammy as if she were really applying for a job. Finally he looked up and pinned her with a keen gaze over the top of his glasses. "A widow. Children in college. How much trouble do they give you?"

Huh. He really meant to keep this interviewlike. "Not much. They're quite good children, aside from being at that rebellious age."

His gaze chilled. "How nice to meet an honest and polite applicant." The compliment was at definite odds with his annoyed look. Why? He knocked the pencil holder off the desk. "Oops. Pick those up while I read the rest of this report."

Pushing her glasses up, she obediently knelt on the gleaming hardwood floor, righted the holder, and put the first pencil in.

He sighed. "So goddamned well behaved. Use your teeth then."

She stared at him and caught his direct look. Realized why. He'd told her to be rude. Honest, but rude. If she were *"quiet or well-behaved,"* he'd choose things she didn't like. Well, he was sure on target with picking up pencils with her teeth. *Ew.*

Must be rude. "You're pretty clumsy, Davies. You should pick them up yourself." She felt...odd...saying that. *"Don't be impertinent, honey. It's important that you're always polite."* Her mama's voice distorted and slid into the Overseer's. *"Sluts don't speak."*

"Miss Madison, are you applying for a job or taking a nap down there?"

"Yes, Sir. I'm so sorry." As she reached for a pencil, his frown stopped her. *Rude. Be rude.* Not knowing what to say, she picked up a pencil and threw it onto the desk. Everything inside her cringed at the action. "There's one."

She caught the glint of approval and threw two more. "Almost done, Mr. Dumb Davies."

His lips quirked. "Enough of that. Come here."

She rose, took a step forward, and realized she was doing it again. Blind passive obedience. "No." She dropped into her chair. "Get on with the interview before I get bored."

His eyebrows went up. "Bored?" He flipped a page. "Small-town girl. Your father was pastor of a church? Pretty straitlaced, I bet."

"That's right." *Why is it so hard to be rude?* "What's it to you?" She sprawled out, her legs extended.

"You're just racking up punishments, Miss Madison. Behave yourself."

Before she could stop, she sat upright, knees together, hands in lap. *"My daughter is a good girl. Did you see how well she sat and listened to the sermon?"*

"Nicely obedient." Sam sounded disgusted. "Bend over and let me see your ass."

Her face flushed. "That isn't fair. I..." *Obeyed you. I was good.* He didn't want her to be good. To be polite. Her brain felt as if it were playing a song with dissonant chords.

"Now. Not next week."

She rose and turned and—*dummy*. She spun back around. "What kind of a CEO are you? That's just disgusting."

He snorted. "Gabi should give you some pointers on how to be insulting." He rose and walked around the desk. "Come here."

The look in his eyes had her backing toward the door. "Uh-uh."

Taking a step forward, he caught her shirt by the front and yanked her to the desk, then bent her facedown over it. Still holding her shirt, keeping her bent over, Sam lifted her skirt and ran his hand over her bottom. "I like the way you just give in. An excellent robot."

Robot? "Let me go, you bastard!" She was learning. She started to struggle.

"Nope." His hand slapped her bottom with a brief sting; then he gave her three more that transformed into lovely sharp pleasure. "Those were for the sassy talk, and so is this." When he ran his finger between her folds, she squirmed uncontrollably as need sizzled through her. He made a hum of approval at her wetness. His big finger circled her clit in a burst of sensation as he teased her.

She was just letting him. She tried to push herself up, but he held her mercilessly in place. And his touch grew more insistent. Her clit swelled as he pressed harder.

When he finally let her up, she was flushed and panting and so, so turned on. With a final hard slap of her bare bottom, he nudged her toward her chair. "I have some more questions, Miss Madison."

She sat in the chair, knees together, back straight. At his raised eyebrows, she flushed. She really was an idiot. "So far your questions haven't shown any intelligence on your part."

He nodded as if in appreciation of the crappy insult. "Church daughter. Raised to be a good girl. Bet you never question if you should obey the person giving orders. You just do what they say, don't you, little girl?"

"I—" She did. "You arrogant bastard, what would you know about being respectable?"

"Bet your husband was real respectable. Conservative. Wanted you to be the same. *Answer* me, Miss Madison."

"He—" Her mouth snapped shut, and she glared. "You can take this job and feed it to your ugly pigs." She rose.

His grin came and went so fast she almost didn't see it. "No, the interview isn't over. Do you even know what you're interviewing for?"

"I... No."

He walked around the desk and grabbed her by the nape of her neck. "Neither do I. Let's see if you have any skills I'd enjoy."

After pushing her into the knee space under the desk, he took his seat, lowered the chair, then moved it forward until his legs bracketed her. With sure hands, he opened his leathers. His cock rose, and she gaped at him. "You want me to suck your—"

"Yep." He slid her glasses off and tossed them on the desk. "A nice blowjob...and quietly, please."

Be rude. Obey, but be rude. He wanted rude, then fine. "Are you sure I can find it? I might get it confused with one of those pencils on the floor."

He choked, even as he pushed a button on the front of the desk.

Obey. Resting a forearm on his knee to steady herself, she licked around the top of his cock before taking it into her mouth. At the taste and feel of his hard erection, desire set up a steady pulse between her legs. The velvety skin was stretched tight, the veins bulging. *Mmmm. Want more.* She lifted her head. "See, tiny dick. Maybe—"

He shoved her head down, forcing her to take it all, effectively muffling her. And he wasn't little at all. She almost gagged as he went deep, but when his hand fisted in her hair and pulled her head up and down, the feeling of being controlled made her insides go smooshie.

"Suck harder."

She did, then defiantly scraped him—gently—with her teeth. Under her forearms, his thigh muscles tightened. Heavens, she'd missed being with him. She inhaled his musky, wonderful scent.

He pulled her hair just enough to give her goose bumps.

Relaxing her jaw, she took him deeper, enjoying the rumble of satisfaction he gave. She could climax just listening to him.

The door creaked open, letting in the noise of people in the hallway. A man said, "You rang, boss?"

Linda froze and tried to pull back farther under the desk. Sam's hand in her hair kept her head bobbing, the wet sounds far, far too loud.

"Yes, would you tell the next candidate that I'm detained," Sam said. "I won't get to her for another hour."

"Of course, sir." The man's voice came closer. "Is there anything I can assist with, while I'm here?"

No. *No!*

Sam glanced at her and raised his eyebrows.

Linda knew she was effectively hidden by the desk, but the sounds of a blowjob... The man knew exactly what was going on. She shook her head frantically, despite the cock in her mouth.

Sam winced, then grinned. "No, thanks, Holt. I don't think I'll have to deal with an overly polite secretary after all."

"Very good. Let me know if you change your mind. I enjoy...interviews." The door closed.

My God, he'd have let that man touch me? She wrenched her head up. "You jerk. How could you have done that?"

He gave her an even look. "A threesome wasn't listed as a hard limit for you. I wanted to see if it was something you'd enjoy." He put himself away, zipped up his pants, and pulled her onto his lap.

She couldn't help but snuggle close. How could the damned sadist make her feel so safe when he held her?

"Looked like you didn't want company, though. Why did you check it as 'possible'?"

"I... At the time, it seemed like an okay possibility." At the time, she'd actually been thinking of ways to make Sam jealous. She sure hadn't thought he would call her on it.

His eyes narrowed, but he didn't say anything.

Letting him think too long might not be a good idea. "So, big boss, what do we do now?" She deliberately squirmed on his very hard cock. Actually, being a bad girl seemed a fine idea. Turning into him, she buried her face in the curve of his neck, inhaling the soap and hay scent before nipping his skin. She undid a button on his shirt and slid her hand in to outline his hard pectoral muscles. His crisp chest hair teased her fingers as she sought out a nipple...and pinched it.

He growled at her, pulled her hand away. "Get back in your chair."

"Ah, come on, Mr. Davies. I'm sure I can be a great secretary." After bouncing on his cock, she pushed off his lap, opened her blouse, and shimmied her bare breasts at him.

As his blue eyes turned to a molten steel color, his whole body seemed to expand.

Uh-oh, maybe that wasn't such a good idea, she thought, even as her skin seemed to burst into flame.

He rose, grabbed her upper arms, and yanked her against him, then took her lips in a kiss so demanding, so wet and hot that her knees buckled. Slinging an arm around her, he kept kissing her, even as his other hand cupped her bare breast. When he rolled the nipple and pinched the tip—hard—a stream of need flowed to her clit. "I can see you want to be punished, girl."

"I... Ah..."

"After that, I'm going to fuck you." She could hear the control in his voice. "Hurt you and fuck you so hard that everyone in the club hears you scream my name."

Oh. God.

After folding his glasses and putting them in his pocket, he lifted her onto the desk. "Kneel up in position."

At the growl in his voice, she felt as if she'd stepped sideways into somewhere softer. Brighter.

Feeling wanted was wonderful. Being understood and still wanted was even better. On top of the desk, she set her butt on her feet. Her hands rested on her thighs.

"Good. Arch your back."

When she complied, his cheek creased with his half smile before he ran his hand over her breasts. His calluses were rough and wonderful on her sensitized skin. "Love these tits, girl."

So blunt. Yet the wash of happiness couldn't be denied.

He tugged at her nipples until her breasts seemed to sizzle. "Stay just like that," he warned before bending down to his toy bag beside the desk. After setting a pair of bandage scissors on the desk, he took a length of rope and circled the base of her left breast several times, slightly tighter than was comfortable. Then he did the right.

Now instead of feeling swollen, her breasts felt as if they'd burst.

His gaze on her face, he fondled each breast and pinched the engorged nipples. Such intense heat lanced through her that she whined and wiggled.

When he lifted breast clamps from his bag, she made a protest that didn't even sound like her. He knew she was sensitive there. Knew she hated those things.

He barked a laugh, and delight gleamed in his hard gaze. "Yes, this will really hurt," he said, openly enjoying how she tried to cringe away. The first one went on, an alligator clamp with a screw. He adjusted the pressure.

"Too tight," she gasped.

"Breathe, Linda. Breathe through it. Take it for me...and for you." Curving his unyielding hand under her breast, he watched her face.

She pulled in a breath, trying to ride the pain. Not a good pain. But his words. *"For me."* She'd do it to please him, to see the approval in his eyes.

"Ready for the next one?"

Tears had pooled in her eyes, and she shook her head no. The shocking bite had lessened, blossoming into a wonderful fiery pleasure, but still...

"Too bad." And he did the other one.

She gasped as the prongs closed on her sensitive nipple, hurting, hurting, and the fact that he'd force her to take the unwelcome hurt shook everything inside her, because she wanted him to push her. To ignore her protests, to make her submit to his will. As he watched her with those mesmerizing blue eyes, she felt as if layers of her skin were being stripped away—a fruit being peeled until only the soft core remained.

He attached a chain between the two clamps, letting the cool metal drop against her skin. "Open your knees."

His gaze never left her face as he ran his hand between her legs, sliding through her wetness. He plunged two fingers inside her. Her pussy contracted around him, pulsing and pulling, sending zaps to every nerve, somehow bouncing off the raw soreness in her breasts and expanding.

He moved closer, sharing the warmth of his body. With fingers still inside her, he used his free hand to grip her hair, tugging her head back so he could take her lips. So he could rub his chest on her clamped nipples, increasing the glorious pain until she whimpered. He took her further, his control over her merciless as he penetrated her mouth and pussy so intimately her head spun.

Thrusting his fingers deeper, he circled his thumb around her clit, pushing her up the slope toward a climax.

As her thigh muscles started to tremble and her insides to contract, he withdrew and stepped back, smiling into her needy eyes. "Pretty Linda." He paused for a second. Then his voice grated lower. "You make me happy, girl. Happy to fuck you." He cupped her cheek and gritted out, as if he drew the words from a bottomless well, "Happy to be with you."

Her heart melted into slush, pooling in her chest. "Sam," she whispered.

"No talking, missy. Moaning is allowed...if you're able."

Able?

He firmly positioned her on her knees and forearms, head down. He yanked her butt up into the air. "Stay there." When he picked up the chain dangling between her breasts, she squeaked at the sharp bite from the nipple clamps. He put the chain in her mouth. "Don't let go."

Hastily, she bent her head so the pull on the clamps stopped, then looked up at him through her lashes. Expression unyielding, he held her eyes, and her whole body sparkled to life.

His lips twitched. "Eager, are you?" He ran his hands down her back to massage her bottom. Warm and caring and wonderful. The hum in her head, in her veins, deepened as if she were falling down a steep slope.

He slapped her bottom lightly at intervals, and she wanted more. Wanted him inside her. Her core felt hollow.

Then he took a flogger from his toy bag. The scent of leather was heady as he ran the strands over her, like tiny fingers trailing on her back and bottom. The falls struck, pattering against her skin. She kept her head down, savoring the massage-like thumps and glorying in it as he hit harder and pain blossomed on her skin. Only it wasn't pain but a driving pleasure. Then down to her thighs and bottom. She moaned as more layers of herself seemed to peel away.

"Good girl," he grated in his harsh voice. "You can take this. Want this. Moan for me now." The flogging grew harder. Each blow surged through her in a sensual inferno, sizzling straight to her pussy and clit, making her insides clench. His laugh affected her the very same way.

He tossed the flogger back onto his bag and removed something else. Gripping her thigh, he pushed a finger inside her. Her vagina clenched around the penetration. Needing. Needing. She moaned.

"Want something in there, girl?" His chuckle was low. Ominous. "At least until I can get there myself?"

She did. Oh, she did. How slutty she was. But it felt so good to simply need with nothing else involved.

Something slid into her vagina, fairly wide, then smaller so it would stay in. Vibrations hit, and her back arched. As her head lifted, the chain in her mouth jerked on her nipples, and the sharp bite of the clamps almost made her come. "Ooohhhh."

His rough hands ran over her shoulders and ass before he nipped the back of her neck. His low voice rumbled in her ear. "Sounds like you're in a good place, girl, and ready for more."

She couldn't talk, not with the chain. Her careful nod satisfied him.

He reached under her, fondling her breasts, reminding her how they were bound, making them throb with the pressure inside.

Two canes came out of his bag. He laid a small, thin one beside her forearm in a visible threat and kept the other. It was leather covered and thick. He tapped it over the backs of her thighs, up her bottom, letting her get acquainted with the feel. *Whack, whack, whack.*

Pushing her, edging her upward, the blows grew harder with a heavy thumping. Her favorite kind of hurting. Then he targeted the same spots he'd hit before. Like the orchestra joining in on a solo, the new sensation drowned everything else out and united the individual pieces into waves of gorgeous pain.

Another harder strike and her head came up, wrenching her nipples. The exquisite blast made her scream around the chain and drop her head back down to ease the pressure. Her arms were shaking. Another blow. *Thump, thump, thump, thump, thump.* Five smacks before he'd pause to let the sharpness of the pleasure swell and ease. Five more. Pause. Over and over.

Through it all, the vibrator never ceased.

The battle to keep her head down, to take more, split her mind, floating her away until it seemed as if her hands were buried in fog. Nothing stood between her and the world. Her shell had cracked open, leaving her exposed. But not chilled. Warm. She was so warm as Sam ran his hands over her. Said something.

"Linda, are you with me?" His voice penetrated, pulled at her, anchored her from drifting completely away.

"Mmm-hmm."

He snorted and pulled the chain from her mouth. "Say my name."

Name? Fuzzy. "S-Sam."

"Good. Take this again." The chain went back in her mouth, and she tongued the cool metal. He caressed her head, rubbed his cheek on hers, leaving his scent behind to flow into her happy place. "You can take more."

Each blow felt as if it should hurt, and tears were in her eyes, yet her whole body throbbed with arousal and need. Each strike of the cane reverberated through her straight to her clit. Her moans increased as she rocked back toward the cane, pleading for more. For more.

But the heavy blows stopped, and he picked up the cane beside her arm. The little one.

His hands pulled her knees apart, opening her, and she clenched as the vibrator jostled inside her.

Then light taps ran up the inside of her thighs, the cane flicking back and forth like a pinball, up and down with tiny, hot stings, just enough sensation to keep her floating. But he never struck her throbbing pussy. Up and up her tender thighs, then down, then up. Never quite...there. She moaned her need.

Her breath caught as he flicked the cane to hit the crease between her thigh and pussy. So close. He struck her labia, even the end of the vibrator, and the impacts surged through to her clit again and again. Never quite there. She gave a high, frustrated whine.

His gruff laugh was sandpaper down her spine, beautiful, wonderful sandpaper. "Needy girl. Let's finish this interview then." The next strikes changed the angle, between her legs, so the tip danced over her upper pussy lips on each side of her engorged clit. Every little blow sent her higher, higher. Then he reached between her legs, closed his fingers on her clit, and tugged.

She came, screaming around the chain as everything inside her blew apart, shaking her, shaking the table. Her back arched, her head lifted, the chain pulled. She yelled again as her nipples blasted shocking, wonderful pain straight to her core.

"Hell of a scream, baby." He pulled the chain from between her lips, then removed the vibrator, making her spasm again. After setting her on her feet, he bent her over the desk. As her legs wobbled, she grabbed the desk edges.

Over the roar in her ears, she heard the sound of a condom wrapper being torn open. A condom? Oh right, the Shadowlands had rules.

"Hang on, missy. I'm gonna take you hard."

She felt the tip of his cock enter. Then he thrust in so fast and deep she went up on tiptoes, her breath whooshing out of her. Her pussy convulsed around him, and he felt so, so good, thick and hard inside. Hot and wet. But he was thrusting too slowly, and she wiggled her hips.

"Stay still." In reprimand, he pulled on the chain and laughed when she moaned.

He reached around her with both hands, loosening the ropes around her breasts. The ropes fell off, and her breasts were freed. As blood surged into her breasts, her pinched nipples felt as if they were on fire. Her swollen breasts throbbed with each beat of her heart.

Then his cock pounded into her, driving her up and up. Securing her around the waist with an arm, he loosened one nipple clamp and pulled it off. Then the other. "Say my name."

Blood poured back in, setting the abused tissues into engulfing brilliant fire. "Saaaaam." Her scream echoed in the room

He laughed and massaged her breasts, making the sensation overwhelming.

Her brain fogged. Her body wasn't hers, was Sam's—all Sam's—responding to his merciless hands and cock. His cock dragged across a spot that made her moan. He angled himself to hit that place, over and over.

As she came again in heavy, clenching waves of pleasure, her head sagged. He filled her completely, mind and body, and when he pressed deep into her, taking his satisfaction, he owned her emotions as well.

MINE. ARMS AROUND his woman, Sam rested his forehead on her back, his cock pulsing inside her. With every small tremor of her body, her hot, slick sheath clenched around him, keeping him there, just past coming, so it felt as if maybe—maybe—he could come one more time.

He figured he'd end up in a grave, but it might be worth it.

Instead, he kissed between her shoulder blades and grinned when her pussy convulsed again.

As he pulled out of her, they both sighed at the loss. Damn, but he cared for this woman.

He did.

He carefully settled her in the corner, disposed of his condom, then grabbed a blanket from a drawer in the filing cabinet. As he wrapped the fuzzy material around her, he touched her cheek gently, pleased to see her contented expression. Still in subspace. Worry-free.

Happy. Far, far better than the way the last scene here had ended.

Some of her euphoria seemed to settle inside him. Putting that look on a masochist's face was definitely the icing on the cake for a sadist.

He kissed her lightly and then cleaned up the room.

After slinging his bag over his shoulder, he opened the door and picked her up. She blinked at him.

"You with me, girl?" he asked, studying her face. The flush of climax had faded, but her color wasn't bad.

"Yes," she whispered. A crease appeared between her dark red brows in an unhappy look. "I came... People watched...?"

Her words were slurred, but, remembering his screwup at the auction, he understood. "Not in public, baby." As he headed for the door, he turned to show her the closed window blinds. He'd pulled them when getting the canes out of his bag. She hadn't even noticed.

"Oh." Her cheek rubbed against him, and somehow without moving, she sank closer in his arms. A snuggler. He had regulars who didn't like aftercare other than water and carbs. Some wanted company but didn't like being touched afterward. Some liked being held.

Linda drowned in being cuddled, always trying to inch closer. He made sure his bottoms had what they needed after a scene. But Linda was different; he damn well loved aftercare with her.

In the main room, he found a secluded chair and settled in. With his free hand, he grabbed the sports drink from his bag and popped the top up. "Drink, baby."

Her eyes were still glazed, but the good little submissive tried to obey. Her lips closed over the bottle cap, making him remember how her mouth felt around his cock. When she sucked in some liquid, just the sound made him start to harden again. He pulled her closer and kissed the top of her head, keeping his grip on the bottle. "More, baby."

"Mmm."

When she'd taken enough to please him, he fed her pieces of a chocolate bar. Alertness started to return to her face.

A small sound made him look up. Rainie stood at the unwritten boundary, checking to see if he needed anything. Good trainee. Despite her brassy personality, she was as finely attuned to nuances as anyone he'd met.

Sam ran his knuckles over Linda's cheek. A bit cooler than he liked. He said to Rainie, "Can you bring a hot chocolate—not too hot—and a beer."

"Yes, Sir," she whispered.

He let Linda drop off again, tipped his head back, and simply enjoyed her soft body. He'd rather have a soft, satisfied woman in his lap than a purring cat any day.

Rainie appeared, set the drinks on the end table, and moved it to the exact spot where he could reach them easily.

He nodded at her. "Good job, girl. You do the trainees proud."

Before she moved away, the flush of delight in her face made him smile. He'd been unconvinced of her suitability when Z had proposed her for the trainee spot, but as always, Z recognized a good submissive sooner than anyone.

Sam jiggled Linda, waited until her attention fixed on him, then held the hot chocolate to her lips.

One sip. Two. He chuckled at her blissful sigh. "Warm."

"That's right, baby." He studied her face. The tiny muscles around her eyes and mouth had relaxed. The tenseness of her neck and shoulders was gone. *Floggers and fucking—a surefire cure for what ails you.*

Still partly in Domspace, he got off on the fact that he'd done that for her.

Her brows drew together, and he had a moment of worry before her big brown eyes lifted. "That so-called interview... You were trying to tell me something."

"I was." After living with a woman who was downright stupid, he valued one who was not. He stroked a finger across the curve of her cheek. Damn, he liked touching her. "Wanted you to catch on to what you're doing."

"But you're a Dom. You're supposed to like obedience." She handed him her chocolate, and he set it on the table.

"I do. But surrender should come from the heart, not from habit, especially at first." Hell, how could he explain this? "You went straight from your preacher family to a conservative marriage. Skipped the rebellion when most kids question—and dump—what their parents taught."

She nodded. "True."

"Then you had the Overseer's slave training beat into you. Lot of programming there, baby."

"Yes." Her mouth tightened.

"Here's your homework. Think about what you're doing. Are you offering your submission or just being a *good girl*? Who do you submit to and why? Who controls your behavior, you or your past?"

He closed his eyes as his own words hit home with even more impact than Z's directive. His past controlled him. Had programmed him.

To hell with that. No more.

"Homework, huh?" A tiny dimple appeared in her cheek. "Thank you for the lesson, Master Sam. And the reward."

He combed his fingers through her hair. Damp at the temples. Silky smooth. "Linda." The words wouldn't come. He couldn't even say the damn phrase in his head.

His teeth ground together. He damn well would. This battle he'd win. For her. For them. "I..." He sucked in air.

"*I. Love. You.*" Each word was hard-won. But audible. He'd said it.

Her eyes widened, then filled with tears. Her hand opened and pressed to his cheek. "I love you, Sam."

He felt as if he'd been dragged behind the plow. For years. Her palm was still on his face; he put his hand over hers. "I'm sorry. About last week."

"I think I understand." She asked gently, "Nicole. Did she...? Why didn't you...?"

Get a divorce sooner. He filled in the rest of the sentence. Little mama with her big heart, worrying about his daughter. "I'd told Nancy I was a sadist. We never played, but she knew. Because of that, I wouldn't have been able to get sole custody." He felt the frustration flood his system. "I couldn't leave Nicole with her—not even part-time—so we...hung on until my lawyer had enough to sway the judge and Nicole was old enough they'd listen to her wishes."

"I'm sorry, honey." She had the softest velvety-brown eyes he'd ever seen.

"She's still around. Takes me a while to get past the memories when I see her. Give me time if it happens again."

Her head cocked, and her eyebrows rose. "I will. As long as you realize that I'll bitch slap you if you give me that 'you're better off without me' bullshit."

His laugh eased a knot in his chest he hadn't realized was there.

A flicker of movement caught his attention. Uzuri stood in almost the same place as Rainie had.

"Uzuri," Sam acknowledged with a sigh. He'd actually forgotten he was in charge of the trainees.

"Sally wants permission to play with Jake, and I'd like help negotiating with a new Dom."

He shifted Linda in his arms and pulled his mind back to reality. They were good girls to remember to check in with him first. But... He studied Uzuri long enough to make her shift her weight nervously.

She needed to learn to negotiate on her own—to ask for what she wanted. "I'll meet you both at the bar in a couple of minutes. Then you'll practice telling me what you want out of a scene before *you* discuss it with the Dom."

"B-but—"

After giving her a warning look that sent her hastening back to the bar, he grinned. The girl was shy, timid with strangers—especially strange Doms—but once she knew someone, all bets were off.

He'd smacked her ass a couple of times for saucy talk. The next night, in the Master's area, he'd opened his toy bag and found it had been emptied and filled with real *toys*. A miniature whip. Plastic handcuffs. A six-inch flogger made of fluffy yarn. A teddy bear in rope bondage.

Its ball gag made of string and a grape had set off the entire roomful of Doms. Probably heard their laughter in Tampa.

After Nolan tied her to a bar stool as punishment for something, she'd filled all the Dos Equis bottles with cranberry juice and somehow put the tops back on. Nolan had spit the sweet stuff all over the well-polished bar, and Cullen had cursed up a blue streak.

Cullen's misstep with the little trainee had resulted in a naked Barbie doll tied to one of his "bar ornament" rings.

Yep, the Dom who won the little brat's surrender would be in for a surprise.

Seemed that life was full of surprises. Sam looked down at the submissive in his lap, feeling as if he'd been in a battle and returned home, safe and sound. "How are you doing, girl?"

"I'm good." She slid off his lap and onto her feet. Her legs were steady, but he regretted the loss of her sweet body already. "I need to get to work. Listening." Her face scrunched up. "I'm so, so glad I didn't hear anything while…"

During their scene? Did she think he'd chosen a closed theme room and shut the windows by accident? Damn, he hated having her at risk. "Be careful. As trainer, I say no more scenes for you tonight. Spend the rest of it waiting on tables. If someone wants you, you tell them just that."

"Yes, Sir."

"And did I mention that you're coming home with me tonight?"

Chapter Twenty-Five

Linda sipped a root beer and studied the papers Marcus had spread over the coffee table in his living room.

In the kitchen, Gabi and Beth were rattling dishes and laughing as they carried lunch out to the patio. "Hurry up, you two. It's time to eat," Gabi called.

Better stop worrying and make a decision. Kicking off her flip-flops, Linda rubbed her feet against the cool tile floor. *Decide.* "So you think the newspaper will settle?"

"Definitely, darlin'." Sprawled in a chair beside the couch, Marcus gave her a flashing smile. "They won't risk the negative publicity of a lawsuit."

"Well." She pulled in a breath. Decision made. She tapped the name of the lawyer Marcus had recommended. "I'll call the lawyer on Monday and get things started." She didn't want publicity any more than the paper did, but it wasn't right what Dwayne had done, and she wasn't the only one who'd suffered. Her anger roused, remembering the tears her babies had shed. "Thank you, Marcus. I really wasn't sure how to handle any of that."

"I do wish I could take them on for you, but I'm glad I could help." He rose and pulled her to her feet. "Let's go get us some food."

He guided her through the kitchen door to a screen-caged pool-and-patio area. Linda took a deep breath of the warm, flower-scented air.

Beth and Gabi sat at the large marble-topped table. Beside Beth, Nolan was drinking a beer and watching a giant inflatable swan that floated in the pool.

Marcus pulled out a chair for Linda and seated himself beside Gabi. "The food looks good, sugar," he said. "Best you eat up, since you'll need energy for tonight."

Gabi grinned. "Yes, Sir." She glanced up at the sky where clouds were filming over the blue. "I was hoping Master Z would open the Capture Gardens, but doesn't look like that'll happen."

Nolan shook his head. "Forecast is for rain and wind starting around sunset."

"Well, damn." Gabi wrinkled her nose. "So what are we going to do?"

Marcus gave her long, slow stare. "I might could figure something out that'll keep you occupied." The lazy power in his voice gave Linda a twinge—made her wish for Sam.

"I just bet you could." Gabi leaned against his arm and gave him a look of such trust that Linda's heart squeezed.

Marcus jerked his chin up at Nolan. "You're not working today."

"No point in being boss if I can't take a day off now and then," the rough contractor said, and his grin flashed briefly. "Never thought I'd have more time off than a fancy lawyer."

"That just doesn't seem right, does it?" Marcus snagged himself one of the sandwiches.

Beth frowned. "He took the time off because I have a landscaping job downtown, and he won't let me be there without him."

"Not with that half-pint crew of yours." Nolan looked at Marcus. "Dan told me about those murdered prostitutes. Not comfortable with her being near downtown."

"Probably wise," Marcus agreed.

Linda frowned. The papers had reported something about the murderer. Sounded bad.

"Is the district attorney's office getting any information?" Nolan asked.

Marcus's jaw tightened. Linda had never seen him so grim. "Not much evidence left behind. The murderer overpowers the victims and ties them up—far too competently. Then he takes his time. The deaths are ugly."

Gabi gave Marcus a concerned look, then scowled at Nolan. "No business at mealtime."

He glanced at Marcus. "Got a gag in the truck if you need one."

Marcus's expression cleared, and he grinned. "Loan it to me tonight."

"You got it." Nolan ignored Gabi's glare and gave Linda an evaluating look. "Anything happen last night?"

Why did he ask that? Had he seen her and Sam in the office room? Her cheeks turned warm, and then she realized he was talking about the spotter. *Way to have your mind in the gutter.* "No interesting voices," she said lightly.

"That's a nice color you got there, darlin'," Marcus said. "Got yourself up to something else last night?"

"I heard Master Sam was in charge of the trainees last night." Beth pointed at Linda with a carrot stick. "And you're a trainee now, right?"

"Sam did supervise us, yes," Linda said primly. Ignoring the laughter, she concentrated on choosing a sandwich. To her relief, the conversation moved on to discussing the high schoolers Beth hired part-time.

As she relaxed back into her chair, Gabi leaned over. "Are you and Sam back together then?" she whispered.

Linda had a feeling she was glowing. After he'd put her in his bed, he'd been...well, Sam, but with a disconcerting new sweetness. It was as if trying to say the words was so difficult that he'd wanted to show her instead.

When she let out a happy sigh, Gabi echoed it. "I'm glad for you...although he scares me a little."

"Really?" Odd, but that had never been a problem. Well, except for when he deliberately got her anxious, and he was damn good at that. But even then, she felt safe with him.

"Will you be at the Shadowlands tonight?" Nolan asked her.

She lifted her chin, despite the chill that climbed up her spine and made her shiver. "I'll be listening all night."

* * * *

Sam stood beside his daughter, looking at the new stable.

"Looks good," Nicole said, hands in her jeans pockets. "Will you breed Galadriel this year?"

"Yep." Sam glanced down at his girl. Prettiest sight in the world. Smart and sweet and talented. Z's words came back to him. *"How about your daughter? Do you discuss your worries about the farm? Or tell her what she means to you?"*

Linda needed those words. Did Nicole? "You doing all right in school?"

"Oh, sure," she said. "All A's except for chemistry." She scowled. "Like I'm ever going to want to dump a bunch of chemicals together in my future career."

Sam grinned, then tried a harder question. "Do you ever miss your mom?"

She gave him a startled look and bent to pet Connagher. After a second of sending the dog into happy wiggles, she answered, head still bent. "Kinda. Not her. Not how she is. But I wish...I wish she'd been... I wish I'd had a mom. She never was."

He ached for the sadness in her voice. Felt like hell that he hadn't done a better job, hadn't been able to divorce the woman and get sole custody much, much earlier. "I'm sorry, baby."

She shook her head and started to walk, his girl's usual response to being upset. Walk somewhere— anywhere. When she was a teen, she'd disappear completely. One of the reasons he'd trained Conn to find her.

He fell into step as she headed for the pond.

"It's not your fault. Hell, you did a lot—more than I realized—at keeping her from messing up my life." She kicked some gravel into the bushes. "Some of my friends had it worse. Like if your mom does drugs, but your dad isn't there to defend you. You were always there, Daddy."

He felt some of the tightness in his shoulders ease. He hadn't totally messed up. He had a momentary thought of how easily Linda would take to mothering his girl; she wouldn't even know she was doing it. Caring was just part of who his woman was.

His woman. Yeah.

But he had his own battles still to fight, and damn, it came hard. "I'm proud of you, Nicole."

The startled glance she gave him sent his gut to clenching. Yeah, he'd screwed up badly, that she hadn't heard that from him before. The path was before him. Did he have the guts to continue?

"Got out of the habit of saying anything," he muttered.

She gave him an understanding nod. "Mother."

"But I—" The words stuck in his throat again. Too many times his ex had begged for him to say he loved her. He'd done so at first but had stopped when the words were such a lie that he couldn't force them out. Z had been right, damn him.

But Sam wasn't a coward. "Love you, baby." The words came out rough.

The way she threw herself in his arms said she'd understood them anyway.

Chapter Twenty-Six

Linda walked through the Shadowlands feeling as if she'd entered a Halloween horror house. Every nerve jangled in fear that something would jump out at her.

The Feds weren't present. Cullen said the FBI agents had flown to New York. One of the Harvest Association's "warehouses" had been found.

Even worse, Sam wasn't there to relieve her fears. Master Z had inspected the trainees for him and said he had problems at the farm. She hadn't realized how much safer she'd felt with him around. Tonight she felt far, far too alone.

Her head tilted at the snap of a whip. Due to the storm warnings, the attendance was down. Master Z had given the Doms a treat and rearranged equipment to clear two huge spaces for the whip aficionados.

In a roped-off area, Raoul was using a long single-tail on Kim. Having seen the damage a whip could inflict, Linda could only stare as the end flicked lightly over Kim's back, over and over, never leaving a mark.

Kim was giggling so hard that her Master snorted, then made the whip crack over his head before swirling it back to snap on Kim's butt. This time it was hard enough to make her jump. And giggle some more.

Linda shook her head. Who would have thought the ex-slave would have fun when her Master used a whip? The cracking sound still made Linda freeze.

Beth came up beside Linda and wrapped an arm around her waist. "He never goes much harder than that, at least not with the whip," she whispered. "Kim enjoys a sexy flogging and even a paddle, but not the whip. He gave her a few stripes when he collared her, and it was so beautiful." Beth sighed. "She proved she trusted him to give her pain, that their relationship and her submission meant enough that she'd risk her worst fears. He proved to her he could hurt her without going crazy and slicing her to pieces."

Linda realized Jessica was on her other side. "Yeah. Raoul loves playing with that whip. The first few times, Kim was stiff and scared, but...look at her. She's going to earn herself a few lines just because she won't shut up."

Raoul walked over and redid the ankle straps, widening Kim's legs. She couldn't wiggle anymore, and her pussy was...awfully exposed.

Linda bit her lip, remembering how Sam had caned her, moving up her inner thigh to hit her labia. What would Raoul do? "Is he going to get mad at her?"

Jessica shook her head. "Watch."

Kim sassed him again. Linda realized he'd moved so Kim couldn't see his flashing grin, and his stern voice didn't convey his amusement. "Chiquita, you are begging me for some pain, yes?"

Raoul had a great voice, Linda thought. Smooth and deep and with that tiny accent.

But she preferred gravel. Harsh with an edge of mean sometimes.

Raoul's next lash made Kim squeak but left only a tiny pink mark.

"Damn, he's good," Linda whispered.

"So's Sam." Beth squeezed her hand. "He and Raoul were showing off out at Cullen's once. I couldn't figure out which one was better." She shook her head. "I still don't like whips."

Linda shivered, remembering the first time Sam had whipped her. It had been at the auction with some triangular leather thing called a dragon's tongue. He'd sure known what he was doing with that. Then again, he also seemed just fine with big and little canes. And his hand. Linda swallowed, feeling heat wash through her. Darn the man, just thinking about him got her all hot and bothered.

As a gust of wind rattled the windows, rain hit the glass panes like a drumroll. The storm was picking up.

"God, I'm glad I don't have to drive in this stuff." Jessica glanced at Linda. "Z's going to keep the place open all night and let people sleep in the second-floor rooms if they want. But if...ah...you don't want company, you can use our guest bedroom."

Company. Linda's lips curved. She kind of liked that room they'd used on the second floor so long ago. "I think I'll be fine." *You got it bad, girl.* "Where's your man?" she asked Beth.

Beth turned toward the bar. Although Nolan was talking with Cullen, his gaze never left Beth for more than a second.

"He really keeps an eye on you."

Beth grinned. "He says I disappeared on him once and it's not going to happen again." She deepened her voice. "'Not on my watch.'"

"Sheesh, I'm surprised he let you come."

Beth glanced at Jessica. "All the Masters showed up tonight. Because."

Because of Linda and her hunt. Some of her fear ebbed.

Jessica put her arm around Linda. "We're here for you too."

When Linda grinned—the little blonde was all of five feet two and didn't look as if she could down a fly—Jessica sniffed. "I'm not going to attack anyone. Our job is just to keep an eye on you. The guys can't follow you around, but no one notices us subs."

Oh. "Thank you," Linda whispered, warmth spreading through her. She glanced over at the bar, caught the bartender's frown, and winced. "I need to get to work. Master Cullen looks like he's going to have a hot-guy hissy fit."

To the sound of laughter, Linda headed for her assigned area.

As time went on, she checked on drinks and took orders and listened. Nothing. Nothing. And more nothing.

Exasperated, she returned to the bar with her drink orders, then had to wait for Cullen.

The giant bartender was whistling along with the music as he poured a glass of wine for a Domme. Finally he wandered down to her. "Got some orders for me, pet?" he asked, leaning a forearm on the bar top.

She handed over her tickets. Some of the trainees could remember who ordered what, but she sure wasn't one of them. Old age, maybe, only—she huffed a laugh—she'd never had a good memory.

Cullen flipped through the notes and turned toward his submissive. "Andrea."

She didn't notice. Dressed in a catsuit that had more parts missing than were present, with cute white ears and a long white tail, Andrea remained intent on the beer she was drawing.

Cullen snorted, then leaned over and grabbed her tail.

Linda winced when she realized the tail wasn't attached to the costume, but to a butt plug instead.

Using the tail as a leash, Cullen pulled his submissive backward. Grinning at the spatter of Spanish profanity from her, he said, "If that plug comes out, love, I'll use a bigger one."

Linda's backside tightened in sympathy.

Andrea backpedaled more quickly.

"When you finish that beer, set up the drinks for these, please, pet." Cullen handed some of the tickets to Andrea before looking back at Linda. "Run along and take more orders. By the time you get back, we'll have these ready."

Clever Dom, keeping her moving. But as a roll of thunder went through the room, Linda frowned. Between the pounding music and the storm outside, she was having trouble hearing. She leaned forward. "What did you say? The music's too loud. I can't hear you."

Cullen hesitated, then even as he repeated himself, he nodded his understanding. Exchanging insults and jokes with the people seated around the bar, he moved toward where Master Z sat at the end.

Before Linda reached the back of the room, the music had changed to something quieter.

* * * *

Damn neighbor shouldn't keep a bull if he couldn't keep him penned up. Still grumbling, Sam turned into the long driveway to the Shadowlands.

Z had promised to watch over Linda when Sam called, but hell. Every minute that passed had increased the tightness in his gut.

And he was late for nothing. Capturing a horny bull in the rainy night had proven impossible. Looked like he'd have a couple of calves he hadn't anticipated.

To top things off, he'd had to bring Conn along to make sure the damn dog didn't try to run the bull off, which was how Sam had discovered the downed fence in the first place.

"You got a death wish, don't you?" he asked the muddy mutt curled up on a horse blanket beside him.

Conn gave a happy whine. Dog loved riding in the truck, and tonight he'd contentedly nap in the cab until Sam had time to let him out for a run. From the sound of it, the storm wouldn't let up anytime soon, and Z would encourage the members to sack out in the upstairs rooms.

With luck—and he'd damn well make that luck—he'd talk Linda into one.

Maybe after Conn got a walk. The soft-hearted woman would undoubtedly want to come out and pet Conn. And she'd get soaked.

A good Dom would order her to strip out of her wet clothes.

A good Dom would spank her if she hesitated.

A good sadist would redden her ass even if she didn't.

Sam parked his truck at the entrance—hell with the parking lot. No one else would be arriving at this point. After a dash to the front, Sam pounded on the heavy door. Locked, as he figured. Ben opened the door and stepped back. "Z said you'd be along. Surprised you came out in this mess."

Like he'd leave Linda here without him? "Surprised anyone did."

Ben took his seat behind the desk. "Most came before it started raining heavy." He frowned. "The lights have flickered a couple of times. We might end up without power."

"Won't that be fun?" Sam shook his head, spattering the floor with drops. The emergency lighting wasn't bright enough for safe scening. Last time the power had gone out, everyone gave up and sat around the bar, Ben included. "You might end up with a drink tonight."

"Sounds good." Ben's ugly face split in a grin. "I'm not into the action, but those corsets? Oh yeah."

Sam snorted in amusement, then entered the clubroom. Cullen and Andrea still manned the bar, although someone would relieve them soon so they could play the last few hours. A lot of the equipment had been shoved into the corners, so Z must have rearranged for some reason.

As Sam walked through the room, he assessed the happenings. A couple of new members were using the spiderweb; rough old Smith and his sub were on the nearest St. Andrew's cross; screams came from the bondage table area where electroplay was happening. Mistress Anne had not one, but two submissives at her feet, one man in a frilly apron with a lacy maid's cap. Would have been better if the guy had shaved first. The other had been locked into an elaborate cock ring and looked near blastoff.

Finally he spotted Linda.

He'd told her last night the trainees could wear the costumes kept upstairs. Apparently, she had. She was damn fuckable in all brown leather, from the bustier that pushed up his favorite assets to the laced-up leather skirt that gave glimpses of garters. Her only jewelry was the trainee cuffs.

Guess he'd better see about putting some ribbons on those cuffs, although he wasn't real happy about that thought.

When he reached her and turned her around, her eyes lit with relief. "I'm so glad to see you." She put her hand on his. "I feel safer with you here."

The feeling of being needed was a heady one. "That the only reason?"

She leaned into him, brushing her breasts over his chest, and murmured, "Perhaps not."

Hell, yes. He pulled her in for a long, hot kiss and let his hands roam over her gorgeous curves. Her pussy was bare under the skirt, and he couldn't resist filling his palms with her soft, round ass cheeks. "Girl," he murmured.

She actually giggled. Putting her hands on each side of his face, she held him an inch from her lips and whispered, "You're the only person I know who can say 'girl' and mean 'I love you and want to fuck you.'" She kissed him lightly. "I love you, Sam."

Damn effective how she could turn a man's brain to mush. He smiled down into her pretty eyes. "Get to work, trainee."

As she laughed and walked toward the bar, he turned to watch. Yeah, the view was even better from the rear. She'd laced the skirt tight enough that it hugged her round ass. Be fun to inch it up to her waist so he could enjoy what was under.

Hell, now he had a hard-on to match the ones Anne's subs sported.

As he moved to where Cullen was mixing a drink, he heard the distinctive crack of a bullwhip. What the hell? "Who's using a whip? And how?"

"Anyone who wants." Cullen grinned. "Z roped off a couple of areas for single-tails."

Well, damn, the evening was looking up. Sam pulled his favorite bullwhip from his bag, adjusted the coil, and clipped it to his belt. "Sounds good."

"Yeah. Z hoped you'd give a demo and lesson for the newer Doms."

"No problem." His favorite kind of lessons. "Trainees okay?"

"They're fine." Cullen jerked his chin to the left. "Uzuri's staring at one of the new Doms."

Sam turned. He'd seen the guy before. Multiethnic, like Uzuri—maybe African-American and Asian. As a farmer, Sam had learned hybridizing made for stronger plants and animals. Made damned fine humans as well.

Uzuri didn't care about a man's race though; she just wanted a man who was gentle and dominant. But Sam had noticed the new Dom had a decided preference for darker women.

After taking the man's order, Uzuri walked back to the bar, hips swaying in a way that no man could mistake.

"Want that one?" Sam asked as she set her tray on the bar top.

Her eyes rounded. "Oh. I—" Her dark skin darkened further. Glancing over her shoulder, she let out a sigh. "He's even better looking than Denzel Washington. But he could have anyone here, so why would he want me?"

Marcus had walked up in time to hear her words. He frowned. "You're pretty as peach pie, Uzuri. Sweet. Lively. Smart."

"Any Dom you've been with requests you again, missy," Sam said.

"Really?" Her face lit up. "They like me?"

Sam's gaze met Marcus's. Yeah, they'd be working on her sense of self-worth in the next few scenes. He'd have to pick Doms who could handle that. He turned to study the new guy. Needed to talk to him.

"But, don't...don't bother that one. I still—"

Sam gave her a look that shut her up. The little mite had worked her way into his affections. He'd damn well be sure she was safe. "You don't have anything to say about it. I'll be talking to him. See if he's worthy of you."

Her mouth dropped open. Then she shocked him spitless with a hug before dancing down to where Andrea was setting up drinks.

Sam heard Cullen's sub whisper, "You hugged Master Sam?"

"My reputation's going to hell," Sam grumbled, giving Linda a quick check before turning away.

"You'd best go beat on someone," Marcus agreed.

* * * *

At the bar, the spotter watched the older redhead—the ex-slave—serve drinks. Yes, that was a slave he'd like to break. To shove his cock in every orifice. Then his knife. Make her bleed.

Aaron shifted on the bar stool as he hardened, and his head began to buzz. It had been a couple of weeks since he'd had any real fun. At one time, he'd been able to wait months between kills, but then he'd linked up with the Harvest Association. His price for targeting potential slaves had been to fuck the unpurchased ones. To kill the damaged ones.

Fine times.

Didn't look as if the redhead would be available anytime soon. He'd heard Davies tell another Dom she was being evaluated and wouldn't be released to play with anyone for a week or so.

Even when she was, Aaron would have to be careful. Sam seemed to have a special interest in the trainee.

In the meantime...perhaps he'd take a trip to Miami and pick up a whore. Indulgently, he watched the ex-slave as she picked up empties from a nearby coffee table, filling her small serving tray. She looked tense.

"Hey, Aaron, got a joke for you."

He turned his attention to the Doms standing nearby. He'd played poker with two of them; a couple he didn't know. "Yeah?"

The man grinned and started, "In a mental institute, there's a sadist, a masochist, a murderer, a necrophile, a zoophile, and a pyromaniac. They're sitting on a bench, bored out of their gourds, looking for something to do.

"'How about having sex with a cat?' asks the zoophile.

"'Let's have sex with the cat and then torture it,' says the sadist.

"The murderer perks right up. 'Yeah. Let's have sex with the cat, torture it, and then kill it.'

"'No, no, let's have sex with the cat, torture it, kill it, and then have sex with it again,' suggests the necrophile.

"The pyromaniac bounces up and down. 'Let's have sex with the cat, torture it, kill it, have sex with it again, and then burn it.'

"They sit in silence. After a minute, the masochist speaks. 'Meow.'"

Along with the other Doms, Aaron roared with laughter, and the redhead stiffened as if someone had pinched her. As if she'd heard something she recognized.

Fuck. Fuck! Aaron spun back to his drink. Before she could turn, he'd set his elbow on the bar and was intently watching Cullen's big-titted submissive. Anyone looking would see he wasn't part of the group of Doms. A glance showed her attention had focused on the men who were still laughing.

His gut turned to lead. Maybe she hadn't seen him on the slave boat, but she'd recognized his voice. His mouth thinned. The other night in the dungeon, had she heard him? Was that why Davies's scene had gone sour? No wonder she was tense tonight.

Was she just afraid, worried she'd heard someone that sounded like a slaver, or was she actually trying to ID him? Fat chance. Too many men sounded alike.

He relaxed slightly. No, if she had been certain, Z would have lined up the entire membership for her. He wouldn't fuck around.

So Aaron had time. He could just go home. Not return until she was gone.

But if the slut told Z now and pointed to the Doms who'd been laughing, one would remember Aaron had been part of the group. A similarity of voice might not be admissible in court, but an investigation would turn something up.

And a search of his apartment would recover the hanks of hair in his bedside table. Souvenirs to liven up his memories as he jacked off. He'd watched enough *CSI* to know that even disposal and a thorough cleaning might not work.

He took a slow sip of his drink as his options decreased.

He'd just have to make sure she never had a chance to hear him speak. No slut was going to disrupt his life. And he'd have to do it tonight.

Tilting his head, he listened to the wind wailing around the building. Easy-peasy to sneak up on her in a rainy parking lot.

He'd wanted to play with her. Now he wouldn't have to wait.

* * * *

God, it was him! The slaver's voice—his laugh. Linda's stomach churned as if she'd chugged a bottle of cheap tequila, and for a second she was afraid she'd vomit. Taking shallow breaths, she forced her body to relax as she looked around. A couple of Doms sat at the bar, sipping their drinks. Not talking with anyone. Not them. Just behind them, four Doms were trading stories and laughing. So...one of the four. But which one?

A trickle of sweat ran down her back. What should she do now? She spotted Sam near the back, instructing a Dom on how to throw a single-tail. Master Z was monitoring a wax play scene that looked as if it wasn't going well.

Cullen was her best bet.

She made her way to the bar, smiling and trying to look carefree, finding a section of the bar that held no one close. She stood, heart hammering, waiting for Cullen.

"You all right, pet?" His appraising gaze ran over her. He'd obviously picked up her distress, although she could swear she looked normal.

"Just a little stressed," she said discreetly. "There are so many people to keep track of." She let her gaze rest on the huddle of Doms.

He glanced at them, and she could see him memorizing their faces and names.

She let her gaze wander over the group, then past. *Don't stare.* Instead, she caught the gaze of a thin-lipped Dom sitting at the bar, sipping his drink.

With a smile, he tilted his head toward the St. Andrew's cross in an invitation to play. The idea of doing a scene right now—knowing the slaver was in the room— made her shudder. And...he was the Dom Sally said had slapped her.

After shaking her head to refuse, she turned to Cullen. "Are my drinks ready?"

"On the way." Cullen patted her hand, his huge one making hers disappear. "You can take a break, you know, love. Master Sam's strict, but he doesn't want you trainees dropping from exhaustion."

Strict. She wanted to be in Master Strict Sam's arms so badly she shivered. "I'm fine." She had to keep moving or she'd flee. Had to figure out which of the men was the spotter. Had to keep him from hurting anyone else.

With a trayful of drinks, she headed toward the tables, almost tripping when the lights flickered, disappeared for a second, then resumed. After a slow breath, she was okay. She had only four to watch now, rather than the entire membership. If she circled around them, eventually she'd figure out which man it was.

The next time she looked, she saw Cullen talking to Master Z. Her tension eased. They'd watch those four Doms. Whichever one of them the slaver was, he wouldn't have a chance to escape. In fact, Z might just line them up for her to talk with. Her stomach went cold.

To her dismay, the group of Doms broke up. Two headed toward the back. One picked up a submissive, and the other asked someone to dance. Most of the stools around the bar were empty now. Probably people wanted to get a chance to play before the power went off.

Oh heavens, now what?

Sam was still in the bullwhip area. Even as he talked to the observers, he looked up and scanned the room. For her, she knew. His gaze hit her like a warm splash of rain, and then his eyes narrowed.

Needing him and his strength more badly than she could bear, she started toward him. A third of the way across the room, she froze as lightning crackled so close she heard the sizzle. The lights flickered and went off. Completely. At least three people screamed, and she heard a shout.

And then the battery-powered, dim emergency lighting came on, marking the doors and along the walls. It didn't help. She still felt as if she were going to jump out of her skin. *Go to Sam.*

As she skirted a couch, the thin-lipped man from the bar blocked her path. He was punching buttons on his cell phone, not watching where he was going.

"Excuse me," she said, looking up into his face.

He grinned. "No. Excuse *me*, cunt."

The voice. *His* voice. *God!* As she tried to run, he jammed his cell phone against her side.

Agonizing pain blasted through her, spasming every muscle in her body, turning the world black.

Chapter Twenty-Seven

The rain hit Linda's face, cold and harsh. *Hurt, hurt, hurt.* She tried to move. Her muscles didn't work. Her head flopped. Her arms were pulled behind her back; her cuffs had been clipped together.

Blinking hard, she realized she was facedown...because she lay over someone's shoulder. And outside.

The slaver...the slaver had her. Everything in her wanted to panic, but her body wasn't hers. Limp and stupid.

How had he gotten outside with her? Past the guard?

As rain streamed down her face, she saw that the ground was grass, not concrete. They weren't in the parking lot. Not in front of the building. She managed to turn her head. Tall hedges, glimpses of a fence. Fountains. They were in the Capture Gardens that Master Z kept closed off except for special times. It was an alarmed fire door. And the alarm...wouldn't work with the power off. *Oh God.*

Thunder rumbled across the sky, the flashes of lightning almost constant. Small solar lights lined the paths. She groaned, tried to move. *Can't let him get away. Can't.*

"Waking up, bitch?" The man rolled her off his shoulder, dumping her on the ground.

Everything jolted. Her head throbbed like someone had used a mallet on her skull.

"Fuck, you're heavy." He rotated his shoulder, his breathing harsh.

She stared up at him. Not one of the four Doms. This man had been at the bar behind those Doms. Her tongue felt fat, sluggish, and her "Why?" came out sounding like mush.

"Saw you listening. Figured it out." He smirked. "I like redheads. Oh yeah. And older bitches. We'll have fun in a minute." He straightened and turned in a circle. "There's a gazebo back here somewhere if I can find it. Got time. With the place blacked out, nobody will notice you're missing until way too late for you. Such a pity."

A second later, she understood. Because he'd taken her out the side door, no one would realize they were in the Gardens. Panic demolished her thoughts until she could only shake. She tried to move, screaming inside her head at her sluggish body. *Try, try!* Couldn't do anything. Closing her eyes against his smug expression, she fought her way free of the fear. Gripped her emotions and held them. She'd lived through this before. Gotten free before.

She forced her hands open. Closed. Again. She had to get her body to work. Pain sizzled through her, too much like the lightning in the sky. The wind whipped the trees overhead. Rain hit her face like hammers, but cold spatter returned a bit of feeling to her body.

"Yeah. The gazebo must be that way." He yanked her to her feet, held her up when her knees buckled.

She tried to jerk away.

"Give me trouble, and I'll zap you again," he said coldly. He patted the cell phone clipped on his belt. "Cute, huh? They make stun guns in all disguises these days."

The cell phone was a stun gun. She closed her eyes, concentrated on breathing, and getting her strength back.

Humming under his breath, he half carried her down the grassy path, past shadowy nooks, arbors and fountains, a swing. A beautiful place and horrible, horrible right now.

"Gonna rip you to pieces, slut. You'll bleed so much even the rain won't wash it away." He squeezed her breast. "Can't wait till Davies sees what I leave of you."

Tears of anger and fear joined the rain on her face. She couldn't bear this. Not again.

No! No panicking. They'd look for her. Sam was there. He wouldn't give up. Neither would she.

* * * *

When the lights went out, Sam ran toward where he'd seen Linda.

"Help!" The high, hysterical scream stopped him. A woman in suspension was panicking and thrashing so hard her Dom couldn't cut her free. Sam grabbed her and held her still as the man snipped through the ropes. One rope. Two.

"Easy, baby, take it easy," the Dom was murmuring. Around the room, other submissives were being set loose. Yells and calls for assistance spread through the room.

Sally appeared in the dim light. "Where's Linda? I can't find Linda!"

Son of a bitch! He couldn't just drop the submissive in his arms. "Sally."

The sub stopped, panting and looking around with terrified eyes.

Fear knotted his gut, and he snapped out, "Find Z and tell him, girl."

Sally ran.

"Last one," the Dom said.

The ropes dropped off, and Sam took the weight of the submissive. As she cried, he set her onto a couch. Her Dom dropped down beside her.

Done. When he turned, he spotted Nolan in the shadowy light with Beth tucked under his arm.

Sam motioned him over. "Find Linda."

"Hell," Nolan muttered, his expression darkening.

Sam headed for where he'd last seen her. No one in that spot. No Linda in sight. Hell with this. He hauled in a breath. "Linda! Answer me now!"

The room quieted, the command in his voice shutting everyone down. No answer. "Linda. Answer me!"

Sharp glass seemed to fill his gut. Where the hell was she? He started for the front entrance.

Z appeared at his side, carrying a heavy-duty flashlight. He handed Sam another. "Cullen said she'd pointed out four Doms, but they're all in the room. Ben says no one came out, and he won't let anyone leave."

"Where the hell—"

"I've got the Masters searching."

A shout came across the room. Marcus's voice. "Restrooms empty."

Raoul's voice. "Theme rooms clear."

"Not upstairs," Dan yelled.

Cullen yelled, "Not danceside."

"Not in the back," Anne yelled.

"He got her out. Somehow." Sam considered. "Your private exit to your yard is locked."

"Yes. The only other way out would be—" Z turned toward the side of the room. The Capture Garden door stood slightly ajar.

"Hell. No power. No alarm." Sam's jaw clenched. The huge Gardens were designed for hide-and-seek games with hedges and hidden nooks. In the dark and rain, it could take hours to find her. If the spotter had her, she didn't have hours.

Conn was in the truck, which Sam had parked right in front. "Start the search. I'm getting my dog."

* * * *

Linda couldn't stop shivering. Her skin was drenched. Her hair hung in cold tangles on her shoulders. She couldn't stand on her own, let alone run.

The slaver—Aaron, he'd said his name was— dropped her onto a bench in the gazebo.

Her hope of rescue was sinking. A tall cedar fence marked the back wall of the garden. "They'll catch you. You should run while you can."

"Gonna do you first." He grinned. "Then I'll cut your hair off for something to remember you by and toss your body over the fence." He tried to yank off her bustier but couldn't work the tiny wet hooks with his wet hands. When he pulled a hunting knife from the sheath at his hip, her breathing stopped.

God, please, no.

But he slipped it under the leather and sliced upward between her breasts. The bustier dropped open. "Much better."

His hands were on her, squeezing roughly. She kicked at him frantically, knocking him back. He grunted in pain, but her bare feet hadn't done enough damage.

Stepping forward, he slapped her legs aside, grabbed her throat. Then his head lifted. Running sounds. A dog baying. "Fuck, they're out here already."

She knew that dog. Conn was here. Exultation filled her. *Scream.* She pulled in a quick breath and—

He grabbed her hair, and his knife pricked her throat. "Scream and you're just meat cooling in the rain."

She choked back the sound, her hands clenching. *Here. I'm here! Please...*

"Too damn fast. Were they watching you, slut?" He slapped her cruelly, the pain sudden and startling, then yanked her to her feet. Before she could recover, the knife was back at her throat. He answered for himself. "I knew you were listening. But you'd already told Z, hadn't you?"

He considered the fence, then shook his head as footsteps advanced directly toward them. "Too late. Bet they have someone guarding the parking lot by now."

Hurry, Sam. Hurry.

Aaron stared down at her with cold eyes. "Guess it's the hostage game. Don't fuck up or I'll slit your throat in front of them all."

He would anyway. She knew it, saw her death in his gaze. He turned as Conn appeared, the dog brought to a sudden halt by the leash Sam held. Z and Nolan were directly behind him. Others followed.

Her hope of being freed was dying fast, but oh, she wouldn't be left alone with this man. Gratitude for that mercy made her eyes water.

In the wet light from the nearby fountain, Sam's pale gaze fastened on her. Fury made his gaze almost glow. "Let her go."

"Don't be stupid." The spotter gave a short laugh. "Back off, way off, or I slit her throat and you watch her bleed out."

"You aren't that stupid." Z's mild voice belied the rigidity of his jaw. "Killing her won't help you."

"Be satisfying though." The knife pricked her skin.

She felt blood trickle down her throat, hot against the chilled skin.

"I'm not going to jail. I heard about the Overseer—getting reamed like a cunt," Aaron said. "Either I get away clean, or I take her with me before I die."

Sam's growl and Conn's snarl sounded in the silence.

The guy laughed. "I never liked you, Davies, but you've got good taste in sluts. Now back off." The knife pricked her harder.

She gritted her teeth. He wouldn't get a noise from her. Wouldn't get anything. Never, ever again. She met Sam's gaze and spoke directly to him. "I'd rather die than let him take me. My choice. My body." *Know that I mean this, my love.*

Sam's face blanked of all expression.

"Shut that yap." Aaron put his hand over her face—her nose and mouth. She couldn't breathe. As she struggled, Aaron yelled at Z, "Back the fuck up. Now."

Blackness danced in her head. But as the men retreated, almost disappearing in the darkness, Aaron removed his hand from her face.

Air. She heaved in a breath, another.

As Aaron dragged her beside him, she turned her head. Everything in her wanted one last look at her Sam. Just one.

At the edge of the clearing, Sam handed Conn's leash to Anne. As the Mistress dragged the dog away, Sam stood alone.

Linda looked at him. *I love you.* Regret swept over her, colder than the dying wind. The rain had stopped, but water dripped from the trees and palms. What might they have had together? Why had she let Sam retreat from her? Now those few days had been wasted, precious jewels of time tossed away.

And her hope of more time with him was fading so, so quickly. Her lips tightened. If the slaver got her to the parking lot, then—but only then—she'd give up. She'd jam her neck on the knife herself. *I'm sorry, my babies. Sam. I hope you'll forgive me someday.*

But never, never, never again would she be a slave.

SAM'S RAGE HAD disappeared, driven down to a hard ball in his gut, waiting to explode. As his mind frantically turned over plan after plan, his heart slowed, his blood turned to ice.

Linda walked on Aaron's right, his right hand curled around her left upper arm, holding her in place. His left hand held the blade against the left side of her throat. The bastard was fully a head taller than Linda was.

There was no surefire plan. None. No time to get weapons, which Z undoubtedly had upstairs. Aaron had made it clear he was willing to die—and kill Linda first.

Sam wanted to wait. Surely there'd be a way to get her free that wouldn't risk her life. She just had to hang in there.

"My body. My choice." She'd spoken clearly. Bluntly. She'd rather die.

He saw only one slim chance to free her. He pulled in a breath against rigid lungs. If his actions killed her…he'd slaughter the bastard and follow. Damned if he wouldn't.

Once back in the shadows, Sam slipped over to Z. He'd need space and darkness. But the approach to the mansion's side door was lit with solar lamps. No way to shut them off.

However, the lighting for the front of the Shadowlands was electrical. Without power, there were no lights.

Z's eyes were black in the dim lighting. "If he's willing to die, there's no good way to take him out before he kills her. We can try, but I doubt she'd survive. "

"I want to take him just past the fence." Sam considered the areas of light and dark. "You make him use the side gate. Follow him. Noisy. Keep his attention on you."

"And?"

Sam unsnapped the bullwhip from his belt.

EVEN KNOWING HER cuffs were clipped together, Linda fought the restraints. She needed—needed—to push the knife away. With every step, she felt the cold metal scrape against the left side of her neck.

She'd lunged to the side to escape his hold, but his hand was big and his grip on her arm was unbreakable. He'd cut her again, whether by accident or anger, and now his grip squeezed her upper arm so tightly the flesh grated against her bone.

Helpless. Her jaw clenched against the screams desperate to escape.

But she'd fight until her options were gone. She let her weight sag and dragged her feet to make the slaver work for every inch of ground.

He didn't want to die. She felt the tremor of the knife on her neck. But she'd heard the spiteful resolve in his voice. He'd kill them both if the men trapped him.

Trembling shook her body. *I don't want to die either.* But she would. *Oh yes.* Even knowing what her death would do to Sam. He'd forgive her. Eventually. The slaver had no intentions of letting her go free; the only question would be when she'd die.

And she'd be the one to decide when. She wouldn't get into a car with him. If he made it to the parking lot... Well, at that point, she'd make sure the only body he'd get would be a dead one.

"Fucking cunt, move your legs." He gripped her upper arm, dragging her forward. The knife never moved from her throat. Her lips twisted in a bitter grimace. Maybe he'd trip and kill her by accident.

"I'll open the side gate for you," Master Z's voice came from behind as they neared the mansion.

"Do it," Aaron grunted, turning away from the door into the clubroom.

Z moved ahead and held the tall wooden gate open.

As Aaron pulled Linda through, leaving the solar lights in the Capture Gardens behind, darkness surrounded them. The wrought-iron sconces along the building walls had gone out with the power.

Footsteps sounded from behind. The Masters hadn't stayed back but were following. Noisily. Nolan's rough curses. Anne's whispered threats. But no gravelly voice. Wanting one last glimpse of Sam more than she wanted breath, Linda tried to turn her head.

Aaron yanked her closer. "You fucking slut, keep your—"

She heard a whistling sound, then a *snap*. Hot wetness splattered across her face and shoulders. The grip on her arm loosened.

Now, now, now. She threw herself sideways, away from the blade.

Unable to catch herself, she landed heavily on her shoulder and frantically rolled.

Over the pounding of her pulse, she heard choking and screaming, the sounds so ghastly that chills raced over her skin.

She was grabbed, and she screamed. Pulled and kicked and fought the ruthless grip. "No. Not again!"

"Easy there, missy."

At the growl in her ear, she froze. *Sam.* His hands were on her. He had her. Panting and shaking, she went limp.

He pulled her into his arms, holding her painfully tight, his face against her hair. His voice a low rumble of curses. "That cock-sucking fuckheaded piece of shit. I'm going to fucking destroy the goddamn motherfucking son of a whore."

He took a breath. "You goddamned scared the shit out of me, girl." And he actually gave her a shake before yanking her into his arms again. His cheek rested against the top of her head as his barely audible chant continued: "I'll rip the fucking asshole's dick off and stuff it down his douche-bag throat. Take my whip and cornhole the bastard peckerheaded fuckwad till his ass whistles 'The Star-Spangled Banner.' Then I'll break the dried-up piece of jackwad's leg off and shove it up his ass." After a minute, Linda untangled the curses and threats, all given in a voice that sounded like a badly tuned gravel truck—the most beautiful sound she'd ever heard.

A man was screaming, close...*Aaron.* She recognized voices. The Masters were there, she thought, the number increasing as others streamed out of the mansion.

Flashlights flickered. Someone retched.

"He's barely got a face left."

"Get an ambulance."

"God, I've never seen so much blood."

"Remind me not to piss Davies off."

Aaron screeched louder.

Marcus's low laugh. "Anne, I do believe that's overkill."

"The fucking asshole doesn't deserve to keep those balls." Anne's hard voice. "Who's got cuffs?"

Over. It was over.

Sam's arms didn't loosen.

She didn't care. She'd stay right there an eternity.

Cullen detached himself from the crowd. He smacked Sam on the shoulder. "You're going to break your woman."

Sam's growl sounded as if it came from two directions. Conn stood behind the big Dom, fangs exposed.

Without moving, Cullen said, "Davies. Call off your damn hound so I can get her hands free."

The arms around Linda loosened slightly as Sam's chest moved with a long inhalation. "Conn. Stand down."

The dog skirted Cullen and lunged into Linda's lap, whining his worry. Wet fur. Warm, solid body.

Master Z appeared. He bent, shining a light so Cullen could see what he was doing. The cuffs were unclipped.

As the men moved her arms forward, her shoulders grated like rusty metal hinges. But she was free. And alive. Her body caught up suddenly, and she started shuddering so hard her bones shook. Everything hurt. Grabbing Sam's shirt, she burrowed, trying to get closer. Closer.

Master Z moved to her side and set a hand on her arm. "Raise your chin, little one."

Cheek against Sam's chest, hands fisting his shirt, she couldn't make herself obey.

"Hell," Sam muttered. "Anne, take Conn for me again."

As the dog was pulled away, Sam tried to shift her.

Ignoring the grinding complaint of her shoulders, Linda wrapped her arms around him. *Never, ever going to let him go.*

Master Z gave a huff of exasperation. "That didn't help. Samuel, we need to see what that knife did."

The chest under her cheek turned rigid, and a merciless grip on her arms moved her back.

More flashlights beamed down on them.

Sam's eyes were pure ice in the increasing light. "Let's see, girl." The anger in his voice reverberated like the bass turned up as he cupped her chin and lifted.

The movement pulled at the burning lines across her neck.

Z touched her neck, then smiled. "All superficial. You did well, Samuel."

"I'm too old for this goddamned active-duty crap." Sam put an arm under her knees and lifted her. "Let's get you bandaged, baby."

* * * *

Above the Shadowlands in Z's third-floor home, Sam held Linda in his arms, where she the hell belonged, he thought. Her face remained as white as the fluffy blanket he'd wrapped around her. Her hair held the only color, much like the brightness she'd brought into his life.

He'd almost lost her. Leaning against the arm of the couch, he pulled her closer. Her legs had tangled with his; her cheek rested against his chest. Her breath created a warm spot on his shoulder, a tactile proof she was alive.

So damn close.

Aaron could have slit her throat. Although the cops had been shocked at what the bullwhip had done to Aaron's face, Sam had been—was still—shaking at how close the bastard had come to killing her.

And she wouldn't have been the first. When she'd told the cops that Aaron had planned to cut off her hair, they'd gone quiet. A call had gone out.

A while later, Marcus and Dan had come upstairs to share what the detectives found at Aaron's apartment. Mementos from the women he'd raped and killed.

She stirred as if detecting his thoughts, then pushed back to look up at him. The bruising on her face made him want to find the bastard and deal out more punishment. "Did I remember to say thank you?" she asked, her dark brown eyes the color of the chocolate she liked so well. He'd need to stock up.

"For what, baby?" He brushed his hand over her hair.

"The rescue." She pulled in a breath. "For letting the choice be mine."

The fabric of the blanket was soft under his fingers as he squeezed her shoulder. Too thin. She'd lost weight in the last week. Since he'd been such an ass. "The choice is always yours." He closed his eyes for a second. "I could have got you killed." He foresaw having nightmares for years about that knife against her throat, the dark trickle of blood on her pale neck.

She flattened her palm on his cheek. "You didn't. And I wouldn't have let him take me. I wasn't going to go farther than the parking lot."

He'd known, goddammit. How could so much courage come packed in someone so soft and sweet? He kissed the top of her head.

"I wondered..." Her forehead furrowed. "Why didn't you wrap the whip around his arm and pull the knife away?"

The cops had asked the same question. Seemed they all watched too many *Indiana Jones* movies.

Sam picked up her arm and bent it, duplicating the position in which Aaron had held the knife. "Need space around the target to wrap a whip. And got to wrap the leather a couple times so it will hold when I pull." He used a corner of the blanket to make a few turns around her wrist, then opened it to show her the length. "There wasn't enough room. The tail would have hit your face."

"Oh." She swallowed. "You knew what you'd do to his...face when you hit him, didn't you?"

"Yes." He tucked the blanket back over her shoulder, hating that she'd gone paler. He'd hoped she wouldn't see Aaron, but of course, she'd looked. "In a scene, a single-tail is used...lightly...even when you intend to draw some blood. With Aaron, I didn't hold back."

Her shiver reminded him that her friend, Holly, had been whipped to death.

"It was a bad gamble, baby. Get surprised by a punch to the face and you're stunned. Paralyzed for a split second. Only a second. But when the whip hit him, it wouldn't have worked if you hadn't jumped away."

Brave, brave woman.

She squeezed his hand and looked at him in a way that made his heart melt. "Thank you for hearing me. And for saving my life." When she took her hand away, he missed her warmth. "I'd better get moving. Will you walk me to my car?"

His jaw clenched hard enough to bust his molars. "No."

"Sam. We can't sit in Master Z's living room all night. It's time to go. I can drive now."

And when she had a belated reaction on the road? When she drove into a ditch, leaving him alone? No damned way. "I'll drive. And you'll come home with me."

Her big eyes widened. Her chin came up. When he saw the bandage, a small circle of red staining the center, his throat loosened so more words came forth. "I want you in my house. Living with me. In my bed."

"But…"

"I love you." The words came easier each time. He curled her closer into him. She was so damned precious. Fragile and strong.

When she didn't answer, he had an uncomfortable reminder of how his silence must have hurt her. He gave her an impatient jostle. "You're supposed to say it back, girl. There are rules."

"Rules?" Her lips tipped up. "My sergeant." Her eyes warmed in the way he'd needed to see, and she whispered, "I love you, Sam. I really, really do."

As he buried his face in her hair, he swore to himself that she'd hear the words from him every single damned day.

Epilogue

Two weeks later

As Linda checked the chicken in the slow cooker for after-church dinner, she smiled at the sound of the children's laughter coming from the dining area.

Nicole was teasing Charles about continuing with his cafeteria job despite the settlement from the newspaper.

"I decided to save the money. It's not that bad, putting a few hours in," answered Charles.

Brenna snickered. "And you get all the girls lined up in a row to flirt with, right?"

"Very true."

Charles. Linda laughed under her breath. Her son definitely had a way about him. Girls had flocked to him even in kindergarten.

As an arm wrapped around her waist, she heard Sam's gruff morning voice. "Good thing I have farm chores, missy, or your cooking would give me a big gut."

She grinned, turning in his embrace to receive her kiss. "Good morning. The kids got here early."

"I heard." He really did growl like her neighbor's dog, Bruno, although a corner of his mouth tipped up, showing he was pleased.

Linda tilted her head at noise from outside. "Is that a car?"

"Sounds like." His brows drew together. "Construction's done. Kids are here. No deliveries are scheduled."

Linda and the children followed him out to the front porch.

A car drew to a stop in the circular drive in front of the house. Blue paint, scraped and faded, a headlight shattered, the passenger door bashed in. A stick-figure blonde emerged.

"Nancy," Sam muttered.

That was Sam's ex? Linda turned to look at Sam. His expression was icy cold...growing more remote by the second. Fear washed over Linda. No. Not again. She took a step toward him.

"Mother." Nicole sounded as if she was winded.

Seeing the fear and anger and sheer misery on Nicole's face, Linda felt fury boiling in her veins. No child should look like that. *Ever.* Last Sunday, the children had flipped through Nicole's baby book. A true mess. Apparently Sam had slapped the pictures in with no attempt at artistry. But he'd tried.

Far too many of the pictures showed a girl with haunted eyes—the same look as she had in her eyes now.

No more. This stopped right now.

Sam started toward the steps.

Linda slapped a hand to his chest, halting him. "Stay here. I'll take care of this." She glanced at her son. "Charles, keep them here."

As she ran down the steps, she heard Sam's rough, "What the hell?"

"Uh-uh," Brenna said. "Don't mess with Mom when she gets pissed off. Seriously."

Linda stalked across the drive.

The blonde scowled, then attempted a smile. "Hey. I'm here to see Sam. Tell him—"

"No." Linda crossed her arms over her chest. Tweaker skinny, teeth rotten, dyed-blonde hair with roots showing, attired in skanky clothing. Poor Nicole. "I live here now, Nancy. You'll deal with me—for about thirty seconds."

"What the fuck?" Shock and anger twisted Nancy's face. She had sweat on her forehead. Hands trembling.

Yes, she was here to hit Sam up for money. Again. "Listen up," Linda said sharply. "This is my family now, and you've screwed up their lives enough. Sam might not have the heart to call the cops, but I certainly will. Leave now. Don't come back. Or I'll dump your ass in jail and press charges." She gave the woman a merciless stare. "You can go through withdrawal behind bars."

SAM STARED DOWN at the two women. "What the hell is she saying?"

Facing him as one unit, Charles and Brenna blocked the steps. He wasn't quite ready to knock Linda's children on their asses. But letting his woman confront his ex...

To his surprise, Nancy wilted under whatever Linda was saying.

Nicole slid up against his side. "She's taking on Mother?"

As Sam put an arm around his daughter, Brenna glanced over her shoulder at the confrontation, then grinned. "She's scary when she goes into Medusa Mama mode." She grinned at her brother. "Remember how the principal begged her forgiveness for giving a detention?"

"Or how she took on that old fart down the block who perved on the kids." Charles glanced at Sam. "An 'I got candy for you, little girl' jerk. He spoke to Brenna *once*, Mom had a 'chat' with him, and he put his house up for sale the next day."

"But she's so sweet," Nicole whispered. "Mother will hurt—"

Sam stared as Nancy retreated from Linda so fast her back banged into her car. She jumped in and slammed the door.

"Mom's sweet right up to the point where you mess with her kids. Then, *look out*. Everyone in Foggy Shores knows that." Brenna took Nicole's hand. "From that smackdown, I'd say you just got adopted."

Nicole's eyes filled with tears.

As Sam pulled her closer, the ice of frustrated anger that had filled his veins melted, and warmth spread from his heart outward. He could only watch as Nancy drove...away.

Hands on hips, Linda waited until the car peeled through the gate. She gave a short nod—task done—and walked back to the porch.

With big grins, her children parted to let her through.

She patted their arms. "Thank you, darlings." Then without speaking, she took Nicole from Sam and wrapped her in a Linda hug, probably the warmest, most caring embrace found on the planet.

Sam's eyes burned, and he looked away.

"Sweetie, you can't help but feel bad, I know," Linda murmured to his girl. "I've lost friends to drugs. It's like cancer. Some can fight back and win. Others—for whatever reason—can't. If she ever turns her life around, then you can see what kind of a person she really is. Until then, I hope you'll let me stand in for her."

When Nicole burst into tears, Sam closed his eyes, hearing the release of years of misery. Of wanting a mother and not having one.

He jerked his head at Brenna and Charles and took them to the stables to introduce them to farm chores. They might as well get used to helping, since their mother wasn't going anywhere.

Ever.

A while later, he released the two kids to play with Conn while he went to the chicken coop. Hard workers, those two. The boy had talked about majoring in criminology—apparently his goal in life had changed over the past year. Well, when he graduated, there were enough Masters in the various law enforcement areas to give him a hand up.

Sam shook his head. When Kouros and Buchanan had driven out to the farm to talk with Linda, they'd obviously felt guilty. Although she'd tried to reassure them, Kouros had still looked haunted when they left. A rough occupation. Maybe Charles should switch his major to agriculture.

Broken fences, unexpected droughts, and foaling were a hell of a lot easier on a man.

Guilt wasn't confined to cops either. When Sally had visited, she'd apologized over and over for suggesting that Linda should be a trainee.

As Sam finished filling the feeders, he heard Linda and his daughter coming toward the chicken coop.

Sounded as if Nicole had returned to normal. She was explaining how she'd learned the facts of life. "I didn't know Daddy could turn so red." She grinned at Sam as she walked into the barn. Her face was puffy from crying, but her eyes were clear. Happy. His girl would be fine.

He sent a look of gratitude to Linda.

"I wouldn't mind seeing him turn red," Linda said. "But did he manage to explain?"

"Hell no," Sam said.

"One of his friends—Anne—took me out for a slushie and told me all about that stuff." Nicole grinned. "Without blushing once."

"Anne? The Anne I know?" From the horrified expression on Linda's face, she'd met Mistress Anne.

He gave her a bland look. "She knows male anatomy. Why not?"

"Ooooh." Her eyes sparked. "We're going to talk about this."

* * * *

As silence filled the house, Sam carried dishes to the kitchen with Conn trailing eagerly after him. Linda was spoiling the hound, slipping him tidbits. Hard to call her on it, since Nicole had been doing the same for years.

A few minutes before, they'd sent the children off, back to their college. Their dinner had been late, but he had to admit, he enjoyed having them all at the table.

Brenna loved to argue but had a lively sense of humor to go with it, and her laughter was as full-bodied as her mother's.

Charles had a protective streak that rivaled Sam's. When Nicole had mentioned walking home from the library in the dark, the boy had scolded her about safety before Sam could get a word in.

Linda had done well with her children. Their idiotic teenager brains might have led them to give her grief, but they were even faster with their affection, with hugs and love you's.

Like a dry plant, Nicole had soaked it up.

Sam had as well. Linda wanted to continue her family's traditional after-church dinners. The idea suited him to a tee.

As he entered the kitchen, Linda was singing the Beatles' bouncy "When I'm Sixty-Four" as she put some oranges in a colorful basket on the counter. He shook his head. Nothing kept his woman down for long.

Coming up behind her, he squeezed her shoulder. "Not sure how to thank you. For Nicole. And Nancy."

Her dimple appeared. "You could give me more of what I had last night. I'm a masochist, you know."

His eyes narrowed on her hopeful face. He'd created a monster. Last night, after using a cane on her, he'd fucked her until around two a.m.

After a second of thought, he smiled slowly. "Be my pleasure. Before you leave, find your favorite toy. Use lube, insert it, wear it this afternoon while you're gone. You'll be stretched and ready for me tonight."

"But…" Delightful anxiety bloomed in her eyes. "Right."

Damn. Maybe he'd haul her to bed early.

Linda picked up a piece of bacon. "Got a treat for you, Conn." She bent to give it to the dog and winced.

Sam grinned. "Someone have a sore ass today?"

"You're such a sadist. And yes, you left bruises."

He knew he had. Earlier in the bathroom, she had been examining a purple spot on her bottom with the half-fascinated, half-pleased look of many submissive-masochists.

He ran his finger down her pretty cheek. "I like leaving marks here and there." Liked knowing she had a few sore spots to remind her of him. A kind of branding.

Unable to resist, he wrapped an arm tightly around her waist and squeezed her soft ass.

She eeped, then groaned as he squeezed harder. Hurting her so nicely. She sagged against him. "Damn you." Her pupils had dilated, and pink swept into her cheeks. "How do you do that?"

"Arouse you? It's not hard." He leaned in and pinned her against the counter with his weight. Her hair had grown long enough for him to get a good grip, and he tugged her head back. After kissing up her neck, he nipped her earlobe, enjoying her sharp inhalation at the bite of pain.

"Sam."

"Mmm-hmm." Running his hand down her front, he explored the V between her legs, then traced over her clit. He could feel it harden despite her tight jeans. And then he let her go.

When she swayed toward him, he took a step back.

Her mouth dropped open. "You're stopping?"

"You have to leave for work in a few minutes, remember? You said you're the only person there this afternoon." And now she could work behind the counter while aching for him.

Her lower lip poked out in a sweet pout. "You want me to suffer all day?"

"Yep." He pressed his erection against her soft stomach. Even sadists had to hurt sometimes. "We both will. And once you're home, I'm going to take your cunt first and then your pretty ass. Yep. I'll fuck you senseless." He pushed against her body again and smiled down into her big brown eyes. "Before that, I'll put you over my knee and turn your ass red." The welts—and anal plug—should make that even more fun. Maybe they'd work on that begging problem she had.

Despite the glare she gave him, her voice came out husky with arousal. "Thanks, Master Sadist. That really will make my day easy."

"You're welcome, missy." Then he leaned forward and gave her the words that erased the glare from her face, the words that came easier every time he said them. "I love you, Linda."

THE END

Loose Id® Titles by Cherise Sinclair

Available in digital format and print from your favorite retailer

Master of the Abyss
Master of the Mountain
The Dom's Dungeon
The Starlight Rite

* * * *

The MASTERS OF THE SHADOWLANDS Series
Lean on Me
Make Me, Sir
To Command and Collar
This Is Who I Am

* * * *

"Simon Says: Mine"
Part of the anthology *Doms of Dark Haven*
With Sierra Cartwright and Belinda McBride

* * * *

"Welcome to the Dark Side"
Part of the anthology *Doms of Dark Haven 2:*
Western Night
With Sierra Cartwright and Belinda McBride

Cherise Sinclair

Now everyone thinks summer romances never go anywhere, right? Well…that's not always true.

I met my dearheart when vacationing in the Caribbean. Now I won't say it was love at first sight. Actually, since he was standing over me, enjoying the view down my swimsuit top, I might even have been a tad peeved—as well as attracted. But although our time together there was less than two days, and although we lived in opposite sides of the country, love can't be corralled by time or space.

We've now been married for many, many years. (And he still looks down my swimsuit tops.)

Nowadays, I live in the west with my beloved husband, two children, and various animals, including three cats who rule the household. I'm a gardener, and I love nurturing small plants until they're big and healthy and productive…and ripping defenseless weeds out by the roots when I'm angry. I enjoy thunderstorms, playing Scrabble and Risk, and being a soccer mom. My favorite way to spend an evening is curled up on a couch next to the master of my heart, watching the fire, reading, and…well…if you're reading this book, you obviously know what else happens in front of fires. :)

—*Cherise*